GHOSTS
OF THE PAST

TONY PARK

First published by AJP in 2019
This edition published in 2019 by AJP

Copyright © Tony Park 2019
www.tonypark.net
The moral right of the author has been asserted.

Ghosts of the Past

EPUB: 9781925786613
POD: 9781925786620

Cover design by Paris Giannakis

Publishing services provided by Critical Mass
www.critmassconsulting.com

For Nicola
and
Edward Lionel Presgrave
soldier, rebel, Australian
1881 – 1905

THE ANGLO-BOER WAR AND THE HISTORY OF
GERMAN SOUTH WEST AFRICA (MODERN-DAY NAMIBIA)

1883 Adolf Lüderitz, a merchant from Bremen, Germany, establishes a trading post at Angra Pequena (later named Lüderitz Bay) on the Atlantic coast of Africa.

1884 Lüderitz requests protection against British expansion and German South West Africa is proclaimed.

1899 Anglo-Boer War breaks out between the Boer republics and the British Empire.

1902 Anglo-Boer War ends with British victory.

1904 The Herero people of German South West Africa rise up against Germany in protest of unfair land and work policies. Some Nama tribes initially side with Germany, then join the Herero. Tens of thousands of Nama and Herero die of starvation, disease and overwork in concentration camps.

1907 Armed conflict between Germany and Nama and Herero ends.

1914 First World War breaks out, South Africa invades German South West Africa at the behest of Britain.

1915 German troops surrender in German South West Africa.

1920 South Africa is granted a mandate over South West Africa.

1990 South West Africa gains independence after a protracted struggle and is renamed Namibia.

2004 Germany offers an apology for the deaths of Herero and Nama during the 'genocide' of 1904–07, but rules out compensation.

2011 Skulls of twenty Herero and Nama taken for research purposes during the genocide are returned to Namibia from a museum in Germany.

2018 The Herero and Nama people launch a class action lawsuit in the US Federal Court against the German government, calling for reparations over the genocide.

AUTHOR'S NOTE

The town of Aus, South West Africa, formerly a German colony, now a protectorate of the Union of South Africa and the British Empire, 1915

This is a story of Africa and of love, which means it will be doubly sad.

My name is Peter Kohl. I am the camp doctor here, administering to more than 1500 of my fellow German prisoners of war. Before the conflict began in Europe and spread like a veld fire to Africa I was a physician and a farmer. If I may record the truth on these pages, I preferred the latter vocation to the former.

I have seen too much bloodshed in Africa. I favour the company of horses and cattle to that of humans, so it is ironic that I am penned here like one of my former livestock.

When I was a free man my neighbours were the dainty springbok, the muscular gemsbok and the sly predators that lay in wait for them. We had to be careful, animals and humans alike, of the desert lion and the brown and spotted hyena, but we knew clearly who our enemies were and we respected them. I miss those simpler days.

In times of war, one side seeks to demonise the other. Accordingly, the South African soldiers who have invaded this colony at the behest of their British masters will soon begin gathering evidence of Germany's wrongdoings as a colonial power.

The subject of their enquiries will be the last war that was waged here, when we Germans fought both the Herero and Nama people, our neighbours in this corner of Africa, who had the temerity to rise up against the Kaiser and fight for their rights. Although this conflict ended eight years ago I can recall the events as if they happened yesterday.

I am writing this account because I am certain I will be brought to trial, for the murder of a man in 1906.

I do not want this story to be published, but it must, nevertheless, be told, for the sake of the people involved and the peace of mind of their families, as much as for the benefit of any vengeful investigator.

In Africa, war is tribal and seemingly never-ending. Before the campaign against the Herero and the Nama, the white tribes across the border – the British and the Afrikaner Boers – killed each other between 1899 and 1902. And it is there, in South Africa, where my story has its genesis.

However, this tale starts at the end, in 1906, when I was sent by my superiors to kill a man who was sleeping with my wife.

PROLOGUE

The desert south of Klipdam Farm, German South West Africa, 1906

The red sand drank his blood, gulped it as fast as it flowed so that once the lions had devoured his flesh and the hyenas had ground his bones in their jaws there would be no evidence that he had ever been here, ever lived at all.

The land would bury what little was left of him until no trace remained, just crisp, wind-carved ripples on the surface of the dune. He tried to speak but his tongue was swollen, his lips cracked. The words wouldn't come. Maybe he made a sound, maybe not.

'Claire ...'

Cyril Blake crawled, hand over hand, and the coarse grains filled his shirt, found their way into his mouth, his trousers, his wound, everywhere. The sand burned his palms. In agony he made it to the knife-edge top of the dune, but when he looked beyond it there was no salvation in sight, just an empty vista with some hardy game. He slithered over like an adder and half slid, half rolled down the leeside.

Behind him he heard the whinny of a horse, then the shouted command of an officer in German.

He had survived through the long night and the cold had replaced the pain of the wound in his gut with teeth-chattering hallucinations. No one would have believed him, if he had ever made it home to Australia, that an African desert could be the coldest place he had ever been.

Now the heat of the day assaulted him and the flies mobbed the hole in his belly.

Blake blinked sand from his eyes. Below him the dry riverbed he had followed to reach this place the day before stretched away to the border and South Africa, just a few dunes distant, but impossibly far in the state he was in. He had once cursed that place, hated it with every fibre of his existence, and had later told himself he would never leave it. It had drawn him in, bewitched him, intoxicated and entrapped him in the same way the smoke from the Chinamen's dens held in thrall the sunken-eyed whores and miners who chased the dragon.

Africa.

Oryx, gemsbok the Boers called them, dotted the valley, nibbling at brittle grass that drained the paltry moisture from the bed. But these handsome beasts were put to the gallop by fifty horses that trotted in confusion, still tied nose-to-tail, along the dying watercourse. He had brought the horses to German South West Africa at Claire's request, to help the rebellion. He had failed in his mission and now he would never see her again. He hoped someone would have the decency to free the horses so that they would not have to face the horrors of war. Perhaps the man who had shot him would come back for the horses; he had left Blake to die while he rode to Klipdam, no doubt to claim the bounty on Blake's head.

Blake managed half a smile at the memory of the woman and was rewarded with the parting of more skin on his lips and the sting of the sweat that tortured the newly exposed flesh. He remembered the taste of Claire's mouth, like nectar.

A shadow brought a moment's respite from the sun and he looked up to see a man standing over him.

'Claire ...'

'Shut up,' said the German officer.

Blake tried to roll, but the movement sent pain shooting through his body. Momentum and displaced sand took over and he slid a little further and ended up on his back, blinking into the sun.

'Don't speak her name.' He spoke near-perfect English. Peter Kohl was a good man, he knew, a doctor. Like Blake, the officer had been talked into donning a uniform because of a need to defend an empire, to vanquish an evil foe that had dared to rise up against the crown.

Utter nonsense.

Blake knew why the officer had come. It was to make sure the bloody job had been done, properly, because the Germans were like that. Everything had to be orderly, by the book, complete and tied up in a bow, even assassinations. Du Preez – he was the one who had fired the bullet that had felled him – followed no such regulations. Du Preez had left Blake to bleed and burn slowly to death under the sun because that's what the man thought he deserved.

'Claire ...' he coughed.

'Enough!' Spittle flecked Peter's mouth and his face turned a deeper shade of red than even the sun had been able to burn him. The doctor took a breath, stilled the tremor in the hand that held the Roth-Sauer 7.65-millimetre pistol. He composed himself, cleared his throat and spoke in a loud, clear voice. 'Cyril Blake, you are guilty of espionage and aiding the Nama people and the criminal Jakob Morengo in his armed rebellion against the lawful government of German South West Africa.'

'Just ... just tell me, Peter,' Blake said.

The officer blinked and Blake wondered if this man, who might have been treating a sick child or tending to a broken arm if he wasn't standing there in his sweat-stained Landespolizei uniform and his scuffed cavalry boots, was crying.

'She is,' his voice quavered, though he spoke loudly, 'dead.'

Blake closed his eyes. 'How?'

'She drowned. It was because of you that she was on the boat. She waited for you, Blake, then she left. You dishonoured my wife and made her a spy against her own people.'

Blake felt his own tears trying to come, but perhaps it was because his body was so dehydrated that his eyes remained dry. His head was reeling. He wouldn't even be allowed the relief of a moment's grief.

'You ... you saw what was happening to innocent people, women and children, on Shark Island, on the railway line *your* people are constructing. You call yourself a doctor and yet still you wear that uniform?'

Peter looked away. If Blake had had the strength, if he wasn't almost dead, he would have tried to get the jump on him, but it was impossible.

'You haven't come to patch me up and take me to prison in Keetmanshoop, have you, Peter?' Blake said.

'No,' Dr Peter Kohl said, loudly enough for his voice to carry across the dunes to the waiting German soldiers, 'I have come to kill you.'

The doctor took careful aim and fired his pistol.

PART 1

CHAPTER 1

North Sydney, Australia, the present day

Raindrops began to spatter Nick Eatwell's back as he cut his eighteenth lap of the open-air North Sydney Olympic swimming pool. The rain annoyed him because he had not brought an umbrella for the walk back to the office.

He remembered something from a couple of decades earlier, when he and Jill had not been married long, on a country road trip. They had watched a cattle dog on the back of a ute. The country was in drought at the time, had been for years, and there had been a freakish sunshower. Fat drops had smeared the dust on their windscreen and the dog, which might never have known rain, found itself pelted by some mysterious substance. He nipped at his back and his fur, trying to chase the drops away. Nick didn't know what had hit him either when Jill had died of breast cancer, eight months ago.

He focused on remembering where he was up to in his laps and used the count to work out what time it was, used the boring repetitiveness and the physical effort of the exercise itself to try and hide the pain. There would be enough of his lunch hour left, still, to have a hot shower, get changed and make it back to the office before two. However, the rain was intensifying and he would get wet again on the walk back.

Nick finished his laps, showered and left the pool. Checking his watch, he decided to brave the downpour. He ran up the road

3

opposite Milsons Point railway station, darting from one awning to the next. A stiff headwind that howled down the man-made canyon of flats and office blocks slowed his progress and drove the stinging drops of rain into his face. By the time he reached the office his shirt and chinos were soaked through. He got into the lift and the woman next to him shook her head. He looked like what he was: pitiful.

The lift doors opened on the Chapman Public Relations office. The millennials, who seemed to need days off because of stress and complained of being bullied when he dared to correct their apostrophes, all had their heads down. Keyboards clattered and soft, urgent conversations were murmured. Jessica, who was young enough to be his daughter, made a point of looking up at the clock. Even on good days coming to work was not something he especially looked forward to. He'd left journalism to make more money, to set him and Jill up for a better life by paying off the mortgage sooner, so they could travel more. Even before Jill died he'd found himself regretting the move; the work bored him and he'd realised happiness was rarely found in a bigger bank balance.

'Oh, Nick,' said Pippa Chapman, the owner of the company, as she came out of her window office and intercepted him on the way to his landlocked work station, 'I was looking for you. Glad you didn't drown out there. Got a minute?'

He was three minutes late. Nick was nearly always the first in the office, after Pippa, and often the last to leave. Pippa was still under thirty-five, had only ever worked in public relations and, to her credit, had built up a reasonable business with her consultancy. In private he called her the pocket rocket. He'd been her star contact once upon a time, when he'd been a comparatively old journalist on a newspaper that was struggling to stay afloat in the digital age. When there had been yet another round of redundancies she had picked him up. He owed her, but she never let him forget it.

Nick followed her into the office. The view of the harbour glittering on a sunny day could lift flagging spirits, but today the water reflected the Harbour Bridge's dull grey and the dreary sky.

Pippa stayed standing, looking out at the unappealing view, rather than at him. 'The tile company walked.'

4

Nick shrugged. 'Typical small-client syndrome – asked the world, whinged all the time and paid peanuts. We're better off without them.'

Pippa turned and her face told him he'd said the wrong thing. 'That's easy for you to say, Nick, you don't have to pay the wages around here. The CEO said you offended him.'

Nick spread his hands. 'I told him that I couldn't sell a turd sandwich.'

'He was launching a brand-new product.'

'Yes.' Nick nodded. 'And he wanted us to get him on breakfast television.'

'You didn't even try, Nick.'

He took a breath. 'I *tried* telling him that we needed to say something newsworthy, maybe run a scare campaign saying that metal roofs are dangerous in high winds or that tiles are better for the environment or some shit like that.'

Pippa straightened and put her hands on her hips. 'Your heart's not in this any more, Nick.'

'In roof tiles? You think?'

'That was my first account when I went freelance, Nick. Tiles helped me build this business, gave you a job.' Pippa drew a deep breath before continuing, 'Nick, we all know what a terrible year this has been for you.'

But, he thought she was about to say, *your wife dying doesn't give you an excuse to be rude to clients.* And she would be right, of course, he had no reason, no right to be picky about what accounts he worked on. Pippa managed corporate and government affairs for a couple of big corporations, but they were cutting their funding. She could not afford to overlook their smaller clients. But the man running the tile company did not like him and he was pushy and demanding. He was always asking why Pippa wasn't at the client meetings. It was an unreasonable gripe, but Nick could see why he would want to have a smart, attractive woman telling him what he wanted to hear rather than a burned-out fifty-year-old setting him straight.

'I'm sorry, Nick.'

'I'm getting better, Pippa,' he said, though he wasn't sure he was.

'I *am* sorry about Jill, Nick, really I am, but that's not why I just apologised.'

For the briefest moment he didn't understand. 'Why, then? What have you done wrong?'

'I ...'

'Pip, please.' His heart started pounding. 'I'm sorry. I'll go back to tile man. I'll grovel and get him back, buy us some time.'

She gave him a sad smile and shook her head, slowly. 'Nick, I'm sorry. I lost the car account as well this morning. We've known for years that they were closing their factories in Australia and it happened. Even if I can get the tile account back I've got to downsize.'

He felt a tightening in his chest and for a moment wondered if it was the beginning of a heart attack. No such luck. She might have felt sorry for him then and reversed her decision.

'Of all the gang,' she went on, though he barely heard her, 'you've got the most experience and you'll find it easiest to get another job. If it's any consolation, you're not the only person I have to talk to this afternoon. I'm sorry, Nick, you're too high-powered for me. I can't afford you any more.'

Which was, he registered, the equivalent of a dumper saying to the dump-ee, 'It's not you, it's me.' It never made a difference.

'When?' he asked.

'You can work out a couple of weeks' notice if you like. I'll pay you all that you're due.'

A few weeks at best, he thought, plus accrued holiday leave which he hadn't taken. He nodded, turned, and started to walk out of Pippa's office.

'Nick ... maybe there'll be some freelance work, maybe I'll pick up another client.'

He nodded but didn't look back at her. He went to his desk, the eyes of the millennials burning into his back, and opened his laptop. He tried to concentrate on a half-finished media release for an advertising company client. Something about a new experiential marketing campaign, whatever the hell that meant.

Nick alternated between flashes of anger and self-pity. He wanted to stand up and go back to Pippa's office and explain to her why she needed him, his contacts and his experience, but he could also see it from her point of view. His expertise and experience had proved invaluable to Pippa, for a while, but now he was an expensive mouth to feed from a shrinking pot. By his own admission he was no good at drumming up new business; Nick was a journalist, not a salesman, and not afraid who knew it.

Unable to concentrate and not willing to give any of his juvenile co-workers the satisfaction of seeing him walking out, he checked his emails.

There was one from someone he didn't know, but the subject line was something a PR man could not ignore: *Seeking Nicholas Eatwell – journalist needs help with a story.* Nick opened it, noting the email address ended in '.co.za'.

> *Dear Mr Eatwell,*
>
> *You don't know me, but my name is Susan Vidler. I am a South African freelance journalist visiting Australia on holiday and business. I am researching a feature on an Australian who served in a unit called Steinaecker's Horse in the Anglo-Boer War in 1902 and later in a rebellion against the German colony of South West Africa, now Namibia, in 1906. My research indicates that you may be the last surviving relative of this man, Sergeant Cyril John Blake. If you are the son of the late Denis and Ruth Eatwell, then you are the man I'm seeking. If so, I was wondering if you might have any documents or other information relating to Sergeant Blake that you would consider sharing with me.*
>
> *Thanking you in advance,*
> *Susan Vidler*

Whoever this woman was she had done her research well because his parents Denis and Ruth had both passed away. The woman gave an Australian mobile number. He called it, grateful for a distraction from what had just happened, and the call went through to voicemail. He left a message saying he was the man she was looking for, and gave his number.

He ended the call and checked his watch. Three hours until he could go to the pub and get drunk. At least, he told himself, he now had a reason other than Jill.

CHAPTER 2

Munich, Germany, the present day

Anja Berghoff looked out the window from her desk in the Ludwig Maximilian University library and saw blue sky. It was what passed for a warm summer's day in Munich and while it would have been nice to be sitting outside in a park she wanted to be somewhere further away.

Namibia.

It was the land of her birth, but her parents had fled in 1990 fearing retribution at the hands of the new South West African People's Organisation government. Even though SWAPO had proved to be magnanimous in its transition to majority rule, following the United Nations–supervised elections, her father, of Namibian-German stock, refused to ever return, and had died proclaiming he had made the right decision.

Anja felt differently. She had been taken from Africa at the age of ten, just old enough to mourn the loss of friends and to appreciate the beauty of the arid but enchanting land in which she had begun to come of age. Germany had been everything that her birth country was not – cold, wet, green, predictable. She had hated it.

Of course, in time she had learned to appreciate her European life, but as impressive as the castles and rivers and snowfields and rich green grass were, they were not a patch on an African night sky awash with stars, the sight of a cheetah stalking its prey through dry golden grass, or the ghostly apparition of one of Etosha's white-dusted elephants emerging from the dark onto the eerie canvas of a floodlit waterhole.

For Anja, the only thing to rival the fascination of Namibia's landscapes and wildlife was its history. She was researching her master's degree in history and her thesis was on the origins of another of Namibia's natural attractions, the wild horses of the Namib Desert, sometimes called the ghost horses.

By a strange chain of events she had found herself wading through once highly classified intelligence documents, which she had obtained online from the national archives. The scans were of letters from a spy based in South Africa at the turn of the twentieth century. What was of interest to Anja was that the agent was a woman, Claire Martin, who, like her, had lived in Namibia, or German South West Africa, as the Kaiser's colony was known at the time.

Claire Martin's life story read like a movie screenplay. She had been born in Germany to an Irish father and a high-born Prussian mother. Her father had fled Ireland after being involved in the Fenian uprising against the British in 1867 and ended up serving on the Prussian side during the Franco–Prussian War. He had married the widow of a Prussian comrade and moved the family to America, where he'd tried to make his fortune on the goldfields in California. After failing there he had taken his wife and daughter to South Africa, and in the 1890s across the border to German South West Africa. There Claire had married the owner of a German shipping company, but he'd gone bankrupt and committed suicide.

In truth, Anja was interested in Claire Martin's later life at around 1906 as a horse breeder in South West, where she and her second husband, Peter Kohl, had had a number of farms and a horse stud, but Claire's early reports about her time as a spy for the Kaiser in 1902 made for fascinating reading. She would have been an unusual and very valuable spy, being a woman and speaking fluent German and English. Plus, while her letters were not directly relevant to Anja's research into the origins of the desert horses, Anja had a theory that something had happened during Claire's time as a spy in South Africa that had a direct bearing on her later life back in the German colony across the border.

Anja saw that Carla, the librarian she usually dealt with at LMU, had returned from her lunch break. She left her notes and laptop and went to the desk to ask Carla if the books she had ordered had been returned.

'Yes, Anja, I have them here for you.' Carla reached under the counter and slid the books over to her. 'What did you say you were researching specifically?'

'The desert horses of Namibia,' Anja said. 'Most people think they're descended from military mounts that escaped or were let go during the First World War, but I'm working on a new theory, that the core group of horses from which the modern ones are descended arrived in the desert some time before then. It's sensitive though; I can't tell you more than that.'

Carla rolled her eyes. 'No need to be so prickly.'

Anja frowned. This woman was not the first person to use that word to describe her. Anja's mother was always saying she needed more friends, and Carla was nice and helpful.

She'd just opened her mouth to apologise when a young man, another student by the look of his ripped jeans and olive-green Bundeswehr surplus parka, came to the counter to ask for assistance. Looking away, Carla picked up a sheaf of printouts and passed them to him.

Anja instead thanked the librarian, took the books and went back to her desk, where she selected the next letter. It was another report from the last months of the Anglo-Boer War, dated 1902. What was becoming clearer in the letters was that Claire Martin had not been in South Africa only to gather intelligence for Germany on the course of the war – which was fascinating enough in its own right – but was also there to facilitate some kind of covert arms deal between Germany and the Boers in a last-minute bid to turn the tide of the war, in which the British had finally gained the upper hand.

This letter, like the others, was addressed to German Naval Intelligence, by way of the Kaiser's embassy in neutral Portuguese East Africa.

On the fourteenth of the month I met with Kommandant Nathaniel Belvedere at an abandoned trading post on the banks of the Sabie River in the low country of the eastern part of the Transvaal. Belvedere is the commander of a battalion of Americans fighting for the Boers against the British. They call themselves the George Washington volunteers. Many are of Irish extraction and have a deep-seated hatred of the British.

Belvedere and a troop of his Americans were part of the Boer force that safeguarded President Paul Kruger out of South Africa when he left Pretoria by train in 1900. Belvedere, formerly a senior manager in a Transvaal goldmining company, was a close confidant of the President. He was to be my contact for the sale of the guns. He intimated to me, once we had established a rapport, that he did not have the funds on his person, but knew the location of enough currency to complete the transaction. I am yet to extract the whereabouts of his money.

Anja set down the letter and opened one of the books Carla had just given her. It was a German-language publication about foreign volunteers who served with the Boer forces. There were a good many of them, not only from America but also from Ireland, Holland, France, Sweden and Germany. Anja thumbed her way to the index and found the name Belvedere. On the listed page she found a photograph of a man with long fair hair, a drooping moustache and pointed beard. He stood in a stiff pose and wore a frown, but Anja detected a smile in his eye. Undeniably handsome, Colonel Nathaniel Belvedere looked like a Wild Bill Hickok character from the American Wild West. The few pictures she had sourced of Claire Martin told Anja that she, too, had been attractive. Anja let her mind wander as to the nature of the 'rapport' the pair had established.

There was no one in Anja's life, romantically, and nor had there been for four years now. She had lived with a man for five years, but unlike her he had not wanted to have children. Eventually, he left. She was almost forty now and as difficult as it was for her she had almost resigned herself to the fact that she would not find a man and have a child. Maybe her mother was right, maybe she wasn't trying hard enough, but for all her longing for a family Anja had become increasingly used to her own space and her own life, which she happily divided between Namibia and Germany.

Maybe, she told herself for perhaps the thousandth time, she would find an intelligent, financially secure safari guide in Namibia who was happy to live with her there during her regular visits. She forced the thought from her head and returned, instead, to the world of Claire Martin and her handsome American officer.

CHAPTER 3

Sabie River, eastern Transvaal, South Africa, 1902

Claire took off her broad-brimmed cattleman's hat as Nathaniel opened the door of the farmhouse, a Colt .45 revolver in his hand. He grinned then stuck the pistol back in his belt. 'Ma'am.'

It was pleasingly warm as she went inside and Nathaniel took her cloak from her. The Transvaal lowveld was much warmer than Pretoria, on the highveld, from where she had ridden two days earlier, and while the May days were sunny and clear now that the summer rains were a memory, the nights were beginning to turn cool. A small fire crackled comfortably in the hearth.

Nathaniel took a step back, his eyes blatantly, proprietorially reacquainting himself with her body. Claire took a step towards him and kissed him.

'We're alone, except for one man, Christiaan, who's keeping watch from the stables,' he whispered in her ear as he waltzed her down a hallway, through a door to a four-poster bed. The building, made of pole and dagga – timber and mud – with a grass thatch roof had once been the home of a Portuguese trader who had established his store in a second building. The property sat astride one of the routes plied by transport riders travelling from the goldfields higher up the escarpment to Lourenço Marques, the capital of Portuguese East Africa, and its port of Delagoa Bay, some two hundred and fifty kilometres further eastwards. 'Christiaan's looking the other way.'

Claire liked the American and she knew he was besotted with her. As he lay over her she shifted and reached for his pistol, which was digging into her belly. She slid it out and placed it on the bedside table.

'My turn.' He kissed his way down her bodice and dropped to his knees on the floor, where he lifted her skirts. 'I know it's in here somewhere.'

Claire put her head back and savoured the feel of his fingers moving slowly up her woollen stockings to the bare skin of her thighs. Nathaniel found the pocket derringer she kept there in the loop of a custom-made leather garter. He pulled it free, and when she looked down over her breasts she couldn't suppress a laugh. He had the tiny gun between his shiny white teeth, like a dog fetching a bone. He took her pistol from his mouth and placed it on the bedside table next to his. He lowered his head again.

She grabbed the posts at the top of the bed with both her hands, her grip tightening and her hips undulating as Nathaniel continued the ministrations hidden by her petticoats. Quite where he had learned his repertoire even she was too modest to ask, but he had clearly been a willing and erudite student. Claire tried to keep her mind on the goal she had set herself, which was to learn where the Boers had hidden the loot that would be used to pay for her guns, but it wasn't easy.

Unable and unwilling to maintain total control, Claire gasped and shuddered and, satisfied he had completed his mission, Nathaniel navigated his way back onto the bed and scaled her. He kissed her and, once she had found her breath again, she rolled him onto his back.

When they were sated a naked Nathaniel led her, wrapped in a sheet, back to the hearth. He moved a Chinese printed screen to one side to reveal a brass hip bath. He topped up the water from a copper.

'Thought you'd never get here,' he said.

Claire saw his cigar box on the mantelpiece. She opened it, took out a cheroot and lit it with a taper from the fire, then drew on it. Claire passed it to Nathaniel, dropped her sheet and slid into the bath.

'That may be, but how do you stand to ga
German artillery to the Boers?'

'It's my late husband's ship that's trans
Portuguese East Africa and it would have been
hadn't reclaimed it. He ran a small shipping
tended and had a terrible problem with gamb
mistresses, as it turned out. He killed himself
for him and he left me with a mound of debts.'

'So you got into the gun-running business t

She gave a laugh that she hoped sounded na
be *that* much from selling cannons to you. No
hope, to buy a parcel of land in German South
a farm, with horses. I've no love for the Brit
Irish, a Fenian – or the way they're fighting thi
my mother's country, gave my father a home, s
to do my bit for the Kaiser.'

'Your bit? How is it that you, a woman, as
are negotiating an illegal arms deal?'

She smiled and raised one eyebrow. 'I've fr
as well as on the docks. Fritz Krupp is a distant

'Aha,' Nathaniel said. She didn't have to
Krupp had built a fortune on designing and m
weapons and warships and selling them to the I
and many customers abroad.

'I've met a few admirals in my time, and
to send reports on the progress of the war her
Naval High Command no one said, "Don't bo
When I got wind that the Boers needed more
might position myself as the go-between, as it w

'You're anything but a silly girl, Claire, and
wise to accept your offer. Our British foes are
that they probably wouldn't even think a woma

Claire smiled briefly in thanks at the comp
not underestimate their enemy. 'There are some
and the government, and the colony of German
who'd prefer it if the Boers won, and they're m
a last-minute shipment of artillery might save th

'Bliss,' she said, reaching for the soap.

He went to a side bar table and uncorked a bottle of whiskey. He poured generous measures into two glasses and came to her.

Claire took her drink, and the cheroot, drew on it again and exhaled the smoke into the glass. She sipped the smoky brew and let it warm her as she reclined in the water. Nathaniel warmed his back by the fire as he took his drink, then bent down for her sheet and fastened it around himself.

'As you were. I was enjoying the view.'

'You, Miss Martin, are incorrigible.'

'Why, thank you, Colonel,' she said, using the English equivalent of his rank, and handed the cigar back to him. 'Tell me, Nathaniel, why exactly are you in South Africa fighting for the Boers?'

He shrugged. 'Lot of my boys are Irish; they've got personal scores to settle with the British. Me, I'm a businessman.'

'I would have thought that as a businessman and an *uitlander* it would not have been in your interest to side with the Transvaal and the Orange Free State?' One of the reasons the two Boer republics had gone to war with Britain, Claire knew, was that President Paul Kruger had denied British and other *uitlander* – foreign – mine workers the vote in a bid to maintain Afrikaner control of the territories the Boers had carved out.

He smiled. 'I was happier trying to bring about change from within the South African Republic than have some big guy – Great Britain in this case – force his will on the little guy.'

'The record of your Washington Battalion would indicate you know something of soldiering as well as business,' she said. In fact, Claire knew a good deal about Nathaniel Belvedere, but her job was to get him to do the talking.

'I killed my first man, a Yankee, when I was sixteen, and while I learned a trick or two I hoped I'd never see another war. The Boers are great fighters but I fear I'm going to be on the losing side again.'

Claire calculated Nathaniel's age. He was in his fifties, but in remarkably good shape. 'You would have been too young to have been an officer in your civil war?'

Nathaniel nodded. 'I was a student of engineering and found myself under the command of an officer by the name of Gab Rains.

He was a brilliant man who turned his m
I helped him develop a new weapon call
was an explosive device buried undergrou
was activated when a man or a horse step
plate. We had quite some success against t

Claire shuddered, and was not quite su
take the time to reminisce about his rol
something so fiendish.

'You fought to protect slavery in Ame
the subject, 'something that the civilised w
Is that your idea of sticking up for the "litt

'Ha!' Nathaniel exhaled and took anotl
the way the British are waging this war yo
civilised, little lady. But, no, I was no plant
give a damn about slavery either way. I wa
North was fixing to strangle the South's e
when I was running a goldmining operatiot
until three years ago, that the English were
ol' Paul Kruger and his burghers.'

She ignored his 'little lady' remark, with
of half an hour ago had earned him som
work to be done. She raised a leg and point
sore from my new riding boots.'

Nathaniel put his drink on the mantel a
lips and took hold of her foot, still drippir
her eyes in a moment of genuine rapture as

'Why are you really here, Claire? Do yo
grudge to settle, like my Irish boys?'

She weighed up how much to tell him. Sl
a business deal with Nathaniel, she had to w
just want payment for the armaments she wa
she wanted Nathaniel to reveal where he w
A good lie, Claire knew, was always based o

'The root of all happiness.'

She smiled, though kept her eyes close
other foot. She could get used to this, she c
so that you can make more money when yc

Nathaniel raised his eyebrows. 'You don't think it will?'

She shrugged. They had met twice before, to organise the logistics of the deal, and it had been during their last meeting that Claire had let Nathaniel seduce her. After their encounter he had confided in her that while he was loyal to the Boers he secretly doubted that any influx of arms or men could prevail against the British.

'No more than you do,' she said. 'But it wasn't too hard to use my family connections to arrange for a consignment of FK-96 77-millimetre Feldcannones, field guns destined for the Schutztruppe in Windhoek to be diverted to Lourenço Marques, where they're currently waiting for you and your lot. Fritz did the deal with me direct, as a family favour, so there's no official paperwork, as it were. I'll take a cut of the payment, and it will hopefully be enough to pay off my late husband's debts. The rest of the money will go into my dear distant cousin's private account in Capri in Italy, where he keeps a villa. I'll be saying goodbye to the shipping business, though, and I'll buy myself a small farm in South West Africa.' More like half the colony, she thought to herself.

Nathaniel gave a sigh and she felt the pressure of his fingers on her lighten. 'So it really is just about the money.'

She opened her eyes and realised she had misread him. Though he may have been disillusioned and had joined the fight against the British because of economic reasons, he was an idealist at heart, a romantic. Claire hadn't thought she needed to win his heart – she had already given him her body – but the truth was she had agreed to spy for the Germans before negotiating the gun-running deal because of something else that had happened to her.

Claire looked into his eyes. She would need to appeal to his sentimental side. 'I have a friend – had a friend, I should say. Wilma was like a sister to me when my family lived in South Africa, during the start of the gold rush. She met a young man, a farmer, and they married. When war against the English broke out her husband joined a Boer commando unit. Wilma was carrying their first child, but some British colonial forces raided their farm, torched it, slaughtered their dogs and took their cattle. Wilma was taken to a concentration camp. You know what I mean?'

'Yes.'

'Wilma wrote to me, managed to bribe one of the guards to get the letter out. She told me she'd had the baby, in the camp, a little boy named Piet. She told me of the horrors – a lack of clean water and decent food; dysentery, measles, other diseases. Wilma asked me if I would try and let the world know of what was going on here in South Africa. I wrote letters to everyone I could think of, contacted the newspapers, and I decided to go and visit Wilma, to petition for her release.'

'And?'

'And by the time I made it to the camp Wilma and Piet were dead. The child died in the big measles outbreak last year and soon after that, Wilma's husband was killed in battle. I don't know if someone can really die of a broken heart, but maybe Wilma just gave up. I was just in time for her burial.'

Nathaniel took her hand in his and looked into her eyes. She saw the war weariness there, and something else, something softer.

Claire changed the subject and asked quietly: 'Is my payment for the artillery here, Nathaniel?'

He looked away. 'No, but I know where it is.'

'Tell me. Maybe we can save time and go there, together, and get it.'

He shook his head, but turned his eyes back to hers and took his cue from her renewed smile. Once more he dropped to his knees and his hand moved under the water in the bathtub.

She placed her hand on his. 'At least tell me there's enough to cover the cost of the guns, Nathaniel.'

He grinned. 'Oh, Claire, trust me, there is *more* than enough to pay for a few cannons.'

'Tell me, please,' she cooed again, then had cause once more to close her eyes and loll her head back over the high metal back of the tub. She removed her hand, giving him free rein. 'Is it far?'

'Close. Less than a day's ride from here. Good things come to those who wait, my dear.'

'Oh, Nathaniel, I don't mind waiting.'

Her body stiffened and her legs straightened over the edge of the tub as the pleasure took hold of her body again. When it had subsided and her breathing had stilled she opened her eyes and saw that he was staring at her.

'Claire ...'

'Yes?'

'You're right. I don't think the Boers have a chance in hell of winning, even if they get your guns.'

'Neither do I,' she said.

'Truth is, I'm sick of war. I lost a dozen good American boys trying to keep the location of the gold meant to pay for those guns of yours secret.' He ran a hand through his long hair and looked away from her.

She nodded, but said nothing. Nathaniel had told her last time that his troop of volunteers had been ambushed by a rogue commando of Boers. Their leader, an old brigand by the name of Hermanus, had given up the cause and set his sights on finding the hiding place of the former republic's gold reserves. Nathaniel and his men had actually been on their way back from delivering a consignment of gold, their wagons empty, but they had been cut down by their erstwhile comrades, with only Nathaniel and Christiaan escaping. He was mulling something over, the same thing as her, she hoped, but she needed him to say it first.

'With the gold, Claire, with just a portion of it, we could disappear forever. We could carry enough to make sure no one could ever find it. I'm probably the last person alive who knows where it is – Christiaan stood sentry near the hiding place and didn't actually go in.'

In? Her mind turned; was the gold in a building, a cave perhaps, an old mine shaft? Her heart beat faster. She watched him intently, wondering if he was laying a trap for her, if she had overstated her monetary motives. Claire realised, though, that he, too, was holding his breath, perhaps waiting to see what she would make of him. Claire had dropped enough hints that she was in this for the money, but she had stopped short of saying she would consider abandoning the deal and simply stealing the gold – all of it. 'Go on.'

He grinned at her. 'I know where the gold is, Claire, and I have the only map in existence.'

*

Anja stretched at her desk in the university library and read the next page of the letter.

> *It became clear to me that Kommandant Belvedere was sug-*
> *gesting a criminal enterprise, that he and I make off with some*
> *or all of President Kruger's gold reserves. Naturally, I would*
> *countenance nothing of the kind, but as this man was display-*
> *ing criminal tendencies I pretended to go along with his plan,*
> *knowing that he would have to reveal the location of the gold*
> *to me.*
>
> *My mission remained clear in my mind: to further Germany's*
> *strategic interests, covertly, by seeing that the armaments reached*
> *the forces for whom they were intended.*
>
> *I was afforded appropriate accommodation at the trading*
> *post, by Kommandant Belvedere, for the evening, but I was*
> *awoken before dawn.*

The collection of Claire's letters to her spymasters was incomplete; the country's archives had been in a building that, like much of Berlin, was bombed during the Second World War, and many of the papers had been burned. There was a reference in this instalment to guns. It was now clear that Claire had been an integral part of a plot to supply artillery weapons to the Boers in a last-ditch attempt to turn the tide against the British, but Anja had read nearly all of the letters she had, and if she didn't find some mention of horses being released into the desert of a neighbouring country soon then her recent weeks of research would amount to nothing more than a diversion – albeit a fascinating one – and a dead end.

> *Kommandant Belvedere's horse was whinnying by the window.*
> *Belvedere sensed danger and, worried by the prospect of a*
> *predawn raid, a tactic favoured by the British colonial forces, he*
> *insisted I leave the farmhouse and ride through the night to the*
> *top of a nearby hill. He informed me he would join me there at*
> *dawn, if all was safe, and gave me his Colt revolver.*

I quickly dressed in a set of men's riding clothes that I carried with my meagre possessions for the purposes of disguise, left the house as quietly as I could and went to the stable. I found Belvedere's Boer sentry asleep. Rudely, I woke him, and told him to report to the trader's house. The man was able to make it to the house without being seen, but when I looked out of the stable door I saw men approaching through the dark. Fearing I would be seen if I took out a horse I left the building and hid in the bush.

CHAPTER 4

North Sydney, Australia, the present day

The afternoon had dragged painfully and Nick left work at a quarter to five.

He didn't care. He no longer had a job.

Susan Vidler, the South African woman who had emailed him, had returned his call soon after he had left his message. She told him it would be no problem to meet him at the Commodore Hotel in North Sydney, some time after five fifteen. He figured it would be better to make small talk with a stranger, and maybe learn something about an ancestor of his, than to get drunk by himself and go back to the flat and look through old photos of Jill until he passed out.

The Commodore was a popular pub and he had left early to be sure of getting a table before the usual after-work crowd descended. When he arrived he walked upstairs from Blues Point Road to the outdoor verandah area, then ordered himself a schooner of beer.

Nick found a seat, took out his phone and checked Facebook and his emails.

'Nick?'

He looked up and saw a pretty face – very pretty, in fact – framed by straight blonde hair. 'Yes, Susan, is it?'

'Howzit?' She extended a hand.

Nick stood. 'Hi.'

'I took a lucky guess,' she said.

'Can I get you a drink?'

'That would be *lekker*, lovely, thanks. Sauvignon blanc?'

'Coming right up.' Nick went to the bar, thinking that at least one thing hadn't turned ugly today.

He returned to the table. Susan sat with her chair pushed back and her legs crossed below a short black skirt. 'Thanks.'

'Nice to meet you,' he said, and sipped his beer.

'You as well. I'm so glad you agreed to meet me. I have to tell you it was quite an effort to track you down.'

'Well, I don't think I've ever heard anything about this relative you're interested in. What was his name again?'

'Blake,' she said. 'Sergeant Cyril Blake. He gets a mention in a book about the history of Namibia, or rather, his alias, Edward Prestwich, appears in the book.'

'Now I'm really confused. You said something about this guy serving in German South West Africa? That's modern Namibia, right?'

'Yes.'

'Australians never fought there, as far as I know.'

Susan leaned forward a little, elbows on the table. Her face became animated and he noticed her eyes for the first time, an almost translucent blue. 'You're right, but Cyril Blake ended up in German South West Africa in 1906, fighting with the indigenous Nama people who, with the Herero, rose up against the German colonial government.'

'Why did Blake join them?'

'That's one of the things I'm trying to find out. It could be that he was sympathetic to their cause, or had some reason to dislike the Germans. It certainly wasn't Blake's war. However, he also seems to have had a business interest in all this.'

'Business?'

She sipped her wine and nodded. 'Blake was a horse trader. Horses were in very short supply on both sides, and there's evidence Blake sold horses to the Nama people. There was apparently a lot of cross-border trade going on between the British-controlled Cape

Colony, part of what's now known as South Africa, and German South West Africa.'

Nick was mildly intrigued, both by the story and by Susan. She was maybe ten years younger than him so she was not some wide-eyed cadet reporter straight out of university chasing her first feature story. He glanced at her left hand; there was no wedding ring. Nick had a vision of Jill in her floral headscarf, forcing a smile, and telling him he should find someone new when she was gone. She had tried to make a joke out of it, telling him to wait at least a year, and had laughed. Still he felt guilty, checking Susan out.

He cleared his throat. 'So, how did you find me – searching online?'

'Yes and no. I knew the name of your great-great-uncle through some other historical research and was able to find his enlistment papers for the Boer War, via the Australian national archives online. His papers listed his mother as his next of kin. I looked her up and later found birth certificates for your great-great-uncle's two brothers through her.'

'I *do* remember my aunt once telling me about three brothers on her side of the family – my mother's side – who had gone to war. One died in France in the First World War and the other's my great-grandfather, who served in Palestine with the light horse. The third one must have been Cyril.'

Susan nodded. 'I found the marriage record for your great-grandfather and great-grandmother through the New South Wales Registry of Births, Deaths and Marriages, online. I then found the birth record for your grandmother and her marriage certificate.'

'Impressive,' Nick said.

Susan smiled and took a sip of her wine, then held up a palm. 'It gets better – well, harder, after that. Because of privacy laws you can't find birth records online for people born in New South Wales less than a hundred years ago or marriage records within the last fifty years. So, I searched Trove, which is in the process of scanning old Australian newspapers using optical character recognition. I found a mention there of your grandparents, a marriage notice that listed them as the parents of the bride, your mother, Ruth.'

'Amazing.'

'It seemed you, or some other descendent of Blake's, were getting harder to find. I searched for other clues and found a website called the Ryerson Index, set up by the Sydney Dead Person's Society ...'

'You're not serious.'

Susan nodded. 'I am. They list death notices from the *Daily Telegraph* and the *Sydney Morning Herald*, going way back. I found a death notice for your father, Denis Eatwell. I'm sorry for your loss.'

'He had a good long life.' *Unlike Jill*. He couldn't shake the feeling of guilt, being in a pub with Susan, but he was impressed with the lengths she had gone to in order to find him. 'So that's how you found me, all via the internet?'

She shook her head. 'Actually, no. This is where fate lent a hand. The Ryerson Index just lists the name and date of the notice, not the text, and Trove hasn't got up to scanning the newspapers from the time your father died. I had to actually go in person to the State Library of New South Wales and look up the *Sydney Morning Herald* edition with your father's death notice on microfilm.'

He leaned back in his chair. 'You flew to Sydney just to do that?'

She laughed. 'No, but I had been meaning to come over to visit friends, and as my queries were leading me to Sydney it seemed like it was, I don't know, pre-ordained or something. The death notice, when I found it a couple of days ago, listed you as Denis's sole survivor and after that the sleuthing was less intriguing – I turned to good old Facebook. There aren't many Australian Nick Eatwells, and when I worked out you weren't a guy in Western Australia, I emailed you, and here we are.'

'That's quite a story in itself, but, forgive me, do you really think it was worth all the effort you went to – given I still don't know much about this guy? And is anyone actually going to run an historical feature about all of this?'

'The story's got more currency than you probably think,' she said. 'Even though the uprising happened more than a hundred years ago it still has implications for Africa and Germany today. For a long time there have been calls from Namibia for the German government to pay compensation. As well as defeating the Herero and the Nama in battle, the Germans set up a network of concentration camps where tens of thousands of people died through overwork, starvation and disease. The worst camp was at Shark Island, on the Atlantic Coast, where terrible things were done. Inmates from the island were also used to build a railway line from the port of Lüderitz to the town of Keetmanshoop and they were literally worked to death. The Germans have gone part of the way, issuing an expression of regret – not quite an apology – but they've stopped short of promising compensation.'

'What do you think?'

Susan shrugged. 'I don't necessarily believe that people today from a progressive, liberal country like Germany should be held accountable for the actions of the Kaiser's regime a century ago, but I can see the local people's point. In either case, a hard-hitting story that shows how abominably the Germans acted will be of interest in both countries, and it'll be newsy as well as a feature.'

'Hmm,' Nick said, not quite convinced. 'The fact that an Aussie fought in this war is hardly going to cause any great ructions in Germany.'

'It might if people here in Australia and in Germany found out that Cyril Blake was murdered on the orders of the German government in 1906.'

Nick felt it. His fingertips twitched the way they sometimes did – not for a good many years now – when he was on to a good story. By good he meant one that sold papers, that got people talking in the streets and pissed off politicians and big businesses. He saw the sparkle in those blue eyes across the table from him and he knew that Susan felt it as well, and it was what had brought her here to a pub in North Sydney.

'The Germans must have been threatened by this bloke.'

Susan nodded. 'There's precious little about him in the archives. Trust me, I've looked in Cape Town, online in Berlin, and even here in Australia. There's not a lot, on paper, that tells us much about who Cyril Blake was and why he did what he did. We know more about his death than we do his life.'

'Really?' Nick said.

'The German military entrapped him. That book on the history of Namibia mentions he was set up by a couple of Afrikaner spies who lured your great-great-uncle into German South West Africa on the promise of a cattle deal. They ambushed him, wounded him, and left him to die in the desert. That's how much they hated the idea of this foreign white man riding with the rebels.'

Nick exhaled. 'Bloody hell.'

'The Germans sent out a military patrol the next day to check on him. Reports from the time suggest your ancestor was still alive, having survived a night in the desert, but he was then executed in cold blood by a German officer.'

'That's a lot to take in.' Nick took a moment to process the shocking revelation. It was one thing to learn of an ancestor who had died in war, in combat, but another altogether to think of someone being murdered. He could see how the German government might not want such a deed resurrected, even today. 'So what do you want from me?'

Susan shrugged. 'I was wondering if there was anything you or your family might have, some sort of papers or letters from or about him?'

Nick frowned. 'I'd never heard of him until just now.' He thought about what he knew of his own ancestry. It didn't take him more than half a minute to work out it was not very much.

Susan reached down to the large brown leather handbag she had brought with her. She pulled out a manila folder, which she slid across the table. 'How about I get us another drink while you have a look through this stuff, Nick.'

'OK.' He took the folder. The journalist in him was interested, but he couldn't help but feel a little weird that a stranger had been picking through his family tree and possibly knew more about where he came from than he did. 'Thanks.'

Susan got up and went to the bar, and Nick opened the folder. There were family trees and printouts from online genealogical research sites, more than one by the look of it. She had obviously spent some time piecing all this together. Stapled to the inside front cover of the folder was a printout of a document which seemed to summarise her findings.

This Cyril Blake, it seemed, was his maternal great-grandfather's brother, his great-great-uncle. Blake had never married and that side of the family had produced very few offspring. Nick himself had no siblings and no cousins from his mother's side of the family. His mother, who had passed away three years earlier, had one sister, his aunt. He looked up from the piece of paper.

'What are you thinking?' Susan set a beer down in front of him and another glass of wine for herself and took her seat again.

The pub was filling up and getting noisier. 'I have an aunt who is really into all this family history stuff, possibly because there are so few of us on her side of the family.'

'I noticed that,' Susan said. 'Do you think your aunt might know something about Cyril?'

Nick exhaled. 'Well, if anyone did it would be her. She's obsessed by our history.'

Susan looked at her watch. 'I don't want to keep you, Nick, if you have to get home to the family or whatever.'

He leaned back in his seat. 'There's no one at home waiting for me. My wife died of cancer eight months ago.'

Susan's face fell and she reached out and put her hand on his. 'Oh, no, Nick, I'm so sorry.'

He nodded. At least he didn't cry any more when he said the words. He looked up at her. 'I'll call my aunt for you.'

'Thank you, I really appreciate it.'

'What about you?'

'What about me?' she asked back.

'Does anyone have dinner in the oven waiting for you, here or in South Africa?'

'No.' She sipped her wine. 'I'm travelling solo and I'm divorced.'

'Sorry,' Nick said.

'Don't be. I'm not,' Susan said. 'Are you hungry? Maybe we can get something together?'

'Sure.' After the day he'd had, Nick couldn't think of anywhere else he would rather be than across the table from a pretty, slightly intriguing woman. All he had waiting for him was an empty apartment and a television and he felt sure Jill wouldn't mind him having dinner with someone, even if it hadn't been a year yet. 'Sounds like a great idea. If you like Spanish food, there's a nice tapas place down Blues Point Road.'

'Love it. I can tell you more about what I'm writing. I think there might even be a book in it. There's even a leading lady in this story, I think.'

'You think?'

'I'm not sure of what exactly happened between them, but there's a half-German, half-Irish woman whose name has popped up a few times in my research, Claire Martin. She was born in Germany, but moved to German South West Africa in the late 1890s. Looks like she and Cyril crossed paths.'

'Sounds like there might even be a movie in it.'

She smiled. 'If you have a look in the folder there's a photocopy of a report from a British Army intelligence officer, a Captain Llewellyn Walters, who served with your ancestor during the Boer War. They were on a raid that was aimed at capturing a Boer leader, an American.'

Nick leafed through the pages until he found the report, written in a neat copperplate. It had been prepared by Captain The Honourable Llewellyn Walters in 1902.

Sergeant Blake and I took up position on a hill overlooking the trading post on the Sabie River where the Boer colonel, Nathaniel Belvedere, and the German spy, Claire Martin, were believed to have conducted their rendezvous. Our intention was to mount a pre-dawn raid while the occupants were asleep. Sergeant Blake seemed unsettled and nervous, his attitude bordering on insubordinate ...

CHAPTER 5

Sabie River, eastern Transvaal, South Africa, 1902

Too many things were not right for Blake's liking, and when things weren't right, the wrong people died.

Blake had never mastered a trade back home in Australia, but three years in South Africa had taught him how to kill and, more importantly, how to survive. He was skilled at his work; he was still alive.

'I don't like it,' he said to the English officer.

'When I want your opinion, Sergeant Blake, I'll ask for it,' Captain Walters replied in a whisper. The binoculars were fixed to his eyes now that the first glimmer of pale orange light was peeking from behind the stark, treeless hills.

Blake was cold, and wet from the dew. The thin horse blanket draped over his back and shoulders had kept his Lee Enfield rifle dry and helped disguise his silhouette, but it had not kept him warm. His sodden khaki uniform and damp undershirt clung to his skin.

Blake had inherited the rifle from a dead English comrade and he considered the protection of his weapon more important than his personal comfort. The Lee Enfield had a smoother, faster bolt action than the older-model Lee-Metford he had been issued with when he first came to South Africa. In Blake's line of work a split second less spent chambering a round could mean the difference between life and death.

Captain The Honourable Llewellyn Walters lay on a waxed cloak with black silk lining and wore a tailored overcoat – the same colour as the Australian sergeant's uniform, but that was where the similarity ended. Walters' shirt was new and starched; his tie done in a perfect Windsor knot; his tunic freshly laundered and ironed; his riding breeches spotless and his boots buffed. Blake's clothes were patched and worn and the leather soles on his boots would soon need replacing. Steinaecker's Horse didn't go in for full dress inspections and it was more important how a man shot and acted in the bush than what he wore.

'Where are the sentries?' Blake whispered.

'Just thank the Lord there aren't any, Sergeant,' Walters replied.

A British sergeant would not have questioned his commander and would have addressed him properly, as sir, but Blake knew Walters had not picked him for this job because of his manners or his deference to superiors. There was very little of that military bullshit carry-on in Steinaecker's Horse, the unit Blake had wound up in after two years of fighting the Boer. The war had changed over the past three years and so had British tactics, thankfully. Walters seemed to belong to the time when ramrod-straight Tommies marched in neat columns towards what they thought were going to be set-piece battles, only to be shot to hell by cunning Boers, lying in ambush in the *koppies* or running circles around them on their hardy ponies. Steinaecker's, and many other irregular horse units, had been set up to play the Boers at their own game and the war had become one of mobile patrols, hunting the enemy and ferreting him out. Blake's unit was slightly more sedentary, its mission to patrol the border of neutral Portuguese East Africa to stop arms and ammunition and other supplies reaching the increasingly isolated Boers from the outside world via the Indian Ocean sea ports to the east.

Blake had seen a good deal of death in his time in South Africa, but the experience had not hardened his heart towards the Boers. If anything, he viewed them more as fellow human beings now than when he had first arrived on this blood-soaked continent.

In the beginning he had believed the tales of the Boers as merciless villains who fired on ambulances and executed prisoners –

greedy Dutchmen out to fleece the empire of the gold that right-fully belonged to the mother country. Now, he saw them for what they were: simple farmers in the main, fighting for their right to self-determination. He didn't necessarily agree that the country should split from the empire, but nor did he see his enemy as devils incarnate. Yet, as his understanding of his foes grew, so did his skills at dispatching them.

'If this bloke is such a senior Boer officer you'd expect him to have an escort, and to post sentries,' Blake said, softly but firmly voicing his concerns. 'It's wrong. Maybe an ambush.'

'I wouldn't have brought you along if I'd known you were a coward, Sergeant Blake.' Walters stared straight ahead through the field glasses.

'All right. Let's get on with it then,' Blake said. He rolled to one side, slung the Lee Enfield over his shoulder and withdrew the Mauser C96 pistol from the holster at his waist. The Mauser, nick-named the Broomhandle because of its long wooden handgrip, was a semi-automatic pistol sold by the Germans to the Boers. The of-ficer who had originally owned it didn't need it any more – he was in a grave near Bloemfontein. Blake liked the Broomhandle for close-quarter fighting, such as clearing buildings, because it had a ten-round magazine – four more bullets than a Webley revolver – and if he needed to use it in open country it had a longer effective range than the standard British service pistol. Despite his misgivings about the raid he was buggered if he would let some Pommy officer show him up.

'Remember, I want the colonel alive.' Walters stood and brushed a stalk of grass from his immaculate cavalry breeches. 'I have infor-mation the American may be keeping company with a woman. She is to be taken into custody as well.'

Bert Hughes, another Australian Blake had picked to come on the mission, had their three horses on the other side of the hill and knew to come as soon as he heard firing.

Blake would have preferred at least half-a-dozen more men, but Walters had insisted that the Boer colonel would be alone. Just what the colonel was doing galloping around the bushveld virtually on his own, and maybe with some female company, Walters had refused to reveal. These days, encounters with Boer commandos were rare for Steinaecker's Horse and their biggest threats usually came from the tough country – riddled with fever and inhabited by man-eating lions, unpredictable buffalos and cunning crocodile – but there had been no sightings of the enemy along this part of the river for months.

'He is an enemy of the crown, who has pledged his allegiance to the Boers, and that is all you need to know, Sergeant.'

Blake left his slouch hat with the blanket. The distinctive silhouette of the turned-up brim would give him away in an instant if they were spotted by a lookout. They moved forward, slowly, and paused behind a stable at the rear of the whitewashed pole and dagga house. Blake looked inside through an unglazed window and saw three horses, all unsaddled. He held up three fingers to Walters, who nodded in comprehension.

Walters re-holstered his Webley revolver and reached into the polished brown leather map case that hung from his shoulder. He withdrew a silver cigarette case, popped a tailor-made cigarette into his mouth and lit it with a match.

Blake shook his head. The bloke was a bloody upper-class idiot, but he did have style. He wondered again how he had landed this ridiculous caper.

Walters replaced the cigarette case and matches and then withdrew a stick of dynamite from a canvas bag slung around his neck. 'Shall we?'

Walters' accent and the aquiline features of his face marked him as a member of a caste and a country Blake would otherwise never have encountered. But the eyes were cold and hard. They could have been Blake's eyes.

'Ready when you are, old boy,' Blake said, doing his best impersonation of a toff.

Walters frowned at the impertinence, and drew his pistol again. They walked to the front of the trader's house, crouching as they passed the shuttered windows, just in case.

The Englishman raised the wick of the dynamite to the glowing tip of his cigarette. The fuse sputtered into life. He placed the explosive at the base of the solid black-painted wooden door of the farmhouse and he and Blake both retreated around the corner of the building.

After the blast Blake was first in, kicking aside the shattered remnants of the door. Acrid smoke and a fog of dust filled the small house.

Blake moved with the Mauser held high, his arm swinging as he entered the first room. A chair was on its back, fragments of a blue and white china vase littered the floor, along with a clutch of sodden wildflowers.

He turned and entered the hallway. A tall thin man in the simple threadbare clothes and crossed bandoliers of a Boer emerged from a room into the hallway. He raised the shotgun in his hands to his shoulder and swung the barrel towards Blake.

All Walters had told Blake about their quarry, Nathaniel Belvedere – other than his name and rank, the equivalent of a colonel in the British Army – was that the man had long, pale-blond hair and a beard. Blake fired twice, both shots hitting the dark-haired man in the chest. The Boer crashed into the doorframe and landed on his back on the floor. Blake followed the body through the door and saw that the room was empty. He returned to the hall, but Walters was in front of him now, charging towards the next doorway.

Walters kicked the closed door and it flew open.

'Get down!' Blake yelled as a bullet whizzed past Walters' head and smacked into the wall.

Walters dropped to one knee. Both he and Blake now levelled their pistols at the stocky blond man who stood naked before them, a Mauser rifle clutched in his hands. He started to work the bolt, but realised he was cornered and dropped the weapon on the mattress of the four-poster bed that dominated the room.

'At least let me cover myself up, partner?' the man said, smiling at Walters.

The man's blond hair reached almost to his shoulders and he sported a goatee beard. The American smiled as he reached for the trousers hanging over the railing at the foot of the bed.

'Slowly does it,' Walters said. 'Search the other building, Sergeant Blake.'

'Where's the woman?' Blake asked the prisoner.

'What woman?' the man asked as he buttoned his moleskin trousers.

'Indentations in both of the pillows, three horses in the stable.'

The man shrugged. 'You're mistaken. There's no one else in the house.'

Blake noticed that the bedroom window was open. The calico curtain billowed as a chilly gust of wind caught it.

'Hurry, Blake,' Walters said, following his gaze. 'Find her!'

'We've got our prisoner. He's the one you were after, isn't he?'

Walters turned red in the face as he turned to Blake. 'I said find the fucking woman, Sergeant!'

Blake was surprised at how quickly the officer's demeanour had changed, not to mention his profanity. He nodded and strode out of the bedroom and back up the hallway.

From the front porch of the farmhouse – the Boers called it the *stoep* – Blake could see Bert galloping over the crest of the hill, their two other horses trailing behind him.

He looked to the whitewashed stables and a horse burst through the open door.

Blake raised his pistol and fired two snap shots. One missed completely, and the other plucked at the rider's grey woollen overcoat.

The rider wore trousers and a wide-brimmed Boer hat. The rider held a revolver in one hand, and half turned in the saddle to fire a wild shot in reply. The horse galloped away. Blake cursed himself for hesitating and arguing with the officer. There had obviously been a third man hiding nearby and he had slipped into the stables while they were searching the house.

Blake holstered his pistol and unslung his Lee Enfield. He raised the butt of the rifle to his shoulder, leaned into the weapon, anticipating the familiar kick, and wrapped his finger around the trigger. The horse and rider were about a hundred yards off. He aimed for the centre of the rider's back.

He started to squeeze.

As the horse reached full stride the rush of passing air snatched the hat from the rider's head. A shock of bright red hair tumbled out in a streaming wake.

'Shit,' said Blake. It was the woman.

He lowered the barrel of the rifle.

The sound of another shot rolled across the hills. Blake turned and saw Bert working the bolt of his rifle, chambering a fresh round.

'Cease fire!' Blake called.

Bert's bullet caught the stallion in his left rear leg and the sleek black animal faltered. The rider was pitched forward as her mount fell. She landed hard on the rocky ground.

Blake ran towards the motionless rider. He cursed out loud. He hated seeing horses injured, but at least Bert had not shot a fleeing woman in the back.

'Get up,' he said as he approached the woman. She was lying face down.

The horse whinnied as it fought repeatedly to stand. Blake brought his rifle back up into his shoulder and fired once. The horse's agony was over.

'Sorry, mate,' he said.

'Get up,' he said again to the woman. He was angry about the death of the animal. He kept the rifle hard against his shoulder. The pistol she had been carrying, an American Colt .45, was lying in the grass a few feet from her, where she had dropped it.

The woman rolled over, as fast as a startled leopard, and her arm flashed up. Blake instinctively dodged to one side and dropped to his knee when he saw another weapon, a tiny pistol, in her hand.

She fired and he felt his left upper arm burn with pain.

The rifle spun in his hands as he brought it down from his shoulder and reversed it in one fluid motion. He struck down hard on the woman's right arm with the butt of the rifle.

'Ow!' the woman said as she dropped the one-shot pocket Derringer in the dirt and clasped her injured arm with her good hand. 'That hurt. You might have broken my bloody arm.'

'Get up or I'll shoot you.' Keeping her covered, Blake stooped to pick up first the Derringer, then the Colt. The words and her accent didn't sound Afrikaner to him.

He glanced at his own arm. The bullet had only nicked the skin, but he would need to patch the tunic and undershirt again.

'Go to hell, you goddamned murdering baby-killing British bastard,' the woman said.

'I resent that. I'm an Australian.' He reached down, grabbed her forearm and pulled the woman to her feet. She struggled against him.

'Quite a looker you've found yourself there, Sarge,' Bert said as Blake marched the woman at gunpoint back to the front of the farmhouse.

The woman cradled her bruised forearm with her left hand. Blake grabbed her shoulder and turned her around. Looking at her again face-on he saw that Bert was right. She had smooth fair skin and her green eyes were flecked with gold. The eyes were ablaze with pure hatred, and her cheeks were as pink as twin African sunsets. Her long red hair cascaded nearly down to her waist.

'What's your name?' Blake asked.

'I'm Claire Martin and I'm an American citizen. You have no right to assault me or hold me captive.'

'What do you reckon, Bert?' Blake asked.

'She put that hole in your tunic?' Bert asked.

'Yeah.'

'Then she's a Boer,' Bert said. 'Just like that one the Queenslanders captured last month. She was dressed like a man and all. Swedes, Irish, the German Brigade, men or women, matters not to me, Sarge. They're all Boers and they'd all fucking kill us as soon as look at us.'

'There's no need for profanity in front of a lady, Bert, even if she was trying to kill us,' Blake said. 'We're taking you into custody, Mrs Martin.'

'It's Miss Martin, you British lackey.' She spat on the ground in front of him. 'And you can kiss my arse.'

CHAPTER 6

North Sydney, Australia, the present day

Nick noticed that while his beer was half empty, Susan had nearly finished her drink and was watching him read.

'Take your time,' she said.

'Almost done.' He turned to the last page of the copied document, written by Captain Walters.

I emerged from the stables, where I had restrained the prisoner, Colonel Belvedere. Sergeant Blake and Trooper Hughes were rudely interrogating Miss Martin. While she was suspected of espionage, the colonials were unnecessarily impugning her honour under the guise of questioning her. I told them to desist, whereupon Blake told me in profane and insolent terms to mind my own business.

Blake walked past me and into the stables. I tried to calm the lady, who was most distressed, and while talking to her, in the company of Trooper Hughes, I heard a scream from inside the stables and then a single gunshot.

When I entered the building I found the American, Colonel Belvedere, lying dead on the ground with a bullet wound between his eyes.

'Bloody hell,' Nick said.

'I know, right?' Susan finished her wine.

Nick thought about what he had read, about this man related to him by blood. Nick had gone through a hard day, losing his job, but, he reflected, apart from Jill's death his had been a life free of pain and trauma. He had never served in the military, and while his family had been touched by war in generations past the casual references in this document to combat and, it seemed, cold-blooded killing, shocked him.

'Are you OK?' Susan asked.

He realised he had been miles away. 'Um. Yes. I guess so.'

'Hey,' Susan said, smiling, as if trying to lift the mood, 'I'm hungry. Shall we get some dinner now?'

'Sure,' Nick said, even though his stomach had just churned.

The sun was setting as they left the Commodore and walked down Blues Point Road, past sandstone cottages with views of the harbour. At the time of the Boer War this had been a working-class suburb, but not any more. There were cafes and boutiques and the office crowd was giving way to locals out for a stroll or a meal.

Nick took Susan to a Spanish delicatessen and cafe called Delicado. The waitress, who knew him by sight, greeted him and escorted them to a table upstairs.

'This is nice,' Susan said as she looked through the menu.

'Yeah. The tapas is good. So, my ancestor killed a man in cold blood?' He was finding it hard to let go of the climactic end to the report he had read at the pub.

Susan looked up. 'We don't know for sure. There are gaps in his personal story and I can't find anything that was written by Cyril Blake himself in his defence, or about what he did during the Boer War and afterwards, in South West Africa, when he fought against the Germans. What's good on the menu? I'm happy if you want to order for us.'

Nick signalled to the waitress and ordered a selection of tapas dishes and a bottle of pinot gris.

'You're going to get me drunk,' Susan said.

'Is that a problem?'

She laughed. 'No.'

Nick was intrigued now by the story that Susan had brought with her. 'So, we don't know if this Cyril Blake was a war criminal or a hero freedom fighter?'

Susan spread her hands. 'Maybe both? We know he never returned to Australia, that he stayed on in Africa after the Boer War ended. There's also a record of him having been charged but not convicted for being in possession of stolen cattle at Upington, in South Africa, in 1906.'

'Great, so he's a rustler as well?' Nick said.

'Your country doesn't seem to mind lionising people with a *colourful* past, Nick. Take Ned Kelly for instance – he's a local hero from what I understand, and then there's Breaker Morant, who shot Boer prisoners of war.'

'Acting under orders, so the story goes,' Nick said.

Susan rolled her eyes. 'One thing for sure is that the German government can't ignore the stain on their history that the war in South West Africa left. They killed thousands of Herero and Nama people. We do know that whatever your great-great-uncle did in South Africa he ended up joining the uprising against the Germans. To the people whose cause he took up he might have been a hero.'

'Or just an ordinary bloke in the wrong place at the wrong time.' The fact was that Nick found himself being drawn in, both by the story and by this attractive woman. He'd almost forgotten that he had just lost his job. 'I can't believe our family never knew about this. It's so ... wild. I wonder what made him sign up for a war in Africa in the first place.'

'Like a lot of Brits and their allies Cyril Blake would have gone to South Africa full of patriotic fervour. His enlistment papers showed he served with the New South Wales Lancers originally. I checked them out. Their unit had been to London to take part in a military parade celebrating the anniversary of the coronation of Queen Victoria and when they were on their way back to Australia war was declared against the Boers and the Lancers jumped ship in Cape Town to join the fight instead of sailing home.'

'So Blake was there for most of the war?'

'Yes, and something in Africa, or maybe someone, kept him there.'

'Maybe he was in disgrace and felt he couldn't go home, or he was on the run?' Nick said.

Susan shrugged. 'I don't know. It was a long shot, but I was hoping you might have something that could tell me a bit more about Blake. Upington, where Cyril faced court, is on the edge of the Kalahari Desert, just across the border from the old German colony, which is now Namibia. So we know he was close to where the insurrection against the Germans was happening in 1906, but not how or why he got involved with it, four years after the Anglo-Boer War ended.'

Their first courses arrived and their conversation fell away as they ate. Nick was hungry and Susan seemed to be enjoying the food.

'What about the woman?' he asked eventually.

'Claire Martin. Yes, her name starts popping up again in the southern part of modern Namibia, not far from where Blake is on the other side of the border in South Africa, once the Nama uprising begins. Claire and her second husband, a Dr Peter Kohl, had a stud farm near Keetmanshoop where they bred horses. They were well off – horses were in high demand then and they also had a couple of cattle farms in the same area. It could be that Cyril Blake was part of a thriving cross-border trade that was going on at that time.'

'This is a lot to get my head around,' Nick said. 'Particularly to-day, of all days.'

'How come?' Susan asked.

He told her what had happened at work.

'You should take a holiday,' she said, 'come to South Africa and learn some more about Cyril Blake.'

Nick laughed. 'I've never thought about visiting Africa. What I will do is contact my aunt, tomorrow, and see if she knows anything about him.'

'Good.' Susan raised her glass. 'Here's to hoping your aunt comes up with something.'

They clinked glasses and drank a toast.

'How long are you in Australia for?' he asked.

'Another week. I was visiting a couple of old schoolfriends who moved here – along with half of white South Africa. I fly back to Johannesburg on Thursday.'

He nodded. The beers and wine had relaxed him and the thought of going back to his flat alone was not appealing. Nick was in no hurry, but it seemed like no time before the waitress returned with the rest of their food and tipped the last of the pinot gris into each of their glasses. Soon they were finished.

'That was great,' Susan said. 'Good suggestion.'

The candlelight caught her eyes and he was momentarily transfixed with possibilities. 'Tell me, what's Africa like?'

She grinned. 'Dangerous.'

'That's what everyone says, with crime and all.'

'What I mean,' she leaned across the table, closing the distance between them once again, 'is that if you come to Africa then you might get hooked, and you'll end up spending a lot of time and money coming back, again and again. It might change your life.'

'To be honest, I could use a change right now,' Nick said, and found he meant it.

She looked at her watch and he felt a little stab in his heart. 'I should get going.'

He finished his wine, trying hard not to show his disappointment. 'Sure, no problem.'

'No,' she held up a hand, perhaps sensing what he was feeling, 'it's not that I don't want to stay out, but I promised a girlfriend I'd go running with her at five thirty tomorrow morning.'

'Aargh.'

'I'm regretting it already.' Susan waved to their waiter.

'I've got this,' Nick said.

'No, please, let me pay half.'

He held up a hand. 'Absolutely no way. Besides, I hope there'll be a next time, and you can pay then. Somewhere fancier.'

She laughed again and he decided he loved the sound. 'Deal.'

While Nick paid the bill Susan summoned an Uber with her phone.

'Here in two minutes,' she said as he put his wallet away and stood.

Nick had enjoyed meeting her, and the dinner. It was a shame to see her go, but talking to his aunt ensured he would be in touch with Susan again, even if it was to say he'd drawn a blank. His guilt over Jill aside, he realised he was way more invested in this ancestor of his than he'd originally anticipated. 'I just hope my aunt comes through with something interesting.'

'Me as well. Oh,' Susan added, 'I meant to tell you earlier. There's a German academic named Anja Berghoff who has also been re-searching Claire Martin and the period of history and the area where Cyril Blake was killed. I reached out to her but she was a bit over-protective of her research. She snubbed me.'

Nick thought for a moment. 'I wonder if it might help if I con-tacted her. She might be interested in hearing from a descendent of Blake?'

'That would be *lekker*. You're right, Nick, she might be more receptive to you, but don't tell her you used to be a journalist – I think she distrusts us. I'll send you her email address.'

'Cool,' he said, wishing she didn't have to leave.

'Well ...' Susan put out her hand to shake and he took it. To his delight, she leaned in and offered him her cheek for a kiss. Nick obliged.

'Night,' Nick said.

Susan kept hold of his hand for a few more seconds. 'It's been *really* nice meeting you, Nick. I hope your aunt does know some-thing as I'd like to see you again.'

They walked out onto the footpath and the car arrived. Nick opened the door for her.

'A gentleman as well,' she said as she got in, her skirt riding up a little and exposing more of her thigh as she shimmied in. 'Thank you again.'

'My pleasure.'

Nick closed the door and watched the car drive off. Susan looked back at him, and smiled through the rear window.

CHAPTER 7

Munich, Germany, the present day

Anja's phone buzzed in her pocket. She took it out and looked at the screen. It was her mother. She let the call go through to voicemail.

Her tummy was grumbling, telling her it was time she left the LMU library and found a sandwich. She had started to pack up when her phone buzzed once more.

Anja sighed. Her mother was becoming mildly forgetful and had probably misplaced something. Anja walked through the library to the reception area, where she could use her phone. By the time she got there the phone had rung out and she was tempted to go back to her desk. However, it buzzed for a third time.

'Hello, Mama, sorry, I was in the toilet.'

'Hmm, ignoring me, more like it ... the gas man is here.'

Anja exhaled audibly. 'Why are you calling me to tell me that?'

'Because, Miss Smarty Pants, you are apparently the one who called the gas company and told them to come and inspect a leak in the basement somewhere.'

Anja was instantly worried. 'Mama, I did *not* call the gas company.'

'But the man said he spoke to you, he called you the "young woman" of the house. He did not call me old, but I found his tone quite offensive nonetheless.'

'Mama, listen to me,' Anja's pulse was pounding now, 'where is this man?'

'He is out the front of the house, of course. Did you think I would let just anyone in? You know there are these conmen who come around preying on old ladies and –'

'Yes, I do know, Mama, we discussed that the other day, remember?'

'Of *course* I remember,' her mother said, raising her voice. 'Why do you think I'm calling you, if not to check?'

'Is he still there?'

'I don't know. I suppose so.'

'Is the door locked?' Anja asked.

'Of course it's locked. Do you think I am a fool?'

Anja bit her lip. 'Did you get a good look at him?'

'I'm going to the peephole now, to check him out.'

'Be careful, Mama.' She waited, fretting, wondering if she should have told her mother she would call the police and then ring her back.

'He's gone,' her mother said.

Anja breathed a sigh of relief. 'Call the police, please, Mama, tell them what happened. I'm coming home right now.'

'Please don't feel that you have to put yourself out, Anja.'

A pair of police officers were at Anja's mother's house when Anja arrived home, somewhat out of breath from her high-speed cycle ride through the Englischer Garten and across the John F. Kennedy Bridge. The police seemed to be finishing up and were trying to extricate themselves, politely refusing her mother's invitation to stay for coffee.

'We'll ask around the neighbourhood, Mrs Berghoff, to see if anyone else has had a visit from this guy,' said the female officer, whose surname was Gunther according to her mother.

'Did you check with the gas company?' Anja asked.

Gunther gave Anja a very tight-lipped smile that told her the police were not stupid. 'Yes. They had no one in the street today. This sort of thing is, I'm afraid, all too common.'

'My mother said the man told her that the "young woman" of the house had called the gas company,' Anja said to the officer.

'I already told them all this,' her mother said.

'Yes.' Gunther nodded. 'It's also a common ploy. Your mother said you went out this morning, to the university, I believe.'

'Yes. I'm a student there, and a tutor.'

The policewoman continued. 'By mentioning you the conman was trying to show your mother that he knew there was another woman in the house, and that therefore he would be more believable. He was probably watching the house for some time. Your mother did the right thing by calling you to check.'

'See, Anja,' her mother said, with a very self-satisfied look on her face, 'not so foolish after all.'

The policewoman shrugged. 'It's likely the guy would have been in and out of the house very quickly. He would have been looking for any cash or jewellery or small valuables lying around, like phones or tablets.'

That was small comfort, Anja thought. As annoying as her mother could be, she felt incredibly protective of her. She put her arm around the older woman's shoulder. 'Were you able to give the police a description?'

'Yes,' her mother said.

The policewoman opened her notebook again, more for show than necessity. '"Dark, like a Turk or a Syrian".'

'All those refugees,' her mother said. 'If you ask me –'

'I'm sure the police officers need to get busy now, Mama, talking to your neighbours.'

'That's right,' Gunther said.

Anja thanked them, and the two officers left.

'I don't know why you want to go back to Namibia so soon,' her mother said as she closed and locked the door behind them. 'Those people have ruined a perfectly good country. They're all corrupt.'

'Yes, Mama.' Anja wanted to defend Namibia to her mother, to tell her of a country that was doing its best to root out corruption and to ensure a good education for its children. Tourists loved visiting the country, with its wide open spaces, good roads and bountiful wildlife. It would be a waste of breath, Anja thought, as she hung up her overcoat and took off her scarf.

'I'm going to the basement to do some work, Mama,' she said. It had been her father's study and she suspected that he, like her, sometimes valued it as a place of refuge.

'Fine, if you'd rather read about horses than talk to your mother.'

Anja sighed and went downstairs. For all her faults and latent racism her mother had loved her father and had kept his desk and study more or less as he had left it. There was a photo on the wall, her parents with Anja as a two-year-old, at the waterhole at Etosha's Okaukuejo Camp, a dusty white elephant no more than ten metres behind them, and a picture she loved, of her father, perhaps in his thirties, shirtless on the beach at Swakopmund on one of the rare days when the water was warm enough to swim.

She sat in his old leather office chair, opened her backpack, and took out some more of the copied papers. Anja began to read where she had left off.

The eastern Transvaal, South Africa, 1902

For the first time in a long time Claire Martin was scared.

A second British patrol had shown up, unexpectedly by the look of it, and two British officers were arguing over her. She knew which one she wanted to win.

'She is *my* prisoner. *My* men captured her,' the reedy younger captain with the evil eyes, Walters, was insisting.

The other officer, a major, had grey hair and a walrus moustache, which he smoothed as he spoke. He had introduced himself to her as Peter Appleton. 'Yes, old boy, and we've seen what your men do to prisoners of war, haven't we, hmm?'

After they had shot her horse and captured her the two Australians had tied her and left her on the ground while they went in search of the captain. From where they had left her Claire couldn't see what had gone on exactly but it seemed the men, including Nathaniel, all ended up in the stables. She had heard a single gunshot. Major Appleton and his nine men had arrived as Captain Walters and the other Australian, Bert she thought his name was, emerged from the stables. Between them they dragged out the sergeant – the one who had captured her in the first place. It was confusing. At first she thought the sergeant had been shot, but he had been knocked unconscious.

Tears had welled unbidden in her eyes when Major Appleton's troopers had brought Nathaniel's body out of the stables. She had guessed him dead. Claire had not loved him, but she had been his lover. There was a difference, but nonetheless she mourned his loss as she willed herself not to cry in front of the enemy.

''Ere 'ere, what's this?' a cockney trooper joked as he turned the dead American's head to one side and inspected the bloody mess where his ear had been.

Claire's stomach heaved. Nathaniel had been mutilated before being shot.

'Enough of that, Soames, you callous oaf,' barked Appleton. 'Not in front of the lady.'

'As I was saying, sir,' Walters continued, 'the woman is my captive.'

'She *was* your captive, Captain. *Was* being the operative word. She was lying alone on the ground unattended when I arrived and you and your ... your *colonials* were up to Lord knows what in that barn.'

'Major Appleton.' Claire sniffed dramatically, looking up at the mounted officer in his saddle. 'This has been a very trying experience for me, I'm sure you'll understand.'

'Of course, madam, of course. May I ask where you are from?'

Summoning her almost dormant American accent, Claire said, 'America, sir. I am a widow – my husband came here to work the goldfields. My cousin,' she dabbed her eyes as she cast a glance at Nathaniel's body, 'was acting as my chaperone until I could raise enough money to return home.'

'I'm sorry for this dreadful disturbance, madam, but I'm sure you'll understand there are certain irregularities which need to be cleared up by the proper authorities. I shall have to take you into custody for the time being.'

'Of course, Major, I understand. But if you could please release these bindings I might be able to tend to myself better.' She raised her bound wrists to him in supplication and blinked twice.

'On your honour, madam, I will have the bindings undone, but your mount will be tethered to mine for the journey back to camp.'

'Of course, Major, on my honour as an American citizen,' she replied.

'See to it, Jenkins,' Appleton said to one of the troopers.

The dismounted soldier pulled out his bayonet and freed Claire's hands. She rubbed her reddened wrists vigorously and gave Nathaniel a last, long look goodbye.

'Sir ...' Walters interjected. 'This woman is not American, she is a Boer sympathiser from the colony of German South West Africa. She is my prisoner and she is playing you for a fool.'

Claire fought hard to hold back a look of shock. He knew a good deal about her. Judging by his behaviour Claire suspected that Captain Walters had a particular interest in capturing and questioning Nathaniel, but she'd had no idea that Walters knew anything of her background. Someone who knew about the armaments deal had talked.

'Enough, Captain! For the last time.' Major Appleton smoothed his moustache again. 'The lady is coming with us and you will follow us and make your report about this ... this business. Rum indeed, to say the least. Talk me through it again – it won't be the last time you'll have to do it today. Jenkins, take the lady inside in case she needs to freshen up before the ride.'

'I'm fine, thank you, Major.' Claire wiped her eyes. She wanted to play up her distress and allowed a few more real tears to flow for Nathaniel. At the same time she wondered if he had cracked under his brief period of interrogation. No, she told herself, otherwise Walters would have ridden off. He was here because he needed her, and if he wanted to question her it was either over the artillery pieces she had promised the Boers, or the way they were going to pay her. If he had been simply a diligent officer doing his duty he would have explained to the major about the shipment of German artillery destined for South Africa, but the fact that he hadn't led Claire to believe that he, like her, wanted to know where the treasure was that would be used to pay for the guns.

'I was questioning the prisoner in the barn when Sergeant Blake barged in.' Walters motioned with a flick of his head to the still-comatose Australian as two troopers laid him across the rump of a horse. His hands were tied. 'Sergeant Blake said to me, "I'll show you how to loosen Old Piet's tongue, sir," and punched the prisoner several times in the face.'

Claire watched Walters through narrowed eyes. She had heard no such comment about 'Old Piet', which was the British nickname for a Boer.

'I see,' said Major Appleton dryly. 'Go on, Walters.'

'When the man refused to say which unit he commanded – our intelligence told us a Boer colonel of American extraction would be visiting this house – the sergeant took out a knife and –'

'Not in front of the lady, Walters. I think we can deduce what happened next from the state of the body.'

'Of course, sir,' Walters said. 'Anyway, the man nearly passed out from the pain. I started to draw my pistol and ordered Blake to cease the torture immediately, but he turned on me. I'm afraid he had me covered with his rifle, sir, and I laid down my pistol.'

'Mmm, not good, Walters, not good, but please go on.'

'Sergeant Blake said words to the effect of "We'll get nothing from this one, he's too tough," and then shot the poor man. While he did that I reached for my pistol and tried to make a move on him.'

'Better, Walters, better,' Major Appleton said encouragingly.

'I don't know if I could have shot him before he got me, and that's the truth, sir, but fortunately the other member of my patrol, Trooper Hughes here, entered the barn at that moment and clubbed the sergeant down with his rifle.'

Bert just nodded, his face sombre.

Claire continued to stare at Walters. He was lying through his teeth. When the major turned his back, Walters briefly returned Claire's gaze and raised one eyebrow in a theatrical gesture. She felt a chill travel the length of her spine.

'I'm sorry you had to hear all that, Miss Martin,' Major Appleton said, as if she was some delicate daisy who would bend in a stiff breeze. 'We are at war and some distasteful things happen in war, but torture and summary execution are not in the Queen's regulations. Please accept my condolences for the loss of your ...'

'Cousin,' Claire said, evenly.

'Yes, cousin. Of course, my apologies,' Appleton said, then turned to his men. 'Soames, Harris, Smith, torch the buildings; leave nothing for the Boers.'

'Sir!' Walters blurted. 'The dead man was a senior Boer officer. I need to search the house and farm buildings to see what documents may have been in his possession. I'll torch the place once I've finished.'

The major frowned. It seemed to Claire he didn't like the impertinent young captain's tone at all. Walters wanted something from the trading post and she wondered if it was the small ceramic bottle Nathaniel had passed to her when she'd made her escape. She had hidden it where no English gentleman would dare look for it and as yet she had not had time to open it. 'No, Captain, you've got some explaining to do back at HQ. You will accompany us now and you can return later today or tomorrow to do your snooping. It looks like there's precious little here to sustain the Boers in any case, but we'll take the spare horses with us.'

Appleton, who Claire suspected had taken something of a shine to her, organised his men to ready one of Nathaniel's horses for her. They set off, Claire's mind racing as the column trotted across the open veld under the warm morning sun. She was acutely aware of Walters' eyes on her from behind. She assumed she and Nathaniel had been compromised, but she wondered how much the captain and the two Australians really knew.

The major's arrival had been a stroke of good fortune for her. She wondered if she could have resisted interrogation as Nathaniel had – if he had indeed kept silent. She told herself she could be strong, but just the sight of the blood on Walters' gloves – not to mention those reptilian eyes – had made her feel faint.

She didn't believe Walters' story, either. She had heard Nathaniel's piercing scream before the sergeant had entered the barn. The oafish Australian had apologised to her horse for putting it out of its misery, so he was hardly the kind of man to torture and execute a prisoner of war in cold blood. He had nice eyes, she recalled, for a colonial lackey.

Claire looked at him slumped across the horse next to her. He seemed at peace, like he was sleeping. His face and hands were deeply tanned, his chin covered in black stubble. She guessed him to be no more than thirty, perhaps around her age, and his thick hair was still jet-black. She wondered what would happen to him. She doubted the British military would take the word of an Australian sergeant over an upper-class English gentleman, and that boded badly for her.

'Major Appleton,' Claire said, as sweetly as she could.

He looked back at her. 'Miss Martin?'

'This is most delicate, Major, but I must answer the call of nature.'

He reached for his moustache with a free hand. 'Of course.'

He slowed his horse and ordered his men, and Walters, to carry on, as he led Claire and her horse towards a large anthill. 'You may dismount, Miss Martin, but please do not try to escape.'

'You have my word, sir,' she said.

Claire dismounted and went behind the anthill. She had thought about trying to gallop away, but the horse they had chosen for her, perhaps deliberately, was in poor condition, so she did not think she could outrun the mounted troopers. Nonetheless, she needed to escape as soon as she could, and to get word to German Naval High Command and her cousin Fritz that the armaments deal was now compromised. That would free her up to pursue her own mission, which would ensure she would make far more than a commission fee for shipping a load of used artillery to some doomed rebels. She squatted down and removed the ceramic bottle.

She uncorked the little flask and upended it. A piece of thin paper, tightly rolled, slipped out and Claire quickly flattened it. As she had hoped, it was the map Nathaniel had mentioned. She took in the town of Komatipoort, which she knew to be on the border of Portuguese East Africa, to the southeast, and a squiggly line with crosshatching, which she was sure was a railroad.

'Miss Martin?' Major Appleton called.

'Coming, Major.' She quickly re-rolled the map, put it back in the little bottle and hid it again. She stood, and as she walked around the anthill she was confronted with the sight of Captain Walters, on horseback, blocking her path. Appleton was waiting politely out of sight, through the trees. The captain had obviously carried on, as ordered, but then doubled back through the bush to catch her unawares. A few seconds earlier and he would have seen her hiding the map. Her cheeks burned.

Walters looked down at her. 'I know you're working for the Germans, Claire. I know what you're up to and I'm watching you.'

Walters pulled on his horse's reins, put the spurs to the animal, and rode off. Claire shivered.

CHAPTER 8

Munich, Germany, the present day

The page of the scanned letter Anja was reading was a fragment, its edges burned, and the damage showed as black on her photocopy.

> *I was not sure how much Captain Walters knew of my mission or my meeting with Kommandant Belvedere, but the raid on the trading post had been deliberately planned to capture the American and, presumably, myself. This meant there was most likely a traitor within the ranks of the Boers. The captain had only spent a short amount of time with Kommandant Belvedere, yet I can only assume Belvedere held his tongue. This, I knew, meant that the captain would be seeking an opportunity to question me about the mission at his earliest convenience.*

Anja smiled at the formal turn of phrase. Claire, clearly a formidable woman, was expressing fear. This Captain Walters had proved himself to be completely ruthless, assuming it was he and not the Australian sergeant who had executed the American colonel in cold blood.

Anja set the paper down and wondered what bearing this information might have on her own studies. Here was a man whose name she had heard before, Sergeant Cyril Blake, entering Claire

Martin's life in 1902 and reappearing four years later at the height of the Nama rebellion as a horse trader and rebel sympathiser.

Anja had heard of Blake from a South African journalist, Susan Vidler, who had contacted her after she had found, courtesy of Google, an article on Anja's research in Namibia's *New Era* newspaper. A young Namibian woman had struck up a conversation with Anja on a previous trip to Namibia while they had both been viewing the desert horses from a hide overlooking the waterhole at Garub near Aus in the country's south. Anja had not realised the woman was a journalist and had been surprised to read a week later about her thesis concerning the origins of the horses. She had learned, since then, to keep her work largely to herself.

Vidler was running to an agenda, to make a name for herself writing a feature that would put pressure on the German government at a time when the Nama and the Herero were renewing their campaign for the Germans to pay reparations for the harm inflicted on their people during and after the colonial uprisings. A class action had even been lodged in the courts in the United States against the German government by expatriate Hereros living in America. The woman had discovered that Edward Prestwich, an Australian mentioned in a couple of history books as having fought on the side of the Nama people, was an alias. The man's real name, Susan Vidler had disclosed, was Cyril Blake and she wanted to know if he had come up in Anja's research. At that time, he hadn't.

In any case, Anja was not interested in politics, nor in sharing her research or findings just yet with another journalist. Her thesis would eventually be in the public domain for anyone to see, but for now she wanted to take her time preparing it and not be led about by a pushy reporter.

Anja heard footsteps coming down the stairs and the door to her father's underground study creaked open.

'Supper will be ready in ten minutes,' her mother said.

'Coming, Mama.'

Anja closed her folder of papers and went upstairs to supper, where her mother served up the plain meal of chicken and potatoes, just the way she liked it.

'I don't know why you need to keep going back over there,' her mother said as they sat down to eat. Anja had wondered how long it would take for her mother to object to her impending trip back to Namibia. 'You should find a nice man here, in Germany, and settle down. Do you know Mrs Mueller's son, Hans, got divorced? He's a catch, no kids, and he works in a bank. You could give up your part-time tutoring job.'

Anja groaned inwardly. She liked her job and her father had left money specifically in his will to allow her to continue her studies for as long as she wished. Neither she nor her mother wanted for much.

'Anja?'

'Yes, Mama?'

Her mother looked down at her food, and then minutely adjusted the cutlery around the plate. She seemed reluctant to meet Anja's gaze. 'You do like men, don't you?'

Anja rolled her eyes and that was enough to settle her mother. They were similar people, both quick to anger. 'I know, you are worried that I am going to stay at university all my life. As I have told you, I do not plan on doing so.'

'Then what will you do? Get a job here? Or are you going to leave me for good and stay in Namibia forever?'

'You know I'm only going for a month, Mama, to do some of my own research and help out with the wild horses monitoring project. As I told you, the horses are at risk of dying out; the spotted hyenas have been taking their foals before they can reach maturity. It's important work and –'

Her mother banged the table in an uncharacteristic show of active aggression. 'No! Your father did not work his whole life to pay for your schooling and your *years* of university so that you can spend your time sitting alone in the desert without a man or a proper job, counting horses.'

Anja clenched her fists.

'It's time for you to come home, for good,' her mother said.

'I *have* a home,' Anja said quietly, but forcefully. 'It is Namibia. I have citizenship there because that is where you gave birth to me, whether you like it or not, and that is where I want to live.'

Her mother's body heaved, as though she was sobbing, even though Anja detected no tears. 'It is true, my worst fear. You would abandon me?'

Anja sighed. 'I don't want to leave you, Mama, but I have a right to decide my own future, what I do with my life, and where I want to live. I'm a grown woman, not a child any more.'

'But don't you see,' her mother reached across the table, 'you are *my* child and I just want you close as I get older and as my time ...'

Anja felt trapped, as she always did when her mother went down this path. She knew how much her mother missed her father and she was such a prickly old woman that she had few friends. There was that word again, she thought, 'prickly'. A psychotherapist friend had told her that what people disliked in others was sometimes a reflection of their own issues. She felt like a prisoner. She wanted to scream.

'You like those horses more than you like human beings,' her mother said. 'You'd be more at home with them than you would be with a man or your own mother.'

On that, Anja reflected she and her mother had finally reached a point of consensus.

CHAPTER 9

North Sydney, Australia, the present day

Nick woke with a trace of a hangover that was quickly diminished with a smile as he thought back over his evening with Susan.

He showered and dressed in a polo shirt and jeans and walked from his one-bedroom flat to North Sydney station, eschewing the bus in order to clear his head. He caught the train to Granville, in Sydney's west. The two suburbs in which he and his aunt Sheila MacKenzie lived were about as different as two places could be and still be in the same city or country.

In half an hour he had swapped the high-rise office blocks and expensive harbourside properties of where he lived for the factories and terraced houses of the landlocked suburbs which had traditionally been a first stop for the waves of immigrants who had sought a new start in Australia. As Nick walked through Granville he saw almost the full spectrum of Australia's multicultural society in shopfronts, cafes and takeaway joints and in the faces of the people going about their Saturday morning business.

He had been to his aunt's place only once before – she had bought it after her last divorce when she and her ex-husband had sold their shared house and both had to downsize. The street was leafy and the early twentieth-century terraces and Federation houses were mostly in good condition or being renovated. He knocked on the door.

'Ah, my favourite nephew.' Sheila, a foot shorter than him, got up on her toes to kiss him on the cheek.

'Your only nephew.'

'Ever the realist.'

'Wait,' he said, forcing a smile, 'it gets worse.'

'Come in and tell Aunty all about it.'

'I lost my job.'

'I'm sorry to hear that, Nick, darling, especially after, well ... Want a beer?'

He checked his watch. It was eleven thirty in the morning. 'Sure. What are you having?'

'Bubbles. It's Saturday.'

'Fair enough.' He went to the refrigerator in the kitchen. Sheila had four cold bottles and he selected one and opened it. She found the glasses, in a box, and he popped the cork and poured.

Sheila raised her glass. 'To the future. May it be better for both of us.'

'I'll drink to that,' he said. 'But today it's the past I'm interested in.'

'Come outside.' Sheila led him through the small kitchen to a narrow yard shaded by a pergola festooned with passionfruit vines. 'I was intrigued by your call. Whenever I've tried to talk to you about family history in the past your eyes just glaze over.'

'Guilty as charged. I met a woman.'

'Aha. I thought you were too handsome to stay single.'

Nick laughed. 'It's not like that. She's a South African journalist. She's asking about a great-great-or-whatever uncle of ours who fought in the Boer War.'

She nodded. 'Cyril Blake.'

'You're amazing,' he said.

'You didn't think so at my birthday party,' she sipped her champagne, 'when I tried to educate you about our family.'

'Well, I'm interested now.'

'Pretty, is she?'

Nick smiled. 'Maybe. But I'm interested in Cyril Blake in any case. Did you know he fought against the Germans as well as the Boers?'

'Yes, nephew, as a matter of fact I did. I actually spoke to your grandmother about him before she died. The dementia was already setting in, but she was able to tell me a bit about him. She told me he'd fought the Germans and gone missing.'

'In Africa,' Nick said.

Sheila looked surprised. 'No, I don't think any Australians were involved in the fighting against the Germans in Africa during the First World War, but there were Boer War veterans who signed on again and fought on the Western Front, so I assumed Cyril was one of them.'

Nick shook his head. 'No, this was in 1906 or some time like that, in the war between the German colonial powers in South West Africa – Namibia – and the local people.'

Sheila set down her champagne. 'But Australians didn't fight in that war. This is amazing stuff, Nick, and really interesting.'

For the first time, when it came to family history, he had to agree with his aunt. 'I don't suppose you have any really old family stuff, do you?'

Sheila put a finger to her lips. 'Maybe. I don't know. I did get a box of stuff from your grandmother, just before she went into the nursing home. There are all sorts of papers in there and I haven't been able to go through them all. While I'm trying to put together the whole family history, I'm only up to the mid–nineteenth century at the moment.'

'What sort of *stuff* was there?'

'Letters, old photographs, keepsakes. There are your grandfather's medals as well.'

'Really?'

She rolled her eyes. 'Yes *really*, Nick. This family history stuff is not all about me trawling the internet for birth and death certificates.'

'I know,' he said. 'I've learned that you have to do some real detective work and that it's not just a mouse-click away.'

'That's true, but that's not what I mean, darling,' she said. 'There are real, tangible links to our past, a lot of them in cardboard packing boxes in this house, you know? This is our *history*, Nick, our people, not just a family tree on a piece of paper.'

He felt bad, now, that he had tuned out of so many discussions his aunt had tried to start with him about where they came from. He was genuinely interested in Cyril Blake, and he was beginning to get an inkling of how his aunt had become addicted to researching their family history. Having lost the person he was closest to he wondered if it was also about having family to cling to.

'So are there any papers that might have belonged to Blake?' Nick asked.

Sheila pursed her lips. 'I'm not sure. There is one bundle that could be of interest.'

'Tell me.'

'Why don't I show you instead? Pour us another drink, and if you want to eat, maybe order us a pizza? There's a menu on the fridge.'

They got up and Nick found himself a beer at the back of the fridge. He saved the champagne for his aunt and poured her another glass, then found the menu on a magnet and called and ordered a supreme pizza and some garlic bread. They met in the lounge room; she came down the stairs carrying a cardboard removalists' box.

'Can I help you with that?'

'I'm not *that* old.'

They each took a seat in armchairs and Sheila put the box on the coffee table between them. 'I think this is the one.'

Sheila opened the box, set the lid down and then carefully began unpacking it. There were black and white photographs, some tied in bundles with string, others in old brown leather frames. Nick saw envelopes with faded elaborate copperplate on them, and folded certificates.

Sheila dug deeper into the box, but she took the time to reverently stack all the items she removed. Nick took a handful of pictures. There were stiffly formal wedding shots and a man in what looked like a light horseman's uniform, with a bandolier strung across his chest and a slouch hat with an emu feather in it.

'Your great-grandfather, in Palestine.'

Nick stared into the innocent face, still untouched by war, and thought that Sheila not only knew these people's names, it was as if she knew them personally.

'Here we are!'

He set down the pictures and looked up. Sheila was smiling, her eyes glittering. '*This* was what I was thinking of.'

She passed a manila folder to him and Nick opened it. Inside were pages of flimsy writing paper, and as soon as he tried to read them he realised they were not in English.

'German,' Sheila said. 'I went through this stuff with your grand-mother years ago,' she continued, sipping some champagne, 'and that's when she mentioned about your great-great-uncle who had been in the Boer War and then gone on to fight the Germans – I assumed in France. She told me she thought those pages were letters or military documents that Cyril might have taken from a dead German. She said she'd found them among her own mother's possessions.'

'Wow,' Nick said. 'I wonder what they say.'

'Me too, and it's been on my to-do list to get them translated, but I'd filed that chore away in my head for when I started research-ing the family's involvement in the war.'

'Do you think I could ...?'

'Nephew, if you want to help your little old aunty and get those letters or whatever they are translated, I would be eternally grateful.'

Nick picked up the first page from the pile of papers. The writ-ing was in German, but there was a date at the top that clearly read '1915'. No doubt that was why his grandmother had assumed the papers came from the First World War, but that still didn't tally with Blake dying in a German colony in Africa in 1906.

'I've got just the person in mind,' Nick said. 'Lili, a German in-tern at my work – well, where I used to work as of yesterday.'

'Sounds good,' Sheila said. 'And it's great to have you on the team. Let's have another drink to celebrate.'

*

On Monday morning Nick showered, shaved and dressed for work. When he had first been told he was being made redundant he had almost told Pippa that he wouldn't bother coming into work the following week, and that she could just give him his payout and he would be off.

After seeing Sheila, he had brought his anger under control. When he thought about it rationally he realised he had not been happy working at Pippa's PR company for some time. He wasn't sure exactly what he wanted to do, work-wise, but he realised now that this could be the chance he needed to make a change. While his options and opportunities were not boundless, he reckoned he could find a job elsewhere without too much effort. He would need to put out feelers and have a look online, but his time with Susan and his aunt had given him something else to concentrate on in the interim.

When he arrived at work, early, he used the copier/scanner to make two copies and scan a PDF of the papers his aunt had given him, then found a pre-paid postage satchel in the stationery cupboard, put the originals in the bag and placed it in the outbox to be sent back to Sheila.

When the intern, Lili, arrived, he went to her desk and asked her if she would be interested in translating some papers for him.

Lili had cast a glance at Pippa in her office and lowered her eyes. 'It might not be appropriate,' she had said in her formal style of English, 'for me to do such a task during working hours, Nick, though you have helped me and I feel sorry for you.'

He had to laugh at her characteristic bluntness. 'Thanks. How about I take you to lunch, Lili, and we talk about it then?'

Again, she looked around her, as if fearing Pippa might overhear. 'You know I am only allowed forty-five minutes.'

He winked. 'I'll make it worth your while. I'm happy to pay you to help me with this, Lili.'

The intern brightened. 'Oh, well, that is another matter.'

At twelve thirty precisely Nick and Lili, who had been carefully watching the office clock, left work and headed to the historic Greenwood Hotel, across the road from North Sydney railway station. Other office workers were taking tables for lunch.

'You know they call this place the drycleaners,' Nick said as they walked in.

'Why?' Lili asked.

'Because it's where all the suits hang out.'

She didn't seem to get the joke and he didn't want to waste time explaining. Seating themselves at a table in the open-air courtyard, they scanned the menu and decided on their meals, Nick assuring Lili that lunch would be his shout. Nick took the folder containing the German papers from his bag and laid it down on the table. 'While I go and order the food, could you have a look at these for me, please?'

'OK.'

By the time he got back, Lili was studying the handwritten sheets intently.

'Anything interesting?' he asked.

Lili read a few more lines then looked up. 'I think so. This is like some kind of memoir or maybe even a novel. But he says he doesn't want it published. It's very interesting – I want to read more.'

He nodded. 'My aunt said my grandmother thought they might have been letters from a German soldier to a family member, during the First World War.'

Lili shook her head, still skimming through the first few pages. 'No, Nick, this is not a letter, it reads more like a story or a history of some kind. The place names are in German South West Africa, which is now Namibia. I have been there with my parents as a child, on safari.'

'Yes!'

Lili looked up and smiled. 'You are excited, Nick?'

'I am.'

'That is good,' she said, 'I have not seen you happy since I arrived at the company.'

He grimaced. Was his dissatisfaction with work that obvious? No wonder he'd been the first one Pippa fired. 'What else does it say, Lili?'

'This covering page is a note from the author. You see the date, 1915?'

Nick nodded. 'Yes, my aunt and I both noticed that and that's why my grandmother thought it dated from the First World War.'

'The author says he is *writing* this manuscript in 1915, but it is about events that happened in 1906. There must be pages missing, or they are out of order, because the story seems to then begin in the middle somewhere.'

'Please, read some for me, now, if you can,' Nick pleaded.

'OK.' Lili took a sip of her water and her eyes shifted left to right. 'This man, Blake, seems to have been knocked out. *When Blake regained consciousness he found himself locked in a cell ...*'

CHAPTER 10

South Africa, 1902

Blake wished he was dead. The pain and nausea hit him like a horse kick as he tried to sit. He rolled to one side and vomited.

The walls were whitewashed stone. The floor of the cell, now stained, was made of cattle dung and water, a local building concoction which set like shiny concrete. Weak shafts of light penetrated the gloom from a tiny barred window set high up on the wall. His bed was a stone slab with a straw mattress. The room smelled of stale piss and, now, fresh vomit.

He looked down at his feet. The laces from his boots were gone, as were his tunic, belt and braces – anything he could hang himself with, Blake thought.

The steel door to the cell creaked open and a Scottish corporal, a guard, filled the doorway. 'Wake up! You've got a visitor.'

Blake blinked. It hurt. The guard stepped aside and Bert Hughes walked in, also minus his tunic, belt and braces.

'You've got ten minutes, no more,' the guard said, then closed and locked the door.

Bert stood in front of him. 'Jesus, you look terrible.'

'I feel worse,' Blake said. 'Are you locked up as well?'

Bert nodded. 'Yeah, I'm in the shit too. Walters came to me with a deal.'

Blake gingerly touched the wound on his head. 'What sort of deal? He's a murderer, Bert.'

'Yeah, right. He says he doesn't want you testifying against him. He wants us to help him get the Yankee woman. Walters says she's a crook and she's sitting on a stash of money she and some Boers robbed from a payroll wagon a couple of weeks ago.'

'I didn't hear anything about that, at least not in our area,' Blake said. 'Why should I believe anything that bastard says? *He's* a crook, Bert.'

'Yeah, well, he says the caper was hushed up. Makes sense, right? Typical army stuff-up. Anyway, Walters says his knackers are on the line as he was the officer in charge of the convoy and he needs to get the money back to save his neck. He says if we get the woman to tell us where she and the American colonel hid the money, that he'll cut us in on a finder's fee. He says he'll tell the major he was wrong about you killing the American in cold blood.'

'*I* didn't kill him, Bert. You know that.'

'Yeah, but Walters will help us if we help him. He says he'll put in a good word for you and you'll be out of here by this afternoon.'

'Bullshit. He set me up, that's why I'm here. I don't trust him. Tell the guards I want a lawyer, preferably an Aussie. Where's the woman?'

'They took her to one of the camps for the Boer women and children – the one near here,' Bert said.

'Bloody hell,' Blake said, shaking his head again, 'people die in those places.'

'What do you say, Sarge? Will you do what Walters wants? If not we're both finished.'

Blake shook his head. 'Fuck him. He's scared and he knows I'm safe in here. As soon as they give me a defending officer I'll tell the law what really happened.'

Bert sighed. 'You won't think about it, Sarge? Walters says there's a *lot* of money to be found and even if he gives most of it back we'll all still do well. He'll just say the Boers spent some of it.'

Blake looked him in the eye, then shook his head, slowly. He glanced down at Bert's boots.

'Corporal?' Bert called. 'I need to get out of here!'

Bert stood and turned so his back was to Blake, and Blake saw how Bert slowly moved his right hand in front of him, just as he heard the key go into the lock.

Laces, Blake thought. Bert still had his in his boots. He wasn't really a prisoner.

Blake jumped up off the bed and wrapped his left arm around Bert's neck while reaching for the other man's right arm.

Bert grabbed Blake's arm with his free hand and then Blake saw what he feared, a narrow-bladed knife half drawn from the pocket of Bert's trousers. Bert kicked back at him, but Blake pulled him to the ground and increased pressure on Bert's neck. Bert had to use his two hands to try and free himself from the choking hold. Blake reached under him for the knife and he got his fingertips on the hilt, but Bert twisted and bucked under him and as Blake drew the weapon it slipped from his grip and skittered across the cell floor.

At that moment the door swung open and the Scottish guard stood there with a pistol raised. 'Put him down, Blake!'

Blake heaved a groggy Bert, who had nearly lost consciousness, upright, using him as a shield. Bert regained consciousness and staggered forward into the corporal, who fired a shot, perhaps accidentally. Bert's body muffled the shot, which went into him. Blake scooped up the knife from the floor and, with the handle wrapped in his hand, punched the shocked guard square in the face.

The corporal fell backwards, burdened by Bert's weight, and his head hit the floor in the corridor with a thud. Blake paused over both of them. He rolled Bert off the jailer. His fellow Australian was dead, shot clean through the heart, and the corporal was out cold.

Blake thought quickly. Walters had sent Bert to kill him and the guard had brought him to his cell with the laces still in Bert's boots. That meant the corporal was at least partly complicit. Blake had Bert's blood on his hands now and it would be his word against Walters'. He'd be charged not just with the killing of the Boer officer, but also with the death of an Australian soldier and the assault of the Scottish corporal. He didn't like the odds.

Blake snatched a ring of keys from the corporal's belt and made his way down the corridor. He came to a room with the word 'armoury' above a steel door and after three attempts found the correct key. Inside he found his Mauser pistol, his rifle, his tunic and belt and his bootlaces. He quickly put the tunic on, then found his matches in his pocket. He returned to his cell and set fire to his stinking straw mattress. The fire would not spread out of the cell and the corporal was on the floor in the corridor, so he'd have clean air beneath the rising smoke.

Blake strode back down the corridor and walked outside. He could see now that the building was an old police station. Behind it was a British tented camp. The perimeter was barbed wire interspersed with sandbag and corrugated tin strong points. He saw his horse, Bluey, tethered to a supply wagon and went and untied him. 'Miss me, boy?'

He put his foot in the saddle, mounted the stallion and headed for the gate. A sentry in a kilt looked up at him.

'There's a fire in that building, Private!' Blake snapped. 'Sound the alarm immediately! I'm off to fetch the medical officer.'

'But, Sergeant ...'

'Now, man! Do as I say.'

'Yes, Sergeant.'

Blake dug his heels into Bluey's flank and galloped away. A bell started ringing behind him.

As he rode he thought about the chain of events that had led to him being locked up and then escaping custody. The raid had obviously been about more than capturing a Boer colonel and the story about the missing payroll wagon didn't ring true. The American must have had information, however, that Walters was prepared to torture out of him. Blake could understand a bit of unauthorised persuasion if there was a good military reason for it, but you didn't get any information out of a dead man.

The raid on the trading post was less than a day's ride from the nearest base, so there was no good reason for Walters to kill the American. Blake wondered now if Walters had ever really intended to bring the American in alive. You didn't cut off a man's ear if you were planning on handing him over to the provost marshal later in the day.

The war had already turned dirty, but Walters had taken it to a new low.

Blake knew virtually nothing about the man. Walters had arrived at Steinaecker's Sabie Bridge camp a few days earlier and the word was that he was an intelligence officer from Kitchener's personal staff. The next day Blake and Bert Hughes had been ordered to front up for a special mission. Blake's troop commander had explained that Captain Walters wanted the two best shots and horsemen Steinaecker's Horse had to offer.

Blake thought about the situation; he had a British captain who was after an American colonel working for the Boers, who travelled without a bodyguard, let alone the battalion he supposedly commanded. The captain was after information so important he was prepared to torture and kill for it and he had corrupted Bert in the process, offering him enough to kill Blake if he did not go along with Walters' revised plan.

There was some truth in what Bert had relayed to him from the captain. This caper, Blake reckoned, was about money, a helluva lot of money judging by the things the captain had done.

Blake had found himself in a dirty fight against an enemy who was clever, connected and ruthless. He was now a wanted man and he needed to find a way to prove his innocence – or Walters' guilt. First, he needed to know more about the dead colonel. He also needed to find the other piece in this confusing puzzle – the woman.

CHAPTER 11

Condor Flight DE2294, Munich to Windhoek, Namibia, the present day

Anja turned away from the couple next to her and switched on her reading light on the Boeing 767-300. She knew she should try to sleep on the flight, but the copied reports from Claire Martin were once more claiming all her attention.

Anja had fended off more questions from her mother as she'd packed.

She would miss her mother – in time. For now she sipped her white wine and opened the ring folder into which she had neatly arranged the photocopies of the historic espionage reports. She was a little sad as she leafed through to the last one she had read, knowing they would soon run out, quite possibly before Claire Martin ever returned to German South West Africa. Anja told herself that even if the reports did not provide any useable information directly related to her theory on the origin of the desert horses, they were more interesting and entertaining than any novel she could have picked up at the airport bookstore.

She found her place and began to read.

The major who had saved me from Captain Walters later handed me over to a more junior officer, a lieutenant. I told this man my cover story, that I was an American civilian. It did me no good.

The eastern Transvaal, South Africa, 1902

'On the wagon, Miss,' the lieutenant said, checking his clipboard. 'Martin, Miss C. You're being transported to an internment camp.'

'You have no right,' Claire persisted, hands on her hips. She tossed a loose strand of hair from her face with a flick of her head and stood her ground. Inside, she was quaking. She knew from what had happened to her friend Wilma that for many women the only way out of one of these camps was in a cheap wooden box.

'Please get into the wagon or the guards shall be forced to manhandle you aboard,' the young officer said.

'Don't you dare touch me,' Claire hissed at the two guards, who leered at her from the shade cast by the wagon.

She still wore her pale buckskin trousers, leather riding boots and blue work shirt. The top button had come loose and, try as she might to keep the shirt together, a flash of pale skin showed whenever she had to use both her hands. As she hoisted herself up into the wagon she caught one of the guards staring at her cleavage. She mouthed a silent obscenity at the guard who, suddenly red-faced, turned away.

One of the guards sat in the back of the wagon opposite her, a Lee Enfield between his knees. The other soldier sat up the front next to the driver. With a crack of his whip the wagon lurched forward.

The lieutenant forced a tight smile and waved. Claire spat out the back of the wagon, past the guard, who shook his head in disgust.

Claire was angry, mostly at herself. There had been no chance of breaking out of the cell block where she had spent the night. After being brought in she'd been questioned for an hour by Major Appleton. From outside the guardroom, where the interrogation took place, she had heard the raised voice of Captain Walters. He was the one she was really scared of. Judging by his simple questions, Major Appleton seemed to have no inkling of her mission or the business with Nathaniel.

At one stage Appleton had stormed out of the room and berated the captain. 'I remind you again, this is my prisoner and I will deal with her as I see fit. You may very well claim to be operating under orders from Kitchener, but until I see any paperwork to that effect you will leave me to finish this business in peace, Captain.'

The reference to Lord Kitchener, the British Army chief, intrigued her. If the raid had been staged to capture Nathaniel – and possibly her – then the fact that their mission had been compromised was the least of it. Captain Walters had told her that he knew she was a German spy, but he had still not seen fit to tell Appleton anything about that or the arms deal Claire was involved in. Walters was keeping quiet about it all, and that made her even more certain that he, like her, was more interested in the payment Nathaniel had been about to make than the guns themselves.

There had been a fire that morning in the cell block. The smoke had crept down the corridor and seeped under her cell door. She had screamed and there had been a good deal more shouting from elsewhere in the guardhouse. She and the other two prisoners – one English and one Scottish soldier – had been hustled out onto the parade ground. There was a great deal of consternation among the guards and she was sure she overheard one of them saying a prisoner had escaped and another had been killed. She wondered what had become of the battered Australian sergeant, and if it might have been he who had fled. But he was the least of her worries right now.

'Where's this camp you're taking me to?' she asked the Scotsman seated opposite her.

'Ye'll find out soon enough. And there'll be some company for ye,' he replied.

'Company?'

'Ye'll see.'

The wagon turned off the main gravel road about an hour later and then creaked and jolted its way up a rutted track. Claire heard hoofbeats as the wagon slowed.

'The farm's just ahead,' an English voice said, presumably to the driver of the wagon. Claire caught sight of a mounted British trooper, spurring his horse along.

She smelled smoke and soon tiny flecks of ash were filling the wagon. As they turned and pulled to a halt Claire gasped at the sight of devastation that greeted her.

The thatch roof of a whitewashed stone farmhouse was ablaze. The heat from the crackling orange flames stung her cheeks.

A young Boer woman, her face gaunt beneath her bonnet, stood in the yard in front of the house and stared into the flames. Two children, a boy aged about five and a little girl, barely walking, clung to her long skirt. She raised a bony arm to her face to shield herself from the heat as the rafters collapsed. Three British soldiers surrounded her and motioned with their rifles for her to leave. She picked up two bags and turned from the blaze.

Three dogs, huge sandy-coloured beasts that Claire recognised as Boerboels, barked ferociously at the soldiers and the burning house, but they were tethered by chains to a steel peg.

Claire saw the white stripes on the woman's grimy cheeks where the fire's heat had cauterised her tears. The woman ushered her children in front of her and took one look over her shoulder. Two more English soldiers with shovels were filling in a hole. One of the men downed his tool and reached into the fresh earth. He shook the dirt from a white-painted wooden cross and rammed it into the ground.

The woman came to the wagon and Claire reached down, offering her a hand. The woman took it with a nod and allowed Claire to help her aboard. The whites of her eyes, Claire saw, were bloodshot and red-rimmed from crying, or the smoke, or both. Her pupils were fixed and lifeless. She stared at the white canvas cover of the wagon as Claire took each of the children from the hands of a British Tommy without thanks. Finally, one of the soldiers threw the woman's two bags into the back of the wagon.

The woman flinched, but remained silent at the sound of a gunshot. There was a second shot, and then a third. The dogs stopped barking, one at a time.

'Round up the cattle,' a mounted officer called to the soldiers. 'Torch the maize. Leave nothing for the bastards on commando. You know the drill.'

The woman turned as the wagon started to move, and stared at the freshly filled grave.

Claire reached across to her, placing a hand on the woman's knee. 'How can I help?'

The woman turned her head and stared at Claire. 'It was my child, in the grave.'

'No! Did they …?'

'No,' the woman said, shaking her head. 'They didn't kill her. She was stillborn, five weeks ago, but the grave was still fresh, you understand?'

Claire shook her head, unsure of what the woman meant.

'The Tommies,' she said in thickly accented English, 'they say that on some farms folk bury weapons and mark them as graves to disguise what's there. They said they had to check.'

'Oh, my God.'

The woman just stared at her, eyes and soul empty. Claire looked at their guard, who turned his face away from them, hopefully in shame. She was in this deal for money but she did sympathise with the Boers, and hated the sight of men in uniform burning and looting a family's possessions, defiling a child's grave, to further the interests of an empire. Her father had been forced to flee Ireland because he had dared defy those who would oppress him and his people.

The little girl started to cry and Claire picked her up and put her on her knee. She drew the child tightly to her breast and rocked her back and forth, moving with the swaying of the wagon. The guards were silent.

'Your English is good,' Claire said to the woman, as brightly as she could.

'My mother was English. I'm glad she's not alive to see all this. The funny thing of it is she didn't approve of me marrying Gerrit.'

'Is your husband …?'

'Alive? Yes. As far as I know. I pray he is. He's on commando.' She glared defiantly at the guard, who raised his head at the mention of Boer troops. 'Are you married?'

'No. Not any more, at least. I'm Claire, by the way.'

'Gerda. Pardon me, but the way you are dressed, you look like you could be on commando as well.'

'No, I'm just an innocent *American* citizen. A neutral,' she said for the benefit of the guard. When he pretended not to be listening, by staring out the back of the wagon, Claire gave Gerda a conspiratorial wink. She was pleased to see the beginnings of a smile cross the young woman's thin face.

'If I were younger, without the children, I would be on the veld. They say there are women riding with the men,' Gerda said.

'So I've heard.'

'If you are not married to a Boer, then why are they taking you to the camp as well?'

Claire did not want to discuss her plight in front of the soldier, so she said, 'I don't know. I'm not part of this war.'

'Everyone is part of this war.' Gerda looked out the back of the wagon and stared at the smudge of smoke on the horizon, all that remained of her home and the resting place of her child. 'You are in Africa, you are part of it.'

*

Claire smelled the camp before she saw it. The rank odour was a mixture of shit, urine, smoke and quicklime. She tried breathing through her mouth, but that hardly helped.

'I have been dreading this day,' Gerda said. She pulled her two children close to her and the little girl, whose name was Henriette, sensed her mother's anxiety and started to cry.

From what had happened to Wilma, Claire knew Gerda had good reason to be concerned, particularly for the wellbeing of her children. Kitchener had ordered his men to start burning farms and rounding up Boer women and children and the elderly in late 1900.

They were called concentration camps. The theory was that by burning their farms and concentrating their women and children and elderly relations in camps, the Boer commandos would be robbed of their support network and forced to surrender. The commandos, however, were adept at living off the land and the loss of their loved ones simply meant they had no reason to stay in one particular area or periodically return to check on their welfare.

Just before they came to the camp itself Claire saw a woman standing in a field of fresh graves. Most of the dirt mounds, Claire realised with sudden horror, were too short to mark adult graves.

This was a children's cemetery. The woman stared listlessly at the new arrivals.

Wooden framed gates latticed with barbed wire were swung open and the wagon creaked into the compound. Hundreds of bell tents, once white and now a rusty red from seasons of mud and dust, were lined up on the gently sloping hillside, which had been cleared of all natural shade. A couple of thin-looking women stopped their toil, carrying heavy buckets, to look vacantly at the new arrivals from below their bonnets.

'Down from the wagons, if you please, ladies.'

Claire looked down and saw a British Army captain reaching up a hand. The man was old for a subaltern – in his mid-forties by the look of him – and Claire wondered if he had been promoted from the ranks. He was hatless and his thinning black hair was stuck to his reddened scaly scalp with pomade. He was smiling, but the grin reminded Claire of a hyena waiting for its turn at a kill.

'I can manage myself, thank you,' Claire said, ignoring the man's gesture.

The captain grabbed hold of Gerda's arm as she clambered down from the wagon, but she shook his hand off.

'Now, now, ladies. No need to be so obstreperous,' he said. 'I'm Captain Davies, the second-in-command of the camp.'

A grey-haired woman in a patched and stained pale-blue dress bustled up to the rear of the wagon. She said something in Afrikaans that made Gerda grin, but which Claire did not understand. Gerda answered back in the same language.

'Forgive me, my dear. We don't get many English here in the camp,' the woman said to Claire in heavily accented English.

'I'm not English.'

'Oh, well, that's all right then. Thank you, Captain, I am sure we will manage by ourselves from here. I'm Hilda,' she said to Claire.

'Claire.'

The captain looked put out. He patted down an imaginary loose strand on his oily head, turned on his heel and marched off.

'He likes to inspect the new ones,' Hilda said to Claire once the captain was out of earshot. 'Be careful around that one, my dear. He and a few of the Tommies from the army camp up the road think we are all so starved of men that we would lift our petticoats for even filthy swine like them. Unfortunately, they're not always wrong in that belief – some of the young *meisies* here sneak out through gaps in the wire in the evenings to trade for food and medicines and other bits and pieces. Come with me, and I'll show you to your tent.'

Claire had looked again at the barbed-wire fence encircling the camp as they walked. It was tall – maybe twelve feet high – but she noted it was in a poor state of repair. Hilda had spoken about young girls slipping out, so it shouldn't be too hard for her to find a means of escape.

'*Ag*, the smell!' Gerda said.

'There are only ten toilets here for just over two thousand people,' Hilda said, still speaking in English for Claire's benefit as they walked.

'My God,' Claire said.

'It was worse when I first got here, five – no, six months ago. The Tommies had dug us an open trench and placed a couple of planks across it. We've built outhouses, but there is always a shortage of timber and lime. The first facilities were badly sited, at the bottom of that slope – the ground is contaminated with filth and it rises up when the rains come.'

'I see,' Claire said.

A bearded man, perhaps in his forties, passed them. He looked Claire up and down but Hilda pointedly ignored him.

'*Hensopper*,' Hilda said, then spat in the dirt. 'Like "hands up", you know? There are plenty of them here as well, the men who surrendered or who do not want to fight. The British keep them here where they are safer from our menfolk. They also try to pay the young women.'

Claire looked about. There seemed to be few guards visible. 'What about security, Hilda?'

Hilda shrugged. 'Not so much. The fence is full of holes and there are not too many soldiers here. Most of us have nowhere to go – our farms and crops were burned and our cattle stolen. Even if we wanted to run we have to eat, so most of us are just waiting here.'

Hilda led them down a lane between rows of grubby tents. 'It's impossible to escape the dirt here and when it rains one is ankle-deep in mud and God knows what else. Over there is the hospital tent. You will see it all in there: cholera, dysentery, measles, smallpox. The diseases hit the children hardest. Many never leave that cursed tent.'

Claire recalled the cemetery and the rows of tiny graves. Occasionally a woman would step out of a tent to check out the newcomers, or look up from her darning or washing, but mostly they were ignored. Claire thought of Wilma, and poor baby Piet, and now she could feel the fear and despair they must have experienced on entering such a place. Claire was determined to escape, and was still fit enough to do so, but it would break her heart leaving these women and children to their fates.

'They say there are more than a hundred thousand of us already penned up like cattle across the country. I don't know if that's true.' Hilda sidled closer to Claire, so that Gerda wouldn't hear, and said, 'But I do know it's the little ones that are suffering the most. The measles epidemic claimed so many children last year; they were underfed and could not fight off the disease.'

Claire nodded, again remembering little Piet.

Gerda must have heard a little of what she said. She clutched her now sleeping daughter tight against her breast and drew her son closer to her. Claire felt a chill run down her spine. Disease was a hidden, foul enemy, from which there was little protection. She *must* get out of this place before it claimed her.

Hilda spoke to Gerda in Afrikaans. To Claire, she said, 'I told her to boil the children's water. Though finding fuel to make a fire is one of our biggest challenges here.'

Claire swatted at a buzzing swarm of blowflies that patrolled around her face. Between two tents a group of children were playing with something on the ground, prodding it with sticks. Claire stopped to take a look.

'*Ag, voetsek!* Get away from that, you children,' Hilda said. The children were prodding a snake – fortunately for them it appeared to be dead. They walked on. 'Here's your tent.'

Hilda held a grubby canvas flap open and Claire stepped into the bell tent. It was hot and sticky inside and the canvas smelled of mildew. The twin odours of perspiration and urine also assailed her senses. A woman in her twenties – painfully thin like most of them in the camp – sat on a straw-filled mattress while she breast-fed an infant. The baby, maybe six months old, should have been pudgy and cherubic by this time of its life. Instead, its limbs were skinny and limp. Its head seemed too large for its body and tiny ribs showed through stretched translucent skin. It was a boy, Claire thought, and his belly was obscenely distended.

'Hello, I'm Claire,' she said. The nursing woman looked up at her slowly, as if the mere gesture was draining her of strength. She half nodded and said nothing.

'This is Kobie,' Hilda said. 'She shares the tent with her younger sister, Magrietta. Where is she, Kobie? Magrietta?'

The woman simply shrugged.

'Magrietta is young, just nineteen or twenty. She is quite a handful. Their father is on commando, a leader, and their mother, God rest her, passed away in January,' Hilda explained. 'I'll leave you two to get acquainted. I'm going to put Gerda and the children in another tent. There's a bed in the corner over there, and you'll find a cup, bowl and a few other bits and pieces that may be of use. There's quite a nice dress there, too. I was going to take it for myself today, but I think it might be more appropriate if you had another change of clothes.'

Claire didn't want to ask to whom the dress, bed, utensils and other odds and ends had belonged. She could guess that the former owner no longer needed them. 'Thank you,' she said. She waved goodbye to Gerda and the children.

Kobie had removed her baby from her nipple and the infant had fallen into a fitful sleep lying across her belly. The young mother had just enough strength to re-button her blouse before she, too, nodded off.

Claire moved to the tent flap and checked outside. No-one was nearby. She closed the canvas again and took up the dead woman's dress that had been left for her. It might once have been quite fashionable, but the bustle and trim had been picked off and the dress itself had been patched and darned in several places.

She took off her riding boots and unbuttoned her trousers. She stripped off the pants and undergarments, as she would have to wash both, and then took off her shirt and camisole. Claire pulled the cotton dress over her head and gathered up her clothes in a pile. The dress felt cool against her bare skin and she found she enjoyed the sensation of not wearing any underclothes. Reluctantly, she pulled her riding boots on again. Now that she was inside the camp she felt less worried about being searched by a British soldier. It was time for her to retrieve Nathaniel's map from its hiding place.

Claire glanced across at Kobie again to make sure she was still asleep. She moved to a corner of the tent and squatted down on her haunches.

'*Verskoon my*,' said a female voice.

Claire looked up, startled, as a young woman came in through the tent flap. Claire quickly removed her hand from under her dress. She felt her cheeks start to burn. 'Um ... forgive me. Sorry, I don't speak Afrikaans.'

'*Verskoon* ... I mean, excuse me,' the woman said. 'But you are not permitted to make the toilet inside the tent.'

'No, no. I wasn't relieving myself, I was ...' Claire stammered.

'Ohhh! Well the other thing is OK,' the woman said, a broad smile crossing her pretty face, 'but I usually wait until the lantern is out in the evening.'

Claire, who did not consider herself a prude by any means, was taken aback by the girl's candour. 'No, I was just adjusting my ...'

'It didn't look like there was anything to adjust from where I was standing!'

Claire's embarrassment was fast turning to indignation. She drew a deep breath to calm herself. 'You must be Magrietta.'

'What did that old cow Hilda say about me? Did she call me a hussy? You talk like a Canadian chap I met ... but I thought they only worked for the English.'

'I'm American, and no, Hilda did not call you any such thing, though she did say you were a handful.' In spite of her irritation Claire found it impossible to be truly angry at the fresh-faced blonde girl. She had managed to find enough food to retain her dimples and these were nicely set off by blue eyes and a cheeky grin. She carried a bouquet of small yellow flowers and a bulging calico bag that clinked when she set it down.

'American! How exotic. Is your husband fighting for us?'

'I'm not married. But I have friends who have served with the Boers.'

'Male friends?'

'Yes.'

'Is there a special one?'

Claire was surprised again at the girl's directness. She guessed youngsters grew up quickly in such a place. 'Not one in particular,' she said, and found she could not hold back a smile.

Magrietta giggled. 'I think we are going to be the best of friends.'

Claire took a gamble. 'Tell me, Magrietta, do you know how to get out of this camp unnoticed?'

'Of course, but it's best done after dark. There are places along the fence where the holes in the wire are easy to get through. Some people trade with the soldiers from the camp up the road. Not the English so much, but there are others – Canadians, Australians, New Zealanders.'

Claire thought again of the Australian sergeant. 'Do you trade?'

'Sometimes.' She opened her cloth bag and pulled out two brown glass bottles and clinked them together. 'Medicines. The nurse in the clinic tells me what she needs – what she can't get by asking the English. I trade with the soldiers for the medicines, and sometimes extra milk and food for Kobie and the baby.'

Claire was about to ask Magrietta what she had to trade with, but then thought better of it. There was no sign of obvious wealth among the meagre possessions in the tent.

Claire also had nothing material to trade, but she needed a lot – a horse, saddle, provisions, clothes, money and a weapon and ammunition. Everything she had needed to complete her mission had been taken by the British when they captured her, except the hand-drawn map that Nathaniel had given her.

'Can you show me where you go to trade?' Claire asked.

'Of course, but ... um, you might want to wash and put some ribbons in your hair first.'

CHAPTER 12

Condor Flight DE2294, Munich to Windhoek, Namibia, the present day

Anja set down the papers and rubbed her eyes.

The lights were on and the flight attendants were preparing the cabin for landing. As a university history graduate, she was aware of Britain's pioneering use of concentration camps during the Anglo-Boer War, and of the scorched earth policy employed against farms, but this was the first time she had seen any primary source material relating to these tactics. It was distressing, and when she had read about Gerda's stillborn baby being exhumed in a search for hidden weapons she had wept enough for the young flight attendant to enquire if she was all right.

The aircraft was on its final approach and Anja looked out the window, not with the sense of excitement of the elderly couple next to her on their package safari holiday, but with the peculiar mix of love tinged with a hint of sadness.

So much blood and so many tears had been spilled over these arid expanses, vast tracts of nothing, that it was hard to fathom how Namibia had emerged as it was today, relatively harmonious and reasonably prosperous by African standards.

Flying into Windhoek's Hosea Kutako International Airport aptly set the stage for any visit to her homeland. Most, if not all, airports Anja had ever flown into were hemmed in by industrial areas or cheap housing – no one wanted to live under a flight path if they could afford not too – but Namibia's gateway was surrounded by sand and camel thorn trees as far as the eye could see.

'Will we see animals here?' the elderly woman next to her asked in German as they touched down and the purser welcomed them to Namibia over the PA system.

'Maybe, on your drive to Windhoek,' Anja replied politely. 'Some buck, perhaps.'

'No lions?' The woman punctuated her question with a laugh, but Anja was sure there might have been a glimmer of hope.

She smiled. 'No. However, there are most certainly leopard living out here, especially in the rocks.'

Her face glowed with hope. 'Really?'

'Yes, but you're unlikely to see them. You're going to Etosha National Park?'

'Of course,' said the man seated next to the woman.

'Then I'm sure you'll see lions there, and maybe leopard and cheetah.'

They both grinned. 'Thank you.'

Anja couldn't find it in her to feel contemptuous or condescending towards the tourists. She had been born here, and even though she affected the nonchalance of a local and had seen lions hundreds of times, it was still a secret thrill for her to see big cats in the wild.

'Are you going on safari as well?' the woman asked.

'I'm based in the Namib Desert in the south so I guess you could say I live on safari,' Anja said.

'Super!' she said. 'Are you a guide?'

'I have been, in the past, but I'm researching the wild horses of the Namib. Have you heard of them?'

'Oh, yes, and we hope to see them on our tour,' the woman said. 'Perhaps we will see you there?'

'Perhaps.'

Anja busied herself changing the sim card in her phone, from her German provider to her Namibian MTC card. A few seconds after she had inserted it the phone beeped with a couple of messages. Anja checked her emails and saw one from someone she had never heard from, a Nicholas Eatwell. She opened it.

Dear Miss Berghoff,
   You don't know me, but I was given your name and email address by Susan Vidler ...

That bloody woman, Anja thought. The journalist was nosey and Anja did not trust her. It was clear she was trying to drag Anja into her stories that were designed to exert pressure on politicians in Namibia and Germany.

Even viewed through the filter of the 'norms' for the time, Anja believed there was no excuse for the cruel and inhumane way the German authorities had prosecuted the war against the Nama and Herero rebels at the beginning of the twentieth century. The incarceration of innocent women and children and the working to death of them and legitimate prisoners of war who had surrendered was as abhorrent as the British policy of rounding up Boer families and the latter atrocities of the Nazis. However, Anja's beliefs stopped short of Germany having to pay reparations for acts that had been perpetrated more than a century earlier. She was media-savvy enough to know that if she said that to Susan Vidler she would be painted as some right-wing extremist.

There was another reason she didn't want to talk to the journalist. The wild horses of Namibia had been the subject of some recent media controversy. The horses' numbers had declined significantly in recent years due to a prolonged drought and predation by spotted hyenas. Opinion was divided on whether more horses were being taken because the drought had weakened them, or because hyena numbers had increased – or perhaps both. The research program Anja had volunteered for involved her and others monitoring the numbers of both species. The Namibian Government had weighed in on the side of the horses, initially trying to catch and relocate hyenas and, later, selectively culling them. There were passionate advocates on both sides of this natural struggle and Anja did not want to be drawn into the public conflict. She read on.

Susan suggested I contact you as she tells me you have been researching the period of Namibia's history that covers the

colonial uprisings of the Nama and Herero people, with a focus
on southern Namibia, near the border with South Africa.

Anja could not see what this man's interest might be and, fearing he
might be another journalist, she was about to skip to the end and
delete the message when a name caught her eye.

I am a descendent of a guy called Cyril Blake, an Australian
who I am told fought in South West Africa against the Ger-
mans and was assassinated by them. As I know you are
researching the conflict with reference to some desert horses I
was wondering if you had come across any mention of Blake
as I have recently become interested in his story, for personal
reasons.

The aircraft had come to a stop and the front doors were open.
People around her were jostling to collect their carry-on baggage
and Anja had to put her phone away and retrieve her daypack.

As she slowly filed through the cabin she thought about what
the man had just written. She had just started reading about Blake,
who had been referred to in Claire Martin's reports to her naval
spymasters. Of course, she was interested in this new connection to
the story, but given that the man had been referred to her by Susan
she was immediately suspicious of his motives.

Why had he said *'for personal reasons'*? Why would he feel the
need to mention that if he was, as he said, looking for information
about an ancestor? No doubt the Vidler woman intended to parade this Nick Eatwell as the aggrieved descendent of a white man
who had been killed by the Germans in 1906, to further sow dissent
between Namibia and Germany.

While she waited for a couple with a baby to unload their co-
pious carry-on luggage from the overhead locker, Anja typed and
sent a short reply to Nick Eatwell saying, as the English would
say, 'thanks but no thanks,' and wished him luck in researching his
ancestor.

When she finally walked through the door onto the open-air
steps leading to the tarmac, she knew she was home. The air was

hot and dry, and beyond the swirling odour of jet fuel was the scent of the bush.

Inside the terminal, after collecting her backpack and clearing customs and immigration she walked into the bear-like advance of her uncle, who was also known as Oom, or 'uncle' in Afrikaans, to everyone he met.

'Hello, Oom Otto.'

'*Ag*, I've missed you,' he said, squeezing her harder.

'Same, Oom Otto. What's been happening while I've been away?'

He took her pack, despite her protest that she could carry it, and they left the terminal. Otto put her bags in the back seat of his double cab Hilux *bakkie*. 'Oh, you know, the same as always. One side of politics calling the other side corrupt, too many people getting killed in road accidents, and the Germans are sending another delegation to express regret or something for the past.'

She nodded. 'Yes, same as always, all right.'

'Your Land Rover's ready to go – well, as ready as a Land Rover ever will be.' He laughed.

'Still a diehard Toyota man.'

'Always. They are –'

'Yes, Oom Otto, I know, *they are very reliable.*'

'Well, what's wrong with that?' He stroked his moustache in a self-satisfied manner.

'Reliability is overrated,' Anja said, inwardly laughing at the way he looked at her with eyebrows raised in surprise. 'Image is everything.'

Otto slapped his thigh with his free hand. 'One thing I'll give you, they are good vehicles for fishing on the coast; all the aluminium doesn't rust.'

'You have to give the British credit for something, it is a very tough vehicle,' Anja said.

'Hah!'

That ended the debate. Otto knew when to retreat gracefully, unlike his sister, Anja's mother. 'Mama sends her love.'

He laughed out loud at their private joke. 'I am *sure* she does. How is she?'

Anja shrugged. 'She is Mama.'

Otto looked over at her again as he drove, too fast, towards Windhoek. 'She loves you, Anja, that's all. It's why she wants the best for you, a nice man, a good job.'

'I already have what's best for me, Oom Otto.'

He nodded. 'I know that, and you know that; all we need to do now is convince my sister that we are right and she is wrong. And we both know …'

'That is never going to happen.' Anja sighed. She and her uncle could make fun of her mother, but Anja knew that her mother really did care for her and, maybe, a tiny part of Anja agreed that finding a man might not be all bad. However, while Anja might have sometimes dreamed of settling down, she knew it could never be in Germany.

Here, in this harsh, empty, sometimes hostile land of burning deserts and desolate windswept coastline, she was home.

North Sydney, Australia, the present day

Nick arrived early at The Greens, an old lawn bowls club in North Sydney that had reinvented itself as a hip indoor–outdoor restaurant, bar and night spot. He had arranged to meet Susan there and had told her that his aunt had given him an old manuscript written by a Dr Peter Kohl. Susan had sounded very interested.

Lili was making headway with her translation and Nick was excited to share the news with Susan.

The table for two he had reserved was outside, in the shade on the edge of the bowling green, and the seating was a couch. It would be quite intimate and for a moment he considered asking for a more formal setting, then thought better of it.

Susan arrived on time, at five on the dot. She looked good, dressed in a blue wraparound dress and matching heels. He waved as she entered the club and made her way outside. He stood and she kissed him on the cheek.

'You seem a bit more upbeat than the last time I saw you,' she said.

He shrugged. 'The truth is I wasn't happy in that job. Meeting you … looking into this old story, kind of takes me back to my time as a journalist and I realised I'd missed it more than I thought. I'll need to find another job eventually, but I've been thinking that I probably needed some sort of change in my life.'

Susan smiled. 'Well that's a really positive way of looking at things.'

'Thanks. Drink?'

'Sure. A pinot gris, maybe? We don't see a lot of that in South Africa and I'm heading home tomorrow.'

'Oh.' His disappointment was genuine. 'I'll get us a bottle, then.'

Nick went to the bar, paid for the wine and returned with an ice bucket and two glasses. 'Is it OK if I say I'll be sorry to see you go?'

Susan smiled. 'That's sweet of you. I kind of feel the same way.'

Nick poured and they clinked glasses. 'I thought you said you were here in Sydney for another week?'

'I did, but I got an SOS from South Africa. I also do a bit of PR work, like you, on the side, and a client-slash-friend of mine in the real-estate industry has an urgent situation he needs some help with.'

'How urgent can real-estate business be? Can't you work from here?'

She shrugged. 'He's working on a big new residential development and there's a lot of opposition to it from the surrounding community. Nothing I can't smooth over.'

'It's a shame you're leaving, though, because I've found some interesting stuff, courtesy of my aunt.'

She took a sip of wine. 'So you said. A manuscript, yes?'

Nick leaned a little closer to her on the couch. 'My aunt had a weighty old document, written in German. She thought it was a diary from the First World War, but it's actually some kind of memoir by a doctor named Peter Kohl and it already mentions my great-great-whatever-he-was-uncle's time in the Boer War.'

Susan sat up straight. 'Nick, that's really interesting. Peter Kohl was the German army officer who killed Cyril Blake.'

'So I've gathered. It looks like Blake met an Irish-German woman –'

'Claire Martin,' Susan interrupted.

'Yes, her. They met each other in South Africa and there was some kind of skulduggery going on.'

Susan raised her eyebrows. 'Go on.'

'Yes. There's an account in the story of the incident that happened in the report you showed me, but it gives a different version. Dr Kohl's version of the story says that after the raid on the trading post the English officer, Walters, tortured and killed the American colonel, Belvedere. If this version is true, my ancestor was framed. He was arrested and locked up, but he escaped, and where I'm up to now, he's trying to prove his innocence.'

Susan looked intrigued. 'Wow, that is an amazing find. Do you speak German?'

Nick explained how he'd given the manuscript to Lili for translation, and that she was hoping to get it done before she went backpacking, but hadn't finished yet.

'I'm sorry I can't stay longer in Australia so you can tell me the rest of the story in person.'

'Me too, but I can email you when she's done.'

They looked each other in the eye, neither of them saying anything for a few long, tantalising seconds. Nick wondered if her heart had started beating faster as well. Susan bit her lower lip.

'It's funny,' she said at last. 'If my research had taken a slightly different path I might have found your aunt instead of you. It would have been nice to meet her. Does she live far from here?'

'Granville, which is on the other side of Sydney, really.'

'She's on your mom's side, right, so she's not an Eatwell? I would have found her if she was.'

'That's right,' Nick said. 'She's a MacKenzie.'

Susan smiled. 'I'm sure she's lovely, but I'm glad my snooping led me to you.'

Nick grinned inside and cleared his throat. 'Do you want a sample to look at now?'

'Yes, please.'

Nick unzipped his daypack and took out the latest instalment, which Lili had brought in to work that morning. 'Before Blake escaped from custody Walters sent another Australian from their patrol to try to get Blake to change his story. When Blake refused, the guy tried to kill him and in a scuffle the other soldier was killed and a guard knocked out.'

'Sheesh!'

Nick smiled. 'He seems like a real tough guy, and honest. So, he breaks out of jail, grabs his horse, and then rides back to the trading post on the Sabie River where the American and the woman, Claire Martin, had been holed up.'

'I know that area, the lowveld. It's beautiful. You should go there if you ever make it to South Africa.'

'Hold that thought,' Nick said, then he started to read out loud.

CHAPTER 13

For the second time in as many days, Blake lay on his stomach just below the brow of a low hill and watched the abandoned trading post, with its small house and stable.

Someone had been back here. There were two bags lying outside the front door of the house; both were open and their contents – clothes by the look of it – were scattered on the ground. Looters, perhaps? Blake thought it unlikely – there were no Shangaan tribal settlements within a day's ride and no Boer commandos in the area.

He scanned the surrounding bush again and reassured himself there was no one else nearby. Blake left his horse tied to a bush and approached the buildings cautiously on foot, his Broomhandle Mauser at the ready.

In the empty stables he saw the overturned chair and the slashed bindings that had held the American. Of his missing ear, there was no sign, but that wasn't surprising as there was hyena spoor on the ground; the animals would have been drawn by the smell of blood.

He entered the main building and saw immediately that the place was a shambles, in worse shape than he had left it. A sturdy timber sideboard had been pitched over. Kitchen cupboards were open and pots, pans and plates were scattered over the stone floor. The crockery and glasses were plain, solid items. There was an air of impermanence about the place – aside from little touches like the spilled flowers and cracked vase he had first seen on the morning of the raid.

And why the wildflowers, if this was a safe place of refuge for fugitive commandos? There was something between the American man and the woman; perhaps the man had placed the flowers as a tender welcome.

Blake walked into the hallway and momentarily relived the moment when he had shot the Boer. His actions had been pure instinct, as instant and as unfeeling as a leopard pouncing on an impala.

Instinct. It was something you couldn't teach a new soldier. If he had it, he would have a better than even chance of surviving life in the bush or on the open highveld. If he didn't, he wouldn't last long.

The door to the main bedroom was closed.

Slowly, he backed out of the hallway into the parlour. He crept out the front door and eased his way along the exterior wall, ducking as he passed each window. Whoever had returned to ransack the house had opened the shutters to give themselves light to work by, but had taken the time to close the bedroom door. The open windows meant the intruder had been there in daylight; maybe he – or she – was still there.

Once at the rear of the house Blake dropped to all fours and crawled until he was beneath the open bedroom window the woman had presumably escaped through. Slowly, carefully, he raised his head, the pistol near his cheek, ready to fire over the windowsill if need be.

He peered inside. The bedroom was empty, but it was not as he had left it.

Tied to the foot of the bed was a large-bore shotgun, its twin barrels pointing squarely at the door. A length of twine ran from the trigger, down over the lower rung of the wrought-iron bedstead and then up to the doorhandle. Anyone opening the door would end up with a gutful of lead shot. It was a clever trap that just added to the mystery of the trading post and its occupants.

Blake inspected the windowsill carefully to make sure there were no other surprises waiting for him and then climbed inside.

There was a wardrobe in one corner of the room and two small chests of drawers on either side of the four-poster. The furniture was made of Tamboti, a tree whose timber was as poisonous as it was beautiful. As in the kitchen, all of the drawers and cupboard doors were open.

Blake untied the twine from the doorhandle and then freed the shotgun from the foot of the bed. He carried the weapon with him into the kitchen and looked out the window. A lone rider was approaching and Blake knew it was Walters.

He stayed low as the captain reined in his horse by the stables and dismounted. Walters drew his pistol as he passed the stable door, then walked around the farmhouse to the front door and entered the building.

Blake climbed out of the kitchen window and hid behind the outhouse, waiting.

After a minute or two Walters came outside. He walked around the house to the bedroom window and peered inside. Blake crept up behind Walters and jammed the twin barrels of the shotgun into the back of the officer's neck. 'Looking for this?'

Slowly, Walters turned his head. 'I heard you escaped.'

'Clearly. You prepared a welcome for me.' Blake relieved Walters of his Webley revolver, tucking the pistol into his belt. 'Time you and I had a little chat, sport. Let's move inside.'

'I can explain, Blake.'

'My bloody oath you're going to explain. To the provost marshal.'

'There's money involved, Blake. More money than you could possibly imagine.'

'So Bert said. Keep moving. Inside.'

'Blake, just listen to me –'

Blake swung the shotgun around and clubbed the officer in the back of the head with the butt, though not hard enough to render him unconscious.

'Bloody hell, what was that for?' Walters wailed.

'Bert, and the American Boer colonel. I should kill you.'

'You don't want to add a real murder to your list of so-far unproven crimes, do you? I can end your troubles with a quiet word to the provost marshal, Blake. I'll tell him it was Hughes who did in the Boer. The package I'm looking for is yours and mine to find and split. Let us talk.'

'You sent Bert Hughes to kill me,' Blake said.

'Sent him to talk some sense into your thick colonial head, more like it.'

Blake heard the crack-thump of a rifle shot and a bullet slammed into the wall of the farmhouse beside them. Blake dropped to his belly and looked in the direction the shot had come from. Walters saw his chance to escape and sprinted away.

'Get down, you idiot!' Blake yelled.

Spouts of dirt rose from the sunbaked yard as the marksman followed Walters' dash. The officer ran to his tethered horse and slid a rifle from its saddle-mounted holster. Instead of aiming at the enemy, though, he worked the action and fired at Blake.

'Bloody hell!' Blake swore. He pointed the shotgun at Walters and pulled the trigger twice, firing both barrels. Blake glimpsed a bearded man running from cover to cover.

The range was long for a shotgun and Walters turned his attention to mounting his horse. Blake, meanwhile, had attracted the Boer rifleman's attention now, and bullets slammed into the earth around him and the wall above his head. Another rifle joined in the fusillade.

The sound of hoofbeats from the other side of the building told Blake the Englishman was on his way.

Across the veld, beyond the stables, three men on horseback were closing on the farmhouse. One pulled up short, about a hundred yards away, and fired shot after shot at Blake, covering his comrades' advance. Blake saw that these men knew what they were doing, and that he was cornered. He rose to his knees and held the shotgun in two hands over his head.

The Boers called to each other in Afrikaans and the two who were moving galloped past Blake and the farmhouse, presumably in pursuit of the fleeing officer.

The third rebel cantered up to the house, directing his horse with pressure from his knees while he held his Mauser rifle into his shoulder, the barrel pointed down at Blake.

His sunburned face was dirty, his ginger beard unkempt and his eyes wide and wild. The man wore no coat or tunic, just a sleeveless garment made of an old grain sack over a long-sleeved undershirt that may once have been white. Two bandoliers of ammunition crisscrossed his wiry torso.

Blake dropped the shotgun and stared up into the man's eyes. He asked himself, if he were in the Boer's position, a renegade living by his wits on the veld, would he bother taking prisoners? *Probably not*, thought Blake. He steeled himself for the impact of the bullet.

Blake started to reach into the breast pocket of his tunic, but stopped when he saw the Boer's finger tense on the trigger of his Mauser's rifle. 'Just getting a cigarette, all right?'

The Boer nodded again and Blake slowly drew out the packet of Wills cigarettes. He took a step towards the horse and offered the pack to his enemy. The man stank so badly Blake had to breathe through his mouth.

The man remained stony-faced for a few seconds, staring at the pack in Blake's outstretched hand. Blake shook out two cigarettes, lit both at the same time and then handed one up to the man on horseback.

'Good, eh?' Blake said, holding the cigarette aloft as he exhaled.

The Boer closed his eyes for a second, savouring the stream of nicotine. He exhaled slowly through his nose. '*Dankie.*'

'No worries,' Blake replied.

'You are not English.'

'Australian.'

The horseman nodded and continued smoking his cigarette. The rifle lay across his lap now, but he still kept it pointed at Blake.

As they finished their cigarettes the other two Boers arrived at the farmhouse on horseback. The three men conversed in Afrikaans and then dismounted. The first man kept him covered.

'Australian, Hermanus,' his captor said to the older man, who looked back at him reprovingly. Blake guessed the older man was the commander, and didn't like his name being used.

'What were you doing here?' the man called Hermanus asked Blake in accented but good English.

His hair was snowy white and fell to his collar. He sported a yellow-stained walrus moustache and long sidelevers. In another life he could have been a kindly grandfather figure, but the pistol in his hand and twelve-inch British bayonet hanging from his belt told another story. He wore a vest made of leopardskin and rough-sewn leather trousers that had come off the back of a buck of some kind. On his head was a wide-brimmed straw hat, such as a farmer's wife might wear to a Sunday picnic, although the zebra-skin puggaree lent it a vaguely manly air.

These were hard men, Blake thought. 'Bitter-enders', they called them, those Boers on commando who would never surrender. Cut off from their women and their farms with no lines of supply, they lived off the land.

'Hermanus, is it?' Blake tried. The man glared at him. 'I'm Blake. I was just looking around.'

'Looking for what? Why do two Englishmen ride out here to look at an empty trading post?' Hermanus replied.

'I came alone, and I'm Australian.'

'We were watching. You and the Englishman, you fought. Why did he try to shoot you?'

'Gambling debt.'

Hermanus raised his pistol and pulled back the hammer with his thumb. 'Time to pay up.'

Blake sensed the old man was not someone to be messed with. 'I was looking for evidence.'

'Evidence of what?'

'Something that would prove who committed a crime. One of your men, a senior officer, was killed here,' Blake said.

'So, is that a crime? You kill our people every day, even our women and children. Why is the death of an American a crime?' Hermanus lowered his pistol a little.

'I didn't say anything about an American, but you obviously know who I'm talking about. Do you know how he was killed?'

Hermanus shrugged. 'What does it matter?'

'He was tortured. He had information that someone wanted badly enough to break all the rules of war to get it. The man who just escaped was the killer.' Blake had no qualms about laying the blame on Walters. The captain had tried to frame him and then have him killed. Besides, Blake had nothing to lose by telling the truth to these desperate men, who looked like they would kill him if they felt he was of no use to them.

Hermanus said nothing.

Blake looked deep into the man's eyes. 'There was a woman, and a younger man with the American.'

'Tell me of their fates.'

'The other man is dead,' Blake said.

'And the woman?'

'Captured and unharmed. For now.'

The old man turned to his companions and appeared to translate what Blake had said, then the three of them conversed in their native tongue for a couple of minutes. They appeared agitated by the news of the woman's capture.

'Where did they take her?' Hermanus asked Blake.

'They took her to the guardhouse where I was imprisoned, but I found out they were moving her to the concentration camp near here. I escaped this morning.'

'Escaped?'

'That woman heard the English officer torturing your friend, heard his screams. She can confirm that I wasn't involved in that business, but the British think I did it and they want to have me executed. I'm safer on the run for now.'

'What do I care about what happens to you?' Hermanus asked. 'I should just kill you now.'

Blake looked the old man in the eyes. 'I reckon you want the woman. I want her as well and, unlike you, I can get to her.'

'Who says we want the woman?'

'Why would you lot come out of the hills to raid a trading post with no stores? There was something – or someone – in this place that people are prepared to murder over. I don't particularly care what it is, but I do want my freedom.'

'You can have your freedom. You are no use to us and despite what you may think we do not shoot prisoners. We will, however, take your clothes and your horse. Strip.'

They may as well shoot me, Blake thought. With no horse and no clothes he wouldn't last long out here in the bush. Even if the lions didn't get him and by some miracle a British patrol found him he'd be swinging on the end of a rope or facing the firing squad before the week was out. 'No.'

'Very well,' said Hermanus. He raised his revolver until the barrel pointed at Blake's eye and pulled back the hammer.

'Think about it. I'm an Australian sergeant. I can talk my way into wherever they're holding the woman and I can break her out. You won't get within cooee of civilisation the way you lot look.'

Hermanus lowered his pistol and spoke again with the others in Afrikaans.

'They say you will lead us into a trap.'

'You saw how the Pommy was shooting at me. I'm on your side for now. The difference is that I can get into the camp where they're holding the woman and I've got half a chance of getting out with her. You can ride off now and leave me if you want – just leave me my clothes.'

Hermanus locked eyes with him. 'You can keep your clothes. You will ride with us to the camp where they are holding the woman – she has something we need. If she is there you will bring her to us. If you fail, I will kill you.'

*

The concentration camp and a nearby army bivouac were half a day's ride to the south. There was a blockhouse on the road that passed between the two encampments, but Blake and Paul, the youngest of the trio of Boers, were waved through without a word.

Paul was dressed in a British Army uniform that had come, in total, from the different members of the Boer commando. It was just as well it was dark, Blake thought, because if a sergeant major got within fifty feet of young Paul and saw or smelled the state of his tunic, trousers or boots, he would be disciplined on the spot. He made Blake's generally scruffy, bush-worn and patched uniform look like he was a guardsman on duty at Buckingham Palace.

Paul had shaved off his beard and his chin was deathly white compared to his deeply tanned cheeks and nose. Blake rode with his pistol holstered – his bullets had been confiscated – and Paul carried his own Lee Enfield, captured from a dead soldier of the Empire in some previous encounter.

There was another checkpoint at the turnoff to the concentration camp. Paul hung back behind Blake, in the shadows. Blake reined in his horse.

'Evening, Sergeant,' said the sentry, a lanky British soldier.

'G'day mate,' Blake said. 'Busy night?'

'Saturday, Sarge. Ladies down t' road are always game for a bit of fun on t' weekend. Been quite a few fellas headed that way tonight.'

'I'll have to make sure there's nothing improper going on then, won't I?'

'Right, Sarge. Though if it's improper you're after I'm told a lady by t' name of Magrietta might be worth asking after.'

'I'll bear that in mind. I'm actually here on official business. I need to talk to a woman who's newly arrived at the camp.'

The sentry nodded. 'Couple o' lasses came in today. One wi' kids and t' other single.'

Blake raised his eyebrows. 'Red-head? Good looking?'

'Aye, that's the one. A pal o' mine said the captain put her in wi' Magrietta. We were hoping she might be as interested in trading as her tent mate,' he winked, 'if you know what I mean, Sarge.'

'I think I do. Where might I find these ladies?'

'Follow t' perimeter fence all the way down to t' south corner. Wire's in a shocking state – folk come and go as they please down there and that's where t' trading's done. Have a good night, Sarge.'

'I intend to, mate.'

Blake thought that if the red-head had plans of escape then a stroll with the infamous Magrietta would be a logical path to follow. It might be easier for him to find her where the inmates did their 'trading' rather than talking his way into the camp proper with the scruffy Paul in tow.

The two of them followed a track that ran along the outside of the camp fence. On the other side of the wire he saw the rows and rows of bell tents. In the distance he heard a violin playing and a woman singing. The song was mournful and Blake was under no illusions that anyone behind the wire was having fun. These camps were repugnant. He reckoned that if he were a Boer whose wife and children had been locked up it wouldn't force him to surrender – rather he'd be like Paul and Hermanus and the other bitter-enders, fighting to the death to see his family freed.

Blake held up a hand to signal Paul to stop. The young Boer spoke very little English. Blake dismounted and Paul followed suit.

'Tie the horses up here,' he said, leading Bluey into the shelter of a stand of trees. 'We walk from here.' Blake pantomimed the action with the first two fingers of his right hand and Paul nodded.

Ahead of them he saw a trio of soldiers walking slowly along the fence line, peering into the camp after every few steps. Beyond the wire he saw that some of the women were ignoring the gawking soldiers, but others were smiling shyly or even waving.

As they neared the end of the line he noticed a woman stoop and pick her way through the barbed wire. A British officer offered her his arm once she was through and they walked off together down a grassy slope.

Blake took off his slouch hat and tried to smooth down his matted hair. He hadn't washed since his false imprisonment at Walters' hands and he was acutely aware of his own body odour. Paul, of course, still smelled like a decaying lion kill after his months on the veld. They would be lucky to get the red-head to even talk to them, he thought.

CHAPTER 14

North Sydney, Australia, the present day

'What?' Susan said, leaning forward, eyes wide. 'You can't stop there.'

Nick shrugged, but grinned. 'That's where Lili got up to. I wonder if there's a German word for cliffhanger?'

'Damn,' Susan said. 'I want to know what happens next.'

Nick gathered up the printouts, tapped them on the table to square them up and put them back in his bag. 'Dinner is what happens next. They do a great burger here if you want to be bad.'

'Bad is good.'

Nick tried to give himself a reality check and tell himself Susan was not flirting with him on their second meeting. 'I'll get us some menus.'

'The burger sounds great. I'm not the sort of girl who messes around when it comes to food and if I like the sound of something – or the look of it – I'm more than likely to throw caution to the wind and go for it.'

'OK.' He stood and went to the bar and ordered for both of them.

'I'm annoyed,' Susan said, slumping back into the couch as he arrived.

'With me?'

'Sort of,' she said. 'It was a long shot, that you or your family might have known something about Cyril Blake, let alone have

103

some sort of records from him or about him, and here, now, on my last night in Australia, you come up with the goods.'

When Nick sat back down their thighs were so close they were almost touching. 'So what do we do? Get Lili to put in some over-time tonight?'

Susan laughed. 'Poor girl, I'm sure your boss works her hard enough as it is.'

'You got that right,' he said. 'That place is – or was, in my case – like a salt mine.'

'Seriously, Nick, I can't wait to read the rest of the manuscript.'

Nick frowned.

'What's up?' she asked.

'It's just that ...'

She let his unfinished sentence hang there for a few moments. 'Just that it would have been nice if I'd stayed around to hear the ending?'

He nodded.

She raised her glass and they clinked. 'It's been nice hanging out with you, even if it was only twice.'

'I feel the same way.'

The silence that descended was companionable, tinged with a bit of regret, at least on his part. He wondered what she was think-ing. Susan looked out across the bowling greens towards Sydney Harbour and Nick followed her gaze; glimpses of silvery water were just visible amid the high-rises on the horizon.

'What will you do with yourself while you decide what to do with your life?' Susan asked.

'I don't know. To be honest, when I thought about you, re-searching this story and the implications of an historical feature on current politics, well, I was a bit envious.'

Susan laughed. 'You and I both know there's no money in jour-nalism. And remember, I still have to do some part-time PR to pay my bills.'

'So you said. Your client in Cape Town?'

She nodded and sipped her wine. 'But let's not talk about work. It's my last night in this beautiful country, at least for now. Part of me is looking forward to getting home to South Africa, but I've come to love this place in a very short time – even if you do have too many rules and regulations.'

'I hear you. It's strange, though.'

'What is?' Susan asked.

'I feel some sort of connection with Africa now, through this long-dead ancestor of mine, even though I've never been.'

'I saw an interview with the author Bryce Courtenay once,' Susan said. 'You know he was born in South Africa but became an Australian?'

Nick nodded.

'I'm paraphrasing, but he said that as remains of the earliest known humans had been discovered there, it was as though we were all of us descended from Africans, that there's a little bit of the continent in all of us,' Susan said.

Nick thought about that. 'Tell me about Africa.'

She sighed. 'Where do I start?'

'What do you miss, what are you most looking forward to seeing?'

'Nothing, that's what I miss. To stand on a *koppie*, a hill, and to look around you, three hundred and sixty degrees, where you can't see another human being, and you know that this is what life was once like, what it should be, what it could be.'

'There are plenty of places like that in Australia, true wilderness,' he said, playing the devil's advocate.

Susan smiled. 'Yes, but we have lions.'

'Touché. Isn't it dangerous, in the bush?'

'Yes and no, depending on where you are and what you do. The stupid don't survive, Nick. There's a sense of living in the moment that's missing here in Australia. You could be camping on the banks of the Zambezi River in Zimbabwe, where there are no fences around the camp grounds, and if you get up in the middle of the night you could be killed by a lion or, more likely, charged by a buffalo during the day on your way to the ablutions block.'

'Scary.'

She nodded. 'It is. And fun. Lots of fun.'

'I get it, I think,' he said.

'Africa's how Australia likes to think it is. We are more in touch with the bush, closer to the land, freer, more adventurous, reckless. It's not all rosy, though. You have too many laws here in Australia; in Africa we don't have enough, and those we do have are treated more as, say, guidelines.'

He laughed.

'It's sad, Africa. Thousands of people are killed on the roads every year in South Africa, and *hundreds* of thousands die of malaria throughout the continent, far more than from Ebola or any other exotic diseases you read about. There are wars and coups, poverty, corruption and crime, murders and mayhem, and yet ...'

'You're not painting a very attractive picture here.'

She held up a hand. 'Hear me out. And yet ... despite all these terrible things, life goes on, Nick. Ordinary, good people face hardships and trauma the likes of which people in Australia couldn't imagine, but they don't give up or complain or crumble. They come together, more often than not at the grassroots level, to find solutions, to make a plan, as we say in South Africa, to help each other.'

Her eyes were bright and she was full of passion. It was odd how she could talk about the continent's problems in one breath and still be inspired by it in the next.

'You'd make a good PR person for South African tourism,' he said. 'You've brought up all the negatives people think of before visiting, and turned them into positives.'

She laughed. 'You'll have to come see for yourself.'

He didn't say anything, as he was fairly sure it wasn't a direct invitation, but a thought had been forming in his mind over the weekend. He had no job for now, and he risked spiralling into a depression thinking about his future and torturing himself over Jill's death. He had money and had been promising himself an overseas trip to try and move on. Jill had told him he should go, before she died. Like talking to other women, though, he had feared he would be racked by guilt, spending their savings on a holiday when that was what he and Jill had planned for later in their lives.

Their food arrived and they fell back on small talk while they devoured their burgers. They had to raise their voices as a DJ had started up, playing some retro tunes from the sixties and seventies.

When they'd finished eating, the wine bottle was also empty.

Nick nodded towards it. 'What do you say to another?'

'I say you're turning me into an alcoholic. And I thought South Africans could drink.'

'Coffee?'

'What are you having?'

'A beer, I think.'

'I'll have one more glass of white, but let me get it.'

'No, I insist.' Nick went to the bar and by the time he came back with their drinks a band had started playing.

'Thanks,' Susan said, having to raise her voice over the music.

'You know,' said Nick, sitting back down, 'I've been thinking about my great-great-uncle. If the manuscript confirms he fought in the uprising against the Germans in 1906 and that he was some kind of hero, then it might be of interest to the media here in Australia.'

'I agree,' Susan said. 'Do you want to help me write the piece?'

He smiled. 'You're a mind-reader.'

'I'd be very happy with that, Nick, especially as I know you're a good journalist. I googled you, so I know about the work you've done in the past, when you worked on *The Australian*.'

'Past being the operative word.'

She reached out and touched his arm. 'No, Nick, that's not what I meant. I didn't mean to suggest that you've somehow gone downhill. I know you've had a rough time lately. This might be just the thing you need, a break before you start another job and a chance to do some investigation.'

'You think?' It was what he had been hoping for. He had been reluctant, though, to muscle in on her story.

'News organisations collaborate on stories all the time these days. With media organisations shrinking they often have to pool their resources. We can do the same thing. This could be a big story and, yes, even a book, one that would sell on both sides of the Indian Ocean, and in Europe, Germany in particular.'

'Thank you, Susan, that's very gracious of you to offer.'

Susan stuck out her hand. 'What's say we go into this as partners, fifty–fifty on the workload and the same split on whatever we make?'

Nick was taken aback. It was a generous offer. However, he didn't need to think about it for more than a second. 'I've got nothing to lose, I just hope I can help.'

'You already have,' Susan said.

They shook hands and toasted each other.

'How about we seal the deal with a dance,' he said.

'That's a bit forward, Nick,' she said, her face serious.

He felt foolish, having overstepped the mark. 'Sorry ...'

'I'm joking,' she said with a grin. 'Let's go, I love this rock and roll stuff!'

Susan jumped up and led him by the hand to the dance floor.

He had learned, for his wedding, but had never been much of a dancer. His spontaneous invitation to Susan to dance had surprised him as well. Susan was a natural and the song called for some old-time moves and it didn't seem unnatural for him to draw her close. He felt a buzz of excitement. She smelled nice, just a hint of perfume, and soon they were both perspiring in the warm Sydney evening air.

The number finished. Susan grinned and fanned her face with her hands. 'More!'

Nick was happy to stay, happier, he realised, as he twirled her, than he had been in months. He forgot about everything and concentrated on the moment, a pretty girl in his arms and their bodies moving in almost perfect unison to the beat. For a moment it felt good to be alive.

'That was great,' she said when the next song ended, 'but I need water, and the loo.'

'Me too, but first ...' He took out his iPhone and swiped to bring up the camera function.

'No!' Susan tried to protest, but he held out his hand and took a selfie of the two of them.

When they reconvened after the bathroom they sat to finish the last of their drinks.

'I've had a great night, Nick. I almost don't want to get on the flight tomorrow morning.' She looked deep into his eyes as she finished the last of her wine.

Nick wondered if she was feeling what he was. 'Where are you staying tonight?'

'The Four Seasons, in the city.'

'They have a great bar,' Nick said. 'I could see you safely to the hotel and have a quick drink.'

'Very gentlemanly.' Her eyes glittered as she smiled and Nick felt his heart quicken.

He ordered an Uber, then they left The Greens and walked through St Leonards Park to Miller Street. Nick's flat was less than two hundred metres away, but he thought that if he suggested going there for a drink it would seem just that little bit too forward. And having a drink or two in the city was fine with him.

A Volkswagen Polo arrived and they both got in the back. Susan was fumbling for the seatbelt as the driver merged into the traffic and headed for the Harbour Bridge.

'Can I help?' Nick said.

Susan moved her hand slightly, and Nick felt for the buckle. Susan was sitting on it and as she shifted, his fingers dug into the warm skin of her thigh. He found the buckle and clicked it home for her. He smiled and found she was looking into his eyes. It was cramped in the back of the little car and they were already close.

Nick felt emboldened by the wine. He leaned a fraction closer to her, and Susan mirrored his action. She blinked and he licked his lips. It was now or never, he thought.

Nick closed the gap between them and she tilted her face to one side to allow their lips to meet perfectly. Their first kiss was soft, but not tentative, more testing. She must have liked it as much as he, because her lips parted.

He shifted as close as he could to her given the confines of their seatbelts. Nick opened his eyes and saw that Susan had hers open as well and they were smiling at him.

They broke apart. 'Your lips are softer than I thought,' she said.

'Is that good?'

'Very.'

They kissed again, and continued exploring each other, hands moving over arms and shoulders and thighs, until the Uber driver pulled up outside Susan's hotel and farewelled them with a grin.

Susan strode across the polished floor, past reception, and Nick followed, mesmerised and increasingly aroused. It had been a long time for him. He felt a needle-stick of guilt, but told himself this couldn't be wrong. She stopped at the lifts and pressed the up button and they stood side by side, hands clasped in front of them.

Inside the lift, alone, Nick gave in and pinned her against the mirrored wall and kissed her deeper and harder than he had so far. Susan clawed at the back of his shirt and, for the first time, touched him through his pants. Nick reached down and ran a hand up her thigh, his fingers unable to linger too long on the soft, cool skin, until he found her pants. She ground against him.

As the chime signalled her floor they tumbled out and along the corridor, laughing at the three attempts it took for her key card to work on the lock.

*

Susan couldn't help it.

She hadn't come to Australia to find a man, at least not like this. She had accomplished her mission, she thought, tracking down Nick Eatwell, descendent of Cyril Blake, but she hadn't meant to fall for him.

Shit, she thought to herself.

And now they were all over each other and this was only going to end one way. Nick seemed like a decent enough guy, if a little down on his luck. She had done better than she could have imagined, not only in finding him, but also in discovering that his aunt had what could be vital information in the old manuscript, and now she was surprised to find that she had feelings for him. She thought of the conversation she'd had with her client in Cape Town and she felt terrible.

Inside the hotel room she wondered if she should cool it, if this had gone too far too soon.

'What is it?' he asked, almost panting.

'It's just ...' *No*, she told herself. It was better not to tell him everything now. Two reasons – one, he would decide not to share the manuscript with her, and two, she liked him too much.

He exhaled audibly. 'It's fine, Susan. If you want to take it slow I'm OK, we can go to the bar and have that nightcap instead.'

Damn it. She was *not* this sort of person and he was a really nice guy. She looked at him. She found him attractive; physically he was in pretty good shape, and when he wasn't down in the mouth he could be fun and engaging. Finding the manuscript seemed to have lifted his spirits, and she was part of that, which made her feel good.

To hell with it, Susan thought.

She came to him again and kissed him. After a while she threw back her head and he kissed her neck and undid the tie holding her dress together.

Since the breakup of her marriage she had been engrossed in her work. In fact, her work had been part of the reason she had split up from Ian, her ex-husband. Susan had been travelling for a good part of the last twelve months and Ian had got sick of it. She had been able to claim the moral high ground when she found out he had been having an affair, but then so had she, with Scott Dillon, her real-estate magnate public relations client.

Scott was handsome, but she had eventually learned he was a pig as far as relationships were concerned. He had been happy to see her marriage fail, but had then started sleeping with his accountant. She needed the kind of attention that Nick was lavishing on her now, and it had been too long since either Ian or Scott had desired her like this.

Susan realised something else, as she ran her fingers through Nick's hair and savoured the feeling of his tongue and lips on the nipple he had freed from her bra. She needed to escape from her work as well, for good. She had a desire to tell Nick everything, but to do so would spoil the moment. *I will when it's all over,* she told herself, making her mind up.

Her dress hung open at the front and she shrugged out of it. In front of her the Sydney Harbour Bridge and the Opera House were lit up and reflected lights sparkled on the water. Susan lifted Nick's head and kissed him on the mouth again.

She moved around him and walked to the window, which was almost floor to ceiling.

Nick trailed after her and as she glanced over her shoulder she saw him frantically unbuttoning his shirt, then unzipping and stepping out of his trousers and underwear.

He paused, then bent down and retrieved his trousers, took out his wallet and slid out the foil-wrapped packet.

She smiled and beckoned with a finger as he rolled on the protection. 'Come here.'

'You don't need to ask twice.'

She looked out at the view as his fingers hooked the elastic of her pants and slid them down. Susan wriggled a little, to help him get them off, and to tease him. She lifted one foot and rested it on the ledge that ran along the bottom of the window.

Nick rubbed himself against her and she ground back onto him. Palms flat on the glass she threw back her head again as he entered her. She wondered if the late-night jogger below, running along the Cahill Expressway walkway, might look up and see her, half naked, pressed against the window.

The thought excited her, as much as the feelings that flooded through her body as Nick gripped her hips. He felt the same way she did, it was obvious. This was a chance for both of them to flee the world they had found themselves in.

For those precious minutes, however long they were, Susan was someone else, someone good.

CHAPTER 15

Windhoek, Namibia, the present day

Oom Otto had a tour that was leaving very early the morning after he collected Anja from Windhoek airport and he had to meet up with his guests the night before they left, for a get-to-know-you dinner.

He was meeting them at Joe's Beerhouse, the capital's number one tourist bar, which was also popular with locals. Anja accepted Otto's invitation to come for a drink, but not for dinner.

Otto dropped her at a guesthouse she had booked in Nelson Mandela Avenue and she forced herself to stay awake during the afternoon. As usual, Otto had loaned her his spare vehicle, a Land Rover Defender kitted out for camping with a roof tent and all the gear she would need for her stay in the desert, most importantly a fridge. One of Otto's friends had dropped the vehicle at the guesthouse. Anja took her copies of Claire Martin's reports outside into the fresh air and found a vacant sunbed by the swimming pool in the walled garden.

The report continued with Claire's tale of life in the Boer concentration camp.

The eastern Transvaal, South Africa, 1902

In the dark, the camp was a different place.

Claire found the foul smell that permeated the place less notice-able now that the sun had set. The fact that she had also washed herself with strong lye soap probably helped. She had been acutely aware of her own body odour all day. Her underthings and riding clothes were still damp, though, so she continued to wear just the cotton dress and her boots. Her own state and that of the camp reminded her that she needed to escape, not just to complete her personal mission, but to survive. To stay in this filthy place would be to die.

'You look so nice now,' Magrietta said, pulling back the flap of the tent and striding in.

Claire placed a finger to her lips and pointed to Kobie who, along with her baby, was fast asleep. 'She's just gone down.'

Magrietta lowered her voice and went to her mattress, reaching underneath. She pulled out her calico bag and from it took a knitting needle, which she handed to Claire. 'Use this to put your hair up, you'll look much nicer.'

Claire did as she suggested and they left the tent. The night air bore a welcome chill, the clear sky studded with glittering pinpricks of light. Magrietta reached into her bag again, then nudged Claire and passed a bottle into her hands.

Claire took a sniff of the open bottle. '*Mampoer!* Moonshine, they call this rotgut in America. You are a very bad girl, Magrietta.'

'This is a very bad place.'

Claire had to agree with her, and took a generous sip of the liquor, home brewed from the fruit of a marula tree. 'Good,' she croaked, handing the bottle back.

'This way, let's go,' Magrietta said, pointing to the fence ahead. 'Look, there's Hettie. She's here almost every night!'

A tall raven-haired girl stood on their side of the fence talking to three uniformed British Tommies on the other. The girl laughed coquettishly and fanned her face with a straw hat.

'A little further along, in that dark patch. That's where the gap in the wire is,' Magrietta explained.

Claire nodded and brushed a lock of hair from her face. 'How does it work?'

'We talk a while. The men bring things to trade. Drink, food, cloth, valuables, medical supplies. We talk some more, then ...'

Claire could guess the rest. 'Is there a particular place you go?'

Magrietta turned her head, so Claire wouldn't see her face. 'There is a small stream, not far. It has a nice grassy bank. We go there to talk, but that is all.'

'Of course.'

'Look, here come some Tommies now.'

Claire saw them. As they came closer to the ambient lights cast by the tents she inspected their uniforms and regimental badges. They were young men, probably only just out of their teens, with bad haircuts. Infantry, by the look of them. She noticed the Lancashire regiment badge. Not only infantry, but also probably poor working-class boys from the north of England.

'Let's keep walking,' Claire said.

'Why?'

'I'm looking for an officer, cavalry, preferably.'

'You do put on airs and graces, don't you,' Magrietta chided.

'What I want will cost a pretty penny.'

'I've a feeling you'll get what you want.'

'I usually do, Magrietta.' Claire smiled.

'What about those two?'

The pair of British officers were strolling along the fence line, smoking and chatting, trying to act relaxed. Claire noticed how every few paces one or the other stole a quick glance through the wire at the women who followed their progress with their eyes. Some of the women wore looks of unconcealed hatred. Others, and not only the young ones, smiled or nodded a mute greeting.

'Good evening, ladies,' the one closest to the fence said as they drew abreast of Claire and Magrietta.

Claire looked him up and down, before he had the chance to do the same to her. He was a young lieutenant, with wavy blond hair and blue eyes, his otherwise pretty face spoiled by a weak chin. His uniform, however, was nicely tailored and his cavalry boots buffed to a high sheen. He was a Hussar. Perfect, she thought. Money.

'It is indeed,' Claire replied.

'A clear night, the sky fairly ablaze with stars. A perfect evening for a –'

'Stroll?' Claire said.

The officer, who was a good three or four years younger than Claire, seemed taken aback and she knew then this pup would be easy to manipulate. He started to speak, but had to clear his throat when only a squeak emerged. 'Indeed, indeed. A stroll would be … very pleasing.'

Magrietta was wide-eyed at Claire's fast work. 'I'll be back soon,' Claire mouthed silently to Magrietta.

'You'll find a gap in the fence twenty yards or so further on, Miss …' the lieutenant said.

'Smith. Jane Smith. So you've come here before?'

The officer's face reddened. Claire walked in the direction he had pointed and he hurried to keep pace with her. Once at the broken section of fence he held two strands of wire to one side and offered his hand as she stepped through. His palm was sweaty and his handshake as limp as an ill-disciplined child's. Claire shuddered and steeled herself for the rest of her performance. 'Thank you …'

'Roderick,' he said, the 'R' coming out as a 'W'.

'What a lovely name. I'm told it's nice to take a stroll along the river in the evenings.'

The officer offered his elbow. 'Then I'd be delighted to show you.'

I bet you would, Claire thought as she linked her hand in the crook of the stranger's arm.

They left Roderick's companion to fend for himself and walked until they came to the stream, where they took a seat side by side on the grassy bank. Frogs croaked and somewhere nearby another couple were holding a murmured conversation.

Roderick leaned over, his shyness gone, and kissed her, his tongue darting in and out of her mouth like a viper's. For all his refinement and the fine cut of his uniform, he still stank like a soldier, of sweat and horse. His hand was on her right breast now.

She felt nothing for him. Claire put a hand on him and found he was hard, bulging against his tightly tailored riding breeches. She cupped it and traced its outline with her thumb. Roderick bit his lower lip and closed his eyes. She fought back a smile and stopped moving.

He opened his eyes. 'What is it?'

She removed her hand completely and leaned out of his embrace. 'I need something, Roderick.'

'Anything. Money?'

'Roderick, how could you?'

'Sorry ... awfully sorry. I didn't mean to imply –'

'A horse.'

'A horse?'

'Yes, one thing I really miss being in this wretched camp is riding. I long to be out on the veld, feeling the wind in my hair. It's so ... invigorating.' She had undone two of the buttons on the bodice of the dress and the swell of her breasts and the outline of her nipples were clearly visible to him as they strained against the fine material.

'I'm sorry, but I really can't help you with a horse.' He reached into a satchel slung around his neck. 'Some nice bully beef, perhaps?'

Claire shook her head and leaned forward and grabbed the hem of her skirt with her right hand. Slowly she raised it, letting her fingers slide the length of her long brown riding boot until her knee was showing.

'Oh, Jane.' He drew a deep breath. 'A horse? Really?'

'You have to help me, Roderick. I'm going mad being locked up here. I just want to remember what it's like to be free again. I'll re-pay you, I promise. In any way I possibly can.' She brushed a lock of hair from her face and smiled at him.

'No, I can't. I'm sure if the camp commandant found out I'd be charged,' he said, yet he leaned closer to her.

Claire continued raising her skirt, until she was sure he could see the shadowed cleft between her legs and the fact that she was bare. Then she stopped. 'If you can't help me, Roderick, then ...'

She left her leg uncovered and moved her hand to her bodice. She toyed with the third button and pouted. Despite his words she could hear his resolve weakening. 'Are you sure you don't want to ride ... with me?'

He exhaled, long and hard. 'All right. Let's go, but quickly.'

Roderick jumped to his feet and held out a hand. Claire grasped it and he pulled her up. He dropped a hand to his crotch to cover his bulging erection and Claire had to turn away to keep from laughing.

'Stop!'

Claire and Roderick both turned and looked up the path that led back to the camp. There were two British officers on horses. One of them held a miner's light up in front of his face so his features were obscured. The other's hand was coming up. Claire saw the pistol.

'Claire Martin! Don't move. You are under arrest.' She saw that it was Captain Walters, the officer from the farmhouse.

Claire pushed past Roderick and ran for the trees.

Walters raised his pistol and took careful aim at her.

'No!' Roderick cried.

Walters fired.

The bullet plucked at her billowing dress as Claire ran, but missed her body. The trees gave way to a ploughed field, which presumably was meant to supply the concentration camp with its meagre fresh rations. Claire hitched up her skirt so she could run faster and the night air was cool on her bare calves and thighs.

The soft ground might slow Walters' horse, but Claire had no chance of outrunning it and she was tiring. Her lungs were on fire and her feet felt like lead as she tried to run across the loose topsoil of the open field. She glanced back over her shoulder and saw that she had not lost the Englishman. She was in the open and every second expected to hear the crack of the pistol once again.

The farmer had ploughed one row deeper than the others – perhaps as a drainage ditch. Claire was still looking backwards when her foot dropped the extra few inches. She lost her balance and crashed into the freshly turned sod.

Walters put the spurs to his mount and as Claire rolled over she saw him looming over her.

'Stay still, you little minx.' Walters dismounted and fell on her before she could get up.

'You're mine now. And you *will* talk to me.'

Claire spat in his face.

Walters released one of her hands and struck her, back-handed, across her jaw. She gasped in shock. Walters raised his hand again for another blow.

'No, stop! Please, I beg of you,' she cried.

Walters checked the blow and wiped his face with the back of his tunic sleeve instead. He stared down at her unbuttoned dress, as did she, and saw her half-exposed breasts rising and falling with every breath. She looked past him and saw that his horse, which he had not bothered to tie, was wandering off.

'Like what you see?' she said.

He ignored the mocking tone. 'What were you doing with that officer down at the river?'

She relaxed a little under him, and felt his grip on her wrist ease slightly in response. *Good*, she thought. 'What do you think?'

He raised his eyebrows. 'Are you a spy or a whore, or both?'

'Neither. I'm a businesswoman and I know how to negotiate for what I want; in this case it was medicines and food for the poor women and children in the camp. You Brits should be ashamed of yourselves.'

'Pah! If you want to negotiate with me, Miss Martin, it would seem I have the upper hand.'

Claire rocked her head from side to side. 'I'm here for the same thing you are, Captain Walters.'

He stared at her. 'You have one thing with which to negotiate. Tell me where it is and I'll spare your life.'

'You won't kill me; if you do you'll never get what you want. Work with me, Captain, and I'll make it worth your while. I can take a little cut, and I'll give you a little something in return.'

She could see he was surprised, having expected more defiance. 'A little what?'

'I'm naked under this dress, Captain. I haven't a penny on me, so there's only one thing I've got to convince you I want to work with you, not against you, and if you hadn't come galloping in on that great charger of yours I would have been putting it to good use right now, as we speak, so I would.'

His top lip curled into a sneer.

'Tell me what you have.' He held the pistol up near her face and cocked the hammer. He relaxed his grip on her wrist with his other hand and ran his fingers down over her breasts to her belly. 'It's a map, yes?'

'Allow me,' she whispered. She opened her legs a little and moved one hand down to the hem of her dress. Walters' eyes were fixed on her breasts again as her other hand went up to her hair.

Walters reached down and fumbled with the fly buttons of his breeches. Claire smiled again as she drew the knitting needle from her bun. Keeping it hidden in the palm of her hand and pressed against the underside of her wrist, she shook her hair free.

'Tell me where it is and I'll go easy on you, girl,' he said.

'Who said anything about going easy?' she asked.

He grinned lasciviously and his warm breath washed over her. He holstered his pistol.

Claire's arm flashed up and she plunged the point of the knitting needle into Walters' neck.

Walters screamed and clutched at the protruding needle. His cries turned to a tortured gurgle as he rolled off her into the soil. Claire jumped to her feet and kicked the writhing Englishman as hard as she could in the groin. He curled into the foetal position to ward off the blows, at the same time as he tried to pull the steel needle free.

Claire looked around for Walters' horse, but she saw it had wandered off even further away. She raised her skirts again and ran as fast as she could in the soft earth. She was breathing hard and heard the crack and the whine of a bullet as it passed within a few feet of her head. Her heart was racing; she had never killed, nor attempted to kill anyone in the past. A kind of lust had temporarily overtaken her as she forced the needle into his skin, but now that madness was replaced with pure fear that Walters would catch her. She looked over her shoulder.

Walters swore at her. With one bloodied hand clamped to his neck he fired again, lower this time; a spout of dirt rose near her right foot.

Claire kept running and heard hoofbeats, but the pistol fired again. Walters could not have retrieved his wayward horse and be riding and shooting again so quickly. Claire risked another glance backwards and saw that the captain had stopped firing at her. Instead, he was turning and raising his pistol to take aim at another horseman who was charging across the field towards him.

Claire was almost at the tree line and when she made it she took cover behind a tree and watched as the horseman bore down on Walters. The British officer must have run out of ammunition or suffered a stoppage. He started to run.

The man on horseback had also run out of ammunition, by the look of it, because Claire watched him draw his own pistol with his free hand and then twirl it on his finger like an American cowboy, so he was holding it by the barrel, like a mini club.

The rider whipped the reins on the horse's neck on either side of the saddle and the beast broke into a gallop. Another mounted man appeared behind the first.

Claire watched, drawing some satisfaction from the wide-mouth look of panic on Walters' face as he ran in her direction. The mounted man drew back his arm and slashed down with the pistol. Claire couldn't help but wince at the loud 'crack' that ensued as Walters pitched forward into the earth. He did not get up again.

She could see, now, to her surprise, that the man who had just struck Walters was the Australian sergeant, Blake. The second man, younger and in British khaki, was riding in his wake.

Behind them both was an officer, with a pistol drawn, and Claire could see that this was Roderick, the man she'd been trying to seduce. He had seen Blake club down Walters and now Roderick was firing.

Claire thought that Roderick must surely catch Blake, who was slowing as he approached her, but then the other rider with Blake dropped back, wheeled his mount and grabbed Roderick, pulling him from his saddle. Together the men tumbled from their horses. The fight between them soon ended when Roderick gained the upper hand and shot the younger man.

Roderick fired a wild shot at Blake, who seemed to be fleeing. Claire stepped from behind the tree and stood in full view of him.

'Give me your arm,' Blake called as the distance between them rapidly closed.

Claire hesitated.

'Your arm!' he called again.

Another shot rang out from behind him and Blake instinctively ducked lower in the saddle. Claire raised her hand.

Blake holstered the pistol and leaned over to the right. He grasped her by the forearm and she matched his grip. He swung her up and around him, leaning to the opposite side of the saddle to counter her weight. She landed on the horse's rump behind him and wrapped her arms around his waist. He spurred his mount into a gallop again.

There were two quick pistol shots fired in succession behind them, but both bullets flew wide of their mark.

'That's him out of ammunition now,' Blake said.

Looking over her shoulder Claire saw that Roderick had given up all thoughts of pursuing them and was rushing to Captain Walters, presumably to give him first aid.

'Hold tight,' Blake said as they approached a fallen tree. The horse took the jump in its stride and Claire was thrown hard into Blake's back as they landed. 'Are you all right?'

'I'm fine,' she said, 'keep riding!'

'I've no intention of staying here. Which way?'

'East,' she said. 'Towards Komatipoort and the border.'

CHAPTER 16

Windhoek, Namibia, the present day

Anja's phone rang. Reluctantly she put down Claire Martin's report. It was Oom Otto.

'Anja, are you coming to Joe's? We're all here.'

Anja checked her watch. She had been so engrossed in the letters that she had lost track of time. Only now did she notice that the sun had almost set. 'Sorry, Oom Otto, I'm coming just now.'

Anja ended the call. As much as she liked her dear Uncle Otto she would much rather have curled up with a Tafel beer in her room and transported herself back to 1902 than make small talk with a bunch of foreign tourists.

However, her mother's admonishments came back to her. She did need to get out more and cultivate a social life. Who knew, she mused as she collected her papers and trudged back to her room, perhaps she might meet a nice single Namibian man and settle down here.

Now that would piss her mother off. She smiled to herself.

Anja took a quick shower to freshen up then walked briskly along Nelson Mandela Avenue to Joe's. The building was nothing much to look at from the outside, more like a factory or warehouse with its wire-topped brick wall, but once she walked around, through the car park, she could hear the bar coming to life inside.

It was not even seven, but the place was already almost full. Joe's was not so much one bar, but more a collection of dining and drinking areas concealed amid a mass of antiques, bric-a-brac and downright clutter. Its eclectic decor ranged from wooden toilet seats glued to the tops of bar stools to a tiny Fiat car that hung precariously over one of the entry ways. The vehicle had been abandoned by some European travellers who made it cross country as far as Joe's before bequeathing their ride to the pub.

Anja pinpointed Otto's mass of thick grey curls and made her way through a coachload of tourists in khaki and leopard print who were waiting to be seated by a harried waitress.

Anja was about to call out to him when a man stepped between two tables to her left and, apparently looking the other way, bumped into her. Beer slopped onto her left hand.

'Hey,' she said, shaking her fingers.

'Oh my, I'm so, so sorry.'

Anja looked up into the man's face now that he was looking the right way. He was taller than her, slim, with thick black wavy hair sporting just the right amount of product. He looked fit and was well dressed, not in tourist clothes, but in slim-fit jeans, a pink polo and expensive sneakers.

'Forgive me.'

'It is fine,' she said. 'You did not spill too much on me.'

'No, but I feel terrible now. Let me get you a serviette. I'm so terribly sorry.'

He sounded South African, well educated, as if he had gone to an expensive school. Whatever his background he was strikingly handsome.

'Really, it is not a problem, excuse me.' Anja finally managed to navigate herself around the polite stranger, who apologised yet again, and made her way through the tourist throng to Otto.

'Hello, Anja!' Otto was an enthusiast and he greeted her as he always did, as if it had been two years rather than two hours since he'd last seen her. 'Come meet my new friends.'

Anja's inner introvert cringed. As a tour guide Otto was part-showman and a bon vivant. He had already memorised the names of the ten people in his group – something that would have taken Anja a week.

If this hadn't been the only chance she would have to spend time with Otto before going back out to the desert, then she would not have bothered. A repeat visitor from Germany began telling Anja about a life-changing experience she'd had in Etosha, when she had witnessed her first lion kill. Anja hadn't even had a chance to go get a drink, and the woman was just centimetres from her face.

'Sorry to interrupt, special delivery. Peace offering.'

Anja followed the eyes and admiring smile of the tourist and looked behind her. It was the good-looking guy who had just bumped into her and he had two glasses in his hand, one of red wine and the other white.

'I'm sorry, I didn't know if you liked wine or which type, but I took a guess and ordered a couple of nice ones. I won't stay, but perhaps you could take one of these off my hands and I'll keep the other.'

Anja was taken aback. If the man hadn't been so handsome, and his smile so genuine, she would have turned him away. Still, she didn't know what to say.

'If you don't accept a glass of wine from this man, then I will,' said the tourist.

Anja also saw the intrusion as a means of escaping the woman. 'OK, white, please.'

Otto bustled back to them. 'Oh, Anja, I see you've met Scott.'

The handsome man smiled at her and held out a hand.

She took it and shook, then looked to Otto. 'You two know each other?'

'Just met,' Scott said, drawing her attention back to him. 'Otto was by himself, waiting for his guests, when I arrived. I saw his tour guide credentials badge and was picking his brains for good fishing spots on the coast.'

'Oh,' Anja said.

'My niece defected to Germany with her mother, but she's one of us, a local, really,' Otto said. 'Anja, Scott, can you excuse me, please? I have to keep doing the rounds.'

'I'll come with you and help,' said the woman who had been talking to Anja.

'Thank you,' Anja said to Scott. 'You may have saved me from a fate worse than death – that is, unless you want to tell me your lion stories.'

He laughed, showing again his perfect teeth. 'Oh, I don't have nearly enough lion stories, though I'm hoping to go back to South Africa with some fishing tales.'

Anja sipped her drink. 'You're here on holiday? Forgive me, but you're not dressed like a tourist.'

'Well I'm from Cape Town, so, no, we don't usually get around in floppy bush hats with leopardskin puggarees. Actually, I'm here working on plans for a new housing estate outside of Windhoek.'

Anja forced a smile. 'Really?'

He laughed. 'Don't look so interested.'

'I'm sorry.'

'It's OK,' he said, 'most people's eyes glaze over when I tell them I'm a property developer.'

'I'm sorry,' Anja said. Ordinarily she would have been looking for a quiet corner where she could escape and read, but Scott was extremely handsome and his eyes were the most beautiful blue.

'What do you do, Anja?'

'Part-time university tutor in Munich, fulltime PhD candidate,' she said.

'What's your thesis going to be about?'

'It relates to the history of Namibia,' she said, her instincts making her clam up again. 'Nothing exciting.'

'I don't know about that! As if being in real estate isn't enough, my friends find my hobby can be quite tedious. I'm into military history, particularly the early–twentieth century conflicts in South Africa and German South West Africa.'

'That *is* interesting,' she said. It was harder, now, for her to keep her cool.

He raised his eyebrows. 'You think so? Can I ask what period or part of the country you're studying?'

'More natural history,' she said, on guard again.

'That sounds cool. One day I want to take a turn through the south of the country. I'm interested in the Nama uprising against the Germans. It doesn't get as much coverage as the war against the

Herero, and also the campaigns of the First World War, when South Africa invaded.'

'I'm staying near Aus,' Anja said quickly, suddenly wanting to keep the conversation going. Scott's attractiveness and his interest in a period that she was currently so focused on were assaulting the barriers she normally threw up to strangers. 'You should check out the military graves near the old German prisoner of war camp.'

He nodded enthusiastically. 'Definitely on my list. I come to Namibia as often as I can, so maybe I'll see you around there?'

'Yes, maybe.' She started to feel tongue-tied and looked down.

'Do you have any plans? Would you like to have dinner? Unless, of course, you want to join Otto and his band of tourists.'

'Er, no, thank you. I mean, yes, please, to dinner.' She felt nervous and quite impetuous, agreeing to an invitation from a stranger so quickly, but she found herself not wanting to let him disappear into the crowd.

'Great. I'll get us a table before this place fills up.'

While Scott was talking to a waitress Anja made her way through the throng of tourists to Otto. 'Sorry, Scott has asked me to have dinner with him.'

Otto gave her a wink. 'I thought you two might have something in common. I think that's a great idea. He's handsome, yes?'

'Oom Otto!'

'I'm pleased to see you socialising with someone other than an old man like me, Anja. Enjoy your evening. I'll look for you around Aus when I pass through there with my clients.'

She smiled at him. 'I'll keep an eye out for your vehicle. I'd be happy to talk to your tourists about the horses if we see each other.'

'Thank you, I'm sure they would love that.'

Otto went back to his clients and Scott came back to her. 'They've found us a table in what passes for a quiet corner here.'

'Super,' Anja said.

The waitress came with menus and led them to their table. When they sat down Scott was framed by traditional fish traps woven from reeds, old German colonial-era Windhoek road signs and antique streetlights. There were reminders even here in the bar that modern Namibia had not forgotten its rich, varied and sometimes troubled past.

Scott perused the menu. 'I'm going to tackle the Eisbein, I think. Otto said it was quite an undertaking.'

Anja smiled. 'I've seen bigger men than you defeated by that dish.'

'Then I'll take that as a challenge.'

The waitress returned and they ordered. Anja chose a gemsbok fillet. 'They're such beautiful antelope I almost feel bad eating them, but they're farmed.'

'Shall we split a bottle of wine?'

'Sure,' she said. Anja was already a little tipsy, but she was enjoying herself so far. Scott chose a South African Zandvliet shiraz from the wine list and smiled, showing his perfectly even teeth.

Anja decided to take a risk and open up a bit about her studies. It was rare to find people outside of the university who were genuinely interested in history, and she realised she could not sit through the entire meal just staring into his eyes. 'I'm looking at the desert horses of Namibia and where they really came from,' she said, and then realised it would sound abrupt the way she'd blurted it out, but Scott looked interested.

'*Really* came from?' He leaned back in his chair as the waitress brought their wine. He seemed to be easygoing yet confident, and Anja couldn't help but notice the appreciative smile the waitress gave him.

'Yes,' Anja said. 'I'm also doing some volunteer work with the wild horses research project, helping with their study of predation of desert horse foals.'

'That sounds fascinating,' Scott said, 'but getting back to the origin of the horses, isn't the most common theory that they're descended from military mounts that were either let go or escaped during the First World War?'

'Yes. Most people think they were British horses from a camp near Garub, in southern Namibia. A German military aircraft bombed the encampment – there is evidence they were targeting the horses – and when their explosives detonated, a large number of horses broke free of their enclosure and scattered into the desert.

Most were not recaptured.' Anja paused. 'However, I think their origins could go further back.'

Scott raised his eyebrows. 'To the time of the Herero and Nama wars?'

'Maybe,' she said, stopping herself, just in time.

Their meals came and conversation was suspended while they tucked in. Anja was anxious because she had inadvertently given away the substance of her own research. But Scott was disarming.

Scott made it about halfway through his huge pork Eisbein, but then pushed his plate away. 'Phew. I'm not giving up just yet, but it's half-time for me.'

She laughed.

Scott wiped his mouth with a napkin. 'What I'd like to find, maybe here in Namibia, is some primary source material about the Nama people's wars, perhaps some oral history handed down from generation to generation. I want to get out into the mountains and deserts where the war was fought.'

'It is amazing countryside,' Anja said, in between mouthfuls. 'It is so stark and ... what is the English word ... for-something?'

'Foreboding maybe,' Scott said. 'Or forbidding, or maybe both.'

'Yes, that is it. Both, I think. It's hot and dry, mountainous, rocky, incredibly hard country for men to survive in, let alone fight in. The Germans were hampered by a lack of supplies, especially water and fresh rations, and they were unprepared for the heat and dust.'

'Whereas the Nama guerrillas,' Scott said, taking up her thread, 'knew the land intimately, could live in it and off it, and were lightly armed and fast-moving. They used classic hit-and-run tactics like the Boers had.'

'Exactly,' Anja said, 'but in the end, like the farmers in the Boer commandos, they were ultimately unsuccessful, not least because their supporters, their families, were rounded up and imprisoned.'

'There are some interesting parallels. It's ironic that the British taught the Germans all there was to know about concentration camps, isn't it?'

Anja nodded.

'Sorry, I hope I haven't caused any offence?'

'No, it's fine,' she said. 'It's just refreshing to find someone who shares my interests.'

Scott topped up her wineglass and poured himself another. 'You say you live in Munich?'

'Yes. It's summer, now, of course, but give me the weather here any day.'

'I think I'd find the desert pretty tough,' Scott said. 'As a Capetonian I'm used to a pretty mild climate.'

She thought he was exaggerating his concerns about life in the desert. Anja could see that Scott was in very good physical shape. He looked more like a rugged outdoorsy type or fitness freak than a businessman, but Anja tried not to put much stock in stereotypes.

Scott took a long look at the remains of his Eisbein, then pushed the plate further away from him. 'I'm afraid I have to concede defeat.'

'I'm not far behind.' Anja finished the last of her gemsbok and Scott poured the remains of the bottle of wine into their glasses.

'It's been lovely meeting you, Anja,' he said, 'but I really think I should get an early night. I have to break my trip to Namibia and fly back to Cape Town tomorrow morning early for some urgent business meetings that have just come up, but I'm coming back as soon as I'm done.'

'I need an early night as well,' she said.

'Where are you staying?' he asked.

'A guesthouse not far from here, in Klein Windhoek.'

'Can I walk you home or organise a car for you?'

Anja felt her heart beat faster and her breath seemed to catch in her chest. This had all happened so fast. 'I … I have a car waiting.'

He held up his hands. 'Sorry, I didn't mean to be forward, or anything other than proper. It's been lovely chatting, Anja.'

'Yes, lovely, thanks.' She got up and walked out and Scott waved to her and went to one of the bars.

A doorman asked if he could organise a car for her and she said yes. He waved to a driver who pulled up within seconds. As Anja got in the car she mentally kicked herself. She had just met a handsome man with an interest in Namibia and its history and she didn't even give him her phone number or ask for his. She didn't even think to get his last name!

No wonder she was single.

Anja gave a start as someone knocked on the window of the car. She turned and saw it was Scott. She wound down the window and he reached inside the car and handed her a Joe's Beerhouse coaster.

'I've written my phone number on here, just in case.'

Anja took it, and smiled. 'Thank you.'

The driver looked at her and she nodded. As the car pulled away, Anja wondered if she would see this handsome stranger again, or if she had just made the mistake of her life.

CHAPTER 17

Sydney Airport, Australia, the present day

'What are you doing here?' Susan said, eyes and smile wide when Nick tapped her on the shoulder from behind as she queued at the Business Class check-in counter for the Qantas flight to Johannesburg.

'I've decided to come to South Africa,' he said.

'You're crazy.'

'For once in my life, yes.' He realised it had been too long since he had done anything spontaneous. Following Susan to Africa was gold standard flying by the seat of his pants. He smiled to himself.

She gave him a light punch on the arm. 'You know, that note of yours that you left next to me on the bed this morning was nice, promising you'd see me again some time soon, but it still felt a bit like you were sneaking out on me while I was sleeping.'

'I wanted to surprise you,' he said.

'Well, that you have.'

They checked in and after passing through security and immigration went up the escalators to the Qantas Club. Susan scouted ahead for two free lounge chairs and Nick went to the bar and returned with two glasses of champagne.

He joined her and they raised their glasses. 'To living in the moment,' she said.

'Bloody madness, more like it,' he said as they clinked glasses.

Susan sipped her sparkling wine. 'Nick, where are you planning on going in South Africa?'

He held up his free hand. 'Don't worry. I don't expect to be tied to your apron strings while I'm in Africa. The truth is, I don't really know and, you know what? I don't care, either. I've got an idea that I'll go and have a look at some of the places where Cyril Blake served. From what you said, that's mostly around the Kruger National Park, right?'

She nodded and sipped her champagne. 'Yes. It's a great place to visit in its own right if you want to go on safari. You can hire a car and drive yourself around if you like.'

'Sounds a bit daunting,' he said.

'Relax, Nick.' She reached out and touched his hand. 'Your average South African family goes to the Kruger Park and drives the family sedan or people mover around the bush on safari.'

'I'll be brave. You're going on to Cape Town, right?'

Susan sighed. 'Yes. I have to go see my client, but to tell you the truth I'm planning on ending our business relationship.'

'Sick of writing press releases?'

'Something like that,' she said, looking out the lounge window over the aircraft coming and going. She looked back at him. 'And after Kruger?'

Nick shrugged. 'By that time I'm hoping Lili will have translated more of the papers my aunt found. With a bit of luck they'll tell the full story of how Blake ended up travelling to South West Africa and how and why he fell in with the Nama rebels. I think it's going to be a fantastic story.'

She nodded. 'It is.'

'What's on your mind, Susan? You were excited at first.'

She finished her drink. 'I didn't expect things to work out the way they have, Nick.'

He looked into her eyes. 'You and me?'

'Yes.'

'Do you regret it?' he asked. He had just wanted to get away, somewhere, anywhere, but Susan was a big part of his impetuous decision to travel to Africa on a whim. He didn't want to feel like a complete fool, but was worried he would if she told him that what they'd done meant nothing and that she didn't want to see him in South Africa.

Instead she reached for him again and took his hand. 'Nick, no, I don't regret what happened. It's just, well, things are complicated for me in South Africa.'

A sudden realisation dawned. 'Oh. Do you have a partner, Susan?'

'No, no, nothing like that, but the PR work I do in Cape Town, it has a way of tying me down. I'd love to be able to hit the road with you, but the client wants me around when I'm in South Africa. I might not be able to walk away immediately, but I'll touch base with you as soon as I can.'

'Gee, it does sound complicated,' he said, though he was mildly relieved.

'It is. As I said, I'm going to ditch the client and finish up, as soon as I get to Cape Town, so maybe your crazy timing is good. Maybe ...'

'You could join me, somewhere on the road?'

She smiled. 'Maybe, yes.' Her mood appeared to brighten.

'Would you like another drink?'

She seemed to mull the idea over. 'Possibly. I need to go to the bathroom first.'

'OK.' Nick picked up a copy of *The Australian* someone had left behind and flicked through the news section.

His phone buzzed.

Nick took it out of his pocket and saw that Susan had just sent him a message, which struck him as odd. He opened it.

Shower room at end of the corridor, on the left. Knock three times.

He grinned, finished his drink, took his bag and went to join her.

CHAPTER 18

Windhoek, Namibia, the present day

Anja was worried. The light in her room in the guesthouse was on.

She was environmentally conscious so never left a tap running nor a light burning for any longer than required. Could she have forgotten? Never.

Perhaps there was a maid in there, or one had visited while she was at Joe's, to turn down the sheets.

No, she told herself. The guesthouse was not classy enough for a turn-down service and chocolates on the pillows. Instead of heading to her room she went to reception, but found the small office closed. She pushed a button on an intercom marked 'night service'.

'Hello, night manager,' a voice said.

'Hello,' Anja said, 'it is Miss Berghoff from room eight. I think someone might be in my room, an intruder.'

'A what?'

'A thief maybe. The light is on.'

'Ah, you must have left the light turned on,' the manager said. 'Happens all the time.'

'No, it does not happen all the time, not with me at least. Please come.'

There was a pause. 'All right. Give me five minutes. I am coming.'

Anja waited, and felt nervous. She patted her pockets and unzipped her small daypack as she waited. With her she had all her cash, credit cards, her iPad and passport, and a portable hard drive with a backup of everything that was on her laptop. She never felt unsafe in Namibia, but she took the same precautions with her valuables as she would have done if travelling in Europe.

She checked her watch, and after seven minutes of tapping her foot the night manager showed up, his white shirt half out of his black trousers. He carried a wooden baton with him.

'All right, let's go.'

Anja fell into step behind the man, who was reassuringly bulky, with thick forearms. They went up the steps to her room, which was located on the upper floor of one of two blocks of rooms. The man stopped near the top and held up a hand.

'What is it?' Anja whispered.

'The door is open.'

Anja swallowed and felt her heart rate increase. 'I would never have left a door unlocked.'

The man took a phone out of his pants pocket and scrolled through his contacts. 'Here is the number for the police. Get ready to call it. Wait here.'

With his little club held at the ready the manager crept slowly up the rest of the staircase. When he was at the door he called out. 'Come out, whoever is in there!'

There was no reply. Anja held her breath, her finger poised over the green 'call' button.

The manager used the tip of the baton to open the door a little wider. It creaked on unoiled hinges. Anja went up the steps until she was just behind the man. When he turned to look back he gave a start at how close she was.

'You scared me.'

'I scared *you*?' she said. 'I'm terrified.'

The man stepped into the room and shoved open the bathroom door, just inside on the right, and put his head and club in there.

'No one,' he said.

Anja followed him in. As relieved as she was that there was no intruder, the room was a mess. Her bag had been opened and her clothes tossed on the bed. Some had fallen to the floor.

'He's moved the mattress,' the man said, pointing with the baton, 'to see if you hid anything underneath. Did you?'

'No.' Anja walked around the room. As she feared, her laptop was gone from its pocket inside her main carry-on bag. 'Damn. My computer.'

'Give me the phone, please.'

She handed it back to the porter, who called the police. He got halfway through explaining what had happened when the call ended.

'What's wrong?' Anja asked, taking a break from sorting through her clothes.

'Damn MTC – the network's gone down.' He tried again. 'No signal.'

She checked hers. 'Same. No signal.'

'I need to go back to the office and call them on the landline. Do you want to come with me?'

Anja looked at the mess the thief had left; the growing feeling of having been violated assaulted her senses. 'No, thanks. I'm going to sort my things and pack them.' She had spent enough time in Africa to know that the police would not be accompanied by a crime scene investigation team, so she had no qualms about going through her possessions. 'Please don't take offence, but I am not going to stay here tonight. I will come to your office as soon as I am packed. I am going to stay at one of the bigger hotels.'

'Suit yourself.' The man turned on his heel and walked back downstairs.

So much for caring for his customers, Anja thought. She would not be giving the place, or its security, a favourable review on TripAdvisor.

Anja put her hands on her hips and surveyed the mess again. She felt a lump rise in her throat, but then told herself to be strong. She needed to do a full inventory of what was left and work out if anything other than her computer had been stolen.

As she folded each item of clothing she imagined a strange man's fingers on her things, her underwear. Anja retrieved her wheelie backpack from the floor and when she laid it on the bed she felt the tears well up. The thief had slashed the linings of each compartment. What on earth had he thought she was hiding in there?

She wiped her eyes. Claire Martin had gone through a war and been imprisoned in a stinking concentration camp and she had been able to go on. Anja drew a deep breath and tried to put the situation into perspective. Claire, she thought to herself again. Anja sorted through her belongings and looked around the room – all of the printouts of Claire Martin's letters were missing. Anja swore.

Why had they stolen those? It made no sense. She had lost a laptop computer, which hurt, but at least she had her hard drive in her daypack. She also had travel insurance, which presumably would pay for a new laptop.

Most importantly, she told herself, she had not been harmed. Burglaries happened every hour of the day in every country in the world; Anja had simply been unlucky, and her situation could have been much worse.

Anja sat down on the bed, picked up the phone on the bedside table and dialled reception. 'It's me, Anja Berghoff, do you have any news for me?'

'The police say they will be here in about twenty minutes. They have asked if you will wait. I have called the Hilton and they have a room. I spoke to the German lady who owns this place, and she says she will pay for your accommodation at the other hotel. I am to organise you a car when you are finished with the cops.'

Anja was taken aback, and touched, at the unknown woman's kindness and understanding. 'Thank you, I'll stay put until the police get here.'

*

Anja looked up from her iPad when she heard the door to her room squeak.

She jumped up and lunged for the door but it flew open, hitting her in the arm. Before she could scream a man barrelled into her, spun her around, twisted her left arm painfully behind her back and clamped his other hand over her mouth. The hand was white, the skin mottled with age, and there was a scar near where the thumb and forefinger met. From the glimpse she had got of him he was dressed in black and wearing a ski mask. She heard the footsteps of another entering the room. She yelled into the man's palm and he twisted her arm harder.

Her kicking and clawing were having no effect, other than increasing the pain in her arm. Just as she tried to rake down on the man's shins the second man came into view again and grabbed her ankles. Together they lifted her onto the bed.

God, no, she thought.

'Don't say a word.' The man who had first grabbed her kept one hand on her mouth. In his other hand was a squat black pistol whose barrel he pressed firmly between her eyes with enough pressure to cause her instant pain. She looked up at him, wide-eyed. 'Hold out your hands or I will kill you now.'

She did not want to submit in any way, but she was terrified they would kill her.

'Roll her over,' the man with the gun said to his accomplice. 'If you scream, you die.'

Removing his hand from her mouth, they turned her and the second man wrenched her hands behind her back. She heard duct tape being peeled from a roll and torn before her hands were bound. The pistol was in the back of her head now, at the top of her spinal column.

'Please, what do you want?'

'Search her bag,' the first man said. 'Quickly.'

'Purse with cash, two credit cards; phone, iPad, hard drive,' said the other.

'Good, take it all.' The gunman pressed the barrel harder into her head and Anja cried out in pain. 'Tell me the PINs for your credit cards.'

She hated the thought of him taking all her money and, worse, her only backup hard drive. But the important thing was to stay alive, and to not anger these men. Cards could be cancelled and she would not be liable for money stolen. She told them the four-digit number.

'Same for both cards?'

'Yes.'

He pressed even harder. 'The truth?'

'Yes, yes, it's the same number for both cards. Please don't hurt me. My hard drive ... please, can you leave it and the printouts you took. They are of no value.'

The man gave a short laugh. 'You don't get to ask for anything. Now stop whining or you'll get something else from us.'

'No, please.'

'Shush,' the gunman said, 'not so loud. We know the cops are coming. This will be quick, and as painless as you want to make it. What are the passwords for your computer and email?'

'What?'

'Don't question me, bitch. Pull her jeans down,' he said to the accomplice.

Anja felt the other man's hands on her bottom, then reaching under her, fumbling for the buckle of her belt and the top button of her jeans. Fear almost paralysed her.

'I'll tell you!'

'Of course you'll tell us. You're not stupid, are you?'

Anja heard a muffled vibration and the man who had been working on her jeans moved his hands.

'Cops are heading down Nelson Mandela Avenue,' the second man said.

The gunman grabbed a handful of her hair. 'Do you want to be brave? Do you think we'll run now that the police are on their way? I have plenty of time to kill you. Ask yourself, is there anything on your computer that is worth you dying for?'

She gave him the passwords.

'Good.'

The gunman held her head up, by her hair, while the second man fixed a piece of tape over her mouth. Hurriedly, they bound her ankles, then left the room.

The tears poured down her face and soaked into the cheap nylon bedspread.

Anja did not know how long it was before the police and the night porter arrived in her room, but it was almost too long to bear. Her mind raced with visions of the men returning to assault or kill her.

A female detective and a uniformed male officer cut her bindings and then the detective ordered the night manager to make her a cup of coffee, or get her something stronger. Anja asked for tea and a brandy then gave the detective a statement about what had happened and what had been stolen.

While waiting for the drinks, Anja called her bank in Munich and cancelled her credit cards. The customer service officer told her, to her relief, that none of her funds had been withdrawn or spent by the thieves.

The detective reviewed her notes. 'You say they asked for your email password?'

Anja nodded.

The detective tapped her pen against her notebook. 'That's a new one for me, but in this age of identity fraud who knows what the criminals are after next.'

'I need to change it as soon as possible,' Anja said, fighting back tears, 'but they have taken my iPad, my laptop, my purse and all my cards, my phone, my hard drive. I feel like everything I have, everything in my life, is gone.'

The female detective reached out and took her hand in hers; the touching gesture made Anja want to cry again.

'You weren't hurt seriously, be thankful for that, praise God,' the detective said. 'Why would someone be interested in your PhD research papers?'

Anja thought about the question. 'I don't know. People say I'm overprotective of my research material, but I didn't think they were worth being assaulted for.'

'What is your research about?' the detective asked.

'The desert horses of the Namib, the Anglo-Boer War and the wars against the Herero and the Nama.'

The detective pursed her lips. 'When we investigate crimes we look for motives. Can you see anyone making money out of your work?'

Anja shrugged. 'No, not that I can think of. I'm protective of it, but is it worth stealing? Probably not. The research papers can be easily found in the German archives.'

'What can you tell me about the men who attacked you? Height? Build? Race? Eye colour.'

'At least one was white, with brown eyes, I think. They wore black clothes, ski masks, and gloves,' Anja said. 'Average height, I suppose, both very strong, muscled. They were behind me or had me face down nearly all the time.'

The detective looked up from her notebook. 'Nearly?'

Anja nodded. 'I got a glimpse of one man's hand. His skin had those liver spots that are common on older people, and he had a scar.' Anja described the location.

The detective made notes.

Anja couldn't see any sense in this attack. Her logical brain also told her that the two men who had robbed her were not starving street urchins. Having ransacked her room they had hidden somewhere, on the grounds of the guesthouse probably, and calmly waited for her to return. They had been quick and ruthless, and, as terrifying as the ordeal had been at the time, she now realised they had not been overly violent, but had rather used just enough physical and mental force to get her to give them what they wanted. In short, they had been professional. She explained as much to the policewoman, and detailed as much as she could remember of what they had said.

'I expect they wanted your email and computer passwords to find out your banking details.'

'I'll cancel the accounts.'

'Anja,' the detective said, leaning closer and lowering her voice a little, 'is there anything incriminating on your computer, something you wouldn't want someone to see? Sometimes blackmail is a motive.'

She shook her head. 'Nothing. Perhaps they confused me with someone else? Perhaps they had been told to raid the hotel room of a rich German tourist and all they got was some credit cards with low limits and a laptop full of notes and a draft of my thesis?'

The detective sat back, closed her notebook and gave Anja a business card.

'Call me if you can think of any other reason why these men attacked you, in particular, and what they might have wanted in your papers and your computer.'

'I will.'

When the police left, Anja's composure cracked and she started to cry.

CHAPTER 19

Johannesburg, South Africa, the present day

Nick woke and had no idea where he was.

The room was blacked out thanks to heavy curtains, but his mind picked up the hum of traffic. He groped around him, feeling for a bedside light switch as he registered that he was in Johannesburg.

His fingers brushed his phone and he pushed the button and the screen lit up. It was four in the morning. He now felt wide awake so he swung his legs out of bed. From the glow of the phone he found the light switch.

The jetlag had woken him. He had forced himself to stay up as late as he could, waiting until he heard from Susan that she had arrived safely in Cape Town, which he did while he was having dinner at a steak restaurant at Emperor's Palace. He had taken the free shuttle bus to the casino complex near the airport and checked into one of the hotels there, the Peermont Metcourt. It was a good place for an overnight stop.

He got up, showered and shaved, and put on clean clothes. At Susan's suggestion he had booked the hotel room and a rental car online from the Qantas Club. His mind replayed their lovemaking in the shower room. He was missing her already. Again, Jill entered his mind. Jill was his soul mate, but he couldn't deny the feelings he had for Susan. Maybe it was just lust, or an infatuation, but meeting her had given him something to look forward to.

Before they had left Sydney Susan had also gone online and showed him how to book and pay for his first four nights in the Kruger National Park. For his first night she had found accommodation for him at Skukuza Rest Camp, which was close to the park's airport. After that he had two nights at Satara camp and one at Pretoriuskop. So far the names meant nothing to him.

'I'll come see you soon, promise,' Susan had said as they had kissed for the last time after collecting their baggage. She hadn't lingered – she needed to rush to make her connection to Cape Town.

Was he crazy? he asked himself.

Maybe. But if this was madness then he wanted more of it. He felt wired, and at the same time relaxed, having been relieved of the crushing feeling of having to face another day in a job he had never really liked. He wondered if this was what retirement felt like. He was realistic enough to know that he would have to find another job some time, but the thought of blowing a good chunk of his severance pay did not bother him right now.

Nick had downloaded a non-fiction book called *Steinaecker's Horsemen* on his Kindle ebook reader, about the unit Cyril Blake had been in during the Boer War. While eating his breakfast and sipping coffee at the hotel restaurant downstairs, he skim-read the book. It soon became apparent that the unit was irregular in every sense of the word.

With a walrus moustache whose nine-inch length was perhaps an attempt to compensate for his short stature, and a penchant for dressing in elaborately ceremonial uniforms trimmed with silver braid and sashes, Ludwig von Steinaecker seemed as colourful as the brigands, hunters, goldminers, traders and chancers he commanded. Steinaecker had a mouthful of jagged yellow stumps of teeth and was known to his men as 'Old Stinky'.

Nick finished breakfast, went back up to his room and fetched his bag. After checking out he waited a few minutes for the hotel's shuttle bus back to the airport. Once he had checked in for his flight to Skukuza he made his way through to departures in the domestic terminal. With another coffee in hand he found a seat and called Susan.

'Howzit,' she said. 'Miss me?'

'As a matter of fact, yes.' He couldn't keep the smile out his voice. 'What are you up to? Are you driving?'

'*Ja*, I'm on Bluetooth. Cape Town traffic hasn't got any better while I was in Australia. I'm just going to have that meeting with my client and end it.'

As someone who had just lost his only source of ongoing income he had a new-found respect for financial security and he hoped Susan knew what she was doing. 'Well, if you're sure ...'

'The money I get isn't worth it for the amount of shit I have to put up with and the things I have to do. Besides, now that I'm on the trail of a really good story again I've realised how much I want to return to journalism, rather than PR.'

He wondered exactly what it was that Susan had to do for this man, or what sort of person he was. She had told him she just had to smooth out some problems, but her sudden flight back to South Africa and her reference to 'shit' she had to put up made her meeting with the client sound more serious than she had initially indicated. Nick felt instantly protective towards her. 'Do you want me to have him horsewhipped?'

She didn't laugh at his attempt at humour. 'As soon as I finish I'm going to book a flight to Skukuza.'

'Great,' he said, feeling genuinely happy.

'There's something important I have to tell you.'

He licked his lips. 'OK. Something good, I hope.'

She paused. 'Important. But, yes, I hope good in the long run. I really like you, Nick. I'll explain when I see you.'

He exhaled. 'Same. Are you all right, Susan?'

'Nervous. A little scared, maybe, but this is for the best. I needed to come back to South Africa to do this in person, but I don't care where we go after I see you, Nick.'

'This is all sounding very mysterious, and a tad dramatic,' he said, trying to keep the conversation light.

'It is serious, Nick, but I want you to trust me that I know what I'm doing. Nick ...'

'Yes?'

'Take care of yourself, please.'

145

'I'll try not to get eaten by a lion or stomped on by an elephant. Oh, and you said buffalo are really dangerous, too, didn't you?'

She paused again. 'I'm not joking, Nick. Africa can be dangerous. Watch yourself, and don't do anything dumb until I see you, OK?'

'All right, I'll wait until I see you to do something dumb. In fact, you can pretty much count on it.'

'Nick ...'

'Yes?'

'I ...'

He felt his tummy flip. He wondered if she was about to say she loved him. His mind turned in time with his innards. Did he love her? Their lovemaking had been sensational, as though their bodies had been made for each other, and they had much in common with their journalistic backgrounds. Now that he thought more about her he realised that from his side of things it was more than just a fling. Not even his thoughts of Jill could change his mind.

'What is it, Susan?' he asked.

'I ... I was just going to say that as soon as I get this done I'm going to go to the bar at the Vineyard Hotel in Cape Town and have a mojito. The barman there is a friend of mine and he's the best, he'll have a drink waiting for me when I get there and I'll call you. You should go there some time.'

She said it so matter-of-factly that he just agreed.

There was a pause, then Susan said quietly, 'Nick. I'm nearly at the office, I'd better go.'

'OK.' Nick thought back over their conversation; Susan's tone of voice. 'You're making me worried about you, Susan,' he blurted.

'Don't be. I'll be all right, once I've seen this through. I'll come find you, Nick. Be careful.'

'What do you mean, be –?'

But Susan had ended the call.

Nick fretted for a while as he finished his coffee, but when he tried calling Susan back his call went straight through to voicemail. He reasoned that she must have gone into her meeting. He read a newspaper and told himself not to worry, and soon it was time to go to the gate for his flight to Skukuza in the Kruger National Park.

He took an escalator downstairs to the tarmac level where buses took passengers to flights servicing regional destinations in South Africa. Nick took a seat while he waited for the Skukuza flight to be called. He took out his Kindle and turned it on.

'What's it like reading one of those little things?'

Nick looked up from the device and at a rotund man sitting next to him. He was dressed in a khaki and blue shirt, work shorts and desert boots. 'It's OK. I still like paper books, but ebooks are good for travelling.'

The man snorted, and said with a strong Afrikaans accent, 'Myself, I read only books made from paper. I like the feel and the smell of a book. From where are you?'

'Australia.'

'I have relatives in Perth, but then again, half of South Africa has family living in your country. My name's Danie.'

'Nick.' They shook hands.

'What are you reading?'

'It's a book about a unit in the Boer War, Steinaecker's Horse. They were based in the Kruger Park area,' Nick said.

Danie nodded. 'I have heard of them. Oh, and by the way, we call it the *Anglo*-Boer War as it takes two to tango, as you would say, *né*?'

Nick smiled and nodded. 'I didn't know that, but thanks.'

'There was a display about those Steinaecker's Horse guys at the camp at Mopani, in the north of Kruger. One of their bases was up there and some archaeologists did a dig there and came up with some stuff. Lots of old whiskey and gin bottles from what I remember.' He laughed.

'Yes,' Nick said, 'from the little I've read so far it seems like they were quite a rough bunch.'

'From what I know they spent more time hunting elephants for ivory and searching for Oom Paul's gold, rather than fighting the Boer commandos.'

'Who Paul?' Nick asked.

'Oom – that's our word for uncle, a term of respect in Afrikaans – and Paul was Paul Kruger, the president of our republic at the time. When he retreated from the British, on a train to Mozambique, they say he took the Transvaal's gold reserves with him, but the gold disappeared. Many people think Oom Paul or his followers hid it somewhere in the lowveld, where the Kruger Park is. Every now and then some *oke* claims to have found it, or part of the hoard.'

'Fascinating,' Nick said. This story had everything – colourful characters, spies, a war, and now even a lost treasure. What Danie had said got him thinking about the pickle his ancestor Cyril seemed to have landed himself in. He couldn't wait for more translations to come from Lili, but in the meantime he had his trip to the Kruger Park to look forward to.

Their conversation was cut short by a South African Airlink ground crew person who called their flight. They picked up their carry-on luggage and made their way through the doors to the bus that would take them to their aircraft.

Nick wanted to call Susan again, but he stopped himself. He didn't want to come across as needy or a worrier.

The flight was short, less than forty-five minutes, and when he landed at Skukuza, inside the Kruger National Park, Nick completed the paperwork to collect a rental car and to enter the reserve.

Leaving the airport he stopped his Toyota Corolla on the low-level concrete bridge across the Sabie River. The bridge was only one lane and he'd had to wait a while for his turn to cross. There were a couple of parking bays halfway along and he pulled into one.

It was an almost surreal experience. On his left a hippopotamus had just wiggled its ears at him and then submerged, and there was a huge crocodile, maybe three metres long, basking on a sand spit by a clump of reeds. For the first time since he arrived he felt like he was truly in Africa.

He wound down the window and carried on, enjoying the fresh air. Once over the concrete causeway he turned left then right, and stopped as a graceful giraffe crossed the road. He was too slow to get a photo, but all the same his heart beat a little faster at seeing this magnificent creature in the wild.

Nick navigated his way to Skukuza Rest Camp and entered via a thatch-roofed gate. He pulled into a car park, got out and checked into his accommodation in the reception building. The woman on duty printed out his reservation form, which included the additional nights Susan had booked for him. Armed with a photocopied map of the camp he made his way to his riverside rondavel, a circular self-contained bungalow.

The river he had just crossed glittered like burnished bronze in front of him and a lone buffalo wandered among the reeds on the other side. This camp was more or less on the site of Steinaecker's Sabie Bridge headquarters. He imagined Cyril Blake standing in this very spot, taking in the same view more than a century earlier. It made the hairs on the back of his neck stand up.

Inside, his accommodation was simple but neat. There was a small kitchen on the verandah outside, with a fridge behind a metal security door; a sign told him baboons and monkeys were a problem in the camp and the fridge was clearly a prime target. He turned the air conditioner on and it rattled and hummed to life. He took his laptop and phone back out to the verandah, powered up the computer and connected to the internet.

While his emails were loading, slowly, he called Susan. The call went through to voicemail again.

'Hi, it's Nick,' he said. 'I hope things went OK with your client. I'm at Suzuki, or Skukoozy, or however you pronounce it. I saw a hippo and a croc on my drive here, and an elephant from the plane on the flight in. Amazing. Look forward to seeing you again soon, and to hearing from you. Bye.'

He hung up, feeling mildly disappointed that she hadn't called him already. He was sure she would.

In his email inbox was a message from Lili. He could see even before he opened it that there was an attachment, which meant more pages. Nick was looking forward to his next instalment, but he decided to stock up on provisions and grab a bite to eat.

Nick walked over to the shop, a large thatch-roofed building that seemed to be eighty per cent souvenirs and twenty per cent provisions, but he found some steak, beers, bread and milk, and the makings of a salad. When he got back to his rondavel he put the food away in the caged outdoor fridge.

His desire to explore Kruger Park was blunted by jetlag and when Nick lay down on one of the beds in the rondavel, ostensibly for a ten-minute snooze, he fell into a deep sleep. When he woke and looked outside the sun was almost touching the horizon. Nick liberated a Windhoek Lager beer from the outdoor fridge. He read the label and confirmed, as he had thought, that it was from Namibia. Blake's story would move there at some point and with luck Nick's journey would keep pace with the old soldier's. Nick set some firelighters and a pile of charcoal in the *braai* in front of his hut – he had deduced the Afrikaans word for barbecue during his shopping trip.

As he took his first sip of his drink, he heard a loud honking sound from downriver and moved to the walkway that ran across the front of his rondavel, for a better view. It took him a moment to locate the source, but the ripples on the shining surface of the river gave the hippo away. What started as a few barely distinguishable bumps emerged slowly and coalesced into a giant creature. The hippopotamus lumbered up out of the water onto dry land, its smooth flank glistening. Nick had read somewhere that hippos came out of the water in the evenings to feed on dry land.

The sight and noise and the timelessness of the setting added to the feeling that he was not just in another country, but another world, another time.

From somewhere far away he heard an eerie *woo-oop*.

'You hear that?'

He turned and saw a man, his neighbour, with a pair of tongs in one hand and a can of beer in the other, smoke rising from the *braai* behind him.

'Yes,' Nick said. 'Is it dumb of me to ask what it is?'

'Hyena,' the man said.

'Wow.'

The man walked over. 'Howzit, I'm Chris.'

'Nick.' They shook hands. 'Is it normal for them to make that weird whooping noise?'

Chris nodded. 'They really don't laugh, like some people say, though they cackle like crazy when they're excited. They patrol the fence here; you might see one.'

Nick smiled and nodded. 'I guess I'm safe if I'm not dead – they only scavenge, right?'

'No, no,' said the man, clearly a local on holiday, 'they are actually very efficient hunters, though they do scavenge a lot. You know they live in a matriarchal society? The lowest-ranked female in the clan is senior to the highest-ranked male.'

Nick chuckled. 'Sounds like where I used to work.'

'For how long are you in the park?' Chris asked.

'A few days, maybe longer if a friend joins me. You?'

'I'm here a couple more days,' Chris said. He started piling the cooked meat onto a plate. 'Enjoy your visit.'

'Cheers, have a good evening,' Nick said.

When the coals were glowing red Nick cooked and then ate his food. He sent another message to Susan, then jetlag caught up with him again and he lay down on his bed and drifted off to sleep with the light still on.

A ding from his phone woke him.

Disoriented, he sat up and saw from his watch that it was ten in the evening. He checked his phone and saw immediately from the notification on the screen that it was from Susan.

Relieved, and heart racing a little, he opened the message.

I am so sorry to have to write this message, Nick. I apologise for not replying to your calls and voice messages, but I have had time to do some thinking and I have to tell you that I will not be joining you in the Kruger Park. It was really nice meeting you in Sydney, but I have to take stock of my life right now and work out what is important to me, with work and my private life. I think it's best if I say goodbye now. Best wishes, Susan.

Nick re-read the message, three times. He couldn't believe it.

He called Susan but the call went straight to voicemail. He left a message and then another.

'Susan, it's Nick,' he tried again. 'Please call me. I can understand, I think, if you don't want to carry on, but I just want to make sure you're OK. Call me.'

He sat for a long while, looking at his phone in disbelief and willing it to ring. He finished another two beers while waiting and his disbelief started turning to anger. It was now morning in

Australia and his phone made a different chime, telling him he had mail. He quickly opened his emails, hoping Susan had sent him a message that way, but there was nothing from her. He saw Lili's unread email so in an attempt to distract and calm himself he read the latest instalment of the manuscript.

CHAPTER 20

The eastern Transvaal, South Africa, 1902

Blake rode hard for another hour, keeping to the open veld and away from the road, where he knew there would be checkpoints, blockhouses and roving patrols. Claire had hugged his back as they rode and he imagined she was cold. She was wearing a simple linen dress and, from what he could tell, little else in the way of petticoats.

He used the stars to guide him and, because he had no better idea, headed southeast. He figured that soon enough they would reach the east–west railway line that led to Komatipoort and that was where Claire had said she wanted to go. It was as good a place as any to aim for. The town was on the border of the Transvaal and Portuguese East Africa, and home to another outpost of Steinaecker's Horse. Even though he was on the run from the British he figured he might be able to get help from one or more of his comrades – several of the misfits under Old Stinky's command had spent time on the run from the law. With Claire as a witness perhaps he could urge Steinaecker or another officer to take up his case and clear his name. They would need food, a horse for Claire, more ammunition, and intelligence about what this Captain Walters had been up to. Blake half hoped the blow to the man's head had killed him, but his rational self told him that if Walters died he would be in more trouble than he already was. He needed to bring

Walters to justice and have his crimes exposed, not to be saddled with another murder charge.

When they reached a narrow stream they dismounted and Blake let Bluey drink his fill. The moon was high and the ripples on the water glittered silver. He knelt and refilled his canteen.

He offered the water bottle to Claire and said, 'Time for some answers.'

'I didn't escape from the British to answer questions from one of their lackeys.' She took the water bottle and drank greedily from it.

'You didn't escape, I rescued you.'

She wiped her mouth. 'I don't know you. I don't owe you anything.'

'Well, I did save your life, so I think at least a thank you is warranted.'

She let slip a smile. 'Very well. Thank you. I need a horse of my own.'

'Are all Americans so pushy?'

'Yes, and because I'm half Irish and half German I'm obstinate and efficient to boot. Now, a horse?'

'I've got an idea where we can get a mount for you. But first, why is everyone after you?' Blake asked.

'I think the real question is, why are *you* following me?' she countered.

He knew she wouldn't budge; she was clearly hiding something that other people were prepared to kill to discover. 'I've been framed over the death of your American friend at the farm, by Captain Walters, the man who was trying to kill you in the field and who tortured and killed your friend.'

She swallowed, and handed back the water bottle. 'What's that got to do with me?'

'You can prove my innocence. Tell the authorities I went into the barn to try and stop Walters when I realised he was torturing that colonel.'

'I can't tell the British authorities anything,' she said.

'Why not?'

'Because they'll hang me. That's why that man Walters was after me. He thinks I'm a spy and a Boer sympathiser.'

154

'And why would he think that?'

'I've no idea, I'm just an innocent civilian.'

More lies, thought Blake, but there was more going on here than just the Brits chasing a Boer sympathiser. It was not enough to explain why a British officer would torture and murder an enemy, and frame Blake and corrupt Bert. 'I'll take you in by force if I have to.'

She gave him a mocking smile. 'You haven't got any ammunition in that Broomhandle Mauser of yours, otherwise you would have used it on Walters. If you had killed him, our troubles would be over and we could go our separate ways. As it is, you probably just knocked him out cold with your little Broomhandle pistol.'

'You know your firearms.'

'I've a cousin in the business, as it were.'

'The British will hang me if I walk in without you as a witness,' Blake said.

'And they'll hang *me* if I walk in with you. Look, I'm sorry, Sergeant whoever you are ...'

'Blake.'

'Well, Mr Blake, I'm sorry, but I've got to get out of this country and back to German South West Africa. If you can help me get east to Portuguese East Africa, I'll go with you to the British embassy in Lourenço Marques and give a statement there.'

Blake rubbed his stubbled chin. 'We should turn ourselves in, get a lawyer and explain things.'

'I told you, they'll execute me. I'm finished with this dirty little war. I want out. I'm going to Portuguese East Africa if I have to walk there,' Claire said.

'If the British don't get you the lions will before you even make the border,' Blake said.

She reached out and put a hand on his forearm. She held his eyes, but instead of defiance, this time he saw desperation. He felt his skin tingle. 'Then come with me, please. We'll stand a better chance with two of us.'

Blake doubted it. He felt sure the woman would slow him down and if she wasn't going to vouch for him then she was little more than excess baggage, but that little touch had made his pulse race like a thoroughbred.

Perhaps seeing Blake's hesitation, Claire appeared to decide to let it lie for the moment. 'How long have you been in South Africa, anyway?'

'Since the beginning, 1899.' Blake unbuckled a saddlebag, searched inside, and fished out a stick of biltong. He cut the dried beef in half and handed a share to Claire. She nodded her thanks and nibbled on the end.

'But why? This isn't your war.'

'I didn't think so at the time either, but then all I was interested in back then was getting into the fight. Now, I don't know. The Boers are just fighting to keep their own country, and I don't begrudge them that, but if everyone rebelled against the Empire there'd be no Empire.'

'And what would be so wrong with that?'

'We've only just become a Federation back home, but I don't know that I can trust the people who have been elected to run a country properly just yet.'

'And you think Britain runs itself or its Empire well?'

'Britain brought education and roads and railways to Australia and to places like this,' Blake said.

'And smallpox, syphilis, rum, guns and those horrible camps where women and children are locked up like criminals but treated worse!'

'All right, all right,' Blake said, holding his hands up in submission; she had a point. He rummaged inside the saddlebag again.

'And where do you stand on burning farms and imprisoning women and children?'

'I've never burned a farm, but I won't lie and tell you I haven't seen it done. I don't agree with it, just like I don't agree with rounding up the Boer women and children.'

His talk was borderline treasonous, but Blake experienced a feeling of relief voicing his concerns about the conduct of the war that he'd largely kept to himself until now.

'Then why do you continue to fight for the British?'

'I'm not fighting for the British. I fight for my mates, for the youngsters who still come over here thinking it's going to be a grand adventure. I fight to keep my boys alive, and because I've seen too many good young men cut down in their prime by the Boers.'

'Spoken like a true man.'

'I like to think that's what I am.'

'You'd be more of a man if you put down your gun and tried to help these people.'

Blake shook his head. 'You're just as guilty as I am. You say I don't belong here, but neither do you – you're just another foreigner keeping the war going.'

She squared up to him, fists clenched by her side and mouth turned down like an angry honey badger – and those things were fierce. He thought she might slap him, but she seemed to take control of herself, let out a long breath and gave a small nod. 'You're right, I suppose,' she said.

Blake was surprised. He had expected this barney to carry on for a good deal longer. 'We need to get some sleep.'

'It's getting cold, but we can't light a fire.'

He was impressed. She knew that the flames and the smell of smoke would give them away. He unstrapped the blanket from behind the saddle and tossed it at her feet.

'I'll manage,' she said.

'I've no doubt of it, but by the looks of things I've got a couple more layers of clothing on than you have.'

Claire blushed and folded her arms across her chest.

Blake tied the horse to a stunted acacia and settled onto the ground. He separated the saddlebags and tossed one across to Claire to use as a pillow. In the distance a jackal howled. He pulled his collar up around his neck, lay back and propped his slouch hat over his face. He heard Claire's footsteps as she moved along the pebbly shore of the stream to do her private business. It was strange being out bush with a woman.

Blake awoke just before dawn, the coldest part of the day. His uniform was wet with dew and his back ached. He sat up, removing the sodden hat from his face. He was alone.

'Shit,' he said.

Apart from the saddlebag he had used as a pillow, everything was gone – the other bag, the blanket, Bluey. He was hungry, so he took the last of the biltong from his bag and chewed on it as the sun came up. He was, he reflected, stuffed.

The bloody woman had left him in the lurch – and after he'd saved her.

Their conversation from the night before played on his mind as he stripped; he was in dire need of a wash. After witnessing Walters kill Belvedere in cold blood and the horrors of the concentration camp, he realised he was finding it harder and harder to justify the war and his own part in it. Voicing his concerns to Claire had only galvanised his misgivings. He realised that at some point the war would come to an end, and he couldn't wait for that day, but in truth, he had been fighting for so long he wondered what else he could do.

Blake loved Africa and that was part of the reason he had stayed. He was drawn to the wide, open country of the highveld, which was just screaming to be farmed again, and the enticing lure of the thick bush of the eastern part of the Transvaal with its big game, exotic peoples, and sheer unadulterated wildness.

In appearance the whole country was not unlike Australia – even Cape Town had reminded him of Sydney – but the country held greater mystery and more promise of excitement and adventure than his homeland. He had actually been tempted by the woman's offer to accompany her to Portuguese East Africa. It sounded an exotic destination. He could be shot for deserting if he crossed the border, but then he had already committed several capital crimes according to the British authorities. That was all academic now, however, as his only chance of clearing his name had vanished along with his stolen horse.

He gasped as he waded naked into the icy stream. Ducking his head under the water, he rubbed the grit from his hair, then came up for air and stood, waist deep, letting the morning sun warm his back. He shielded his eyes and looked to the north. Two riders were approaching across the veld at a gallop. He strode from the water and reached for his pistol, even though it was empty. He made no attempt to cover himself as the by-now familiar figures closed on him.

Hermanus reined in his horse, and the old Boer commander pointedly avoided staring at Blake's unashamed nakedness.

'Where is the woman?' asked Hermanus.

'You tell me,' Blake said.

'What do you mean?'

'She left with my horse, sometime in the night.'

'Headed which way?'

'Something tells me you know the answer to that question,' Blake said.

Hermanus looked to the east. 'Put that bladdy pistol down, man, I know there are no bullets in it.'

Blake lowered the weapon. Hermanus spoke to the younger Boer in their own language.

'Where is Paul?' Hermanus asked Blake.

'Lost him near the camp. Took a bullet, I think. He was a good lad.'

Hermanus grunted. 'Why didn't you come to the rendezvous point, like we agreed?'

'We were being chased,' Blake said. Truthfully, Blake had thought he could outrun the Boers as well as the British.

'That bladdy woman.' Hermanus sighed.

'You can say that again.'

The other Boer dismounted and, while Hermanus covered Blake with his rifle, the man scooped up Blake's uniform, under-shorts and boots.

'Wait a minute. You can't leave me here naked.'

'Thank God that I don't shoot you,' Hermanus said. '*Kom, kêrel,*' he said to the younger man, who stuffed the uniform into a grain sack with evident glee and climbed back on his horse. Hermanus spurred his mount and the two men galloped eastwards.

Blake sat on a rock and shook his head.

CHAPTER 21

It was still dark when Nick woke, hungover. His phone told him it was four in the morning.

Jetlag. The only good thing about it was that it helped if you wanted to get an early start. This way he could be at the gate to Skukuza camp when it opened, at dawn.

He got out of bed, showered and made a cup of coffee in the outdoor kitchenette. It was chilly this time of morning. With fingers wrapped around the steaming cup he looked out over the Sabie River. He felt despondent; Susan hadn't replied during the night and it seemed he would be left to his own devices in the Kruger Park and for however long he stayed in South Africa.

He went back inside and found the map book he'd bought the day before and while he waited for gate-opening time, he planned his first drive into the Kruger Park. As well as seeing some animals he wanted to get a feel for the landscape that Blake would have patrolled on horseback. Even though Susan had broken things off with him he had come this far and was still interested in learning more about his great-great-uncle.

In his book on Steinaecker's Horse Nick had read about the Selati railway line that had once passed through the park, and he decided it would be a good, historic route to follow if he could find trace of it. Designed to service the goldfields at Sabie and take

160

produce to the coast and ports of Portuguese East Africa, it was an expensive folly and a tribute to the ingenuity of conmen and corrupt politicians.

The contract for the line's construction had been awarded at a price based on the length of the track laid, and its designers had therefore built in miles of twists and turns, inflating the price until it became one of the most expensive stretches of railway in the world. The line had been impractical and short-lived. The goldfields had never lived up to their promise and passenger services through the wildlife-rich lowveld were all too often interrupted by collisions with big game. The line had eventually closed.

Nick heard a weird noise that sounded like a cross between a baby howling and a screeching bird. He ventured outside again and saw a furry shape bounding along his roof. He checked the back of the map book, which had illustrations of common animals, birds and reptiles of the Kruger Park. He identified the noisy culprit – a small primate called a greater bush baby; to him it looked similar in size and build to the brush-tailed possums that roamed Sydney gardens and rooftops by night.

As the sky started to turn from black to grey he got ready to leave, making sure he had his map, camera, binoculars and some snacks and water for the drive. In line with the warnings he'd read, he checked that all the windows of his rondavel were closed and secured, and on his way out he locked the front door.

Nick got into the car and found when he reached the gate that he was far from the only early riser; a queue of about a dozen cars was already waiting for opening time, engines idling.

When the gate finally opened Nick followed a course southeast from Skukuza camp. He wound down the windows of his Corolla and enjoyed the crisp coolness of the morning air and the clear blue sky. If the day was anything like yesterday he knew it would be hot soon enough.

As he rounded a bend he saw a phalanx of elephants crossing the road, fifty metres in front of him, and braked. Big ones, females, he guessed, shepherded babies across and a particularly tall cow gave him a long stare and tossed her mighty head at him, shaking her ears.

Nick felt a charge of adrenaline as a mid-sized straggler took a few steps down the road towards him and blew a shrill trumpet blast from his trunk. When Nick was sure the whole herd had crossed and moved into the bush he tentatively edged forward. Looking to his right he saw that the family had melded into the trees and was peacefully feeding.

As lovely as the sighting had been he couldn't fully enjoy it knowing that he would be alone for the rest of his safari. He'd been on his own for eight months, and had allowed himself, if only briefly, to think that he might find companionship again. The prospect of sharing his time in Africa with a pretty, bright woman had made this trip not just a spur-of-the-moment folly, but something he was genuinely set to enjoy. That hope had been dashed with Susan's cold text, and he felt more alone than he had in a long time.

Nick had misread Susan, completely. Perhaps she had seen their time in Sydney as nothing more than a fling, or maybe she had been initially caught up in the whirlwind then had a change of heart on returning to South Africa. She had told him to take care of himself, to be careful. Had she been trying to tell him to guard his heart? he wondered. The alternative was that something had happened in her meeting with her client to change her mind, or perhaps she had a partner.

Susan had told him that she would explain something to him when she saw him again. Had she simply suffered cold feet? Nick let out a sigh.

Further along he came to a turnoff that led to a big granite outcrop, called Mathekenyane. He saw that another early-morning driver had made it to the top and, consulting his map, he realised it was a lookout spot where he could get out of his car. Nick took the turnoff and drove to the top of the hill. The other tourists were leaving as he got there, which meant that when he got out he had the expansive view all to himself.

He had a commanding 360-degree view of the brown African bush, and if he closed his ears to the sound of a passing game-viewing vehicle below and the khaki-clad visitors chatting on board he could just about imagine himself alone, like Blake, sitting astride a horse, looking for wily Boers and dangerous game below.

Nick set off again, generally heading towards Crocodile Bridge camp, which was close to the town of Komatipoort, another of Steinaecker's outposts, and the border with Mozambique.

On a stretch of dirt road he found the remnants of the ill-fated railway line. It was an embankment, clearly man-made, but the tracks had long ago been pulled up. Had Cyril ridden his horse along this stretch of railway?

Despite his nagging feelings of anger and worry over Susan he did his best to enjoy the day's lazy drive.

Crocodile Bridge camp was much smaller than Skukuza and had an intimate feel about it. The temperature here was hotter and the air felt thicker. Across the river he could see cane fields. He went to the entry gate by the camp and worked out that he could exit the park, but return the same day, without having to fill out any more paperwork.

'How far is Komatipoort?' he asked the woman behind the gate reception counter.

'Not far, maybe twenty minutes.'

That was good enough for him. He had only basic supplies and he figured he could get some more food and drink in the town. Nick left the park and drove across the river, pausing on the low-level concrete bridge to watch a buffalo wading in the shallows, then carried on through the cane farms until he came to the town of Komatipoort.

Other than Johannesburg, and he had seen little of that city, this was his first experience of Africa outside of a hotel or a national park. The traffic was slow, not due to congestion, but more as if movement was an effort. He worked out who to give way to at a four-way stop intersection, and cruised past general dealers and workshops with signs in English and Portuguese, no doubt due to the proximity to Mozambique. There were shops selling seafood; prawns seemed to feature. A woman with a striped bag of goods on her head sashayed gracefully along the footpath, making the task look effortless, while young men lounged outside a seedy-looking bar.

He lowered the window and smelled cooking chicken and chilli – peri-peri. He stopped at a shopping centre with a SPAR supermarket and parked the car.

Nick's tummy rumbled and he decided he needed fortification before shopping. There was a Wimpy burger restaurant in the centre so he went in, took a table for one, checked the menu and ordered a toasted sandwich.

While he waited he checked his messages. There was another transcript from Lili, which lifted his spirits a little. Interestingly, there was also an email from Anja Berghoff, the prickly German PhD student he had contacted, at Susan's suggestion, to ask if she had any information about Blake and Claire Martin. Anja had politely but firmly fobbed him off. What did she want now? he wondered.

Dear Mr Eatwell,

I am writing to you because I have reconsidered your offer to share the information you said you had about your ancestor, Sergeant Cyril Blake. My own research has suffered a setback – I have lost most of my recently acquired primary source material and it will take me some time to recover it. In the meantime I am in Namibia and while I intend to carry on with my fieldwork as planned I would very much like to learn what you have discovered.

Yours sincerely, Anja Berghoff

The tone was very formal, once again, but this time she was not telling him to piss off. In fact it sounded like she needed him. He wondered what had happened to her research and how she had lost it. She'd left a phone number at the bottom of her email, with a prefix that he guessed was Namibian. He might phone her later, he thought. No, he would text her and get her to call him if she was that desperate.

He opened the last message from Lili and the latest translation.

CHAPTER 22

The eastern Transvaal, South Africa, 1902

'It amazes me how you've stayed alive so long,' Claire said, looking down at a naked Blake.

Blake opened his eyes. 'What kept you?'

He sounded cool, but she knew he was surprised to see her. Blake was lying on his back, on a large flat rock by the side of the river, basking like a lizard in the still-warm afternoon sun. He made no move to cover his nakedness. Claire sat astride a new horse, with Bluey tethered to hers. She had swapped her second-hand dress for more practical men's clothing, once more.

'Aren't you going to get dressed?' she asked.

'Your Boer friend, Hermanus, showed up this morning and stole my uniform, though he kindly left me my empty pistol. He's looking for you, just like the British are. I told him I had no idea where you had gone. Where did you get to?'

'I slipped away without you waking and now I was able to ride right up to you while you were asleep. It's a wonder you weren't killed by the Boers years ago.'

'Who says I was asleep this time?'

She made no attempt to avert her eyes, although she was pointedly not looking at that part of his body, at least not now that she'd had a good eyeful already.

'A gentleman would have covered himself – if he was aware of a lady approaching.'

'A lady wouldn't have come this close without announcing herself. Besides, I don't think it's a gentleman you're after.'

She raised her nose at him. 'Who says I'm after anything?'

'You came back. And you said it yourself, you need help getting through the bush to Lourenço Marques. You won't need a gentleman for that trip; you need someone who knows where to cross the border without getting caught.'

Claire harrumphed and untied the calico bag attached to her saddle. She hated it when a man was right, but fortunately it didn't happen often. However, as much as it pained her to admit it, she did need help right now. She was still alive because she knew her limitations as well as she knew her skills.

They would have to pass through dense bush inhabited with a menagerie of dangerous creatures, and she had never lived or worked in the malaria-ridden bush of the Transvaal. These treacherous lands were also home to bands of renegade Boers, bandits, poachers and fierce Swazi and Shangaan tribesmen. It was no place for a single woman, not even one of Claire's calibre. Nathaniel's map would take her even deeper into the bushveld, away from the main east–west road and railway route, and along a disused spur line. She would need the help of a man like Blake – his bravery, his brawn and his Broomhandle Mauser would all come in handy.

'What I need is another horse, another gun and someone who knows how to use both,' she said.

'You've found the right bloke, Missus.' Blake rolled off the rock and opened the bag. He nodded in satisfaction at the coarse woollen shirt, the moleskin trousers, riding boots and broad-brimmed hat.

'It's Miss.' Claire wasn't sure why she'd bothered to correct him.

Blake pulled on the trousers and slipped on the boots. The fit for both was close enough. 'I'm pleased you brought civvy clothes. How did you pay for these?'

'I stole them,' she said. 'We couldn't have had you swanning about Portuguese East Africa in a British uniform.'

He raised his eyebrows as he buttoned up. Claire tugged on Bluey's reins and pulled him up alongside her. Reaching into the holster on the saddle she withdrew a rifle and tossed it to Blake, who caught it one-handed. She let her eyes linger on his broad chest as he examined the weapon.

'Holland & Holland double. I'm impressed you got away with this. Did you use your feminine charms?'

She frowned at his apparent lewdness. 'Nothing of the sort. I found a trading store and the Greek storekeeper was dead drunk.'

Claire reached into her saddlebag and withdrew a leather bandolier stuffed with shiny fat brass cartridges for the rifle. 'They're .577 nitro express,' she said, throwing him the belt. 'One of those rounds will stop an elephant.'

Blake caught the belt and slung it over his arm and pulled the leather-covered recoil cushion of the big hunting rifle to his shoulder. He sighted down the barrels. 'You do know your weapons and ammunition. It's good for shooting dangerous game but you've got to be close, less than a hundred yards for an accurate shot.'

'There will be plenty of dangerous game where we're going.'

'I don't doubt it.' Blake paused, and seemed to be weighing up his options. 'Look, I don't know what your game is, but it looks like I'm out of the war for now. If I get you to Lourenço Marques in one piece, will you come with me to the British Consulate and sort out this mess Walters landed me in?'

'I will,' she said.

Blake nodded. 'Then you've got yourself a marksman and a horseman.'

Claire smiled and tossed him a box of bullets. 'Oh, and I got you some 7.65-millimetre rounds for your Broomhandle Mauser.'

He grinned. 'I'm impressed.'

'This is business, Mr Blake. Nothing more, nothing less. You get me to LM and I'll put in a good word for you with the British. That's it.'

'Fine by me,' he said, pulling his new hat lower down over his eyes to shield them from the afternoon sun.

They rode until it became dark and Blake lit a fire to keep the lions away. He judged them to be far enough from any road or the rail line to take the risk.

'What's it like, the bush, where you patrol?' she asked him from across the flames.

'Uncle Paul Kruger proclaimed the whole area a reserve in 1899. It's full of game. We won't go hungry down there, but it's dangerous country. Plenty of lion, as well. We should be able to make it through the worst of the bush in a couple of days. Once we're across the Lebombo ranges – the border with Portuguese East Africa – we'll cut south again down to the railway line and the road to LM.'

Claire nodded. Blake stared into the fire, silent. He was a handsome brute, she thought, but there was more to him than just another hard-drinking, foul-mouthed soldier. He clearly had sympathy for the innocents in this conflict, and no matter the reason, he had already risked his life to save her. She remembered what he had said about fighting for his fellow soldiers – his mates – rather than for a cause. That was nice. She was now fighting for her survival, and for money, and she wondered which was the greater evil, risking all to steal something that didn't belong to you, or risking your life for a cause you didn't truly believe in.

'What are you thinking about?' she asked after a while.

'A man can't go through life branded as a criminal, or worse, a coward.'

'Isn't it better to be a live coward than a dead hero?'

'Ah. Now you're talking about life and death,' he said. 'That's a different thing altogether. I've seen too many good men go to their death because they wanted to be a hero. The word means nothing to me. There's nothing wrong with turning and running if it's the sensible thing to do. That's how the Boers fight and they're damn good at it. Fire a few shots then melt away.'

'Well, you're not fighting any more, so it's academic.'

'True, but something tells me I shouldn't be hanging this up just yet,' Blake said, slapping the Holland & Holland by his side.

They slept but woke before dawn to the sound of a pair of male lions calling to each other from either side of their little camp. They hurriedly packed and rode away, and reached the Crocodile River, upstream from Komatipoort, at noon. The river was about fifty yards wide, swirling and brown. Blake dismounted and led Bluey down to the sandy bank. He could see in the shallows how the bottom dropped away steeply.

'Too deep to ford,' he said.

'There must be a bridge nearby.'

'At Komatipoort, but there's a blockhouse there, manned by our lads. Can you swim?'

Claire bit her bottom lip, then nodded. She was not a confident swimmer, but she did not want to show weakness in front of the Australian.

'I'll go across first with my horse, then come back for you.'

'I'll be just fine.'

Blake shrugged then walked about fifty yards upstream, scanning the bank with his eyes.

'What are you looking for?'

'Drag marks.'

'What sort of drag marks?'

'Crocodiles. A croc drags his tail when he walks in and out of the water.' He walked a few paces, stopped and pointed. 'Yep. Here, see?'

Claire joined him and stared down at the prints in the mud and the squiggly trail the tail had made.

'Get your rifle out and cover me. Watch for the eyes – that's all you'll see of it, if you're lucky.'

'If *you're* lucky, you mean.'

Blake sat down on the sand and pulled off his boots. He tied them to Bluey's saddle and unbuttoned his shirt. He started to undo his trousers, then appeared to think better of it.

'Don't stop on my account, Mr Blake, I shan't watch,' Claire said, turning away, 'this time at least.'

Blake shrugged again and undid the fly buttons. He tied his clothes into a bundle and secured them to the saddle as well. Then he took the hunting rifle from its bucket and grabbed Bluey's reins with the same hand that held the weapon, and plunged into the water without hesitation.

Claire turned back, scanned the river for crocodiles and secretly marvelled at how easy he made the task of swimming the river appear.

She averted her eyes when he started to emerge from the water, but not before sneaking a peek at his body. Broad shoulders, muscled buttocks. It was just as well he was too far away to see the colour in her cheeks.

'Decent now,' he called.

She looked up and saw he had his trousers and boots on. He had dried himself with his shirt and it was now draped across his horse's saddle, drying. The hunting rifle looked like a toy in his big hands. His normally wavy black hair was plastered flat, making his face look less wild, more sleek and refined.

'Your turn to look away, now, Mr Blake.'

He turned.

Claire stripped down to her stolen chemise and bloomers, rolled her riding clothes into a bundle and fixed it to the saddle as Blake had done. She also tied her new Mauser rifle high on the saddle. She waded into the water, but her horse was less willing than Blake's. She doubled back and, looking down, noticed how the silk bloomers clung to her thighs. 'Don't turn just yet.' She finally coaxed the horse into the water. 'All right, Mr Blake.'

Claire tried hard not to panic, but as she began to swim she couldn't help but swallow mouthfuls of river water as her horse thrashed about. The third time it happened, she coughed wretchedly and at that moment the horse whinnied and tossed its head. The movement pulled her down again. She struck out wildly with her free arm and eventually got her head above water. 'I'm all right,' she called, but she felt herself beginning to lose control.

*

Blake turned and saw that Claire was having a hard time of it right from the start. Occasionally her head dipped below the water's surface and, when she re-emerged, she coughed and spluttered. He took a few steps closer to the water's edge.

Blake laid the rifle down on the sand and started to pull his boots off again.

'I'm fine,' she repeated.

Blake ignored her and waded into the water up to his knees. Then he stopped, swore, and turned and ran back up the bank.

He scooped up the rifle.

'What is it?' Claire called.

Blake brought the heavy rifle up into his shoulder in one fluid movement and pulled the trigger. The rifle kicked his shoulder and a geyser of water erupted not six feet from Claire's face. She shrieked and flailed her arms faster. In the process he saw that the wet leather reins had slipped from her hand.

'Crocodile!' he yelled.

Blake had been tracking the beast's eyes, but now they were gone. He doubted he had hit it with his first shot. It would have seen the horse and would be diving now.

'Forget the horse, Claire. Swim!'

He paced down the bank and saw the snout break the surface near the horse's rump. Blake fired again, sending up another spout of water. The bandolier of ammunition was tied to the saddle.

The gunfire had spooked Claire's horse and the frightened animal thrashed in the water. Claire went under again.

Blake dropped the rifle, ran down the bank and dived into the water. When he broke the surface he saw that the horse was between him and Claire. The crocodile appeared again, but this time, to Blake's horror, the killer was suddenly behind Claire.

Blake struck out for her, cutting off the horse. The confused animal turned and started swimming alongside Blake, towards Claire. Blake grabbed the horse's mane and let it carry him towards her. Claire stopped swimming and looked around.

'Keep going!' Blake commanded.

'Something brushed my leg!' she screamed, her mouth filling with water as she slipped below the surface.

Blake reached across the saddle, grabbed the Mauser and then kicked away from the horse. He flailed his way towards her. 'I'm coming!'

He was aware of the crocodile's bulk off to his right now, creating a mini bow wave as it effortlessly navigated its interception course towards the floundering woman. Blake reached Claire first, though, and trod water by her side. He grabbed a handful of her hair and pulled her to the surface. 'Swim, damn it,' he ordered her, and thrust her towards the bank. He followed her in until his feet touched the sandy bottom.

Blake turned and saw the eyes again. He backed up the bank, but stumbled and fell over Claire who was on all fours, coughing and retching up river water.

Blake rolled over and worked the bolt action of Claire's rifle as the crocodile propelled itself from the water, jaws wide again.

The rifle was still by his hip but Blake pulled the trigger and the Mauser jumped in his hands. The bullet entered the soft flesh of the crocodile's upper jaw and exited out the top of its snout. Its head snapped to one side and the reptile rolled back into the water.

Blake used the weapon to help himself stand. His hands were shaking. He walked unsteadily up the bank.

Claire got to her feet and was staring at him, mouth half open. The colour had drained from her face. He dropped the Mauser and folded her into his arms. They held each other tightly.

'It's all right now,' he said.

As his heart rate slowed he became aware of the heat of her body, the hard nipples pressed against his chest through the wet silk. It had been too long since he had held a woman. Just the feel of her made him feel better, made him want her.

Seeming to remember herself, Claire stiffened in his embrace and placed her palms on his chest. 'Please! Mr Blake,' she coughed again. 'Thank you, but excuse me!'

She turned and stormed off up onto the grassy bank. She sat down and drew her knees up to her chest and wrapped her arms around her legs. Blake stood on the sand, hands on his hips. He heard splashes and turned to see Claire's horse disappear beneath the surface of the water.

Blake retrieved Claire's sodden bundle of clothes which had come loose during the attack and snagged on the branch of a sycamore fig tree overhanging the water. He carried them back to where she sat. 'At least we didn't lose these. Let's get going.'

She looked up at him, took a deep breath, and nodded. Blake saw that tears had started to brim in her eyes.

'You all right?' he asked.

Claire looked away from him as though embarrassed by her show of weakness.

'I love horses. It's my dream to have a big farm, a stud, and breed them, one day.' She looked at the river where her mount had vanished. The tears began to flow.

Blake came to her and took her in his arms, and she sobbed into his chest.

CHAPTER 23

Komatipoort, South Africa, the present day

Nick looked around the single-storey outdoor shopping mall complex. He tried to imagine what it might be like to tangle with one of the crocodiles that he had already seen in the Sabie River.

Cyril Blake had rushed into the river without hesitation and taken the beast in almost hand-to-hand combat. He must have had feelings for Claire, or was it simply a soldier's instinct to protect someone in trouble?

Nick wondered if he would have had the courage to do something like that.

He went back to his little car and set off for the Kruger Park again. After a few minutes his phone rang and he pulled over to the side of the road. His heart skipped as he fished it out of his pocket, hoping it was Susan calling to say she had reconsidered her decision. Instead it was a number he didn't recognise.

'Nick speaking.'

'Mr Eatwell?'

'Yes, who's calling?'

'It is Anja Berghoff here, Mr Eatwell. I am wondering if you can please agree to share the information you have about your relative Cyril Blake who fought in German South West Africa in 1906.'

174

Why should I? was the first thought that popped into Nick's head. The woman had been downright rude to him in her reply and he did not think her tone had been something that had been lost in translation. 'Why is it so important now?'

'Because ... because I have lost all my research material.'

He heard her voice crack. 'So you said in your email. How did you lose it?'

'Well, not lost, exactly; it was stolen from me. Last night, in Windhoek.'

'Didn't you have a backup of that as well, on a portable hard drive or on email?' It was the sort of question, he realised, people always asked when someone had lost a file or their photos. He knew, full well, that he was the last person who could criticise – he was hopeless at backing up his work.

She sniffed. 'My laptop and my hard drive were both taken, and the criminals forced me to give them my email password. The thieves accessed my account and deleted everything.'

'That's too weird.' This did not sound like an opportunistic crime. 'You say they "forced" you?'

'Two men came to my hotel room, robbed it while I was out, and when I came back they attacked me. They ... tied me up and threatened to kill me. They didn't touch my credit cards or bank accounts, although I was able to cancel the cards very quickly.'

'Bloody hell.' Susan's final words, a warning to be careful, came back to him, and he wondered if she'd meant more than just to be careful of the wildlife. 'Who would want that stuff?'

Anja blew her nose. 'I don't know. But they threatened to kill me.'

'Over some stuff about desert horses?'

'Yes, but my current research material covered much more than that. It dated back to the conflict in German South West Africa and the Anglo-Boer War. I was tracing the life of a woman called Claire Martin, who is linked to my study on the origins of the desert horses.'

'Claire ... yes.'

'Your papers mention her?'

'Yes.' She had gone from borderline distraught to pushy quickly. 'Susan Vidler gave me your email address. She said that you snubbed her when she asked you to share information.'

'That woman is a journalist. She is rude and she just wants a sensationalistic story.'

Nick was not sure how he felt about Susan right now, but he bridled at Anja's blunt criticism. For one thing, it was the pot calling the kettle black as far as he was concerned. 'Whatever. Have you tried calling or emailing Susan since you lost all your data?'

There was a brief pause. 'Yes. Both. She has not replied to me and there is no answer when I call her phone, which is not surprising, as I also did not return her calls or emails in the past. She is ignoring me.'

You and me both, Nick thought. 'So you came to me.'

'Yes. This is not easy for me, Mr Eatwell, Nick. I know I could have been more polite to you, but I have worked very hard on my thesis and now it's gone. Please understand, I have spent months amassing this material and Susan wanted me to just give it to her so she can write an article. I was not even sure if the information I had on Claire Martin was eventually going to help with my thesis, but finding it was like conducting an archaeological dig – you brush away the layers and hope you will uncover something of value.'

'OK,' he said uncertainly.

'I am sorry, Nick. Please accept my apology. I am lost right now. Please can you help me?'

His earlier anger melted; he sensed apologies were not something Anja Berghoff issued every day.

Before he could answer she carried on. 'Please. Whatever I have, if I can find it again, you can look at, if it helps you. May I please ask what it is you have?'

'It's a manuscript of some sort, written by a German doctor named Peter Kohl, long after the war against the Nama. In his foreword he says he is writing while a prisoner of the South Africans and the British during the First World War, in 1915.'

'That is very interesting!'

'You sound excited,' Nick said.

'Oh, yes. Peter Kohl was Claire Martin's second husband. Her first husband killed himself. If Peter Kohl is writing about your ancestor, then he must have known him,' she said. 'What time is it there?'

'About the same time as where you are, I expect?'

'Oh,' she said, sounding surprised. 'You are in Namibia?'

'South Africa. I'm having a look at where my ancestor fought during the Boer War, in the Kruger Park. I was supposed to be travelling with ... a friend.'

There was silence for a few seconds. 'With Susan Vidler?'

She had a quick mind, Nick thought, but he didn't really feel like explaining to a stranger how he had just been dumped. 'Maybe. I mean, we had no fixed plans, but she said we would catch up.'

'Hmm.' Anja said nothing more.

'What?'

'This is strange,' Anja said. 'I get robbed, for my research, it would seem, and you are supposed to meet with a journalist who is interested in material we each have and who is now not returning either of our calls.'

'You think there's a connection?'

'I don't know, but something else just occurred to me. My mother's house was almost robbed, just before I left for Africa, by a man pretending to be from a gas company.'

Nick checked his watch; he calculated that he needed to start driving again if he was going to get back to Skukuza camp before the evening sunset curfew, when the camp's gates were closed and tourists needed to be back at their place of accommodation. 'I need to drive.'

'Where are you now?'

'At a place called Komatipoort. You know it?'

'Yes, yes I do,' Anja said. 'Claire Martin referred to it in the documents I have – had. She was a spy for the German government, you know?'

'I gathered she was a spy of some kind,' Nick said. He wanted to know more but he wondered if she was playing him. 'We don't drive and talk on mobile phones where I come from, and this cheap rental car of mine doesn't have Bluetooth. I need to get on the road, Anja.'

'It is the same in Germany,' she said. 'Talking and driving is frowned upon, but in Africa everyone does it. That is possibly why there are so many accidents. But if you want to know more about Claire Martin, I am happy to tell you what I know. Do you have plans to come to Namibia?'

'I don't know,' he said, truthfully. The whole trip had been a half-baked idea, though Susan had dangled the prospect of journeying to the place where Cyril Blake had been killed, in southern Namibia, near the border of South Africa. 'Maybe.'

'I know the area where Blake died in 1906,' said Anja, as if reading his mind. 'Claire Martin and her husband had several farms not far from there at the time.'

He didn't bite. 'I need to get moving. I'll think about your request, Anja.'

'One more question, please, Nick. Who else has a copy of your manuscript?'

'My aunt – she has the original, and a young woman in Australia who is helping me with translations.'

'Maybe tell them to be careful. I could be worrying for nothing, but thank you, Nick, I hope to hear from you. I have a new email address as the thieves hacked my old one. I will send it to you via SMS and maybe you would consider emailing me an electronic copy of the manuscript if you have one?'

'I do have a PDF copy.'

'Good. This is the right thing to do, to share our information,' she said.

Then why didn't you when you had the chance? he wondered.

Nick ended the call, put the car in gear and raced to the Crocodile Bridge entry gate as his phone pinged with the message Anja had just promised.

An hour into his driving a big male lion walked across the road in front of him.

Nick was transfixed by the sight of rippling muscles, the fulsome red-gold mane, the eyes that sent a chill down his spine when they seemed to lock onto his through the open window of the little car. He sensed movement in his peripheral vision and turned to see a tawny-coloured lioness emerge from the long grass on the opposite side from where the male had come from.

The lioness walked up to the male and bumped heads with him. When the big boy did not respond she raised a paw and swiped at his face. The male growled. The female turned and presented herself to him, lowering herself to the tarmac in front of Nick's car. The male came behind her, squatted down and entered her, biting down on the lioness' neck as he did so. It was over in seconds and the female snarled and stood, gave Nick a filthy look, then walked back into the grass.

Nick checked his watch. Despite the thrill he'd felt at what he'd seen, he needed to go.

He thought of Susan, and how nice it would have been to share something so exciting, so intense with someone else.

CHAPTER 24

Sydney, Australia, the present day

In Sydney it was midnight and Lili was feeling the buzz and giddiness of one too many shots at the Manly Wharf Hotel.

With the ferries finished for the evening she had taken a bus from Manly to the city and then changed to a train that would take her to her share house in Newtown. She was regretting not taking an Uber, although her credit card was possibly already over the limit after tonight's partying.

Lili unzipped her daypack and took out the sheaf of photocopied pages. The extra money Nick was paying her to translate came in handy for partying. Lili found the spot she was up to and started to read.

The eastern Transvaal, South Africa, 1902

Blake rode slowly, sparing Bluey, as there were once more two of them on the horse's back, along with their meagre possessions.

Claire had dressed in her soaking clothes, and though she started off by gripping the rear of the saddle to steady herself as they rode, she eventually put her arms around his waist. It was only sensible. Her riding clothes were sodden and, as the afternoon breeze picked up, she huddled closer into his back for warmth. He found himself enjoying the heat of her body through his shirt.

'Let's stop,' Blake said. 'We'll chance a fire.'

'Not on my account,' she said. 'I know it's risky.'

He ran a hand down his face. 'Then on my account. I'm knackered.'

A lion called in the distance, its two-part grunt managing to sound mournful and terrifying at the same time. The bloody things were everywhere in this part of the country.

'I've heard tell that sound carries for several miles,' Claire said casually, although Blake could hear the uncertainty in her tone.

Blake dismounted, tethered Bluey to a tree and unstrapped the bedroll from the saddle. 'Depends on the countryside. Sound doesn't travel too far in this thick bushveld. That fella's probably close, no more than half a mile at most.'

Claire shivered. Blake gathered some leaves and twigs and Claire fossicked for dead wood. Blake knelt, struck a flint, and coaxed a flame with his breath.

Claire set down the fuel she had collected. 'Will the fire help?'

'Keep him away? Maybe. It won't hurt. Don't stray far; you might not come back.'

'Thank you, you're very reassuring.'

He placed the wood on the flame and, once it caught, stood to admire his handiwork and warm his hands. 'What we need is a bottle of rum.'

Claire wrapped her arms around herself. 'I'm cold.' Blake unfurled the blanket from the bedroll and tossed it to her. She caught it and wrapped it around herself. 'I can't ... stop ... shivering.'

'Get out of those damp clothes,' Blake ordered. 'You're wetting the blanket as well. You'll never get warm that way.' He turned around. 'Tell me when you're ready.'

'I'm decent,' she said, after a few moments.

Blake smiled for the first time since the river crossing. God, but she did look beautiful, with her hair in disarray and just a glimpse of pale shoulder showing from under the blanket she was wrapped in. Claire stared into the fire.

He was starting to feel the cold as well, his back damp and chilly from where she had been pressed against him. He rolled down his sleeves and did up his top button. He searched for some more dry wood and fed the fire.

'That was brave of you, to dive into the river to help me,' she said. 'Brave, but stupid.'

'You're welcome. Why stupid?'

'You don't need me to get where you're going.'

'I need you to help clear my name,' he said.

'But you risked your life to save a virtual stranger. I don't know that I would have done the same thing in your shoes.'

'War makes you do some stupid things. In my army we'd rather die than run away and leave a man in danger.'

'Ah, so that makes me an honorary man now, does it? Men. That's why so many of you never come home from wars. Brave, but stupid. Women are smarter, you know?'

'More ruthless, you mean?'

She pondered the comment a while. 'Some people would think we're too soft, the fairer sex and all that rot, but yes, I'd probably agree with you. I don't think we do things out of some false notion of fair play. We protect our own, like a lioness would, but we keep our eye on the mission, on the way ahead. Also, we rarely get to fight in proper armies, so history hasn't shown how we'd act in a military situation, other than the likes of Joan of Arc and Boudica, and they fared quite well by all accounts.'

Blake stared into the fire and nodded. It was an interesting choice of words – mission – that she had just referred to. 'So, are you a fighter, Miss Martin?'

'If I fight, it's for peace.'

'Doesn't sound like those two words go together too easy.'

'Of course they do. Like love and hate, fire and ice, night and day. You can't have one without the other. God, I could use some brandy right now, I'm still freezing.'

Blake stoked the fire, but he, too, was shivering now. 'We can't keep this going all night, you know, there are Boer and Brit patrols all through this valley. We're too close to Komatipoort.'

Claire reached across to the rock where she had draped her wet clothes. In doing so she exposed a slender arm and the swell of the top of her right breast. 'The clothes are still cold. They're starting to get a dew on them, as well.'

'Best roll up in that blanket and get some sleep, then.'

'What about you?'

He shrugged. 'I'll be fine.'

Claire lay down and rolled onto one side so she was facing away from Blake, then flicked one side of the blanket away from her.

He stared at the smoothness of her back, the skin glowing pale gold in the firelight; his gaze followed the swell of her hips and the top of the cleft of her buttocks. 'Hurry, Mr Blake, it's cold, but don't get any ideas. Keep your clothes on and we shall both survive the night.'

He lowered himself to the blanket and now that he was there Blake didn't want to move away from the warmth of her back, nor put his arm between them. Instead, he slowly reached over her body, drawing her into an embrace.

She shivered against his body. 'I'm still cold.'

'You can wear my shirt.'

His desire for her was growing, literally, as he lay there, and he didn't want her having to slap him when she felt him. He rolled onto his back and started unbuttoning his shirt.

'Well, if you're not going to hold me then I'll take you up on your offer of another layer.' She turned over and looked at him. He fumbled with one of the buttons. 'Let me do that.'

He lowered his hands and felt her fingers brush the hair on his chest as she undid it. She moved on to the next button, unbidden, looking at what she was doing, not at his eyes.

'You would have died for me, Blake, in the river?' she said in a low voice.

'Right now, I reckon I'd do just about anything for you,' he said. He reached out, slowly, with his hand, like he might to a wild creature, not wanting to spook it. She didn't flinch and as the back of his hand, his fingers, caressed her cheek, she kept her eyes on him, but didn't move. 'So soft,' he said. She gave an almost imperceptible nod, so he continued. 'This place, Africa, it can fill your head with visions of natural beauty that you wouldn't think possible and then the next minute you'll come across a burning farm or the bloody aftermath of a gunfight. What's missing is this, something tender.'

'You may be talking to the wrong woman if it's tenderness you're after, Sergeant Blake.'

She smiled, but she licked her lips as well, betraying her nerves. He wondered if she could hear his heart. Blake moved his hand, slowly again, so as not to startle her or break the moment, until his fingers were behind her neck. He started to draw her to him and she shifted. For a moment he thought he'd gone too far, but then she was on him.

Blake rolled with her and their mouths came together. She ran her fingers under his shirt, up and down his back as he drew her to him, no longer embarrassed by his lust. She pressed her naked body against him then reached between them to unbutton his trousers. The night air was so cold that she pulled the blanket over them, so that not even the firelight could guide them. It was fingers and palms, mouths and lips that did the exploring as she helped him slide out of his pants. They laughed as they fumbled until he found the place that was as slick as moss on a polished river rock and as hot and wet as a Transvaal summer.

The lion called again in the distance and the excitement of it seemed to spur her on, rather than make her look about. They were lost to the sensations as he entered her, as she grabbed him, as he drove and she rode. Her body was lean and strong beneath that soft pale skin and she met his strength with a force of her own. At one point she bit him, as he'd once seen a lioness do to her mate, and the short sharp jolt sent him over the edge.

Blake looked up at her, red hair glowing like the flames behind her, the stars framing her face as she gasped for air.

He drew her to him and wrapped his arms around her.

'Yes,' he whispered in her ear, 'I would die for you.'

CHAPTER 25

Skukuza Rest Camp, Kruger National Park, the present day

Nick made it through the gates of Skukuza with three minutes to spare. Just a few kilometres short of the camp he and three other cars had been bailed up by a big bull elephant, who then took it upon himself to lead them towards the camp in a frustratingly slow conga line for a quarter of an hour. He stopped by the camp store and bought some more provisions and a bag of firewood.

When Nick arrived at his rondavel he was greeted by a stern-faced man in national parks uniform, and a cleaner slopping soapy water out of his room onto the verandah.

'Hello, how are you?' the man said without much feeling.

'Fine, thanks, and you?' Nick said. 'What's happened?'

'Baboons. You must have left your window open.'

'No way. I read the sign and I made sure I closed and locked all the windows and the doors.'

'It is easy to miss one window, and that is all it takes. I will show you.'

Nick stepped over the bucket and felt bad at the dirty marks his shoes left on the still wet, freshly cleaned floor as he followed the parks man inside.

'See here, how they have bent the metal frame of the window?'

Nick stepped closer and saw how one of the panes of glass was missing, presumably swept up now by the cleaner.

'The baboons grab it,' the man demonstrated, 'if it has been left open enough for them to get their fingers in. Then they bend it until the glass breaks.'

'Yes, but I didn't leave it open.'

The man nodded slowly and smiled, as if implying: *That's what they all say.*

Nick was annoyed, not only that the man didn't believe him, but that the baboons seemed to have ransacked his bag. His clothes and belongings had been heaped on the bed.

'You are lucky,' the man said.

'How so?'

'They usually shit everywhere. These ones must have been disturbed before they could do their dirty business.' He laughed.

Nick felt uneasy. Sure, some baboons could have found some canny way to get in, but the theft of Anja's research and Susan's cryptic warning were preying on his mind. When the man had left and the woman had finished cleaning he surveyed the room and went through his clothes, folding and sorting. He didn't seem to be missing anything and he repacked, now wondering if he was being overly paranoid. To calm himself he went back outside and drew on some nearly forgotten boy scout and camping holiday skills to light a fire. He remembered a rainy weekend in a borrowed tent on the New South Wales south coast with Jill, not long after they had met, him trying and failing to coax a flame out of sodden wood and damp paper. The memory saddened and unsettled him again.

At least this fire had crackled nicely to life. Nick got himself a beer out of the fridge and took another look inside the rondavel. What he could *not* see, on the polished concrete floor or the bedspread or the window ledge or walls was any sign that any baboon or monkey had been inside. There were no dirty hand or footprints, no scuffs, and, as the national parks guy had pointed out, no smelly calling cards. He wondered if a human could have been rummaging through his possessions and left the mess and open window to make it look like primates were responsible.

Nick took out his phone and thought more about the men who had assaulted and threatened Anja. He didn't know why an academic's papers could be so valuable, but it certainly seemed as if that was what the thieves had been after. Susan had told him to be careful, but was there something she hadn't told him?

He checked his watch and did the calculation; it was two in the morning in Sydney. He thought about his aunt, Sheila. He didn't want to worry her needlessly, but the story of Anja's robbery played on his mind.

Nick got another beer, took out his laptop, sat down and turned it on. He thought about Anja Berghoff. He had been annoyed at her initial rudeness, but after talking to her he felt for her, having endured a robbery and assault and losing all her research material.

He decided to bring Anja into the loop. He found her new email address that she had sent him, then emailed a scan of the original manuscript to her, along with Lili's translations to date.

Next he went to Facebook. His aunt was addicted to the social media platform. He opened the messenger box and saw that despite the late hour the green dot next to her profile picture was illuminated. He clicked on her and the dialogue box from their last chat opened. He saw that she had been on just five minutes earlier.

Hi Aunty, are you awake? He typed.

The rippling dots next to her name told him she was typing a message. *Unfortunately yes, bit of a drama at home.*

Nick closed down Facebook on the computer, picked up his phone and put through a voice call on messenger.

'Hello?' Sheila said.

'Aunty, is everything OK? Are you all right?'

'Yes and no,' she said.

Nick's tummy lurched. 'What's wrong.'

'Well *I'm* fine – I'm at the caravan at Norah Head.' Sheila kept the van at a park on the New South Wales north coast. 'But I got a call from my neighbour, Russell, a couple of hours ago saying my house had been broken into.'

'Bloody hell.'

'Exactly. Russell was coming home from the pub, half pissed, and noticed the side window was open. He heard noises inside and called the cops. He waited outside, watching my place, and saw the burglar leaving. He tried to stop him but the guy king hit him in the face. The police arrived and called an ambulance – Russell's got a broken nose – but the robber was long gone.'

'Did they take anything?'

'Funny,' Sheila said, 'Russell's wife Bev checked the house for me when she got back from the hospital just a little while ago. Bev said the burglar had turned the place upside down, but the TV's still there. Russell said the guy wasn't carrying anything, so maybe he got spooked.'

'How about all your family tree stuff?'

Sheila snorted. 'The bastard trashed my filing cabinet. Bev said there was paper all over the study floor, ankle deep she reckoned.'

'The manuscript?'

'Got that with me,' Sheila said. 'Your parcel arrived just as I left for the coast. Why do you ask?'

Nick exhaled. 'I hate to sound paranoid, but I think that might have been what the crook was after. A German woman researching the same stuff was held at gunpoint here in Africa and forced to give over all her documents and passwords, and my bungalow here in the Kruger Park was trashed today. The rangers here reckoned it was baboons, but I'm not so sure.'

'Over old documents? Really? Why?'

'No idea,' Nick said. 'I can't think what would be in this stuff that would be so valuable, but I'm going to try and find out. Meanwhile I think you need to be careful. Tell the cops what I've told you.'

'They'll think I'm crazy,' she said.

'Maybe, but I'm worried about you.'

'What about the girl who was doing the translation for you?'

'Lili.' Nick had been thinking the same thing. 'She's my next call.'

Newtown, Sydney, the present day

Lili's phone rang.

She had just got off the train at Newtown. The suburb's vibrant nightlife was buzzing around her; the area was popular with

students, hipsters and late-night partygoers. She ducked into the alcove of a small apartment block to partly shield the call from traffic
noise and the sound of live music coming from the pub next door.

'Hello!'

'Lili, hi, it's Nick.'

'Hello, who is calling please? I can't hear you.'

'Lili, it's Nick!'

'Nick? Are you in Africa? I finished work today, no more time
in the salt mine as you called it –'

'Lili, please, listen to me. Are you OK? Is everything all right?
Has anything unusual happened?'

She thought about the question, her mind slow to process it,
even though she had worked out that her English was even more
fluent after she'd had a few drinks. 'Unusual? No, only this phone
call. And my internship was always going to finish today. I had
hoped that Pippa might keep me on, but now I suppose I have to go
and pick fruit in the middle of nowhere or –'

'Lili, do you have the manuscript with you?'

'Yes, of course. I have the copy you gave me in a folder. I was
just doing some reading on the train.'

'Has anything happened at your share house in Enmore or wherever it is?'

'Newtown. All is fine, thank you for asking, but what is your interest, Nick?'

'Where are you now?'

'Nearly home.'

'Do me a favour, please. I know this will sound crazy, but please
just call one of your flatmates and ask them if everything is all right
at your house.'

'It's Friday night, Nick.' Lili laughed. 'Most probably they are
all out partying.'

'This is serious, Lili.'

'I don't know what you're talking about. What do you mean
"if everything is all right"? You're being weird, Nick.' She started
walking. 'I am nearly home in any case.'

'Lili, listen to me, be careful. You could be at risk. I'm worried
someone will try to break into your house, if they haven't done so

already. My aunt's house has just been burgled tonight, your time, and a German woman, an academic I've been in touch with who has been researching Claire Martin was also robbed, here in Africa. Something's going on. Someone is trying to get hold of the manuscript, any papers about Blake and Claire Martin. You have to take this seriously.'

'OK, OK, Nick. I'm walking home now. I am almost at my house.'

'Lili, if there's no one home, don't stay there. Find a friend you can be with and –'

The line dropped out.

Lili stopped and looked at her phone, swaying slightly. She'd really had too many shooters. She waited a minute, then tried calling Nick's number, but it wouldn't connect.

Lili thought about what Nick had said, about his aunt and the academic being robbed. Surely it was just a coincidence? This was Australia, she told herself, not the wilds of Africa. As much as she was enjoying reading the manuscript she could not think of anything in it that could be of monetary value to anyone.

She turned into her street, a row of terrace houses which had nearly all been restored. Her place, which she shared with three other girls and a guy, looked dark from the outside. As she had told Nick, it wasn't unusual for everyone to be out on a Friday night, even at this late hour.

She put her key in the lock, opened the door and stood there, listening. The house was dark, but she could hear no one rummaging through drawers or cupboards.

Lili shook her head, flicked on the light switch and looked around. All in order in the hallway, kitchen and lounge room. She felt better so she took off her heels and walked upstairs.

Lili paused to look in Emma's room and saw that it was neat as always; Lili joked that Emma could have been German as well. Jason's looked like a bomb had hit it, but that was perfectly normal. Lili smiled; if a burglar had been through there no one would ever know.

Lili opened the door to her bedroom, dropped her heels, and was about to put her hand over her mouth, when someone beat her to it.

CHAPTER 26

Aus, Namibia, the present day

Anja was at the Klein-Aus Vista Lodge, near the small settlement of Aus, checking emails on the new iPad she had bought in Windhoek when the message from Nick came through. While she had never had anything but fond memories of Namibia's capital city, she was now quite pleased to be some six hundred kilometres south of it and back in the desert landscape of southern Namibia.

It might be nothing, she told herself, but the scanned manuscript was all she had to work with right now in terms of primary source research material. She opened the document, quickly worked out where Lili had got up to in her translation, and began to read.

Komatipoort, South Africa, 1902

A steam locomotive's whistle tore through the dawn chatter of birds as they reached the outskirts of Komatipoort. Despite being based at the Steinaecker's Horse encampment at Sabie Bridge, Blake had travelled to the outpost here on the border a few times so he knew the place fairly well.

'That's the town, or what passes for it,' Blake said.

Claire saw the squat shape of a standard British Army block-house made of timber, tin and compacted earth. Somewhere beyond that would be the border post.

They followed a track that crossed the main railway line, once Blake had scouted ahead on foot and had a good look eastwards and westwards to make sure no train or foot patrol was approaching. He got back on the horse, with Claire behind him.

'Where does the Selati line begin?' Claire asked.

Blake looked over his shoulder as they trotted on. 'That line's been closed for years; never got off the ground, in fact. The company that built it went bankrupt about eight years ago. Why do you want to know where it is?'

'I've a slight problem,' she said.

Blake shook his head. 'I don't like the sound of that, and don't care, we're sneaking across the border, tonight.'

'Well, in point of fact,' Claire said, 'I need to make a short detour along the Selati line.'

'Nothing up there but lions and fever,' he said. 'No detours.'

'Blake ...'

'Claire ...'

She found it hard to suppress a grin or keep the colour from her cheeks when she thought about the evening just gone. It had been nothing short of thrilling, making love under the stars, and his lovely body had kept her warm through the night.

Nathaniel had been a bit of a master of technique, but in Blake she encountered just the right mix of strength and tenderness. She could tell he liked women, and knew his way around them, but there was none of the brashness or borderline arrogance of the American. There was a sadness about Blake, brought on by the years of war, no doubt, and it had felt as if he was clinging to her the way a drowning man might to a life preserver. He had held her tight and closed his eyes even tighter when he was inside her, as if he was using her to escape something awful. When he had opened his eyes and looked at her it was like she was suddenly coming home to something. She didn't mind that feeling a bit.

Didn't mind the rest of him, either, truth be told.

Claire took a deep breath. She would have to trust him, and after last night she felt she could. The fact was that she needed him, not least of all his physical strength. 'I can guarantee you that it will be worth your while if you come with me up that railway line.'

'I'm more interested in clearing my name and not ending up in front of a firing party than whatever caper you've got going.'

She shook her head. 'Trust me, you'll be able to hire the best barristers in the land if you stick with me.'

'Last night ...' he said.

'... was grand,' she whispered in his ear. 'Now don't be spoiling it with silly words and do as you're told like a good soldier and take me up that railway line.'

'No.'

Claire frowned into his back. She needed him to do as she wanted, and the best way to make a man do that was to make him think it was his idea.

'If you could do anything in the world, Blake, go anywhere, what and where would it be?'

In spite of the abrupt change of subject, he didn't even need time to ponder. 'When I lived in Sydney I used to watch the toffs sailing on the harbour. I thought, that's what I'd do if I could: build a boat and learn to sail. I'd travel the world.'

'There's a boat up that spur line.'

He laughed. 'You're crazy.'

'No, I'm not. There's –'

Blake held up his hand, then reached into the leather bucket on the side of his saddle, drew out the Holland & Holland side-by-side. He opened the breach, took two fat cartridges from the belt and slid them into the barrels. He snapped the rifle closed.

Claire peered around his broad back and saw a man in British uniform riding hard and fast up the track towards them.

The man was waving a scrap of white fabric above his head. 'It's over, it's over!'

Blake reined in his mount and the man slowed as he approached them.

'Put that bloody gun away,' the man yelled. 'Your lot have given up.'

'He thinks you're a Boer, thanks to your civilian clothes,' Claire said into Blake's ear.

Blake nodded. 'I'm Australian,' he called.

The man pulled on his reins as he drew abreast of them. Claire could smell the liquor on the rider's breath from six feet away.

'Australian? Wait, I know you; Blake, isn't it?'

Blake nodded and lowered the hunting rifle.

'I'm Toner, Daniel,' the man said. 'I was at Sabie Bridge for a couple of months last year.'

'Ah, yes,' Blake said. 'What were you saying? It's over?'

'Yes, Sarge, the war, it's done. We can all bloody well go home. Old Piet Boer's finally given up. We got a signal today saying the Afrikaners have signed a peace treaty at Vereeniging. It's bloody over!'

Blake exhaled as Claire's mind raced. There were bound to have been other people close to former president Paul Kruger who would have known the secret location of the republic's gold, and with hostilities over they might come looking for the treasure. She had to act quickly.

The man, Toner, raised his eyebrows. 'What are you doing in civvies, Sarge?'

'Long story,' Blake said. 'What are your orders, Dan?'

'Orders? My orders are to find more grog. We've been on the stuff since we got the news. Come down to the Big House by the border and join the party, old boy.'

'We may very well do.'

'And the lady's very welcome,' Dan said.

'I'm sure,' Claire said over Blake's shoulder. 'Cyril, ought we not to be moving along?'

Dan burped. '*Cyril*. One thing I remember, ma'am, is no one's supposed to call him that.'

'On your way, Dan,' Blake said.

Toner grinned and nodded and rode on, past them.

'Well now,' Claire said, 'that's a turn-up for the books. After all these years. It makes it even more important for me to take that trip up the Selati line.'

Blake looked back at her. 'And why's that?'

'If it's the party of the new century that's going on down at the border,' Claire said, 'then tomorrow will be a hangover to match. It'll make it easier for us to slip through to Portuguese East Africa. But, unless you want to join in the celebrations with a bunch of drunken soldiers, I suggest a scenic detour for now.'

She hugged him and gave him a squeeze.

'Is this something to do with whatever your mission was?' he asked.

'There's a treasure waiting up that spur line, Blake, and it's ours for the taking. If we don't move now someone else will get to it.'

'A treasure? I guessed this was about money. You're a thief?'

Claire pursed her lips. 'More like a freebooter, a pirate of old. Think of this as spoils of war.' She held her hands wide. 'I want what was promised to me – I was in the middle of doing an arms deal to supply German cannons to the Boers – and now that the war's over I'm going to be left high and dry and penniless. Look, Blake, my father had to flee Ireland because of the greedy and unfair policies of the British, and my husband killed himself over gambling debts. This is my shot at a half-decent, honest life.'

'You just want what you were owed?'

She smiled. 'Perhaps a small commission on top. I'll make it worth your while as well, cover your expenses as it were. There'll be enough for your boat.'

He narrowed his eyes as he looked into hers for a few long moments. 'Very well.'

'Oh, one more thing, Blake.'

'Yes?'

'We're going to need to borrow a cart, a big one, with a couple of strong horses.'

Now he rolled his eyes at her, but she knew she had him hooked. She rewarded him with a smile and a wink and though he shook his head he couldn't hold back a laugh. Maybe it was the end of the war that was allowing him to relax and follow her, or maybe he was as drawn to her as she was to him.

Blake was able to navigate by memory to Steinaecker's camp in Komatipoort, known as the Big House, and, as Toner had given them reason to expect, there was the sound of much revelry from the building. There wasn't even a sentry on the gate or the stables, so Blake and Claire helped themselves to a couple of sturdy if ageing carthorses and what looked like a farmer's covered wagon that had probably been liberated from some Boer homestead. Claire told herself she would find a way to return the horses and wagon, if not to Steinaecker's forces, then to the rightful owners.

Claire took the reins of the wagon horses and Blake rode ahead, out of camp and back along the main east-west railway line until they reached the junction of the defunct Selati line.

They turned off and followed the line on its winding north-westerly course. The tracks were rusted from lack of use and grass and the occasional young tree grew from amid the leadwood sleepers. The gravel road that ran alongside the line, and which had been built to aid construction, was washed away in some places and in others blocked by fallen trees. These obstacles took time to circumvent in the wagon.

'I hope this isn't a bloody wild-goose chase,' Blake called back from his saddle.

'You'll get your goose, as well as your golden egg and your boat if you stick with me, *Mister* Blake.'

He smiled and turned his face up to the sun. 'I like the sound of that much better than "Sergeant". However, the army's got long arms and a longer memory. I still need you to help me clear my name, Claire.'

'You help me with my wee errand and it'll be my pleasure to vouch for you, Blake.'

Claire drove the wagon with the map next to her. She had done her best to estimate their speed and worked out that the first landmark she was seeking should come into view soon.

She saw it.

Ahead the line took a sharp curve to the right – one of the many needless deviations in the line that had earned the conmen who developed the Selati railway their ludicrous payment. On the bend was a prominent *koppie*, a rocky hill with a large baobab growing out of the crown.

'We need to leave the line here, Blake,' she called ahead.

He waited for her to catch up and Claire found the narrower, even rougher track that wound around the *koppie*, off to the right.

An elephant trumpeted loudly from somewhere ahead in the bush. Blake raised his right hand and Claire caught up with him then pulled on the reins to stop the horses.

'What is it?' Claire asked.

'Elephants hate lions. Whenever they see or smell them they trumpet and try to chase them away.'

'Oh my goodness!'

As if on cue a lioness bounded down the track towards them. Blake's horse shied, rearing up on its hind legs. Blake held tight and pressed his knees together and told his horse to stay calm.

'They're fine, Claire,' Blake said. 'Stay still on the wagon and they won't hurt you.'

Easy for him to say, Claire thought, her heart pounding as a second, third and fourth big cat followed by half-a-dozen small cubs trotted around them, through the bush.

Claire knew full well there were more dangers ahead, and most likely behind them as well.

*

Private Daniel Toner had been heading for a trading store on the outskirts of Komatipoort that served the transport riders and other travellers, catching thirsty men and horses before they rode into the town proper.

The store was deserted and locked when Dan arrived, but seeing he was under orders to bring back more grog and it was the end of the war, he took the law into his own hands and shot the padlock off the front door. Once inside he helped himself to as much whiskey and gin as he could stuff in his saddlebags, plus a bottle he took for the road.

He was three sheets to the wind on his way back to Steinaecker's camp when he came across a pair of British officers and four raggedy-looking Boers. He waved his white flag above his head.

'It's over!'

Dan took a swig from his bottle and reined in his horse. He burped. 'Hello, sir,' he said to the British captain at the head of the mixed bag of troops.

'Private,' the officer said.

'War's over, sir, the Boers have signed a peace –'

'Clearly,' the captain said, gesturing to the men behind them. 'These men have surrendered to me.'

Dan took in the Boers. They were a tough bunch by the look of them, the eldest dressed in a coat made of leopardskin. It was odd, he thought, that the Boers still carried rifles in their hands and pistols in their belts. Perhaps the captain had taken their ammunition or had allowed them to keep their guns on their word that they accepted the war was over. He, however, had been told to disarm any Boers he met on the road. The word was that some of the so-called 'bitter-enders' might not respect the order to lay down their arms.

'You want me to escort these men to our camp, sir?' Daniel asked.

'No. They'll be fine with me. I'm looking for two people, Private, an Australian sergeant and a red-headed woman. She's Irish, but talks like a Yankee.'

Daniel looked sideways. He didn't know Blake well, but he was a soldier, from the ranks, and this toff was an officer. His immediate loyalty was to Blake. 'Can't say as I recall meeting such a pair, sir.'

The officer drew a Webley revolver from its holster, thumbed back the hammer and pointed it at Dan between his eyes.

'Bloody hell, sir.'

'You're lying, Private. Where are they and where were they headed? Across the border?'

Daniel's eyes went to the other officer, the younger lieutenant who had trotted up on his horse to the captain's side.

'I say, Captain Walters, is this entirely necessary? The poor fellow says –'

The captain swung in his saddle, his gun hand moving with him, and shot the lieutenant in the chest. The young officer toppled from his saddle and landed with a thud in the dust. He was groaning, blood frothing at his lips, when the captain shot him in the head.

'Yes, Roderick, it was necessary.'

Dan looked around for the quickest escape route, but the Boers raised their rifles and pointed them at him. 'Drop your weapons, *Engelsman*,' the one in leopardskin said.

Dan freed his Lee Enfield rifle from his saddle and tossed it to the ground.

'Now, Private,' Captain Walters said, shifting his aim point back to between Dan's eyes, 'Australian man and a red-headed woman, if you please. Time is of the essence.'

'Y-yes, sir ... I saw them. They were heading towards town. I fell asleep on the side of the road for a while, near the Selati line, sir, in the long grass. I woke up to the sound of a horse and cart, sir, and I saw them again. They were on one horse before but now they had a wagon as well. They went up the branch line.'

'How long ago, Private?'

'About an hour, no more, sir.'

'Good man.'

Dan breathed a sigh of relief. 'Thank you, sir.'

Walters pulled the trigger.

CHAPTER 27

Skukuza Rest Camp, Kruger National Park, the present day

Nick barely slept. He had tried calling Lili again several times, but could not get through to her.

He was frustrated because he didn't know Lili's address and he didn't know the names of any of her friends. Pippa might have it, but when Nick looked online at Australian directory assistance he couldn't find Pippa's landline – he assumed it was an unlisted number. He had tried Pippa's mobile, repeatedly, but he knew she had a house in the country, near the wine-producing town of Mudgee northwest of Sydney, and a signal at her place, he had learned when he once needed to contact her on the weekend because of a client emergency, was non-existent.

Still jetlagged, Nick was fully awake at four in the morning. As much as he had wanted to explore more of the areas where Blake had served he felt he needed to do something more than sightsee. Something was definitely not right and Nick knew Susan would have some answers.

Given what had happened to his aunt and Anja, and now Lili dropping out of contact, he wondered now if something bad had happened to Susan. Whatever had gone on with her he told himself he needed to see her in person.

He got online and found there was space on the next flight to Cape Town, which left from Skukuza Airport at 11.20 am. He booked a one-way ticket, not knowing where he would end up after that.

As the sun was rising he walked around the camp to try and calm his nerves. He followed the Sabie River and watched a troop of vervet monkeys sitting in the sun grooming each other, stretching and yawning like little humans starting a new day. Then he walked through the camping ground, feeling envious of the local families and foreign couples enjoying a simple holiday.

As he weaved his way to the big reception building he saw that it also contained a bank. He stopped to draw out money and his phone rang.

'Nick?' said Pippa's voice as he answered. 'I got your messages, all five of them. You're in Africa?'

'Yes, South Africa.'

'I came into Mudgee town, to have dinner. You want to know if I have Lili's address?'

'Yes, please. I think something may have happened to her, Pippa.'

'What makes you think that?'

'She was helping me with something, a story, and a woman here in Africa who was interested in the same stuff was assaulted and robbed. I'm pretty sure someone broke into the place where I'm staying and tried to rob me, but covered their tracks.'

'*Pretty sure*? Nick,' Pippa said, and he could hear her exhale, 'this is Australia, not Africa. People get attacked all the time in South Africa according to all the Saffers I know.'

'My aunt's house was robbed – she also had access to the material that Lili, the woman here and I all have. Also, the woman who was mugged here foiled an attempt by a guy to rob her mother in Germany. Pippa, look, it'll take me a long time to explain all the ins and outs. Do you have Lili's address?'

'Yes, I do, but only at the office. There's a copy of her tax declaration form at work, but I don't have her details with me.'

'Fuck,' Nick said.

'Hey, I'm trying to help here,' Pippa said.

He ran a hand through his hair. 'Sorry. Is there any chance you could get to the office?'

'It's a five-hour drive from here and I'm on my way to dinner on a Saturday night, Nick. I can't just pop down the street.'

'When will you be home?'

'Sunday afternoon or early evening.'

'Could you go then?'

'Nick –'

'Please, Pippa. I called Lili and I was waiting on the line while she was heading home after a big night. The signal went out here and I haven't been able to get through to her even though I now, clearly, have reception. She knew how worried I was about her and she hasn't called me back.'

'She's barely out of her teens, Nick, a young girl on a working holiday. She's probably still sleeping off her hangover – either that or she doesn't want to call you in South Africa because she's worried about the cost.'

'Then why is her phone not answering?'

'Flat battery?' Pippa asked.

These were plausible answers but Nick was worried for Lili and he didn't seem to be able to get Pippa to take it seriously.

'You have to do something, Pippa.'

'No, Nick, I don't. Neither of you works for me any more and, to tell you the truth, I was getting a bit worried about you. You seemed depressed and stressed at work, and –'

'And so you fired me. I get it.'

'Calm down, Nick.'

'Don't tell me to calm down. A young woman's life could be at risk. She might have been injured.'

'Yes, and you might just be overreacting. I've had enough of this.'

'Wait –'

Pippa ended the call and Nick swore again and walked back towards his riverside bungalow. He knew she thought he was a flake, and maybe he was. It was possible the string of crimes was unrelated.

But Anja had been robbed of her research, print and electronic, and there seemed to be a crossover with the material in the memoirs that his aunt had given him. A criminal had almost talked his way into Anja's mother's home, Sheila's place had been burgled and his rondavel had been trashed – if not by baboons then by humans. That meant that if someone had tried to rob him they might very well still be here, in the Kruger Park. He looked over his shoulder; now he really was being paranoid, he told himself.

There was no one following him.

Nick remembered Anja saying that her attackers had ransacked her hotel room and later come back for her. Suppose the person who had searched his hut was waiting somewhere for him? He slowed his pace and stopped within sight of his rental car and rondavel.

Everything looked fine. His neighbour was gone.

Nick remembered the man saying he was in the park for another two nights. He wondered if the man might have noticed something suspicious. Nick went to his hut, circled it, not really knowing what he was looking for, then went inside to pack his bag.

When he finished he went back out, taking his notebook and pen. He thought he would slide his name and number under the neighbour's door, asking him to give him a call so he could ask him more about the alleged baboon raid and if he had maybe noticed anyone hanging around, acting suspiciously. However, when Nick went to the next rondavel a woman in national parks uniform came out sliding a bucket and mop with her foot.

'Sorry,' he said, 'I just want to leave a message for the man who is staying here.'

'Sorry, sir, this man has checked out,' the cleaner said.

'I thought he was staying a couple more days?'

'The man, he said he had to go home early, some emergency with his business.'

'Oh. Thanks,' Nick said.

Nick gave his rondavel one last check, in case he had forgotten anything. When he was done he drove towards the entry gate but on a last-minute impulse he turned into the parking area in front of reception. He got out and went to the reservations desk.

'Morning,' said a young woman with ornately braided hair.

'Hi.' Nick took a seat in front of her and took out his booking confirmation form. 'I wonder if you can help me, please. I was staying next to a man here in the camp and he left this morning. I really need to get in touch with him and I wonder if you could please give me his contact number. I imagine you'd have it with his reservation.'

'I'm sorry sir,' the woman said, 'I can't give out that sort of information.'

Nick had expected this response and had already thought up a cover story. 'The guy left his gas bottle and cooker behind and I want to let him know I have it.'

'We have a lost property office here, sir, you can leave the gas bottle with us.'

'I don't want him to have to come back to Skukuza if he doesn't want to, and he was very helpful to me. It would also save you the trouble of having to contact him. He was in number ninety-one.'

The woman frowned, and Nick hoped she hadn't seen through his lie immediately, but he smiled gormlessly at her and she began tapping her keyboard with glittery nails.

'Ninety-one. Mr Human.'

Nick remembered the man's first name. 'Yes, Chris.'

'The woman shook her head. No, Charl. That's an Afrikaans name.'

'Yes, yes, of course. I must have misheard – I'm from Australia so maybe it was his accent.' *Bullshit*, Nick thought. He had taught himself, as a young journalist, to remember people's names. He felt a jolt of adrenaline. His neighbour had given him a false name – he was now as sure of that as he was of having locked the rondavel's window before leaving. Something definitely didn't add up.

'Sure,' said the woman. She tapped her keyboard some more and looked at her screen. She smiled. 'I am sure he will be back today or tomorrow for his lost property. He's staying at another camp tonight, not far away.'

Nick was about to say to the woman that Chris – real name Charl – had told him that he was staying in Skukuza for a few more days. He had lied about that as well. 'Can you tell me where he's staying next?'

The woman's mouth turned down again. Nick thought she was debating with herself how much more information she could or would release.

'Maybe I can take a drive to his camp or meet him halfway?' Nick suggested.

The woman looked at him and must have judged him to be harmless. 'It says he will be at Satara camp on the twenty-second and twenty-third and then Pretoriuskop on the twenty-fourth, then his booking ends.'

Nick swallowed. Charl had Nick's exact itinerary, yet he had lied to him.

'Is there something wrong?'

'What? Oh, no.' Nick thought the colour might have gone from his face. He stood, his legs a little shaky. 'Thank you.'

Nick left the reception building and went back to his car. It was only a few kilometres from the camp to Skukuza Airport and on the way he passed a trio of giraffe which looked inquisitively at him from over the tops of the low trees they were browsing on.

A few kilometres on, two male impalas ran across the road, one chasing the other, forcing him to brake suddenly, and he realised that despite the turmoil in his mind and his fretting over not hearing from Lili he needed to be aware of his surroundings.

Be careful, Susan had warned him.

The low-level bridge over the Sabie River was clear, but he slowed and stopped briefly, looking once again at the old bridge that had carried the ill-fated Selati rail line.

There was something here, back then and maybe now, that Blake and Claire Martin had become involved in. They were two people on the run, but for more than the crimes they had committed in the course of their wartime duties. There was something that the English intelligence officer, Llewellyn Walters, had been prepared to kill for, and there was something in the papers that he and Anja had been entrusted with that someone was prepared to rob and threaten violence over.

The airport was not far once he'd crossed the bridge and he parked, handed in the keys for his rental car at the Avis office and checked in. While he waited to board his flight to Cape Town Nick checked his emails and found two from Anja – each contained her rough translation of the two chapters following where Lili had got up to.

The first focused on Blake and Claire making their way along the disused Selati railway line – the same route he had taken to Crocodile Bridge camp and Komatipoort, but in reverse. The chapter ended with the soldier the pair had met on their travels being killed by the ruthless Captain Llewellyn Walters.

The small departures area of the terminal was open on the side that faced the runway and overlooked a tasteful water feature. Scores of small wooden birds were suspended from the thatch roof above him. It was as serene and beautiful as an airport building could be, and here he was, just reading about coldblooded murders being committed on the day a war had ended.

Nick opened his computer, and while he waited for it to come to life he thought again about how Charl's itinerary had exactly matched his own. Along with everything else that had gone on, this was too much of a coincidence.

The last piece of the puzzle clicked into place. Only one person other than Nick knew that his aunt and Lili had the manuscript, and that he'd been in contact with Anja Berghoff. That person also knew his exact itinerary in the Kruger Park, because she had helped him book it.

Susan Vidler.

CHAPTER 28

Claire's stomach rumbled, but she was too excited and nervous to even think about raiding their meagre stock of food in the saddlebags. The track they were on petered out as they ascended a particularly rocky section, at the foot of a *koppie* made of impressively large boulders. They could take the wagon no further.

Claire reasoned that the cave noted on Nathaniel's map must be close, as even with a good number of men it would be hard work ferrying the gold from the wagons.

'End of the road?' Blake said.

'We have to go on foot from here,' Claire said, 'but we must be very careful. I'll take the lead.'

Blake dismounted and took his rifle. '*Koppies* like this are good leopard country. Are you sure you want to go first?'

Claire worked the bolt of her own rifle. 'I'll be just fine, thanks.'

Blake tethered Bluey to the wagon and followed her, his eyes and his rifle barrel moving in a continuous arc, left, right, ahead and behind them. Claire moved as briskly as she dared, her eyes down, watching her feet and checking the hand-drawn map.

She held up her free hand and Blake stopped behind her.

'What is it?' he whispered.

She pointed to the ground. There was a pile of rocks that might have looked natural unless one knew to look for it. 'Move off the track, to the right, and skirt this part of the path. There's danger here.'

Blake came to her and Claire pointed to some notations on the map.

'"STT"? What does that mean?' Blake asked.

'It took me a while to remember,' Claire said, 'but on the night before your raid, Nathaniel made a point of telling me about a terrible weapon his superior officer had developed during the American civil war. It's called the sub-terra torpedo – STT.'

'What the hell is it?'

'Buried explosives, detonated by stepping on a hidden metal plate.'

Blake dropped to one knee and carefully examined the ground near the rock cairn. He snapped a leafy twig from a nearby tree and used it to brush away some soil. Just as Claire had warned, a rusted metal plate came into view.

Blake gave a low whistle. 'Tell me again this is worth it.'

'Your boat and my ticket to a brighter future. It's worth the effort, trust me.'

'If I don't get my bloody legs blown off.'

Claire set off again and the path climbed steeply, up into the *koppie*. She stopped and reached out, touching the surface of a granite boulder.

'What's that? Paintings?'

She nodded. 'Yes, as noted on the map. They're by the bushmen. Maybe a thousand years old.'

They both paused to look at the detailed, instantly recognisable images of kudu and sable antelope, lions, giraffe, elephant and rhino. The animals were all to scale and faithfully rendered, but the people were larger than life and abstractly depicted. Claire walked around the boulder.

'Here it is.'

Blake joined her, still scanning the rocks above and below them for ambushers or pursuers, then followed her into the gloom.

'Have you a match?' she asked.

He held his rifle in the crook of his arm and struck a light. Claire picked up an old bundle of rushes tied with twine and held them to the fire. The rudimentary torch caught light and illuminated the interior of the cave, revealing dozens of wooden boxes stacked atop each other.

Blake bent to inspect the writing.

'Ammunition, artillery shells.'

'Give me your Mauser,' Claire said.

Blake looked up at her, dubious, but pulled the pistol from its holster. 'This isn't the bit where you kill me, is it?'

Claire smiled and took the pistol, cocking it with the ease and confidence of a born soldier. She pointed it at the padlock on a box on the top of the stack.

'Claire! You'll kill us if that lot goes off!'

Claire fired before he could stop her and the shot assaulted their eardrums in the confined space. She knocked the remains of the lock away with the smoking barrel of the pistol then opened the box. Blake, now holding the torch, peered inside and brushed away some of the straw that had been used as cushioning material.

'Bloody hell.'

The gold ingots inside reflected the warm orange of the flames.

Blake looked up, his eyes roaming over the stacked crates. 'How much is here?'

'I'm told about two hundred thousand pounds' worth, give or take,' Claire said. 'Kruger's gold was split into ten shipments and this is just one of them. The other loads were sent to different secret locations, each with a detachment of trusted Boers to guard them, in this case loyal American volunteers. And in case you're wondering, this little lot weighs about a ton.'

'Blimey,' Blake said, then looked into her eyes. 'You're going to nick a ton of gold?'

Claire smiled. 'I'm not here for the fishing, Blake. Paul Kruger's government is finished, but if you think I'm going to let the English have this lot, then you're wrong. This stuff belongs to no man, Blake. It's booty, spoils of war, call it what you like. Question is, are you in?'

He licked his lips. 'I am.'

'Then let's get moving.'

Blake hefted the nearest box, then paused. 'How are we going to get all this across the border?'

Claire frowned. 'I was a spy, you know, Blake? I've greased a few palms already, at the border and on the docks at Delagoa Bay.'

'What was the gold supposed to be used for?'

'Krupps 77-millimetre cannons, made in Germany. Fritz Krupp's a cousin of mine. The Boers would have moved them through the bush, overland. No offence, Blake, but you Steinaecker's Horse boys have a reputation as a bunch of drunken layabouts and poachers, so the burghers figured they would have been able to slip the guns under your noses without too much trouble.'

Blake shook his head, but smiled. 'Who else knows this is here in this cave?'

'No one,' Claire said. 'Nathaniel and his man at the trading post were the only survivors of the detail that moved this consignment of gold here on President Kruger's direct orders. Nathaniel's men were ambushed by a bunch of Boer rogues, a commando of *bittereinders* who are more bank robbers than patriots. They're led by a wild-looking fellow in a leopardskin coat called –'

'Hermanus.'

Claire nodded. 'You know him?'

'He's the one who was looking for you in the camp.'

'That figures. Hermanus hoped to capture at least one of Nathaniel's boys, but they fought like tigers and took out most of the desperados. Nathaniel was able to get word to me and I met him at that trading post you and Walters raided. Nathaniel was tough and brave, Blake.'

'I know,' Blake said. 'He withstood torture.'

She nodded. 'To give me time to get away.'

'And what about Walters?' Blake asked.

'That bastard's crooked as well,' Claire said, 'the devil incarnate. I heard he's been roving the veld, looking for Kruger's gold. He tells people he's on official business, but the way he treated Nathaniel ... He's no more working for the interests of the Crown than I am. So, the choice is, which bunch of thieves deserves the treasure more – us, Hermanus and his cutthroats, or Walters?'

Blake didn't need to answer the question. He set off down the narrow passageway leading to the mouth of the cave carrying the first box of gold. They had a lot of heavy lifting to do, about fifty boxes' worth, he reckoned.

Claire had moved ahead of him and stuffed the burning torch into a crack in the wall to give them light to move the boxes by. For the first time Blake noticed an irregular-shaped object in a natural rock alcove by the entrance to the passage. It was covered in an oil-skin. Blake set down the crate and lifted off the waterproof cover.

'Claire,' he called softly behind him, 'come take a look at this beauty.'

*

Hermanus stood in the overgrown track that ran parallel to the Selati line and looked down at the ground, where Adriaan, his tracker, was pointing.

Adriaan was nineteen, but he was as ruthless as any of the remaining four men in the commando and the best tracker of the lot of them. He had been at war since he was sixteen.

'They turned off here, Oom,' Adriaan said.

The ground was rocky and Hermanus only pretended he could see what the boy was looking at. 'Lead on.'

Adriaan nodded and, clutching his Mauser, moved off, eyes scanning the ground ahead of him.

Hermanus motioned for Wikus, brave but brash and twice Adriaan's age, to file in behind the youngster. Wikus would watch over the boy's head while he tracked.

They came to a covered wagon, with a horse tethered to it. Hermanus moved past Adriaan and Wikus, but they, and Frik and Willem, crowded behind him to peer into the back of the cart.

Hermanus tried to lift the box closest to the rear of the wagon. 'This is too heavy to be ammunition.'

'The gold?' Frik said.

Adriaan studied the ground. 'They are coming and going, Oom, the man and the woman. They are getting tired, their feet are slipping as they carry the heavy boxes. There is sweat on these stones.'

'They won't be watching too carefully,' Wikus said.

'Move off, same order,' Hermanus said, 'and be careful, Wikus. This woman has outsmarted plenty of people so far, even that devil of an Englishman.'

Wikus snorted. 'And we sorted him out.'

They had left Walters tied to a tree, near where the Selati line met the main tracks. Hermanus told Walters they would come back for him, as they would need him to talk their way through the border and any British military checkpoints. Hermanus had said that he would still get a cut of the gold, if they found it, though it would be much smaller than Walters had expected. Hermanus would, in fact, kill Walters as soon as they were safely across the border into Portuguese territory.

Adriaan walked slowly along the rocky pathway, continuing to read the signs on the difficult ground.

*

Llewellyn Walters had been tied to a leadwood tree with his back against the trunk and his arms and hands wrenched behind him. He had no doubt Hermanus and his Boer brigands would kill him as soon as they felt he was no longer of use to them.

He heard voices.

'Hello!'

From around a bend in the winding track that followed the course of the railway line came two Shangaan hunters. One carried an assegai, a short stabbing spear, and the other an ageing Martini-Henry rifle, slung across his back.

The men came to him and, after initially chuckling at his predicament, the man with the spear cut through the rope securing him to the tree.

Walters rubbed his wrists, which were raw from his attempts to loosen the rope, and shook his hands to bring back the circulation. He nodded his thanks to the man with the spear and, through pantomime, asked if he could inspect the weapon. The hunter laughed and handed over the spear. As soon as it was in his hands Walters brought the tip up and stabbed it under the man's ribcage into his heart.

As the man staggered backwards his companion was struggling to shift the heavy rifle over his head. Walters pulled the assegai from the dying man's body and rammed it into the rifleman's neck. As the man fell, clutching at his throat, Walters relieved him of his Martini-Henry and set off up the track.

*

Blake had not survived nearly three years of war by dropping his guard. Whether consciously or subconsciously his eyes were always roving, searching the veld for signs of danger, even as his back and arms protested at the weight of the boxes.

As he left the rocky pathway he caught a flash of movement ahead. He dropped to one knee and set down the last crate of gold he would have to load on the wagon. Looking over his shoulder, he saw that Claire was making her way from the mouth of the cave, down the slope. She was watching her feet. She was a strong, fit woman, but she was struggling to carry her final load.

He snapped his fingers to get her attention and looked to her as he drew the Broomhandle Mauser from its holster. Claire didn't see him, but a man came into view. He was studying the pathway in front of him, but when he next looked up he saw Claire. He opened his mouth to call out, but Blake had already taken aim. He fired, two quick shots.

The man fell backwards, both rounds in his chest. Chaos broke out.

Claire dropped her box of gold and ran back towards the cave mouth for cover. Blake got to his feet and ran forward, which he hoped was the last thing his enemies would be expecting. He heard a crack and felt a whoosh of air beside him as a bullet came close.

Blake dived and rolled, crawled to the nearest tree then popped up, looking for a target. He saw a man running, fired a snap shot, but missed.

Another man with a rifle emerged from behind a tree and fired. Blake answered with two shots, at least one of which hit the man, but not seriously, because a few seconds later Blake felt another round whiz past him from the same direction.

He crawled over the rocks to get away from the man's fire and search for a new vantage point and targets. With his semi-automatic pistol he had the advantage of being able to fire faster than his opponents with their bolt-action rifles. He willed himself to stand and, firing on the run, emptied his magazine at the two men who both came out from behind cover to take aim at him.

As he ran he caught a brief glimpse of Hermanus, distinctive in his leopardskin coat, but the old rogue was too clever to expose himself long enough for Blake to draw a bead on him.

Out of ammunition, Blake turned and ran back up the pathway. When he got to the place where the small cairn of rocks had been laid he took a mighty leap. Exhaling with relief when he landed, he carried on up towards the cave. Blake heard the Boers yelling in Afrikaans behind him. He prayed their bloodlust was up.

Blake ducked behind a boulder before he reached the cave mouth, which was still out of sight to anyone coming up the path.

*

Hermanus skirted the pathway and climbed a freestanding boulder, which gave him the advantage of a few yards of elevation. The top of the rock was smooth and flat and he lay down.

Adriaan was down, dead, probably.

'Frikkie, go forward, man,' Wikus called from the ground below. 'I'll cover you.'

The ground erupted.

*

Blake hunkered down as the buried explosives detonated. When he looked up he saw there was little remaining of the man who had just stood on the devilish device.

There would be confusion below and the Boers would have checked their advance. Blake got up and, with his Mauser reloaded, moved down the pathway again.

A man stumbled into view. He must have been close behind the man who had detonated the underground torpedo as he looked dazed. Nevertheless, he raised his rifle and aimed at Blake.

He was too slow. Blake fired two shots and one found its mark, knocking the man over. Blake searched for a new target.

*

Hermanus took careful aim at Sergeant Blake, then squeezed the trigger.

The Australian fell backwards, shot in the gut. Blake raised his pistol and fired off a couple of rounds in Hermanus' general direction.

Hermanus was not a man who enjoyed seeing animals suffer and he felt the same level of pity for Blake. The man had been a worthy adversary. He worked the bolt of his Mauser rifle, aimed at the man's head, then fired again.

Blake stopped moving.

Hermanus slid down from the rock and made his way past his men. Wikus was still alive, but he would not be so for long. Hermanus stopped by him, looked into Wikus' pleading eyes, then shot his friend in the head.

He passed the body of young Adriaan, such a shame, and the smoking remains of Frik. He felt his rage start to build, but kept it at bay.

'Come out, Claire,' he called.

There was no answer.

He reached Blake, passing Willem's body on the way. Hermanus hadn't seen Willem go down, but he assumed Claire had got the better of him during the gunfight; she was not to be underestimated. He could see that his bullet had hit the Australian's head as blood covered his face. Hermanus nudged Blake's body with the toe of his rough handmade *veldskoen*, but there was no response.

'Claire?'

'I'm coming nowhere,' she yelled back.

'Claire, my men are dead and so is Blake. It's just you and me. It will take two of us, at least, to move the gold through the border.'

You have my word, as a gentleman, that I will not harm you. I need you, Claire.'

Hermanus knelt by Blake's body and picked up the Mauser pistol the sergeant had dropped. 'I'm going to come forward, Claire, and I'm going to toss you my rifle. I want you to do the same, as a sign of good faith, and then we'll talk.'

He moved forward, slowly, and stuffed Blake's pistol in the rope belt that held up his ragged trousers. Soon he would exchange these pauper's clothes for finery. He moved between giant boulders and saw now that there was a passage leading to a darkened opening ahead.

'I'm throwing my rifle, now, Claire.'

He tossed his rifle so that it clattered near the entrance.

'Slowly,' Claire said back from the dark. 'I want to see you with your hands behind your head.'

'Very well,' Hermanus replied, 'but toss out your rifle, and Blake's.'

He heard her unloading the weapons, which was good, and then the rifles clattered into sight, a Mauser and a Holland & Holland side-by-side. The big hunting rifle would be a useful addition to his collection, he thought.

Hermanus drew Blake's Broomhandle pistol from the small of his back and held it, ready to open fire, with his other hand behind his head. 'I'm coming in.'

'Slowly, mind,' Claire said.

He had thought he might try to take her alive, to help him move whatever was left of the gold, but she was as dangerous as a cornered leopardess. Better, he thought, to kill her.

Hermanus came to the entry of the cave proper and stepped into the gloom. He blinked and he knew it would take a moment for his eyes to adjust.

'I'm here,' Claire said.

He didn't need to see her to kill her at such close range. He started to move his hands, bringing the pistol to bear, and as his eyes grew accustomed to the dark he saw a flash of movement in a natural alcove off to the right of the entrance.

'Just as I thought,' Claire said.

Hermanus pivoted and found himself looking down the barrel of a Maxim machine gun, mounted on a tripod, with Claire Martin sitting behind it. The last thing on earth he saw was the woman's grim face as she pushed down the firing mechanism and blew his body back out of the cave mouth.

*

Claire stepped over the shredded remains of Hermanus, trying not to look at the Boer commander's body. She consoled herself with the knowledge that it was him or them, and that Hermanus had already proved himself a traitor and a murderer by ambushing and killing most of Nathaniel's troop of American volunteers. She ran to Blake, knelt down beside him and cradled his head in her lap. He was still breathing.

She wiped the blood from Blake's face and found that the bullet had creased the side of his skull, by his temple, but not penetrated his head. Of more concern, apart from the fact that he was out cold, was the hole in his side. She took the hunting knife from his belt and cut through part of his shirt, balled it and held it against the wound to staunch the blood. Hacking off more of his clothing, she managed to knot together enough pieces to make a bandage, which she tied around his body.

She drew him to her, her lower lip trembling as his blood stained her clothing. She kissed his cheek. 'Please don't die, my love.'

Blake was not a small man, but she had to get him to the wagon. She bent down and managed to roll him onto her shoulders and lift him in a fireman's carry. She staggered under his weight, nearly falling a couple of times on the loose rock, but managed, at last, gasping, to lay him on the tailgate of the cart.

She ran back and retrieved the fallen weapons, including Blake's prized Broomhandle pistol, tossed them into the wagon. Fear and anger infused her with new strength and determination and she hefted and loaded the last two crates of gold that she and Blake had been carrying. With Blake's horse tethered to the cart she climbed aboard and set off.

Blake came to, briefly, then lapsed back into unconsciousness as the heavily laden cart juddered and swayed about. She was getting close to where they had turned off the main road when Captain Llewellyn Walters stepped out into the path of the oncoming horses and discharged a shot into the air over their heads.

Claire's heart sank. She didn't know whether to scream or cry.

'Where's the Australian?' Walters reloaded the single-shot Martini Henry rifle he was holding.

'In the back, wounded,' Claire said. She could see no point in lying to the Englishman. 'He's out cold and shot in the gut; he's no threat to you, probably won't make it.'

'You've got the gold,' he said.

'No, just boxes of ammunition.'

Walters laughed. 'I should thank you, for doing all the loading for me. By the look of the way this wagon's sitting on its springs I shan't even bother asking if you got all of it. What of the Boers?'

'You can go up the line and take a look for yourself, if you're minded,' Claire said with a toss of her head. 'But the vultures have probably found them already.'

Walters grinned, all the while pointing his rifle straight at her. 'War's over, Claire. We can be friends now. You'll still need help getting your cargo out of South Africa.'

'Oh, and you're going to help me, are you?'

'There's more than enough for two people on that wagon. Let's let bygones be bygones.'

'You were going to rape me, when you had the chance, and you killed Belvedere.'

He shrugged. 'There was a war on.'

'So that makes it all right, does it?'

'We're no longer foes. Step down from the wagon now, there's a good Irish *cailín*.'

She bridled at his condescending tone and words, but held her tongue. They were both criminals and she would be as likely to hang as he would for stealing this much gold, but Walters had cut Nathaniel's ear off before murdering him and had set Blake up to be killed in prison. If she was bad, this man was evil. A flicker of movement through the bush had caught her eye. She looked over her shoulder. Blake was secure in the back of the wagon, but one bloodied arm was hanging out the back.

'What is it?'

She saw it again, a blur, pale brown, like British khaki, well camouflaged against the already dry early winter leaves.

'I need to check on Blake. Or perhaps you'd like to, if not to make sure he's not lying in wait for you, then at least to put him out of his misery, one soldier to another.'

'You Irish are all heart, aren't you?'

She kept her hands up, but looked to the other side of the wagon. There was another flash, on the opposite side of the track. It was a pincer movement, being executed with precision, stealth and a sense of urgency that would put the best soldiers on the veld to shame.

'What are you looking at, girl?' Walters moved to the back of the wagon and lowered his rifle in order to check under the tarpaulin that covered Blake.

Claire saw her chance. She dropped her hands and flicked the reins on the rumps of the two horses and they jumped forward. At the same moment she ducked to one side.

Walters fired, though because he was using only one hand his rifle bucked high and the bullet whistled over Claire's head – had she still been sitting upright it would have gone through her back.

As she neared a bend on the track Claire risked a look backwards.

The first of the lionesses that she and Blake had seen on their ride into the cave was on Walters, who was screaming.

CHAPTER 29

Nick had a spectacular view of Table Mountain as the pilot of the SA Airlink Embraer banked the aircraft and lined up for his approach to Cape Town International Airport.

Nick had managed to read Anja's translation of Blake and Claire Martin's story on the flight. It was clear, now, that Claire had found and stolen a tenth of Paul Kruger's missing hoard of gold and if there was more information to come that pointed to where some of the treasure was hidden, then that explained the value of the manuscript.

They landed and Nick made his way to the baggage carousel. While waiting he did a quick internet search and worked out that a ton of gold was worth more than sixty million US dollars in today's money. *Worth robbing*, he thought. Next he typed in 'Kruger's Gold' and found a barrage of hits. The internet listed plenty of stories about possible locations of the missing gold and failed attempts to locate it. There were claims of people finding evidence of the gold from as far apart as a dam near Pretoria to various spots hundreds of kilometres away in the Kruger Park, and the Bourke's Luck Potholes in the escarpment overlooking the lowveld. His bag appeared and he put his phone away.

Nick had got online at Skukuza Airport and booked a rental car. He took his luggage and made his way out of the terminal, hitching a ride on a golf buggy shuttle via a tunnel that led to the car companies.

He needed to find Susan, but with the exception of her mobile phone number, which he had tried maybe twenty or thirty times, he knew next to nothing about the woman he thought he had fallen for.

Nick had googled Susan, repeatedly, but found very little to go on. From his journalistic eye, it was as if she, or someone else, had scrubbed the internet clean of her presence. He knew that she had worked as a journalist on local newspapers back in the early 1990s, but this was before virtually everything written for newspapers ended up online.

Susan had told him that she had worked for various public relations consultancies in recent years and he had confirmed that from a story online about an award she had received for a PR campaign for BMW motorcycles seven years earlier. Other than that there was no mention of her or the services she offered. She had, he recalled, said that most of her work was as a subcontractor to other companies, so that would explain why she was not listed in the staff profiles of other agencies.

Susan had also said she was a freelance investigative reporter, but he could find no recent articles with her name on them. Perhaps her story on the push for reparations from the German government was going to be her big splash. However, when he googled 'reparations from Germany for Namibia' he came up with more than 130,000 results. This was not new news.

Or maybe she was a liar.

As he followed his satnav's directions through heavily congested Cape Town traffic, he tried to recall all the conversations he'd had with Susan, about Cyril Blake and about Nick's own friends, relatives and acquaintances.

Her questioning, now that he thought about it, had all seemed like small talk, albeit detailed. He'd put the continual questioning down to her being a journalist, as well as someone getting to know another person they were supposedly attracted to.

Susan *had* shown an interest in Sheila's passion for genealogy and he had also told her Sheila's full name and where she lived.

221

Susan had wanted to know about Lili, too, and Nick had told her what he knew with no reservations.

Nick had booked into the Vineyard Hotel, another of Susan's recommendations, in the event that they ever got there together. There was no chance of that now.

He just wished he could at least talk to her.

He remembered their last conversation, which he had been playing over in his mind. She had mentioned the Vineyard. *The barman there is a friend of mine and he's the best, he'll have a drink waiting for me when I get there and I'll call you*, she had said to him. Funny, Nick thought, what stayed in his mind. He had fallen for Susan but recalled nothing else about her family or friends other than the mention of the barman.

Nick found the hotel and noticed as he pulled in that Table Mountain seemed to loom over the building from behind. A porter met him and unloaded his bags and a valet took his keys and rental car. The porter took him to his room, and as soon as the man was gone Nick made his way back through the lobby to the bar.

Nick took a seat and ordered a beer.

'Just arrived?' asked the barman.

'Yes, from Skukuza in the Kruger Park.'

'On safari. Nice,' said the young man.

'Yeah, would have been nicer, except a friend of mine cancelled on me.'

'Sorry to hear.'

'Me too. I got stood up.'

'That sucks, man,' the bartender said as he took up a wineglass and began polishing it.

'It does,' Nick said. 'The truth is, I'm worried about her. My friend was supposed to call me and tell me when she was getting on a flight from Cape Town to Skukuza, but all I got was a very short, sharp text, telling me she wasn't coming and that basically our friendship was over.'

'Weird.'

'Yes,' Nick said. 'Actually, she told me she used to come to this hotel a lot.' Nick took out his phone and opened the camera applications, scrolling through the images to the selfie he had taken of himself and Susan after their dance. He enlarged it, cropping himself out of the frame, before handing it over so that the bartender could see it more closely. 'Do you recognise her, by any chance?'

The barman's eyes flashed with anger as he gave the picture a quick glance. He tossed the phone on the bar, towards Nick. 'You people. Are you a reporter?'

'Hey,' Nick said, pocketing his phone, 'I just wanted to know –'

'You can't leave her in peace, can you?' the barman said, his fists clenched on the counter. 'I don't care if you're staying here. You people will try anything.'

'You know Susan?' Nick said.

'Yes. And I've already spoken to the police *and* some journalists. I sent them packing, because they weren't guests. To you, I have to be civil.'

'The police ...? Look ...' Nick looked at the barman's name tag. 'Zack?'

The barman folded his arms. 'Yes.'

Nick took the phone out of his pocket and showed Zack the photo in its original form. 'You can see better, in this picture, that Susan and I knew each other. I was supposed to hear from her a couple of days ago and she never called. I got a text message from her, basically breaking up with me. I don't know what was going on between you two and I don't really care, but –'

'We were *friends*,' Zack said, his shoulders sagging. 'I'm gay.'

Nick saw now that the anger was leaving Zack, or, rather, being swamped by another emotion. His lip was trembling and his eyes were red, glistening.

'You knew her?' Zack asked.

'Yes, we met in Australia. All I'm trying to find out is where she is and if she's OK. I'd really just like to have a talk with her and she's not answering my calls. She said she loved the mojitos here ...'

Zack exhaled, lowered his head, then looked up again. A tear rolled down his cheek. 'My God, you don't know, do you?'

Nick felt his stomach drop. 'Know what?'

'Susan's dead.'

PART 2

CHAPTER 30

Upington, South Africa, 1906, four years after the end of the
Anglo-Boer War

Blake was as far away from the rest of the world as he could be
and still earn enough to be able to get a drink, a woman and a
bath. And that was fine with him.

A bell tolled in the small tower of the Dutch Reformed Church,
the oldest and most substantial building in the haphazard scatter
of rough mud-and-timber single-storey structures that lined the red
Kalahari sand and rock strip that was known as Schroder Street.

Blake led a mob of twenty horses, tethered nose to tail. The
chains he used to hobble the animals each night were now draped
around their necks and the metal links clinked with every step. The
street was empty, all sensible humans and beasts hiding in the shade
somewhere to escape the midday sun.

The whitewashed church had been built by old Reverend
Schröder some thirty years earlier. He'd supposedly come at the behest of the local Nama, to bring them education and religion. In
Blake's experience hard drink, disease and death came hot on the
heels of missionaries.

Blake ignored the pealing and rode on further to the second-
grandest place in town, the Upington Hotel.

The main thoroughfare was wide enough to turn a bullock cart,
but that's where its grandeur ended. A drunk sat on the ground,

sleeping in the shade of a wagon, propped against one wheel. A donkey, another of Upington's insensible residents, brayed as if to announce Blake's arrival. This place, he mused, was the polar opposite of where he'd served in South Africa. Where the bushveld along the border of Portuguese East Africa had been thick, emerald green in summer and teeming with wild animals, Upington was in the middle of a desert. Its source of water, and the only reason the town existed, was the Orange River, which slithered slowly, like a fat puff adder, through the lifeless landscape. A fringe of green clung to the river's banks but beyond that was a waterless nothingness.

The proprietor of the hotel, Willem Erasmus, known as Rassie to all, stepped out into bright glare, a picture of incongruent finery in his bowler hat, clean white shirt and bow tie. 'Meneer Prestwich, right on time.'

Blake gave Rassie a crooked grin in reply to the standing joke – time meant nothing in the desert and Rassie had no more idea when Blake would be back in Upington than Blake did himself. 'A drink, Rassie, for me and the horses.'

'Some fine Irish whiskey?'

Blake smiled and nodded, knowing there was nothing fine behind Rassie's bar. The word 'Irish', though, was enough to make him think of Claire again. It happened less frequently these days, but still the occasional word or a glimpse of red hair would remind him how meeting her at that abandoned trading post had changed his life.

When Blake had regained full consciousness in 1902 in the Portuguese hospital in Lourenço Marques the first thing he registered was a nurse addressing him by the wrong name.

'You are Edward,' she had said, smiling and speaking her accented English slowly and a little too loudly, as if she thought him simple. 'Edward Lionel Prestwich. It says so on the papers that were with you when the lady brought you here.'

The papers listed his unit as Steinaecker's Horse and Blake was lucid enough to realise that Claire must have found him a new identity. But there was no sign of her.

From the nurse he learned that he had been operated on by Dr Machado, a physician of some renown, and, though Blake had been close to death, the doctor had been able to save him. He had vague memories of Claire's face, coming in and out of focus as he gained and lost consciousness. Blake's other vivid memory from that time immediately after his surgery was of fire and smoke. He had thought it a nightmare, but the nurse told him there had been a fire in the hospital and Dr Machado had died, bravely trying to rescue a patient who had been left in a burning ward. Although she had managed to rescue his Broomhandle Mauser and Bluey, left in a stable near the hospital, Claire Martin herself had vanished, leaving no word of where she was going or how he might contact her.

Penniless, Blake had recovered then worked a passage on a cargo ship from Lourenço Marques to Cape Town – he remembered Claire letting slip that the ship she would board from Portuguese East Africa would take her to the Cape. As well finding Claire he wanted to clear his name, but to do all that he needed wages. He had contacted a lawyer and learned that Captain Llewellyn Walters had narrowly survived a mauling by a lion on the day Blake had been shot at the cave. Walters had recovered and become, ironically for the war criminal he was, a colonel in the Cape Mounted Police. The lawyer wanted money to pursue the case, and so Blake had found work with an old comrade from Steinaecker's Horse, who had returned to his family's farm in the Cape at war's end.

When he had almost saved enough to pay the lawyer's fees the man had had a change of heart, telling Blake he no longer believed he could prove Walters was a murderer and that Blake was innocent. Furthermore, the lawyer advised Blake in an urgent whisper to get out of Cape Town. Blake had never been one to run from a fight, but at the same time he'd been looking into a business venture. On the farm he was in charge of the horses and he had learned that there was good money to be made trading animals with the inhabitants of the neighbouring colony of German South West Africa. The local people, the Herero and the Nama, had risen up against their colonial masters in 1904 and war had broken out. Both the rebels and the German military, the Schutztruppe, needed horses, and the Cape Colony was teeming with the mounts of thousands of British and colonial soldiers who had sailed home without them.

As Edward Prestwich the horse trader, Blake was now making a reasonable living and would have been lining the lawyer's pockets if the man hadn't been murdered in the course of a backstreet robbery near the Cape Town waterfront. While Blake still clung to hopes – albeit fading ones – of clearing his name and perhaps finding Claire, he found his new life suited him.

More than the money, he was drawn to the vast emptiness of Africa. As harsh and unforgiving as the landscape was, the quietness helped still some of his memories of the war and dull the pain and bitterness he felt over the way Claire had used him.

Blake had found, or rather lost, himself with his new name on a new border, this time close to the frontier with German South West Africa, a remote corner on the African continent where the chilly waters of the Atlantic pounded a treacherous shoreline backed by vast sandy deserts.

War had followed Blake, or perhaps, he thought as he dismounted outside the Upington Hotel, it had been the other way around.

Upington in the remote north of the British-ruled Cape Colony, near the border with the German territory, was a hub for the horse trade and, for those like Blake who thought it worth the risk, a nice sideline in cattle rustled by the rebels from German farms.

'Dawie!' Rassie called. In response, a Nama man dressed in patched cast-off clothes trotted around from the back of the hotel. The Nama's homelands straddled this side of the border and the nearby German territory. Unlike the dark-skinned tribes Blake had encountered in the Transvaal, in the east of the country, Dawie's people were of a light brown complexion. The Nama had traditionally been nomadic pastoralists and most of them had converted to Christianity and adopted the Dutch settlers' language and dress. 'Take Kaptein Prestwich's horses and tie them out the back. Fetch feed and water.'

Blake waved hello to Dawie – the title 'Kaptein' he had used was the Nama's term for a leader or a chief – and tied his own mount to the hitching post. He turned away as a burgher, one of the local farmers, rode past in a carriage pulled by two horses. The man didn't exchange a greeting; everyone knew that Edward Prestwich had come to South Africa to fight the Boers, and while the war had been over for four years now, with the British victorious, it had not been forgotten everywhere.

Blake took off his felt slouch hat and slapped it against his trousers, raising a mini dust cloud in the process. After he'd sluiced the dust from his throat he would soak his body, and maybe someone else's, in a bath.

'Come, try the new whiskey,' Rassie said.

Blake walked inside the hotel. It was fetid, smelling of booze and smoke, unwashed bodies, sin and sick, but it was an oasis compared to the thirstlands he'd trekked through the past week.

'Will you be trading those horses for cattle, Eddie?' Rassie set two scratched glasses on the wooden counter and poured for the two of them. There was no one else in the bar.

'No. The Germans will be paying me handsomely for those fine mounts.'

Rassie snorted. 'Nags more like it, but if you do pick up some cattle remember old Rassie has many hungry customers to feed, eh? Maybe your friend the "Black Napoleon" has some nice fat beasts ready for the slaughter?'

Blake raised a glass to the barman. Rassie was always fishing for information, but Blake had learned to play his cards close to his chest. He'd been arrested once before for *allegedly* trading in illegal cattle, and while the prosecution had not succeeded due to a witness not being able to make it to court, he was now more careful to keep his business to himself. The fact was that the horses were destined for the 'Black Napoleon', Kaptein Jakob Morengo, the leader of the Bondelswarts Nama clan in German South West Africa and sworn enemy of the Kaiser. The Germans had given Morengo his nickname due to his tactical prowess as the most successful guerrilla leader in the south of their colony.

Rassie sipped his drink and set his glass down. 'A Landespolizei officer came from Keetmanshoop two days ago, asking about a herd of cattle that had gone missing from across the border.'

Blake threw back his whiskey in one gulp and set the glass on the bar. He didn't care about the Landespolizei; they were barely capable German part-time coppers. Rassie refilled his glass. 'Well, you know it wasn't me, this time. I had a proper alibi.'

Rassie smiled. 'I won't ask where you got your horses from.'

Blake shrugged. 'Legal and cheap. Four years on and the Cape's still overrun with horses from the war.'

'And why didn't you go home to Australia, Eddie, along with all those other Tommy sympathisers? You never have told me.'

Blake wiped his lips with the back of his hand. It was a good question, and one he'd given up trying to answer for himself. 'I don't know. This place, Africa, gets under your skin.'

Rassie shook his head and clucked. 'Nee, man. Thorns get under your skin, flies' eggs, worms, bullets. This place just cooks you, *braais* you until you're red on the outside and black on the inside. You've spent too much time in the desert, Eddie. Your brain is fried, man.'

'Maybe.' The second whiskey was working, dissipating the aches of the long ride. There would be more pain tomorrow morning, in his head, but it would be worth it.

'For how long are you back, Eddie?'

'A week, maybe two.'

'Your palace awaits you,' Rassie said.

Blake laughed. He had a rough mud-brick rondavel with a grass roof behind the pub where he kept his meagre possessions. It was the closest thing to a permanent home he'd had since he'd left his tent at Sabie Bridge – he had never felt at home on the farm in the Cape. 'Thanks. Can you get Dawie to draw me a bath?'

Rassie winked. 'Of course, or I could fetch you a girl?'

Blake shook his head. 'I think I need some sleep first, but thanks all the same. Maybe tomorrow.'

'Sure. There was a new woman in town, what, four days ago?'

'Come to make her fortune?'

Rassie shook his head and poured himself another drink. 'No, a *white* woman, from South West. She rode with a Nama guide.'

'She was from across the border?' Blake was mildly curious; women were scarce enough in this frontier town and this was news that could rival the relief of the siege of Mafikeng during the war.

Rassie took a sip. 'Didn't tell much, but asked plenty. Wanted to know where she could buy some horses. She was also asking around about cattle; she said a herd of hers had been stolen by the Nama and her theory was that they'd been brought across the border and sold here.'

Blake gave a half-smile. 'I wonder where she got that idea?'

Rassie looked heavenwards. 'The good Lord only knows.'

'Even though the Nama don't target German women she's either very brave or very stupid riding down here in search of a few cows and horses.'

'She wasn't German,' Rassie said. 'Dawie said she spoke to her servant in German, but to me she spoke English, with a strange accent. I met an American once, in Cape Town, a sailor off a ship. Could have been like that, but not as strong.'

'Hmm,' Blake said, affecting nonchalance. He tried to stop the glass from vibrating on the bar top as he set it down. 'What'd she look like?'

'Red hair. Skin would have been a lovely marble, if she hadn't been riding so long. But she looked like she'd spent plenty of time in the sun, not like one of those homely *Fräuleins* the Germans ship into Swakopmund and Lüderitz to populate their little colony.'

Blake licked his lips; his mouth was parched again all over. His heart beat faster. He took a breath to steady himself and concentrated on forming his words casually. 'Get her name?'

Rassie shook his head. 'Sadly not.'

Rassie would have tried, Blake told himself; he was too inquisitive not to. Had the woman hidden her identity deliberately? 'Did she find her cattle?'

'You say *I* ask too many questions, Eddie.' Rassie gave a chuckle. 'But to answer yours, no, she didn't, but I took the liberty of telling her I knew a man who was on his way here from the Cape who might be bringing horses and cattle. Shame for me you only brought the nags. This foreign woman might be interested.'

'Where is she?'

Rassie shrugged. 'Maybe back across the border where she came from, or trying some of the local farms.'

Blake took another drink with Rassie and he forced himself to stick to the small talk while all he wanted was to know more about the red-headed woman. Maybe it was just the mention of

Irish whiskey that had got him thinking about Claire again and his mind had jumped to conclusions; he told himself that even in this corner of Africa there would be a reasonable number of farmers' wives with hair that colour, even though he couldn't think of any off the top of his head. Rassie ordered Dawie to fetch water for Blake's bath.

When he'd finished drinking in the bar Blake undid his saddlebags, hefted them onto his shoulder and walked to his hut. It was as palatial as a jail cell, but it was somewhere he could rest up when he was in Upington. He unbuckled his pistol belt, hung up his Broomhandle Mauser, and peeled off his dust and sweat–encrusted clothes.

Dawie must have had word that he was on his way, for the wood-fired boiler had already produced enough hot water for him.

Blake eased himself into the tin hip tub, savouring the stinging heat that worked its way into his tired joints and dirty pores. He scooped a double handful of water, closed his eyes and sluiced it over his hair.

The door creaked.

'Give a man some privacy, Dawie.' Blake heard the door close again, but he knew someone was still in the room – he caught the scent of soap, and that was definitely not coming from Dawie. As he craned his head he saw her.

Liesl dropped to her knees behind him, rested her hands on his shoulders and kissed him on the cheek. 'Hello, Blake. How are you?'

He covered her hands with his. For the briefest of moments he had allowed himself to think that it might have been Claire coming in, that she had been searching for him and finally found him. Seeing Liesl, however, was something of a relief. If it had been Claire he would not have known which emotion would have come to the fore first. He had sought to dim her memory with half-a-dozen women in the past four years, but Liesl was by far the prettiest. 'Fine and you? I hope no one saw you slip in.'

'Dawie did, but he knows about us. He told me before you went away. He thinks you're a good man.'

'Hah. I always knew he was a poor judge of character.'

Liesl picked up a cake of soap from the floor beside the bath and lathered a flannel. 'You are, Blake. You help us. You brought horses this time?'

'Yes. And don't make me out to be some kind of saint, Liesl. I'll be selling those horses to your uncle.' Liesl was the niece of Morengo, though she kept that quiet on this side of the border.

'Hmm-mm.' She started washing his chest, reaching around him. 'And I know from my uncle that you don't really make any money. You take the cattle Uncle Jakob steals, sell them, and you take a percentage. The horses you give him for free.'

'Where have you heard all this rubbish?'

'From Uncle Jakob. He also likes you.'

'Was Morengo here, in Upington?'

Liesl took hold of his right forearm, lifted it, and scrubbed it, from fingertip to armpit. 'Briefly, yes. He escorted some more of the women and children here, so they could get to one of the British refugee camps. He was hoping to see you.'

'Why does the Black Napoleon want to see me in person?' The Germans had put some three thousand Marks on Jakob Morengo's head, so he was a careful man. Most of Blake's dealings were done through Morengo's underlings.

Liesl moved her mouth closer to his ear and lowered her voice. 'Uncle Jakob has learned the Germans are planning an attack on his base at Narudas. As well as the horses you have brought he needs more, as well as ammunition and food. He also wanted to move some of the women with small babies and the old and infirm to safety.'

'Jakob's got spies everywhere, so he's probably right about the Germans.'

Liesl picked up his other arm. Her movements were slower this time and she hadn't drawn back from him. He felt her breath on the back of his neck as she washed him. Fortunately the water covered his midriff.

'Yes, spies *everywhere*. I followed a German patrol last week, while you were away, watched them steal three horses from the Spangenberg farm.'

Blake reached over and encircled her slender wrist in his right hand. He turned his head so he could look her in the eyes. 'Do *not* do that again, Liesl.'

The girl pouted. 'I'm old enough to do my share now – nineteen. I counted the soldiers, and I got close enough to hear them talk, at their camp, and found out the name of the man who led the patrol.'

Water sloshed over the side of the tub, wetting her long dress as he swivelled. He let go of her hand but wagged a finger at her. 'You must *stop* this nonsense immediately. If the Germans catch you following them they'll shoot you, or worse.'

Liesl jutted out her chin. She had the look of a wilful child, but the eyes of a caracal cat and the body of a grown woman. 'This is not just about making money, Blake. I am the niece of a kaptein and I am *not* going to spend my life working as a maid in a bar full of drunken farmers.'

'You're safe here, Liesl.'

'Yes, safe, but a slave, just not to the Germans. Anyway, I'm not going to spy any more.'

He exhaled and slid back lower into the tub. 'Good.'

'I'm joining Uncle Jakob's forces. I'm going to fight and I want you to find me a nice horse.'

Blake thumped the side of the tub. 'I am not going to help you get yourself killed, Liesl.'

Liesl said nothing more for a minute or two, as she re-lathered the washcloth and gently pressed him forward so she could scrub his back. When she'd finished he slumped again and closed his eyes, thinking that he had put her in her place.

He remembered the first time he had seen her, crossing the border from German South West Africa with a score of other refugees. Her clothes were rags and her limbs skeletal. For all his bluster Rassie had a decent heart and he had taken her in as a maid. One night a drunken farmer named de Waal had grabbed her around the waist while she was picking up glasses in the bar. Blake had stood and suggested de Waal let her go. When he didn't and, instead, ground himself against her from behind, Blake had knocked him unconscious.

Liesl had filled out and grown enough to turn the head of more than one church-going burgher, and Blake had suggested to Rassie that she might be better put to work out of sight, cleaning the few rooms the barman kept. Blake and Liesl had become friends, and their friendship had eventually blossomed into something deeper. He had told her his story and his real name one night after drinking too much in the bar, and he'd found that sharing his burden with someone else had helped ease it. He started bringing her things – fabric, soap, a mirror, ribbon – when he made his trips up from the south with more horses. Having learned that she could read he also brought her books, which she loved more than anything else.

'I'll be sad to say goodbye to you, Blake.'

He opened his eyes. 'Liesl, you don't know what war is like.'

She stopped washing him. 'I've seen my people driven off their land, chased into the desert where they starved. Some of my friends have been killed, fighting.'

'Not women.'

'No, the Germans kill women by working them to death, or they die of the pox in these camps people are talking about. I'm a woman, yes, but that doesn't mean I can't fight. I can ride and I can shoot and I can get past German patrols in a way a man can't. I want to live in my homeland.'

Blake sighed. He'd seen too many young people die fighting for someone else's cause, but Liesl had been forced to leave her birthplace. In some respects, he mused, the Nama were like the Boers during the war with the British, fighting to protect their way of life, even if a far-off monarch didn't like the way they were going about it. He felt for her, but he couldn't bear the thought of that pretty face, that smooth skin being torn apart by bullets or shrapnel.

'Maybe you don't understand that, Blake – what it's like to fight for your own land. Maybe you don't like Australia. You told me you came from a place by the sea, where it rains, and where the grass is green and the cattle are fat. You told me of this place and it sounds like the Eden the pastors talk about, yet you are here, in the thirstlands. Why?'

'I told you before, Liesl, I was wrongly accused of killing a man during the war against the Boers and one day I need to clear my name.'

'*One* day.' She shook her head. 'Your war was over four years ago. You can go home. You can find a lawyer to plead your case.'

'For that I need money, more than I've got. There's still a bounty on my head – that's why I'm here, where nobody knows me.'

'Except me. I know you're not Edward Prestwich. Don't try and stop me leaving to join my uncle, Blake.'

He heard the implied threat in her voice, that she might black-mail him to get him to help her ride off to her death. He saw the determination in those eyes, which had set like amber – golden and beautiful but hard at the same time. In all the months since that drunken night in the bar he hadn't regretted sharing his real identity with her. Until now.

'I think you're not just here for money, Blake.' She stood and he saw how the fabric wet with bath suds clung to her young body. He remembered her skin, as slick and sweet and golden as honey.

Her father had been a German, a kindly man who had died when he'd fallen from his horse at Keetmanshoop in South West Africa, and Liesl had overcome the jibes of her relatives about her parentage and earned the respect and patronage of her important uncle through her actions. Morengo might love his niece, but he was also canny enough to know that he could use her, if not as a spy then in some other role where she could help his insurrection.

'My father would not have supported what is happening in my country now. He would have fought, even against his own people. He believed in justice, and that the Nama should have their share of the good land. I think you're here because you want to help us.'

'I'm here to make enough money to get out of this bloody desert, clear my name, then buy a boat and sail away to some place where it rains.'

She shrugged. 'If you say so.'

Blake stood, water cascading onto the floor, and stepped out of the tub. He went to her, dripping. He wondered if he should get a towel, but Liesl just stood there, looking him in the eye. She was young, but she was stubborn.

Like Claire.

However, it was Liesl who came to him and put her arms around him. She stood on her toes to kiss him and now her dress moulded itself to his body. Liesl took a step back, reached for the hem and pulled the sodden garment over her head. Now she was the same as him, bare, wet, in need of someone.

Blake took her to the bed and fell upon her, taking her, with the reverence of a worshipper and the single-minded surety of a bird of prey. She scratched at his back, her nails a match for her feline eyes. He had to hold the bedhead with one hand to stop it banging on the wall – he didn't want Dawie or Rassie's face appearing at the window.

Liesl clung to him and they rolled so that she was on top. Blake looked up at her, his hands almost encircling her waist as she brushed the hair back from her face and grinned down at him. He raised his fingers to her mouth as she began to moan, but she repaid his attempt to keep her quiet by biting him. The flash of pain sent a jolt to his mid-section and they collided together. Claire had done the same thing when they made love, he reflected afterwards.

When they were done they lay still in the afternoon heat, side by side. Blake, weary from days in the saddle, fell asleep, and when he woke an hour later, Liesl was gone. He drifted back into a deep, dreamless slumber.

A knock on his door woke him. He got up, pulled on his long underwear and hooked one suspender over his shoulder. He picked up his Broomhandle Mauser and opened the door a crack. It was Dawie, and outside the sky was turning pink.

'Mr Edward,' Dawie said, 'Liesl sent me. She says you must come to the river, by the punt.'

Blake rubbed his eyes. He always felt bad when he woke after being on the booze in the afternoon – it was better to keep drinking. 'Did she now.'

'Very urgent, sir. She says her uncle will be there.'

'Righto.' That meant business, not more of the girl's foolish idealism. Liesl had not let on that Morengo was still in town – she was playing a child's game of espionage that he feared would end in tragedy. Blake finished dressing, went out and decided to walk to the meeting point.

Upington's dusty main street was empty. Behind him a few farmers were already drunk enough to be singing in the hotel. Blake had put on his coat; the one thing he'd learned about deserts was that they were as cold as a banker's heart at night. Though he was right-handed he wore the Mauser on his left hip in a reversed holster. He kept his hand on the pistol grip under his coat, ready to draw. Liesl wasn't the only spy in this *dorpie*; the Germans paid former Boer guerrillas for information on rebels from German South West Africa moving back and forth across the border. There was no shortage of men desperate enough to try to collect the bounty on Morengo's head.

He carried on along empty Schroder Street, and past the church he came to the track that led down to the horse-drawn punt, the only means of crossing the Orange River. It didn't run at night. A man stepped from behind a tree trunk.

'Mr Blake.' The man touched the tip of his broad-brimmed hat.

'Prestwich,' Blake said. 'I told you my name last time we met, Kaptein.'

Jakob Morengo smiled broadly. His face was darker than most of the Nama he led because, Blake had learned from Liesl, her uncle was half Herero. He wore a three-piece suit, well-fitting but dusty from riding. 'Yes, so you did, but my niece has informed me of your real name.'

Liesl showed herself from behind the same tree. She had changed, he noticed, from her simple dress to a pair of men's trousers, a shirt and an old khaki jacket. A hat like her uncle's made sure that anyone who viewed her from a distance would think she was a slight man, perhaps even a bushman in western clothes. It seemed she was serious about joining the fight.

'Why did you go and do that?' Blake asked Liesl.

She jutted her chin out. 'For the same reason you told me.'

'What did I tell you?' He wasn't even sure he knew himself.

'You're sick of hiding, Blake, tired of running from the law; even if you can't clear your name you want to come out from behind the mask you hold up.'

'Is that so?'

Morengo smiled. 'She has quite a way with words, don't you think? It must be all the books you have lent her. For that, I thank you. Everyone deserves a good education, no matter the colour of their skin, their tribe or their gender.'

'Very forward thinking,' Blake said, 'radical, even.'

'My uncle speaks six languages and he's the first kaptein to allow women to have a say in his council meetings,' Liesl said. 'He studied in Germany.'

'Ironic, wouldn't you say,' Blake said, addressing Morengo, 'that it's a mark of honour in your niece's eyes that you were given an education by the people you're trying to kill.'

Jakob gave a small laugh. 'I met good people in Germany, many of whom believe that the Nama and the Herero and the other peoples of our country have been treated unfairly by the colonists. I was pleased to learn more of their language and their culture and I am sure if the people I met knew the full extent of what was happening across the border, pressure would be brought to bear for peace. Until then, we must fight.'

'Even young girls?'

Morengo looked briefly to his niece, his smile disappearing. 'She is a woman. She has a mind of her own. And courage.'

Blake felt the implied insult hang in the air, but let it dissipate. 'I've got your horses.'

'And I will bring more cattle, soon. I have some in the Karasberge. They will be here in the Cape Colony within the week.'

'Fair enough,' Blake said. 'But why have you come in person this time?'

'I need more, Mr Blake, or may I address you by your real first name?'

'Just Blake.'

'Very well, *Blake*.' Morengo seemed uncomfortable with the suspension of polite convention, but carried on. 'You may call me Jakob, not Morengo. As my niece told you, I believe, the Germans are coming for my forces. I'm expecting a two-pronged attack from Keetmanshoop in the northwest and Warmbad in the south, by the end of the month.'

'Not long.' Blake looked at Liesl. 'You have spies everywhere.'

'Quite,' Morengo said. 'But so do the Germans. They know that our *kraal*, where our women, children and cattle are, is in the Karasberge, at Narudas.'

Blake nodded. He'd driven horses and taken cattle to and from various locations around the Karas Mountains, known locally as the Karasberge, but had never been to, nor been told the location of Morengo's headquarters. 'You're either foolhardy or you trust me a great deal, Jakob.'

Jakob gave a broad smile. 'I am no fool.'

'Didn't think so. Why are you telling me this?'

'I need more guns and ammunition and I need to return to the *kraal*. I don't have the time or the spare men to set up a meeting at some other location. I want you to bring the arms to me, in person.'

'How many rifles?'

'Fifty, with a hundred rounds of ammunition for each.'

Blake gave a low whistle. 'That's a bit different from running cattle and horses. Riskier. More expensive.'

'I can barter, find you more cattle if you want, but that will take time we don't have. I can pay you.'

Blake raised an eyebrow. 'What with?'

'Gold.'

'Serious?'

Morengo reached into a leather satchel that hung from a strap around his torso. He took out a gold ingot and handed it over.

Blake hefted the bar, knowing instantly from its all-too-familiar weight that it was real; he had shifted enough of the bloody stuff with Claire. He held it up to the moonlight, inspecting it more closely. 'South African. Where did you get this?'

Morengo smiled. 'I was raiding a farm for cattle and food and I found this, in a strongbox, in a stable. The owner of the farm left in a hurry; she was probably in the process of hiding or retrieving the treasure when my men and I arrived.'

She. Blake's heart punched the inside of his ribs. 'How many more of these did you find?'

'Enough for fifty rifles and five thousand rounds. Perhaps a few more of each when I need them.'

'So this could be an ongoing business relationship, you're saying?' Blake went to hand the ingot back, trying to keep his hand steady at the same time.

Morengo held up a palm. 'Keep it. This relationship can last as long as the war, until my people have their freedom. That is worth all of the gold in South Africa.'

'Where's the farm, where you found the gold? What did the woman look like?'

Morengo laughed, from deep within his belly. 'Oh, Mr Blake, you should be on the stage.'

He licked his lips, his mouth parched again, as it had been when Rassie had mentioned seeing a red-headed woman in town. 'You're quite a character yourself, Jakob.'

Jakob became serious again. 'How long will it take you to get the guns?'

'A week maybe?'

Jakob stroked his chin. 'Close to the end of the month. I hope I have that long. The German columns do not move fast; the desert wearies them and my scouts delay them. As quick as you can, please.'

'I'll ride out tomorrow,' Blake said.

Liesl, who had retreated behind her uncle as the two men negotiated, stepped forward, hands on her hips. 'Is that what it took to make you join our struggle, a bar of gold, Blake?'

'I'm not joining anyone's war; one was enough for me. But I believe your people have a reasonable beef with the Germans and your uncle here and the other Nama I've traded with have been as honest and honourable as cattle thieves can be.'

'Rare praise indeed,' Jakob muttered.

Liesl turned to her uncle. 'We should ride.'

Jakob ignored his niece. 'Come to the Karasberge, within five days, if you can, Blake. Liesl will find you and guide you to Narudas and our *kraal*. I hope you have the weapons by then, but she will wait for another two days after that – no longer. If you have not arrived by then I will assume you have run off with my gold and I will send men to kill you.'

'I'll be there, within the week.' Blake needed to learn more about that gold and its owner. He would push himself and Bluey hard to meet the deadline. Bluey was getting on in years, but he was a tough, loyal horse.

As Morengo and Liesl melted back into the shadows along the bank of the Orange River, Blake held the ingot tight in his hands.

CHAPTER 31

Cape Town, South Africa, the present day

Nick zipped his fleece tight to ward off the chilly wind coming off the water as he made his way down a footpath lined with tall palm trees that led to the Table Bay Hotel.

He had driven to the Victoria and Alfred Waterfront, Cape Town's tourist hub, and killed twenty minutes wandering around the shopping precinct until his appointment with Susan's ex-husband, Ian Heraud. The hotel had a prime spot on the break-water, and as Nick approached it the swirling white tablecloth of clouds fluttered briefly enough for him to get a glimpse of majestic Table Mountain in the background above the hotel's long blue roof.

Zack, the barman at the Vineyard, had heard Susan mention Ian's name and his job as a food and beverage manager at the rival three-hundred-room hotel, and Nick had telephoned him. Reluctantly, Ian had agreed to meet him.

As he approached, a well-groomed man in a dark suit came out and stood, looking about. Nick saw from his nametag that this was the man he was looking for. 'Ian? I'm Nick.'

'Howzit?' The two shook hands. 'Mind if we walk? I need a smoke.' Ian coughed as he took out a pack.

'No problem,' Nick said.

They retraced Nick's steps to the breakwater as Ian lit up.

'Nothing like a bit of fresh air,' Ian said.

'Thanks for seeing me.'

Ian nodded. 'You said you met Susan in Australia?'

'Yes, in Sydney.'

'I didn't know she'd been over.'

'Yes, she came to research an Australian connection for a story she was writing, about the Nama and Herero people in Namibia suing the German government for reparations.'

'Hardly breaking news,' Ian said, drawing on his cigarette and exhaling. They kept up a brisk pace, because of the cold. 'She never showed any interest in that sort of thing when we were married.'

'I'm sorry for your loss.'

He snorted. 'I lost her three years ago. She left me for another guy, and the bastard had the hide to show up at her mother's place while I was there comforting her, even though they'd broken up. Susan was still in contact with him. Rich *doos*. She worked for him.'

'Had she been doing some PR work for him lately?'

Ian paused and stubbed his half-smoked cigarette out on a litter bin, then fished a handkerchief from his pocket and blew his nose. 'Fucking flu, and smoking's not helping. I don't know. She did *PR* for him when she was sleeping with him behind my back. I never really knew what that meant, or what it achieved. Do you?'

'Used to be my game, until recently,' Nick said. 'Not any more.'

They resumed walking along the edge of the grey sea. Gulls screeched overhead. 'I don't know what else she was doing. We never had kids so we didn't talk much after the divorce. She tried to patch things up between us – not get back together, but she made an effort to be friends, after she and Scott broke up. She was a better person than me, better than him, that's for sure.'

'Scott?' Nick asked.

'Yes, Scott Dillon. He was the *other man*. When she left the newspaper she went to work for Scott's real-estate company.'

Nick thought a moment. 'I've seen that name.'

Ian nodded. 'No doubt. After Pam Golding and Seeff he's probably the next biggest real-estate company in the country; you see his posters everywhere. He made his money in property development. Susan was his head of communications, and then his mistress. Dillon's wife found out and left him – helluva huge divorce settlement, but Dillon decided he didn't want to marry Susan, or maybe vice versa. I heard he ended up with his accountant at some point, but probably dumped her as well.'

'Where can I find him?' Nick asked.

'His office is in Sea Point, but he told Melanie, Susan's mother, that he was off to Namibia again. He's doing business up there, apparently, and he's a big game fisherman and hunter, likes long rods and guns. Compensation, I reckon.' Ian laughed scathingly.

'That must have been tough, seeing him at her mother's home,' Nick said.

'I wanted to hit him. Should have. Now all I feel is empty. I wasn't a perfect husband, but who knows why people do what they do? I miss her.'

They had circled back towards the hotel. *Me too*, Nick thought. He shook hands with Ian, whose shoulders started to shake.

Nick didn't know the guy but he reached out and put an arm around him.

'Hijacked – killed for her bloody car.' Ian couldn't hold in his tears. 'I never would have wished for anything like this to happen to her, you know?'

'Yes,' Nick said. 'I know.'

Ian broke away from him and blew his nose again. 'Sorry.'

'Don't be. Look, thanks for meeting me, Ian. I appreciate it.'

They shook hands again and Ian headed back down the stately avenue of palms. As Nick started to walk away, Ian called over his shoulder. 'Funeral's in a week or so. You've got my number, call me, I can give you the details when I have them.'

'Thanks.'

'Oh, and Nick?'

'Yes?'

'Cape Town might look like a slice of Europe, but this is Africa. Be careful.'

Nick collected his rental car and drove to Cape Town airport. He caught a golf buggy to the terminal and his hands were jittery as he checked his emails on his phone. There was one from Anja, confirming that she would meet him in Aus, in Namibia, whenever he made it there. She reiterated her condolences over Susan's death.

Nick had booked himself a ticket to Upington, where he would hire a car and have a look at where Cyril Blake had lived, and then drive across the border into Namibia. He checked in and went to his gate.

Be careful, Ian had said.

While he waited for the boarding call Nick looked up the website for Scott Dillon's real-estate company. He needed to learn more about Susan's last meeting with him, about her state of mind. The burglary at his aunt's place, the attacks on Lili and Anja and the ransacking of his hut in Kruger by his lying neighbour all seemed to be linked, but now a murder had occurred. He was still worried about Lili and hoped Pippa would have some news for him soon. Nick needed answers.

He found a number and dialled and he was presented with a frustrating array of numeric call options. Eventually he managed to speak to a human being and asked for Scott Dillon's personal assistant. He'd just managed to get through to the person he wanted, a Lisa Jordan, when the first boarding call for his flight was made.

'Hi, I'm sorry, I don't have much time, but I really need to speak to Scott Dillon or get a message to him, please. My name is Nick Eatwell. Mr Dillon doesn't know me, but it is very important.'

'Sir, I'm sorry, but Mr Dillon does not take calls from people he doesn't know; perhaps I can help you if you tell me what it's about, or I can direct you to one of our offices,' the PA said with the practised cool of an experienced corporate gatekeeper.

Nick drew a breath. 'It's about Susan Vidler. I know about their history and that Scott recently visited Susan's mother, Melanie.'

There was a pause, presumably as Lisa regained her composure. 'I'm sorry, Mr Dillon isn't in at the moment, he's travelling –'

'To Namibia, I know. Fishing, etc. Listen, Lisa?'

'Yes, Lisa is my name, sir.'

'Can you just get a message to him, please? Susan Vidler's boyfriend, Nick Eatwell, from Australia, needs to talk to him, urgently please. I'll give you my mobile number and email. Maybe you can get a message to him and ask him if he wants to contact me.'

'This is quite irregular,' Lisa said.

Another call was made for his flight and Nick got up and presented his boarding pass, his phone wedged between shoulder and cheek as he gave Lisa his contact email and number. 'Please,' he said as he ended the call, 'this really is urgent.'

Nick boarded a bus that took him and his fellow passengers to their aircraft. On board he set his phone to flight mode. Attached to Anja's email was her translation of the next few pages of the manuscript, which he opened once he was seated. It seemed they were working together now, officially.

Nick rested his head against the aircraft window and let his mind wander. What a journey his great-great-uncle had been on. He imagined Blake, the disillusioned ex-soldier, on the run, taking on an alias, and then becoming involved with a local girl. It was as though he had turned his back on the rest of the world and the conventions of the time. Was he a romantic adventurer, or just a common criminal? Maybe a bit of both.

The afternoon South African Airways flight, one of only two per day, left at four thirty-five and took an hour and twenty minutes. As someone who had grown up in a city and had never ridden a horse, Nick had no concept of how long it would take to ride that distance, particularly if he was droving – was that the term? – a team of horses or a herd of cattle along the way. In the terminal he'd checked the distance – nearly eight hundred kilometres by road, apparently. The money must have been good, Nick thought.

Nick turned his thoughts to Susan. It was too early for him to have said he loved her but he had been immediately drawn to her. The time they had spent together had been fun and he had really been looking forward to getting to know her better in the Kruger Park and wherever else their travels might have taken them. He had barely had time to absorb the news of her death, let alone grieve for her. Still jetlagged, he dozed off, but woke in a panic. In his dream he had seen Susan, lying dead in a hospital morgue.

The captain announced that he'd started the descent into Upington, and Nick checked his watch. He wondered if Pippa would make good her promise to check up on Lili. It was 2 am in Sydney, on Monday morning. He would have hours to wait, worrying about what had happened to his young German friend.

The landscape below had been uniformly golden brown and empty, but as the captain turned the plane Nick saw reds in the distance, the sands of the great Kalahari Desert.

They landed and Nick was surprised by the chill in the air as he walked down the aircraft stairs. By the time he collected his baggage, found the rental car desk and signed the documents that would allow him to take the vehicle across the border into Namibia as well, it was nearly dark.

'Can you recommend somewhere to stay, please?' he asked the woman behind the desk.

'There are plenty of guesthouses, B&Bs, and a big Protea Hotel,' she said. 'A friend of mine manages a place called Libby's. It's on Schroder Street, the main road into town. It's a yellow building, you can't miss it.'

'Thanks.'

His phone's GPS took him into town. There seemed no shortage of guesthouses, just as the rental car woman had promised. He found Libby's guesthouse and despite the late hour he was given a friendly welcome and shown to a room that looked fine.

He took up the offer of dinner, rather than organising a takeaway or driving into town to see what was open. He dropped his bag in the room and was walking through the courtyard to the dining area when his phone rang. He looked at the screen – no caller ID.

'Hello?'

'Mr Eatwell?'

'Speaking.'

'It's Scott Dillon here, how are you?'

'Ah, Mr Dillon ...'

'Call me Scott.'

'OK. Thanks for getting back to me so quickly.'

'My PA, Lisa, told me you said it was urgent. Plenty of people will use the "u" word to try and get through to me, but Lisa is usually able to sort out the pretenders. She said you mentioned Susan.'

'Yes, I did.'

'Terrible shame about what happened. I know it happens a lot, but I still can't believe it ...'

'I'm from Australia, Scott, and I'd heard about the crime rates in South Africa, but I guess I must have been in a bit of a bubble here so far. Crime happens everywhere, though, right?'

'Um, yes, I guess,' Dillon said. 'But, listen, Nick, if I may call you that?'

'Sure.'

'Nick, I was badly shaken by Susan's death. Lisa says you said you were her "boyfriend" and I'm not sure what you know about me, but Susan and I worked very closely together and her death has hit me hard. I'm actually on my way to Namibia on business, as I believe you also know. So, I'm sorry to sound blunt, but what exactly did you want to talk to me about that is so urgent?'

The truth was, Nick didn't know exactly; it was just that something didn't feel right. However, one of the skills he had learned as a journalist was to think on his feet when interviewing someone, rather than writing out a voluminous list of questions in advance. Like all reporters he had also learned to ask open-ended questions, those that couldn't be answered with a simple yes or no.

'Susan and I flew from Sydney to Joburg together and she left me to fly on to Cape Town, for a meeting with her last remaining public relations client, you. After that she was going to come up to the Kruger Park and meet up with me. How was she when you saw her?'

'She was Susan. Smart, professional, efficient as always.'

'Didn't seem worried by anything? It's just that, well, I got close to her in Australia, and I had the feeling something was troubling her.'

'Well,' Scott said, 'according to Lisa you seem to know that there was more to Susan's and my relationship than just work. We were together for a while, after her marriage broke up. I think I got to know her pretty well, Nick, and I can say that she didn't seem worried about anything in particular when I saw her.'

'Then why was she planning to end her business relationship with you?'

Dillon answered immediately: 'Because the project we were working on had run its course. Susan put together a media and local government relations strategy for a new golf estate development I'm working on. When we met she told me that while she had been happy to do the up-front work she didn't want the hassle of dealing with local newspapers, residents' groups and municipal politicians and bureaucrats over the development. She was also trying to resurrect her journalistic career working on a feature set in Namibia.'

'Yes.' There were a few moments of silence, each man waiting for the other to fill the void. 'She told me that she had to return to South Africa from Australia because her client had an urgent situation and needed her help.'

'Well,' Scott said, drawing out his answer, 'my development is pretty time critical and I may have told her that I was in a hurry to implement the strategy. Like I say, she pulled out, but I don't overuse the "u" word either.'

She could have told him she wasn't going ahead by phone from Australia, Nick thought. There was something Scott Dillon wasn't telling him, maybe something Susan had hidden from himself as well. 'Did she have any enemies, Scott?'

'What are you now, Nick, the police? This sort of shit happens in Africa, my friend. I'm sorry to have to open your eyes to it. The hijacking was nothing short of a terrible tragedy; Susan was in the wrong place at the wrong time. I know what you must be going through, but if there's nothing more specific you want to ask me, then I'd like to grieve in private.'

'Whereabouts in Namibia are you going?' Nick asked. 'I'm heading there as well. Maybe we could get a coffee or a beer.'

'Nick ... I can understand how you must feel, having only just met a fantastic girl and then having lost her, but I don't know that we're going to have a friendly walk down memory lane if we get together. I hurt Susan when we split up, and for that I was very sorry. We managed to stay friends and have a business relationship despite all that, largely because she had a big heart and was very forgiving. I'm feeling her loss very keenly and I want some time alone. Besides, I'll be out fishing a lot of the time, in between meetings and site inspections.'

'Where?'

Scott gave a small laugh. 'A good fisherman never reveals his secret spots. I know this is tough on you, but I think I've given you enough time for something that's not really urgent.'

'Yeah, I can see it from your point of view. I think the urgency for you has gone.'

Now the pause. 'What do you mean by that?'

'That you got what you wanted – a married woman – and then you got sick of her.'

'Goodbye, Nick. I think you need some time to cool off.' Scott ended the call.

Nick was annoyed at himself for getting angry. He thought about calling him back, but Dillon's direct number hadn't come through on his phone and Lisa, the PA, would now be under orders not to put him through, so there was little point trying the general number. Dillon either had no involvement in the robberies and attacks on people who had access to the missing manuscript – in which case he would write Nick off as a crackpot – or he had got the message that Nick was on to him. There was also the possibility that Susan really had been the victim of a random crime.

He went through to dinner, too lost in his thoughts to engage in conversation with any of the other guests in the dining room. None of them looked like contract killers or professional burglars, he thought, but then again 'Chris' who had stayed next to him at Skukuza, had looked like any other middle-aged guy in South Africa.

Would the person who had ordered the burglaries and robberies of his aunt, Anja and his rondavel in the Kruger Park go as far as killing someone? If Susan had been informing on him and had passed on the whereabouts of the copies of the documents, had she had a change of heart? Was it possible, he wondered, that someone other than Susan had sent him the breakup message, someone who wanted to throw him off any investigative trail?

Nick had two beers with dinner, then went to his room. He channel-surfed cable television for a while, then gave up trying to find anything interesting or distracting. He worked out that it was still too early in the morning in Australia to call Pippa to see if she'd found Lili's home address.

Nick checked his phone before turning out the lights and saw that Anja was working late. It was clear she understood that time was of the essence. Her emailed translations were coming thick and fast and, despite plenty of typos, the story of Blake's time in this same place seemed more important than ever. He opened the document and started to read. While Lili had laboured to translate the manuscript in full, Anja was summarising, to save time, Nick assumed, and wrote in the same direct manner in which she spoke.

It was Claire Martin who had come to Upington, ostensibly in search of cattle that had been stolen from her by Nama rebels.

She owned a number of farms across the border in South West Africa and had married a doctor who was also an officer in the Landespolizei – the reserve police force – Peter Kohl, the author of the manuscript.

CHAPTER 32

Keetmanshoop, German South West Africa, 1906

Claire dismounted outside the Schützenhaus, the newly completed shooting club building that served as a social hub for German farmers and military officers in Keetmanshoop.

A mini dust devil tore up the street and enshrouded her briefly. She spat dirt and a Schutztruppe captain, coming down the stairs, looked away, in disgust probably, then back at her as recognition dawned on his face. He touched the brim of his Südwester grey felt bush hat, pinned up on the right side with a black, white and red imperial cockade. 'Frau Kohl.'

'Hauptmann.' She walked past him, ignoring his disdain for her manners. It sometimes seemed to Claire that pretty much everything she did, from wearing long pants when riding to cutting her hair short to mitigate the effects of the oppressive heat was frowned upon by most people she met. Even though she was half German she knew she was viewed as a foreigner. In this colony folk prided themselves on being more German than their relatives back home – that is, when they weren't screwing their native maids. She walked up the steps, noting yet another frown as she pushed open the door to the bar, which was reserved for men only.

She heard Peter's laugh before she saw him and knew exactly where he would be at this time of the day: holding court at the bar. As her eyes adjusted from the glare of the late-afternoon sun to the dim, comparatively cooler interior, one of the four Schutztruppe officers around Peter saw her and cleared his throat. Kaiser Wilhelm glared down at her disapprovingly from a portrait on the wall.

'Madam, please ...' the officer began.

'Oh, shut up with your stupid rules,' she said in German.

Peter spun around, sloshed some beer out of his glass as he set it down on the bar and opened his arms wide. '*Schatzi*! Welcome home. Even I was starting to get worried about you.'

'I'm fine.'

He strode to her and took her hands in his, then lowered his voice. 'Come, let us sit outside so as not to bother these young farts. These regular officers straight off the boat from Germany are so formal.'

All Claire wanted was a drink. It was times like this she missed America.

Peter led her outside to the rear of the club where there was a watered lawn and some trees, a mini oasis in the parched lands around them and the dust-covered cluster of buildings that passed for the town.

Peter was in uniform and he, too, looked like he had been riding, slightly dishevelled but as handsome as ever. He called a barman and ordered a fresh beer for himself and one for her. He leaned forward and kissed her on the mouth.

She tried to maintain her scowl but failed. She returned the kiss, without passion, but Peter still smiled. 'It's good to see you. Did you find your cattle?'

She shook her head. 'No, but I've an idea they're across the border in Upington.'

'There is too much theft going on, so the officers tell me.' He slapped his thigh. 'I am going to put in an order for a nice new English stallion from Upington myself.'

She frowned at his laughter. Peter made light of everything, even the bloody war. 'You've been out on duty?'

The waiter came with the beers and she and Peter clinked glasses. '*Prost*. Yes, a patrol was ambushed by Morengo's Nama and one of our boys was wounded. We rode out to meet them and I operated on the man, there in the desert, can you believe it?'

He was a good doctor and the district was lucky to have him, she knew. 'Yes.'

'He will live, I think. We were celebrating in the bar just now.' Peter looked around again then whispered: 'And the gold?'

'No sign of that either,' she said, 'though I couldn't just walk into the Upington Hotel and say, "Where's my gold?" now, could I?'

His eyes widened. 'You actually crossed the border? Claire ...'

'Of course I crossed the border. Everyone does, Peter. It's part of the reason why your lot can't catch the Black Napoleon and his troops. He leads you a merry dance.'

Peter nodded vigorously. 'Yes, this man, Morengo, the *Schwarzer* Napoleon, I like him. You know, they say he speaks six languages and was educated in Germany. Even these young bucks in the bar have a grudging admiration for him. I think he is a worthy adversary.'

'Hmm,' Claire said, 'that may be, but he's also stolen a substantial portion of my fortune, Peter.'

He waved a hand in the air and took a long sip of beer. 'Pah. I am sure you have plenty more hidden away somewhere, though hopefully not in the stables again, hey?' He laughed, then hugged her to him. 'We won't starve, Claire, and if you get hungry we can leave the farm and go live in the bush. I will hunt for us, like a bushman, wearing only a loincloth and carrying a bow and arrow – maybe with a gun for the lions – and you will lie by a river with no clothes on like a Himba, smoking dagga and raising little orphan Nama children who will call you Mother.'

Claire broke free of his embrace and punched him in the arm. 'Stop teasing, Peter. What do you know of our financial situation?'

'I'm sorry.' He looked as though he meant it. 'I did not mean to make a joke about you not falling pregnant.'

'Oh, that.' It was her turn to wave away an imaginary fly. 'Don't worry about me having babies.'

'I would like a son, or a beautiful daughter one day, but I am happy as we are.'

She sighed inwardly and gave him a small smile. Peter had been considered one of the best catches in the colony when she married him three years earlier; men outnumbered women by twenty to one.

The colonial society in Germany sponsored young girls of modest means to take the long sea voyage to South West Africa, where they were placed in positions of domestic service with farmers, in the hope that the pairing might lead to what the Germans considered a proper marriage, between white people. All too often, however, the young *Mädchen* learned their would-be suitor might have one or more African concubines already. Peter had confided to her that venereal disease was one of the most common ailments he was called on to treat, among the farmers and soldiers. Peter was as near to perfect as a man in this part of Africa could be, but he was acutely aware of it and so were several ladies of good breeding, and a couple of their daughters. He had a roving eye, of that there was no doubt, and Claire knew he'd been unfaithful to her more than once.

In truth, she was not as happy with their current arrangement as Peter was. As a former spy she could rationally tell herself that Peter served a purpose and had been a means to an end – she could not have bought so much property in South West Africa without him on her arm and people were less suspicious of a doctor coming into money. They had put it about that one of Peter's great-aunts had died and left him a large inheritance.

Peter had been her doctor when she arrived in the port of Lüderitz in German South West Africa, after leaving Blake in Portuguese East Africa and fleeing with the gold. Peter had clearly been infatuated with her from the moment they met and she had allowed him to strike up a friendship with her – it was always good to be friends with a doctor, she told herself.

While Peter had made some romantic overtures, some subtle and some less so, she had waited a year, with increasing impatience, for Blake to make contact with her. Blake had still been recovering from his surgery and lapsing in and out of fevered consciousness when Claire had learned that Captain Llewellyn Walters had survived his encounter with the lioness and, even in a reportedly weakened state, had been asking about her and her cargo on the wharves at Delagoa Bay. Walters had put about a fanciful story that Claire and a gang of renegade Boers, whom she had subsequently dispatched in cold blood, had robbed a British Army payroll wagon and she was wanted by the police and military in South Africa.

Claire decided it was too dangerous for her to wait for Blake to mend and had left a note with Dr Machado, the competent surgeon caring for him. In the letter she told Blake to contact her, should he wish, via the port authorities in Lüderitz, German South West Africa.

She had heard nothing from Blake and her own letters to Dr Machado had never been answered. Claire had resigned herself to the fact that Blake was not coming. As saddened and disappointed as she was, she liked to think of him back in his native Sydney town; the alternative, that he not recovered from his wounds, was too much to bear.

Peter, meanwhile, had proved himself – as a suitor at least – devoted, attentive and persistent.

Before they married she had told Peter a mix of truth and fiction about where her fortune had come from. He had been fascinated to learn of her work for German naval intelligence as a spy, and of her connections to the Krupp family. She said she had profited from an arms deal late in the war, but as the transaction was highly secret the colonial authorities in German South West Africa had never known about it. Everyone else who was in on the deal or knew about it, except for Captain Walters and, possibly, Blake, was dead. Even her poor cousin Fritz was gone; he had committed suicide back in 1902 after a German newspaper got wind of the homosexual orgies he was holding with young Italian men at his villa in Capri.

Claire did wonder if Walters would come after her one day, but one thing about living in a remote corner of a German colony was that she figured she would have advance notice if a lion-scarred British officer came snooping about trying to find her. Thanks to her first husband she had a network of contacts at the port of Lüderitz, and she and Peter were well known throughout the government and military upper echelons due to the fact that most of the horses they bred ended up serving the war effort. If Walters did make his way to South West Africa she would hear of it, and he would not leave the colony alive.

Peter had no idea of the true size of her fortune nor about her largest cache of gold, which she'd had to abandon at Lüderitz when she had nearly been caught smuggling the crates of ingots into German South West Africa four years earlier. The precise location of that dumped treasure was known only to her and for now, at least, she was sure the gold was still safely hidden.

Peter had loved the intrigue that she had fed him, and Claire was happy with the story too, because it painted her not as a criminal but as a canny profiteer who had taken no more than was her due. Peter was a young doctor who had come to the colony with little more than the clothes he wore due to a series of foolish investments, and he half joked that if he returned to Berlin there was a jealous husband of a high-born lady who had threatened to kill him. Finding a woman of means who, if she was immodest enough to admit it, looked good on his arm, was a godsend to Peter.

However, Claire was lonely now in her marriage. Peter's infidelities were one reason and her own decision not to have children – something else the colonial authorities no doubt secretly whispered about – left her with little in life other than her horses to truly care for.

'Sometimes I think our horses are your babies,' Peter said, breaking into her thoughts and, like many a husband, reading them.

'I'm going to ride home and bathe,' she said.

He squeezed her hand. 'You always seem to be riding off somewhere, but at least this time it's home.'

She detected the note of sadness in his voice, as if he were telling himself that he couldn't be blamed for straying if she kept up her roving ways.

The truth was that despite them owning three farms, she felt unsettled. As terrible as they had often been, she missed the days of the war in South Africa, where she'd had free rein over her life. She had thought that land, something her Fenian father had been denied and her first husband had been unable to provide, would give her a sense of freedom and belonging at the same time, but it had not been so. Running one farm was hard work, even with a good supply of gold buried here and there, but managing three along with their attendant staff and their families during a time of war presented a never-ending litany of chores, scares and tiring conundrums.

But it was not just her business that was to blame for her lack of time with Peter. This new war with the Nama was escalating and

Peter, as a doctor, was called on so often in his role as a Lande-spolizei officer that he was employed almost fulltime by the army. Peter had always had his medical practice, now in Keetmanshoop, and while he liked the *idea* of being a farmer, she had always done the lion's share of the work managing their properties. Even so, his military service had added to her list of duties. She couldn't be everywhere at once and it was hardly surprising that the Nama had been able to make off with so many of their cattle, not to mention some of her gold that the rebels had stumbled upon in the stables.

Claire didn't feel afraid, riding the desert landscape alone or with Jonas, her Nama labour manager for company on longer expeditions; Jakob Morengo of the Nama had made it plain in his statements and deeds that they did not target German women and children. Claire was becoming increasingly worried, however, that the same code of chivalry was not being followed by the Germans when it came to dealing with the rebels.

Jonas had told her that when the *kraals* of Morengo and others had been raided, by Schutztruppen in search of fighters, their huts were being burned and the women and children rounded up and taken away. It was a chilling echo of the so-called 'scorched earth' policy that the British had employed to defeat the Boers in South Africa. In some instances, Jonas said, innocent Nama people had been killed on the spot.

Claire mounted her favourite mare, Roisin – a good Irish name – and cantered down the main street of Keetmanshoop and out into the arid emptiness. She gave the horse its head and tried to push the worries from her mind. It didn't work – she kept seeing the women and children in the concentration camps that the British had set up to house the Boer families; she smelled the filth again and saw the tiny graves.

She feared the Germans had learned from their neighbours across the border how to fight a guerrilla war – starve the rebels of support by rounding up those closest to them.

At the same time Claire felt the theft of her cattle as a personal affront. She had been careful to ensure that the Nama who worked on her farms were well looked after, with decent housing, fair pay and plentiful rations. She knew some farmers were not as caring, nor as lenient; Claire would refer cases of theft or other criminal behaviour to the local head man, but too many of her neighbours boasted of making use of the law that allowed them to discipline recalcitrant workers with their fists or a *sjambok*, the rawhide whip. She'd made a name for herself as a softie and a snob for walking out of drinks or dinners at the Schützenhaus when the men started laughing or boasting about such things.

And she was unsettled for another reason. There was talk among the soldiers – Peter had relayed it to her – of an Australian who traded cattle and horses with Jakob Morengo and the other Nama. It was no secret that some of the English-speaking farmers across the border in the Cape Colony were sympathetic to the Nama cause, or perhaps just anti-Germany, as most Brits seemed predisposed to be. On her brief visit across the border she had asked the barman in the Upington Hotel for information on this mysterious Australian, but not even she had been able to wheedle a name out of the man. It was probably a case of one criminal protecting another, although she could hardly be critical of that sort of behaviour.

When Claire arrived home, Sylvia, her cook and maid, appeared in the hallway, apron on and the smell of chicken roasting in the wood-fired oven wafting from the kitchen. They exchanged pleasantries and Claire asked for a bath to be drawn.

As Claire undressed she found herself thinking of Blake. Many Australians, she told herself, had probably stayed on in South Africa to work the goldmines, perhaps even to trade in horses, and she had no reason to believe Blake would still be in Africa, let alone so close to where she now lived. All the same, the memory of their lovemaking under the stars came back to her.

Sylvia departed and Claire lowered herself into the bath, the heat of the water almost a match for her thoughts. If by chance he was on the continent of Africa, then why had he not contacted her? She was certain she had not been Blake's first woman, but had she been wrong to sense that there was something different about that time between them? Perhaps it was just the tumult of war, the shared risk, that had made it seem so vivid, so exciting, so … important. As enjoyable as her liaisons with Nathaniel had been, she had been half acting, manipulating him while telling herself she cared for him. But Blake had rescued her, had risked his life for her.

She closed her eyes, trying to surrender to the soothing steam, but her mind kept turning. *Why did he not even try to find me to collect his share of the gold?* A week ago she had been busy unearthing one of the old ammunition boxes of gold when the Nama cattle raiders had been spotted approaching the farm. While the rebel commanders had decreed that no white women be attacked, she was not going to put herself at risk by trying to take on a dozen or so men who had ridden hard and fast into the farm. On hearing of the force's imminent arrival she had taken Sylvia and Jonas – lest the rebels take it into their minds to shoot him as a sellout – away in the carriage. Claire had only had time to loosely scuff some dirt over her hidey-hole in the stable and the horsemen had obviously noticed her shoddy work and exhumed the ammunition box full of Paul Kruger's gold bars.

Ever since, she had been worried that more rebels might come to the farm, this time not looking for livestock, but for more of her buried treasure.

'*Schatzi?*' Peter's voice boomed through the high-ceilinged farmhouse, echoing off the wooden floors. 'Sylvia, you are dismissed. We will be fine for the rest of the evening.'

The door of the bathroom flew open and he grinned down at her, a bottle of champagne in one hand and two crystal flutes in the other. He set down the glasses on her dressing table and opened the bottle.

'I couldn't stay at the bar, thinking of you in the bathtub!' He poured for them and handed her a glass. 'Cheers, as the English say.'

Claire lay her head back on the edge of the bath, closed her eyes and took a sip. Bliss. She forced her worries from her mind. Peter was good fun, and a tiny part of her wished he had been faithful to her so that she could have learned to love him properly, and forget about Blake.

For now, though, the feeling of him tipping a jug of warm water through her hair, then working in and lathering the soap while she sipped champagne, would do.

CHAPTER 33

After breakfast at Libby's guesthouse Nick used his phone's GPS to find the Kalahari Mall, where he stocked up on provisions for his road trip and bought a paper map of Namibia and a road atlas of Southern Africa at the Bargain Books shop.

Electronic devices were good for getting from point A to point B, but useless for situational awareness. He wanted to take a soldier's – or perhaps a rebel commander's – look at the distances he would have to cover in the next few days, and where everything was in relation to everything else.

He had his second cup of coffee for the day at the Mugg & Bean in the mall while he studied his map. The first thing that hit him was the vastness of the distances that Blake had travelled in the course of his business in this part of Africa. The area that Steinaecker's Horse had covered had, at first, seemed large to him, but in comparison to the wide empty lands of the Northern Cape and Namibia it was like comparing a suburban backyard to an outback cattle station.

The map showed him that Jakob Morengo and his rebels had roamed over hundreds of kilometres. The Karas Mountains – there were in fact two ranges, the main one, and a Klein, or small, Karasberge as it was called on the map – seemed huge in area. It was easy to see how Morengo, with his local knowledge, could have hidden from the Germans for so long in this empty corner of a largely un-inhabited colony.

Nick's phone rang and he saw that it was Pippa Chapman.

'Lili's in Royal Prince Alfred Hospital,' Pippa said.

Nick's stomach flipped. 'God, no, is she –'

'She's OK. She was mugged, in her house. She wasn't answering her phone so I went to her home in Newtown. Her flatmates filled me in the whole ordeal.'

'But she's all right?'

'She was knocked unconscious. The doctors are keeping her an extra day for observation because she was still a bit woozy. I've called her parents in Germany – they're apoplectic, as you can imagine.'

'But Lili's OK?'

'Again, yes, Nick, but the doctors want to make sure. She's quite shaken up. She had her backpack stolen; the cops interviewed her. Lili told me to tell you that she's sorry for not listening to you.'

'Any other message?'

'Yes. I'm getting to that. She said to tell you that she's sorry but they got all your documents. What have you two been up to, Nick?' Pippa took an audible breath. 'Are you involved in something criminal?'

'No.'

'Well, if whatever you and Lili were doing has got her hurt then I think you need to take a good long look at yourself.'

'Thanks, Pippa, I really do appreciate you checking up on Lili. I'll take it from here. Bye.' He ended the call. He didn't need his ex-boss to tell him that he needed to take stock of his life.

He tried Lili's number again, but it went through to voicemail. He left a message telling her to call him, day or night, and to just let the phone ring and hang up and he would call her straight back.

He looked at the map and the atlas, opened to the page that showed Upington and the Northern Cape. Further north across the border in Namibia was Keetmanshoop, where Claire Martin had fetched up as a wealthy landowner married to a doctor. It was a big jump from spying for the Germans, and running guns to the Afrikaners. And, of course, she spoke of her 'fortune' and another cache of gold hidden near Lüderitz somewhere on the coast.

Gold.

For as long as man had mined and smelted it they had also stolen and killed for the stuff. He thought of the guy on the flight to Skukuza telling him about the legend of Kruger's gold and his own check of the internet, in Cape Town, about the ongoing interest, even to this day, in reported findings of the Boer republic president's missing treasure. What he needed now was more information about Scott Dillon and how he might link to all this, before he confronted the man in person.

He typed 'Scott Dillon' into his phone's internet browser. The first few pages all related to real-estate sales so Nick searched under 'News' instead. Again, most of the stories were pieces speculating about the South African and international real-estate markets, though a few from business publications pointed to the falling share price of Dillon's company. It appeared he had overextended in golf estate developments, which seemed to be going out of style. Nick found another two entries that looked interesting.

Real-estate mogul's fire sale to pay off ex, was a gossipy piece from the *Sunday Times*. Nick opened it.

Scott Dillon's no stranger to auctions, but yesterday it was some property of a different kind going under the hammer in an auction of some of the real-estate titan's most valued personal items. On the auctioneer's block were rare pieces of memorabilia once owned by President Paul Kruger, including items of clothing, a desk, and a diary. Sources close to Dillon say the one-hundred-million-rand divorce settlement ordered by a judge when Dillon split from wife of fifteen years Joanne has cleaned out Dillon Real Estate's cashbox.

Bingo, Nick thought. So, Dillon was into collecting Kruger-era memorabilia, including the former president's personal papers. Also, it was more speculation about his financial state, reportedly parlous. Here was a man who could certainly use some gold.

The other piece that was interesting was from an online edition of *House & Home* from a few years earlier, in happier times for Scott and Joanne. A picture showed him sitting in a lounge with her on the arm, draped over him, in a sumptuous living room. It was a profile piece about the celebrity couple's home and their lifestyle. Nick scrolled down the page.

'Scott's a mad keen collector of South African history, especially around the Anglo-Boer War,' Joanne says, gesturing to a huge book-case and a number of 'very valuable' objects and records ...

Nick checked his watch. He needed to get moving.

Leaving town, the trappings of the twenty-first century fell away rapidly. Even flying along at a hundred and twenty kilometres per hour he started to feel the isolation of the landscape. Away from the Orange River the vegetation became stunted and mean, the ground rocky and thirsty. He was no farmer but he imagined farms needed to be huge here, as in the Australian outback, to support a viable herd.

From what he knew from Susan's research into the death of Blake and his own checking of the map, the Australian had been killed much further north of Upington, closer to the border between modern-day Klein Menasse on the Namibian side and Rietfontein on the South African side. He recalled her saying that the patrol that had ridden out to check on Blake, and subsequently executed him, had left from Klipdam, on the German side.

Nick crossed countries instead at Ariamsvlei, which was closer to Upington, with the Karas Mountains on the other side, where the 'Black Napoleon' had waged his guerrilla campaign.

He thought of Lili as he drove; he felt terrible that she had been hurt as a result of her involvement with him, but relieved that she seemed to be fine. Anger began to bubble inside him and he gripped the steering wheel hard. He still didn't know who was targeting him and the people in his life who had been touched by the story of Claire Martin and Cyril Blake, but it had become personal now. Nick had never been one to pick a fight, always avoiding bar-room punch-ups and conflict of all kinds. Now he wanted to find out who was responsible for this series of burglaries and assaults – perhaps even a murder – and exact some form of revenge.

The Karas Mountains popped up out of the surrounding flat, stony country as though God had plonked them there as an after-thought. In the distance they appeared a hazy blue-grey. Nick saw on his map that a detour from the main B3 road onto a side road, the D203, would take him through part of the mountain range.

He left the tar, and the gravel road took him on a winding trail that followed the course of dry riverbeds between flat-topped mesas that appeared red up close. The mountains, if they could be called that, did not seem particularly high, but this struck even his non-military mind as perfect ambush country.

Nick could picture canny rebels, intimately acquainted with the land, scaling these rocky cliffs and raining down fire on German horsemen forced to take the easy way through the valleys. Apart from the odd sheep farmer's hut there was no real sign of life in these barren hills. The little vegetation was clustered along the parched watercourses. In the summer, when the seasonal rain came, perhaps they flowed, but now, when Nick stopped to stretch his legs by a sandy riverbed, there was no sign of moisture.

It would have been a good place to fight a war, Nick mused, with few civilians hardy or foolish enough to scratch out an existence here, but from the last papers Anja had translated it seemed Jakob Morengo had brought his Nama people, women and children, and their precious livestock to these very same desolate hills.

Nick looked around and savoured the silence. Morengo must have known that what waited for his band's supporters was far worse than any privation this harsh natural environment held in store for them. To stay in their homeland meant imprisonment and, most likely, death.

So, Jakob Morengo had brought his people not through the wilderness, but into it, and in doing so he had dangled a target too big, fat and juicy for the German military to resist. Here was a man who cared for his people, but at the same time he would have been acutely aware of the risks. There were only two outcomes to this strategy, neither of them great – death or a stay of execution. Because even if Morengo could turn back the German columns that he knew were coming his way, how long would it be before the Kaiser's men rallied themselves and returned to finish them all off?

Nick looked forward to reading Anja's next email as soon as he was back in internet range.

CHAPTER 34

Garub waterhole near Aus, Namibia, the present day

Even in her puffer jacket, fleece, gloves and beanie, Anja was shivering as she brought the night vision binoculars up to her eyes.

The icy wind whistled through the open sides of the rock-wall viewing hide, twenty kilometres from Aus on the road that led to Lüderitz, a further hundred kilometres away. She needed no reminding that Aus was regarded as the coldest place in Namibia.

She picked up the mare and her tiny newborn foal, moving across the open expanse of desert sand. The mother stopped every few steps to bend her head and feed on the miserable shoots the desert produced. The thirsty youngster tried every time to drink.

Anja's stay in Namibia so far had been traumatic and as cold and desolate as this part of the country was, she found the emptiness of the desert and the sight of the horses helped calm her. She might have lost nearly all of her research, but she had a copy of Nick's manuscript and here, in front of her, were the real-life progeny of the horses she was researching. All was not lost for her, but the horses themselves were in trouble.

Even though Namibia's desert-adapted lions were famous – infamous to farmers – for the long distances they travelled in search of food and mates, they were not present in this part of the country.

Instead, the number one threat the wild horses faced was spotted hyena. The last thing Anja wanted to see was a foal or an elderly horse brought down by a clan of hyena, but she was interested in how alert the horses were, especially at night.

In recent years a protracted drought and increased predation by hyenas had led to the horses' numbers dropping dramatically, to less than a hundred animals. It was rare these days, Anja knew, for a foal to survive to anything approaching maturity so seeing this little one in front of her was even more special.

In her notebook, by the light of a torch covered with a red lens so as not to startle the animals, she noted the number of times per minute that the mare looked up from feeding to survey her surrounds. Anja watched, counted and recorded until the mare and her foal strayed beyond the range of the binoculars. The horses' departure gave her an excuse to get back to translating the manuscript on her new iPad.

It still irked her that she'd had to spend a small fortune on new equipment before the insurance payment came through, as well as set up a new email account, but being out here with the horses was soothing. She forced her fears from her mind and concentrated on the job at hand.

Anja heard a loud whinny and looked up from her iPad. She took up her night vision binoculars and her heart thudded. A spotted hyena, distinguishable in the full moon by the round slope of its back, was making its way across the plain.

Through the green glow of the device she made it out more clearly.

A desert stallion trotted into her field of view, stopped and tossed its head.

Anja panned left and right, searching for the mare and her newborn foal, and cursed herself – she had been so engrossed in reading the manuscript that she had neglected her fieldwork.

The mare was leading her foal towards the waterhole and the hide which overlooked it; perhaps, Anja theorised, she associated the hide with humans and safety. Anja knew, however, that spotted hyenas were brazen – given half a chance they would take a chop off a *braai* if no one was looking.

Anja's heart pounded. She had seen the carcasses of horses that had been preyed upon by hyenas, and pictures and videos of a hyena chasing a horse, but she had never witnessed a kill herself. Now that the prospect loomed before her she felt the mix of emotions that confronted tourists when they had the chance of seeing a kill in the wild. On the one hand it was exciting and her elevated pulse rate confirmed that fact, but on the other hand she felt a bond with the desert horses and the thought of seeing one taken, especially a foal, horrified her.

The hyena circled the three horses, watching and waiting. It paused and raised its head, sniffing the breeze, which was coming from behind Anja, towards the predator. The hyena probably had her scent now, but it showed no sign of backing away from the hunt.

Anja wondered what would have happened if the hyena was not alone, if there were two or three of them, or more. Hyenas had a reputation for being scavengers, which they certainly were, but few tourists knew that they were also adept hunters. Several years earlier she had seen four hyenas chase down and kill an impala in Etosha National Park. The clan had acted in perfect synchronicity, two of them swinging out as flankers and the other two chasing down the fleet-footed antelope. It had been over in seconds and had been one of the quickest, most efficient kills Anja had ever seen.

She feared for the foal.

The night's chill forgotten, Anja stood, elbows braced on the rock wall of the viewing hide. The hyena moved across her field of vision and around behind her. The mare whinnied and the stallion pranced up to her, as if to check on her and the foal. The little one, oblivious to the danger, tried to drink, but the mother stamped her hoof.

If they galloped away now, Anja thought, the hyena would chase them and probably catch the foal, if not the adults. Anja looked over her shoulder. The hyena was four metres away, mouth open as if grinning, curved teeth shining in the moonlight. Part of Anja wanted to throw a rock at it, to scare it away, but she was a scientist, and as heart-wrenching as it might be to see the foal killed or maimed, she could not interfere in nature.

She bit her bottom lip. *Haven't we done that already?* The desert horses should not have been there in the first place – hell, some people would say her people, the Germans, should not have been in South West Africa, though she did not believe that. The horses, whatever their origins, had adapted to the desert, just as her people from Europe had learned to live in Africa. Efforts had been made to manage the horse population in the past, including culling or capturing and removing some animals to ensure genetic diversity. Even now, in the middle of a drought, donors were providing feed for the horses, here at this very hide, to ensure they did not starve to death. The horses were a tourist drawcard, as well as an accepted part of Namibia's fauna.

Another debate had raged between supporters of the horses on one side and hyena researchers on the other. The 'horse' people had petitioned the Namibian Ministry of Environment and Tourism to intercede, either allowing them to relocate the horses to a safer area or to dart and move the hyenas. When the latter had been tried and failed – hyenas were canny creatures and not easy to trap or sedate – some hyenas had been culled. This had infuriated those on the predators' side.

So why couldn't she scare this hyena away? Anja asked herself. Who would know, or care, if she did? The tourists who would coo over and snap pictures of this little foal would probably thank her if they knew she had intervened to save it.

Then Anja thought of the hyena. Judging by its size she guessed it was a female as these tended to be bigger than the males and dominant in the clan structure. It probably had cubs somewhere, in a den in some rocks. The little ones, a uniform dark brown when new born, and cute like little bears, would be relying on their mother to nourish them with milk, and for that she needed to feed herself. Who was Anja to interfere and begrudge a hyena a meal? The hyena, after all, was native to Africa, and if it was a question of rights then surely the predator had more right to be here, and to eat, than the prey?

But were there now more spotted hyenas in this part of the desert because the population of introduced wild horses supported them?

It was too much to take in and besides, the hyena was making its move. It came around from behind the hide to the right flank, showing itself in the moonlight. The mare tossed her head and the foal, at last, seemed to pick up the presence of danger. It trotted a few metres, but its mother rounded it up.

The stallion shot away from the female and foal, galloping straight at the threat.

The hyena stood its ground and whooped at the moon.

The stallion stopped short and reared up on its hind legs, forelegs kicking as if it was going to strike down at the hyena, which snarled in return.

Anja picked up her camera and in her rush to get to the right-hand end of the hide she kicked over a Thermos flask of hot coffee. The metal container clanged noisily against the rock wall and concrete floor.

The hyena, hearing the man-made noise, turned and ran. The stallion gave chase, for a hundred metres or so. Anja, swearing at her clumsiness, glanced out of the hide in the other direction and saw the mare and foal galloping away to safety.

Once her heart rate had returned to normal, she returned to reading and translating Dr Peter Kohl's manuscript.

When she looked up again the hyena, which had circled back to the hide, was glaring at her. Danger was never far.

CHAPTER 35

The Karasberge, German South West Africa, 1906

Ambush country, Blake thought as he led the horses laden with rifles and ammunition through the moonlit night.

Whenever he crossed the border to do a cattle or horse trading deal he kept his wits about him. The money was good, and while he tried to salve his conscience with the thought that he was helping what seemed to be a good cause, Blake never forgot that he had truly crossed a line and was now a criminal. While he wouldn't kill another person over a herd of cattle he knew there were men out there who would, and the German Schutztruppen would shoot him on sight if they caught him running guns to the Nama.

He looked at the land as a soldier would. If he was leading a patrol he would stick to the high ground as much as possible, but that was impossible with his train of pack animals. He scouted for cover from his vantage point on Bluey's back, identifying places where he might be able to take shelter and return fire if he was shot at.

As he rode along the dry sandy riverbed he scanned the top of a natural wall of black basalt, the rocks as square and precise as if they'd been kiln-fired and laid. He felt a chill under his long oil-skin coat and rested his right hand on the grip of his trusty old Broomhandle Mauser.

There was an oddly familiar tingling in his fingertips that he didn't normally get from a cattle or horse deal, no matter how crooked the characters involved.

It was excitement.

He hated to admit it, but a part of him knew he had never felt as truly alive, as sure of himself as he had when he'd been out in the veld facing the prospect of contact with a Boer commando at any moment. He felt it now, the intoxicating mix of fear and anticipation. The wanting and not-wanting were like a drug, better even than opium.

'You're early.'

Blake's horse whinnied and he pulled up on the reins. Liesl stepped from behind a boulder on his left. She held a Mauser rifle and the moon glinted on her smile.

He touched the brim of his hat. 'Been watching me long?'

'About an hour, across the plain.' She lowered her voice. 'I'm glad you came, Blake, but there are half-a-dozen of my uncle's men hiding around here also watching you – and me.'

He nodded. He had not been about to kiss her, if that was what she was worried about. He sensed from her tone of voice that whatever they'd had was over now, in any case. That didn't stop him caring for her, or worrying about her being out in the desert with the rebels.

Liesl whistled and a pair of armed men emerged from the valley ahead of them, one trailing her horse.

They led him through the mountains, along more of the riverbeds, and then slowly upwards, along narrow paths of loose rock that would have been invisible to someone who'd not been brought up in this part of the world. Up and over a couple of saddles they trotted and walked, slowly, quietly, carefully, until the pre-dawn brought an even more bitter cold to the riders' bones.

Blake smelled wood smoke, and as they crested yet another rise he saw Jakob Morengo's clan spread out before him in a high, windswept U-shaped bowl surrounded by rocky flat-topped ridges.

Cattle were penned in *kraals* made of thornbushes and the people had made close to a thousand temporary homes out of branches, blankets and woven grass mats. It was a mean settlement, but at least it had been, up until now, a place of safety. Women with bundles of firewood on their heads, men cleaning rifles and children marching and playing with sticks for Mausers eyed Blake as Liesl and her escorts led him through the camp.

They came to a canvas tent, patched and old, but one of the more habitable structures on the plateau. Jakob Morengo was outside, dressed in his suit pants and an undershirt, braces hanging down. He was shaving in front of a mirror hanging from a tent pole. A canvas wash basin hung in a tripod.

He looked over at them as Blake dismounted. 'Welcome, how are you, Mr Blake?'

'Blake. Fine, and you?'

'Fine, fine, fine. Good to see you.' Jakob rinsed his blade. 'Please allow me to finish. A soldier should shave every day, water permitting, don't you think?'

Blake shrugged. 'The Boers didn't bother in their war, and nor did we, at least not in the irregular units.'

'Quite right! Help yourself to coffee. Liesl, perhaps you would do the honours?'

'Of course, Uncle.' She took a battered pot off a pile of coals.

'What I mean,' Jakob finished his last stoke, rinsed the blade and wiped his face, 'is that it was quite right that you copied your enemy. The strengths of the Boers were their knowledge of the land, their ability to travel light and move fast, and to hit hard and then run. At the same time the British were marching in a column, in three neat files, and shaving every day and burdening themselves with useless equipment. It was only when you colonials started playing them at their own game that you had some success.'

'Thanks for the history lesson,' Blake said dryly, 'but I was there. So why are you shaving, because you want to be seen in the same light as a British or German general?'

Jakob laughed and took a cup of coffee from Liesl, who also poured one for Blake. 'No. But I don't discount the Germans, nor underestimate their power.'

Blake drank some coffee; it was good.

'I see by the look on your face that you're surprised to taste coffee this good at the tent of a black man.' Jakob put on a white shirt and buttoned it to the top.

'I'm surprised to taste coffee this good in the Karas Mountains.'

Jakob smiled. 'I developed a taste for it in Europe. I was a clerk on the mines, in South Africa, and worked for a German company in Windhoek. The director was a kind man, forward thinking, who believed Africans would one day inevitably move into managerial positions beyond being the boss boy in a house. I made friends, but I noticed that the Germans prize order and precision over everything else. Rules must be obeyed, projects completed, accounts kept, and plans followed – everything is enforced with discipline. It's the same with their military operations.'

'I've heard the same said of them,' Blake said.

'I shave,' Jakob pointed at him with the razor blade before folding and putting it in the inside pocket of his suit jacket, which he then shrugged on, 'because it speaks of discipline. I want my men to see that I take pride in my appearance and my hygiene. However, the Germans run into trouble when Africa interferes with their love of order.'

'How so?' Blake sipped some more coffee.

'They find the climate here extreme – the summers hotter than anything they have ever known and the winters colder than they expected, or came equipped for. Patrols in the field suffer from a lack of water and fresh food and the men become louse-ridden and prone to disease as a result. My men are used to living in the wild, but I have to remind them to stay healthy, to keep clean, and to exercise self-discipline.'

'Good advice,' Blake said.

'But when I shave I think not like a Boer on commando, but as a German commander would.'

'And what do you think?'

'I think the Germans are following orders, and their orders are not merely to defeat me and my rebels on the field of battle. If their mission was as *simple* as that they would adapt their tactics, use smaller, more mobile patrols, enlist more of the disgruntled Boers and arm and equip them as fully fledged commandos. No. The Germans don't just want to kill or capture my men and me, they want to crush my people entirely. They want to send a message to the rest of the colony and indeed the world that native people dare not rise up; that the price of rebellion is annihilation.'

Blake thought about that. As horrible as the concentration camps had been in South Africa, Kitchener's intention had not been to wipe out the Afrikaners – though thousands had died of disease and hunger – but to deny the commandos their support. 'That sounds ... extreme.'

Jakob nodded. 'It's happening. You know, the Herero began this rebellion, and we Nama, even our best-known commander, Hendrik Witbooi, initially fought on the German side against the Herero. Our two peoples never particularly liked each other – my own parents, one from each tribe, suffered prejudice from both their families for marrying someone from a different culture – and in the past we had been at war. However, the Nama saw how the Germans treated the Herero when they had defeated them in battle and it shocked them into changing sides. Nama warriors were ordered to slaughter Herero prisoners and the Germans drove the women and children into the Omaheke Desert where they died of thirst and starvation. Some of those who tried to return to their lands in surrender were gunned down on the express orders of the former German commander, Lothar von Trotha. Others, we hear, are being sent to camps like the one on Shark Island at Lüderitz where they are worked to death.'

It sounded barbaric to Blake, but Morengo was now playing to a wider audience – his senior men had gathered around him, drawn to the charismatic leader's raised voice. Part of war was about demonising the enemy, but Blake knew from his own experience that things were never black and white in war, and that the other side was not always as evil as the politicians would have them believe. 'So what will the Germans do now?'

'They are coming, as I predicted when I saw you at Upington. Two columns, one from the north, the other from the south. They are bringing mountain guns – light artillery – and Maxim machine guns. You know yourself that you don't fight lightly armed mounted men with artillery and heavy machine guns; we move too fast, and I for one have no intention of throwing my men at some fixed position the Germans may take up.'

Blake looked around the plateau at the makeshift shelters, a woman breastfeeding a baby, two small boys with sticks chasing each other, a young girl stirring a pot of porridge. 'They're coming for your people.'

'Yes. To teach us a lesson.' Jakob looked around and waved his other men closer. 'Gather round, let us plan.'

Blake had seen some bad things during his war against the Boers. There had been individual instances of savagery and the business of burning farms and imprisoning civilians had turned his stomach, but he'd never heard of British forces shelling or machine-gunning innocents. If what Jakob was saying was right then the Germans were taking this fight to new depths.

Liesl caught his eye and glared at him, hands on hips, as if to say, 'I told you so'.

Jakob called to one of the young boys who Blake had been watching, and when the lad came to him the leader took the boy's stick. When the child pulled a face Jakob wagged it at him in mock anger. 'Go to your mother. Stop playing at war.'

Jakob walked around his tent; Blake and the others followed him. Morengo indicated with his stick for them to form a semicircle around a dozen or more piles of rocks that had been stacked on a piece of bare flat ground. Blake noted that several stacks formed a horseshoe and he realised he was looking at a three-dimensional map of where they were in the mountains.

'You approve, I see,' Jakob said.

Blake nodded.

'The Germans will need many wagons for their arms and ammunition and other supplies. Their most likely routes of approach are here, and here.' Jakob pointed to valleys leading into the Karasberge from the north and west respectively. 'They will make for the high ground on two sides of where we are and open fire on our people with the mountain guns.'

Blake pinched his chin between two fingers then raised his eyes to Morengo. 'Too late to head for the border with South Africa?'

Jakob met his stare. 'If I'd wanted to run we would have done so months ago. Some of our people have crossed into the Cape Colony and are now in British refugee camps. They struggle to survive on the food the English can spare for them. We have been pushed off our grazing land into these hills. We will not be pushed further.'

So that was it, Blake realised. Morengo wanted this battle as much as the Germans did. 'You've got what, a hundred, hundred and fifty men?'

Jakob rested his hands on this stick. 'One hundred and thirty-three.'

'The Germans won't come with less than a company from each direction; they'll need that many men to protect the guns. You'll be outnumbered at least two to one, probably more like three.'

'Precisely. So what would you do, Blake? Where would you try and stop their advance?'

Blake was not a general, not even an officer, but he'd led count-less patrols where the tactics had been left to him. There were a few truisms a soldier learned the hard way – stick to the high ground, don't attack a defended position with less than a three-to-one ad-vantage in numbers, and never volunteer for anything. He shook his head. 'You don't have the firepower to stop them, not even one of their columns.'

'So what would you have me do, run away?'

It was Blake's turn to smile. 'Yes.'

CHAPTER 36

Grünau, Namibia, the present day

Nick checked into a B&B called the Withuis, white house in English, outside of the small town of Grünau.

He stayed in the eponymous building, an old farmhouse on a larger working farm. It had been built in 1912, but walking on the creaking wooden floorboards, running a finger along the cast-iron wood-burning stove and looking out over the wide empty spaces of Namibia, he wondered if this was the paradise that Claire Martin had envisaged when she'd reinvented herself from German spy to respectable landowner and doctor's wife.

Nick settled into a leather armchair, and while he waited for dinner, which the owners had arranged to deliver to him at seven, he used the house's wifi to search for more information about Scott Dillon, real-estate mogul and former lover of the woman he thought he had loved.

He found and read a couple more articles online about the divorce of Scott and Joanne Dillon. It had been acrimonious, to say the least, with Joanne alleging multiple infidelities on Scott's part. Joanne, according to one story, owned an art gallery in Cape Town's Victoria and Alfred Waterfront, which is where Nick had parked his rental car while meeting with Ian Heraud. Nick googled it and found a generic email for Joanne Dillon Fine Art.

It was after hours, so there was no point calling the gallery, and he doubted Joanne sat in the premises selling paintings to tourists even if it was still open, but he clicked on the email address and composed a new message.

Dear Ms Dillon,
My name is Nick Eatwell. I am an Australian journalist currently visiting southern Africa. I'm interested in some information about your ex-husband Scott's business interests and was wondering if you would be willing to talk to me, either on or off the record.
Yours sincerely, Nick Eatwell

What the hell, he thought, she would probably ignore the email, but if she was still mad at Scott then maybe she would get in touch. It certainly seemed she had been more than ready to dish the dirt on him in the media during their divorce. He added a 'PS' saying that he was in Namibia at the moment and giving his local mobile phone number.

There was a knock on the door and the farm owner brought in dinner on a tray wrapped in a blanket to insulate it from the cold night air. Nick thanked him and polished off the venison pie quickly. He was halfway through his malva pudding when his phone rang. When he looked at the screen he saw it was from a South African number.

'Hello, Nick speaking.'

'Mr Eatwell?'

'Yes.'

'Howzit. It's Joanne Dillon here. You emailed.'

He was surprised she had replied, and so quickly. 'Yes, I did. How are you?'

'Half drunk as it happens, how are you?'

Nick smiled. 'On my second beer. I was wondering –'

'You want to know about that bastard ex-husband of mine. Are you writing about the golf estate that's failing in Australia, or the one he's trying to inflict on the people of Windhoek?'

Nick didn't know anything about a development back in his home country, but he knew not to blow a lead when it was handed to him on a platter. 'Among other things. It seems he's in trouble.'

'For years now.' He heard a slurp on the other end of the call. 'He's been sailing close to the wind for a long time, since before we were married. I bailed him out, which is one of the reasons I needed him to pay up – I barely managed to hang on to our home in Constantia – but he still owes me money from the settlement, so I don't want to ruin him, just make him pay.'

'I see.'

'Do you? You probably see the smooth businessman, the philanthropist giving money to save-the-rhino charities and buying sanitary pads for disadvantaged schoolgirls so they can stay in class, not the crooked businessman.'

'Crooked?'

'Well, let's just say Scott bends the rules until they almost snap, and he has curried favour with more than one town planner here in South Africa. I imagine there's less tolerance for that sort of corruption in Australia?'

'We like to think so,' Nick said, 'but it doesn't stop dodgy developers and councillors and local government staff trying to get into bed with each other.'

'Sounds like my ex; he'd try to get between the sheets with a black mamba if he thought it would get him off, or get him off the hook.'

Hell hath no fury, Nick thought, though he was still surprised by how candidly Joanne was talking about her ex to a stranger, let alone a journalist. 'I saw that he was recently auctioning off some of his historical memorabilia.'

Joanne snorted. 'Fancies himself something of an expert on Paul Kruger and the Anglo-Boer War. The fact is, he's more interested in money than anything else.'

'Is it very valuable, that stuff?'

'Kruger's diary and the papers he was auctioning?' Joanne asked.

'Yes.'

'To diehard collectors, yes, reasonably valuable, but the papers were of no use to Scott. He was less interested in history and more in Kruger's missing millions. Have you heard of Kruger's gold?'

'I have,' Nick said, 'just recently. So, your ex-husband is a treasure hunter?'

'A wannabe, yes. He was obsessed with it. He used to keep files on all the spurious reports of finds of the gold that have come up over the years. He dragged me along on holidays in the lowveld and anywhere else the gold might have been hidden. He was desperate to find it, and now he's desperate for money.'

'How desperate?'

Nick heard her take another drink. 'If Scott thought he had a genuine line on the gold, something hard, or even something new, he would do anything to get hold of the information and to keep it from anyone else.'

'Anything? Like what? Would he resort to the use of violence, theft maybe?'

There was a pause. 'Be careful, Mr Eatwell.'

'Nick. Why? I'm just researching a story.'

'So you say. Tell me precisely what your story is about.'

He had to think fast. 'Susan Vidler.'

She let the name hang there, between them, for a few long seconds. 'What about her?'

'She was Scott's PR woman. You heard she died.'

'Shot in a hijacking, yes.'

'Yes ... it was tragic. I met her, in Australia.'

'Did you now? Pretty woman.'

He didn't bite. 'She asked a lot of questions.'

'She was a freelance journalist as well as a public relations consultant, and though I hate to speak ill of the dead, she was a whore as well. You're a journalist, so you know your people ask lots of questions for a living. Who did you say you write for?'

Nick bridled, but kept his anger in check. 'I didn't. I'm also freelance. I got a sense Susan was after more than just some background for a feature story she was working on.'

'Scott was probably paying her to put a positive spin on his failing golf estate in Sydney. He thought all the South Africans living in Australia would miss their gated complexes and golf courses, but most of them, it seems, were trying to get away from those sorts of developments in the first place. The project was going down the toilet, and your environmentalists – greenies I think you call them – didn't like the idea of bulldozing bush on the New South Wales north coast to put in putting greens.'

'Susan didn't say anything about that development to me. She was interested in history, in the Boer War in fact.'

'Maybe Scott was on to a new lead. Why did Susan contact you about that stuff?'

'I've got my own interest in the period,' Nick extemporised. 'Would Scott pay someone to hurt or rob a person to get hold of information he wanted?'

Another pause. 'Do you know how cheap it is to hire a hit man in this country, Nick? Do you remember the case of the guy from the UK who had his new bride killed on their honeymoon?'

He did, vaguely. 'Are you saying your husband would hire a hit man?'

'I'm saying, Nick, that he would do whatever it took to get what he wanted. You need to be careful.'

'You're not the first person to tell me that.'

'Who was the first?'

Nick didn't want to say. 'I'm a big boy, I can look after myself.'

'That depends.'

'On what?'

'On how much you know and how much my ex-husband wanted whatever you have, or are chasing. There was a journalist investigating him in Cape Town. He ended up dying in a home invasion robbery.'

'Are you saying ...?' He was shocked that she might be hinting that Scott had something do with a killing, but he cautioned himself that it might just be the alcohol talking.

'Just be careful, Nick. Get back to me if you learn something new. And if you're talking to Scott, tell him I'm sorry about Susan. I hated her, but no one deserves to go like that. Funny ...'

'What is?'

'She drove like a maniac, like a Formula One driver. She'd taken defensive driving classes, as well as self-defence and advanced shooting classes. She always carried a gun, at least she did in South

Africa. Of all the people I knew, she would have been the least likely to get taken without a fight.'

Nick's mind whirred. 'Did she do more for your ex-husband than PR?'

'Apart from fucking him, you mean?'

He grimaced. 'Yes, that's what I mean.'

'You know she had her PI's licence?' Joanne said.

'She was a private investigator?' Nick couldn't hide his shock.

'*Ja*, she did all the kung-fu and driving training stuff when she was doing PI work, in between journalism jobs. As you know a good journalist has to be able to dig, maybe even go undercover sometimes.'

The revelation had left him speechless. Had Susan been working not as a reporter but as a private investigator when she'd tracked him down in Australia? Journalists in the UK had a reputation for either engaging or acting like undercover investigators, or resorting to phone hacking, but he'd never resorted to such tactics. *Was it really Scott Dillon who wanted information about Blake?*

'Nick? You still there?' Joanne slurred.

'Yes. Sorry. Go on.'

'I had my suspicions, when we were married, that as well as sleeping with Scott, Susan might have been in on some of his shady deals. I know she was involved in meetings with politicians and bureaucrats in South Africa over some of Nick's property deals. I think she might have been the, what do you call it, bagman, or rather bag woman, in a few of those projects.'

Nick didn't like what he was hearing and still couldn't or didn't want to believe it. *Was she investigating me?*

'Still there, Nick? Or have I frightened you off this time?'

'Still here.'

'Did you try to contact Scott direct?'

'I might have,' he said.

'No need to be coy, boy. That was a mistake. Scott despises journalists, except those who work for glossy property magazines. If he took your call or got back to you then that means he's worried about something. Normally he would have avoided you like the plague and wouldn't have been seen anywhere near you unless he was courting you. Plenty of people have tried to expose his shady deals and failed.'

Nick wished, now, that he had contacted Joanne before calling her ex-husband, but it was too late. 'Any more advice?'

'Same as before. Be careful.'

Joanne ended the call before he could ask another question.

Nick checked his emails. There was one from Anja, telling him she had to take a break from translating because she'd had an eventful evening. He called her.

'Hello?'

'Anja, it's Nick.'

'Oh, hello. I'm out in the desert, studying the wild horses. I saw the most amazing thing, a near-miss attack by a hyena on a foal.'

She sounded breathless, girlish in her excitement, quite different from the reserved manner of her emails and the formal English of his other calls to her. 'Interesting. Look, I think we should meet up sooner rather than later. I'm near Grünau, at a place called the White House. Do you know it?'

'Of course. You are not far from me.'

'I want to go back into the Karas Mountains again, first thing tomorrow, to find the place where the big battle between Morengo and the Germans took place.'

'Narudas. It's on the eastern side of the Karasberge. I've got a rough idea where it is. I'll check with my contact at Klein-Aus Vista Lodge and SMS you some GPS coordinates for your satnav.'

'OK, thanks.'

*

Anja was tired, coming down from the adrenaline rush of seeing the hyena stalking the horses. She walked out of the hide and set a camera trap on a pole near the waterhole then went back to the shelter, got into her sleeping bag and curled up on the hard floor.

She woke with the sun, after just a few hours of sleep, got out of the bag, stretched and went and checked her infra-red camera. She was actually relieved that there were no pictures, which meant she had missed no more action.

Anja cleaned her teeth and ran a brush through her hair. Then she put the kettle on her gas bottle and portable burner and made coffee, which she drank with a couple of rusks for breakfast before packing up her things. By the time she was pulling away from the hide the first of the day's tourists were arriving to get dawn photos of the desert horses. Anja felt a pleasant warmth inside, despite the freezing conditions, when she saw the mare and foal approaching the water point.

In the car she called Ulli, the head researcher based at Klein-Aus Vista and, as she'd hoped, he gave her some coordinates for Narudas farm. Anja SMSed the coordinates to Nick, who responded that he had received them. She calculated that they would arrive at the spot about the same time.

She drove as fast as the old Land Rover would go, just nudging the speed limit, the sun visor lowered against the rising sun as she headed eastwards on the main road towards Keetmanshoop. The Karasberge emerged on her right as she skirted the northern edge of the mountains and, eventually, she turned off onto a gravel road that led into the range on the eastern side.

Ahead of her, parked on the side of the road was a small white sedan, with a tall man standing outside. He waved to her as she pulled up. She got out of her four-by-four, bringing her new iPad with her.

'I'm imagining you're Anja, as there's no reason for anyone else to be out here.' He had a wide smile.

'Hello, yes, I am Anja.' She held out her hand and he took it. She gave him a firmer handshake than he was expecting, she thought. She held up her iPad. 'I was busy last night, as I mentioned, with my research, but if you like I can translate for you here, now, as I read.'

'Sure, that sounds great, and nice to meet you at last.'

'Yes, nice to meet you, as well.' She felt a little nervous and awkward.

'So, do you think this is the battlefield?'

She looked down at the screen, opened the document, and started skipping ahead in the manuscript, speed-reading while Nick stood staring out at the rather barren rocky landscape.

'Dr Kohl mentions a conical hill, shaped like a breast,' she said, then blushed.

Nick pointed. 'Well, that one over there sticks out.'

She looked up and out across the landscape, unwilling to meet his eyes while her cheeks burned. 'And a ridge, in a horseshoe shape. I think we are in luck, Nick. We are looking over the site of Jakob Morengo's *kraal*.'

Glancing sideways at her, Nick said, 'I'm really sorry about what happened to you, Anja, about the robbery and everything. I feel like it's my fault.'

She shook her head, touched by the genuine sincerity she heard in his voice, and finally looked into his green-brown eyes. He was a bit older than her, she thought, and handsome in a slightly unkempt way. 'It is done. It is a shame we had to meet this way, but I am glad I got a chance to read Dr Kohl's manuscript. Unless all the incidents, the robberies that you mention are coincidental, which seems unlikely, then there must be something of great value to someone in this document.'

'I've got a line on who that might be,' Nick said.

Anja raised her eyebrows. 'Someone looking for Claire Martin's gold maybe? That's the only thing of value I've seen in the manuscript so far.'

'Paul Kruger's gold, as a matter of fact,' Nick said. 'There's a real-estate mogul in Cape Town, Scott Dillon, who's an Anglo-Boer War history nut and would supposedly do anything to find that lost treasure. You've heard of it?'

She nodded. 'Of course. Everyone who has been in the Kruger Park area knows the story, but it's widely believed to be a myth.'

Nick shrugged. 'Well, let's see where the story takes us.'

Anja looked down at the screen again and started to translate. She smiled. 'Dr Kohl has once more inserted himself into the story here.'

Anja started to read aloud, but stopped when something came back to her that Nick had just said. 'You say this man's name is Scott?'

'Yes, why?'

'I met a South African called Scott in Windhoek. He said he was something to do with property development. What does he look like?'

'I don't know, really,' Nick said, 'I've only seen some pictures of him online. Dark wavy hair, a bit of a pretty boy, I suppose. I'd say women would find him handsome. Apparently he has plans for a golf estate near Windhoek. I wonder if it could be the same guy?'

'This man was very attractive. I met him in Joe's, a bar, and he was very forward with me, making friends, but in a gentlemanly way. He asked me a lot of questions about my work.'

'He seems to come to Namibia often,' Nick said. 'Do you think …'

'I need to look online.' Anja took her phone out and checked the screen. 'No signal. I will check later, but I'm worried, Nick. I met this Scott on the same evening I was attacked. If it's the same man, perhaps he was looking for your manuscript? Perhaps he knew we'd been in contact with each other and deliberately delayed me while the other men searched my room?'

'You might be right. That sounds too targeted to be a coincidence. Scott Dillon is the only link I have to Susan Vidler, and she knew where my aunt lives, and that Lili had a copy of the manuscript as well. Plus, of course, she had been in touch with you, and asked me to contact you, too. You may not know this, but Susan was working for Scott, possibly as a private investigator.'

'Really?' That surprised Anja, but it made sense. The woman had always seemed particularly nosey, even for a journalist.

'Yes,' said Nick slowly, clearly still thinking. 'And if it was Scott Dillon who was behind the attacks and robberies, then we have to assume that he now has the manuscript, stolen from Lili, and is working from the same information we have. If there are clues to where Claire Martin might have hidden her share of Kruger's gold, then Dillon may well be following them up.'

'What will you do, Nick? Do you want to confront him?'

'I think so. For now, though, we need to work out exactly what is so important in this manuscript.'

CHAPTER 37

Narudas, German South West Africa, 1906

D r Peter Kohl coughed and spat, his saliva thick with dust, as he reined in his mount at the centre of the horseshoe-shaped ridge overlooking the valley. The long ride from Keetmanshoop was over, but there would be no rest. Non-commissioned officers gave softly spoken orders as the mounted column of Schutztruppen reorganised itself for the attack on Jakob Morengo's *kraal*.

The breath of men and horses hung in the air, harness buckles clinked, and from along the line came the snicker of Mauser rifle bolts being worked as rounds were chambered, ready for action. A cone-shaped hill, which instantly reminded Peter of one of Claire's perfectly shaped breasts, caught his eye in the ghostly pre-dawn light.

He missed his wife and he missed his life on the farm, both of which he now realised he had taken for granted for too long. It was cold, but at least he had an extra layer over his police reservist's uniform, a long oilskin mariner's coat he had bought in Cape Town.

Peter had tired of war in a very short time, just the week it had taken the German columns to march and ride from Keetmanshoop and Warmbad to these godforsaken hills. Below them was their Nama quarry.

A horseman approached and reined in next to him. Peter saw that it was Hennie du Preez, one of the Afrikaner scouts who rode with the Germans and, sometimes, spied on the Nama people and their sympathisers for them. Du Preez had fought in the Boer War, against the British, and had chosen to move to South West Africa rather than live in a South Africa run by his enemies. 'Morning, Doctor. A good day for some shooting, don't you think?'

Peter gave a small nod, but he was not looking forward to more blood and bodies.

Below them Peter saw hundreds of *matjieshuise*, mat houses, wooden-framed structures covered with mats woven from reeds. From each little home came a straight plume of smoke that lined the pale pink dawn sky. Here and there, for it was still early, Peter saw women, the early risers of the African family, wandering about. One had a bundle of wood on her head as she walked, another stirred a pot. His stomach grumbled. What he wouldn't give now for an Eisbein in the Schützenhaus, and a cold beer. Instead, dinner and breakfast were tinned beef and biscuits.

'It looks quiet,' du Preez said, 'but von Deimling needs to be careful. That Jakob Morengo is as clever as Christiaan de Wet. I'd best be going, Doctor.'

Du Preez touched the brim of his hat and gave a more formal salute to the overall commander of the one thousand–strong German force, Colonel Berthold von Deimling, who, with an entourage of half-a-dozen staff officers, stopped next to Peter.

'Let's hope there is not too much business for you today, Herr Doktor Kohl,' Colonel von Deimling said.

Peter lowered his glasses and forced a smile. 'Today the Black Napoleon will meet his Waterloo, Colonel.'

Von Deimling frowned. 'If you were not a reservist, or if you rode with us more often, Herr Doktor, you would know that I forbid the use of that ridiculous nickname for this common outlaw.'

'Sorry, sir.' Peter wondered if von Deimling had overheard and reprimanded du Preez for likening the black man to Christiaan de Wet, the canny Boer leader whose highly mobile commandos had caused the British so much trouble.

Morengo had certainly drawn the first blood against this force. The guerrillas had hit von Deimling's column in the rear, where they had least expected it, on the ride down from Keetmanshoop. Riding out of the setting sun, a score of Nama on horseback had sailed into the wagon train carrying the Schutztruppe's ammunition and food, firing from the saddle at men and horses.

The wagon masters, cooks and storemen bringing up the rear had been armed, but their rifles and pistols were not within easy reach. Their officers might have been scanning the mountaintops and ridges for ambushes, but the last thing they expected was a fast-moving flying column riding up in their own tracks. The toll had been savage.

As a doctor in a frontier colony Peter had seen far more blood-shed than he might have in the wealthy suburb of Berlin where his family lived, but this attack had shaken him.

Until now, apart from some minor injuries and the time he had ridden out into the desert to save a young trooper who had been wounded in an ambush, the war had largely been an abstract concept for him, something discussed by young braggarts in the bar, tales of gruesome native savagery and soldierly courage. This was young men dying painful deaths, and despite rushing from casualty to casualty, he had been able to do so little for them. Eighteen had died and another twelve men were wounded, six of them badly enough to be sent back to Keetmanshoop on a wagon. Peter felt like he had failed the men and his commander so the colonel's rebuke hurt him doubly.

He felt angry at the rebels. He himself had treated many Nama patients who had gravitated to his and Claire's farm when they'd learned he was a healer. Some of the other settlers thought him foolish and soft, but he saw the local people as just that – human beings who deserved his help as much as any German farmer or his wife. Now he cursed them for stealing his cattle, for rising up against the Kaiser. Peter had thought Morengo a noble fellow, again, in the abstract, fighting for his land and freedom, but now he wondered why the Nama had not found some more peaceable way to make their case.

When he closed his eyes and looked into his heart, and saw the pleading eyes of a nineteen-year-old German boy calling for his mother with his dying breath, Peter realised he wanted revenge.

He studied the huts. Again he noticed that nearly all of them had a cooking fire outside.

'No sign of Morengo and his criminals,' Colonel von Deimling said.

'They will be hiding in the hills,' Peter said.

'Of course they will be, Herr Doktor. What we need to do is bring them out. Leave the strategy to me and I will leave the butchering to you.' The colonel spurred his horse and galloped off, his smirking staff officers in his wake.

Peter felt chastised yet again. More than ever he just wanted to focus on healing and farming, rather than the business of war. It brought out the best and worst in men and so far, in his limited experience, he had seen only the worst. The young Schutztruppen in the supply train had died without great bravery or sacrifice. There had been no rallying counterattack or acts of gallantry, just chaos and blood. After the attack, he had winced as an officer had walked along the column dispatching wounded, thrashing horses. More than one young soldier had cried at that act alone.

Returning to the task at hand, Peter continued to study the *kraal* below through his field glasses as riders were dispatched to the various units under von Deimling's command, to put the commander's plan into action.

Peter shifted his gaze and watched a troop of artillery unlimbering their mountain guns. The crews worked with practised speed, setting up the small but deadly cannons, removing ammunition from wagons and stacking it. Officers and non-commissioned officers sighted the guns and gave the command to load.

Further along the ridgeline half-a-dozen of the Maxim machine guns – terrifying weapons Peter had so far only seen fired in training – were being set up on tripods. A sergeant had let him fire one during a shooting practice, and the vibrations through his arms and the smell of cordite and hot gun oil had left him in no doubt that this was a true manifestation of the meeting of warfare and modern manufacturing, a machine that could kill quickly and en masse.

Peter scanned the rocky hills, which were turning pink in the dawn, and the still deeply shaded ravines and valleys. He mentally traced the trajectory of the guns and tried to identify their targets. So far he had seen no armed enemy on foot or horseback.

A red sun was visible through the haze above the flat peaks to the east as Colonel von Deimling gave the order to attack.

There was a series of ragged booms and a sound like material being torn as shells left the battery of mountain guns. Peter lowered his binoculars to get a wide-angle picture of exactly what the guns were targeting. His jaw dropped. From the high plateau below he heard the crump of distant explosions and saw dust clouds mushrooming between and directly on the humble dwellings of the *kraal*. Von Deimling had given the order to shell the civilians.

Peter heard the chatter of the Maxims and watched for their fall of shot. Here, too, the gunners were raking the mat houses of Morengo's followers.

A cloud of dust to his right told Peter that a company of Schutztruppen were on the move, their horses galloping down a narrow pass towards the plateau and the killing field below them. The German soldiers were mounted infantry, rather than cavalry, which meant they dismounted to fight, instead of riding through the enemy's ranks. Peter saw the men rein in their animals as they came to the edge of the plateau. Here and there a soldier gathered the mounts of his comrades while the rest of the force moved quickly into an extended line and started moving towards the rows of houses on foot, rifles up and ready.

Peter scanned the battlefield, if it could be called that, and saw maybe fifteen or twenty women and children running from the advance. He wondered what had happened to the rest of the civilians – if Morengo's band numbered between 150 and 200 then surely the number of dependents would be a multiple of that, perhaps a thousand or more wives, children and elderly people? Had so many been killed in the barrage?

The mountain guns and the Maxims adjusted their fire to keep their shower of shrapnel and bullets ahead of the advancing Schutztruppen.

Peter swallowed bile, imagining and trying to prepare himself for the sight of eviscerated women and children in the obliterated, smoking remains of huts. He had wanted revenge, but not like this. He kicked his horse and followed the same trail the soldiers had just negotiated.

His heart pounded with a mix of excitement, fear and dread. Peter stayed on his horse as he passed the Schutztruppen who were holding the mounts of their fellow soldiers, at the same time dimly registering that the guns had fallen temporarily silent; the skirmishers must have worked their way across most of the plateau. He caught up with two riflemen, one of whom kicked in the flimsy door of a house that had survived the artillery bombardment. The man went inside the dwelling, but came out, shaking his head to his comrade.

'What do you see?' Peter called down from his horse.

'Nothing, sir,' the man said. 'Nearly all these stinking huts are empty. There are cooking fires, but no food, no pots, no sign of people. We came across a couple of bodies, old people by the look of them.'

Peter looked across the plateau. The hairs on the back of his neck stood up. 'Get back to your horses, mount up!'

'The natives have all gone.' The soldier put his rifle between his knees, took off his Südwester hat, and reached into his pocket for a pipe. 'With respect, you're the doctor, sir. We take our orders from our officers. We were told to clear these huts and we've done so.'

'It's a trap,' Peter said, the realisation hitting him. Von Deimling was so intent on crushing the rebellion, on sending a message to Morengo by targeting his women and children, that he hadn't seen that the camp was all but deserted. 'Goddamn you, I said get on your horse.'

The soldier laughed at him. Peter drew his pistol and the man reached for his Mauser.

'Be careful where you point that peashooter, Doctor,' the man said, working the bolt of his rifle to chamber a round.

Peter looked up, checking the ridgeline partly encircling the plateau. He heard a rattle of rifle fire and a bullet smacked into the ground next to the foot of the man who had been mocking him.

'Shit!' The soldier spat out his pipe and ran to the matting wall of the hut he had just searched. The flimsy dwelling might have provided some concealment, but it couldn't stop the bullet that tore through the reeds and into the man's chest.

Peter dismounted. The man's comrade dropped to the ground and crawled towards his friend.

'Help me get him up on my horse,' Peter said.

The soldier was almost at the wounded man when another bullet brought up a fountain of earth near his hand. He stood, turned and ran towards where his own horse was rearing up, trying to break away from the man left to guard it. The fleeing man pitched forward as a round took him in the back, through his heart, killing him.

Peter dropped to his knees next to the wounded man and unslung the canvas satchel full of medical supplies he kept on him. It had been severely depleted after the first attack. He ripped open the wounded soldier's uniform tunic. A wheezing noise was coming from his chest and blood was frothing and bubbling around the bullet's entry wound. Peter knew the man's lung had been punctured and that there was little he could do for him. He figured that if he could make the hole airtight the man might at least be able to breathe more easily.

'Shoot ... shoot me, Doctor.' The man coughed, his lips bright red. 'Don't let these savages finish me slowly.'

Peter shook his head. He doubted the guerrillas firing on them could be more barbaric than men who deliberately shelled and machine-gunned civilian homes. He tried to think what he might use to seal the man's punctured lung. Ideally it would be something waterproof, but flexible.

His coat. He took the hunting knife he wore on his belt, lifted the hem of his sailor's overcoat and cut away a square patch. He rinsed the wound and the material with water from his canteen and then placed the material over the wound. Immediately, the gurgling stopped and the lung seemed to draw the oilskin in against the wound, sealing it. Peter secured it with a bandage around the man's torso and tied it off.

Around him, Schutztruppen were either running to get their horses, firing up at the hillside, or coming back past him, once more on their mounts. He called to a man still on foot. 'Come, help me.'

The man obeyed and together they lifted the soldier who had been shot in the chest. They walked with him, supporting him under his shoulders, and were nearly at Peter's horse when the man between them shuddered and pitched forward, dead.

Peter turned, drew his pistol again and fired blindly up the hills. How could they shoot a wounded man in the back?

*

Blake worked the bolt on his Lee Enfield, chambering another round. He called to Morengo. 'Tell your men to stop aiming for the wounded.'

'They would have massacred our women and children if they had still been there.'

Blake nodded. 'I know. But look at it this way. If you wound a man it takes two others to get him off the battlefield. You're tying up more Germans by wounding them rather than killing them.'

Morengo gave the order in Afrikaans, the common language of his band.

Blake took aim at a man on a horse who was waving a hand around, an officer probably. He breathed in, then out halfway, and squeezed the trigger. The man's horse reared up at another sound or shot and the officer was jerked out of the line of fire. Blake felt nothing, not disappointment at missing, nor relief; this was just a job. It was funny and scary how easily he had settled back into the business of hunting and killing. He worked the bolt again.

The Germans were getting organised below, most of the Schutztruppen now back on their horses, their officers trying to find a path up the hills to get to the rebels.

They would fail. Morengo had used his unparalleled knowledge of these barren hills to execute the plan he and Blake had agreed upon. Most of the women and children had been evacuated the night before. With their belongings piled onto donkeys they had left under the cover of darkness, making their way up steep, winding paths that were barely visible even in daylight. They were a mile away now, making their way along a shadowed ravine en route to a new location.

To make it look like the *kraal* was still fully inhabited they had lit cooking fires at nearly all of the huts before dawn. A few people, those too infirm to move swiftly by night, had agreed to stay. The ruse had worked and, as Morengo had predicted, the Germans had wasted precious shells and bullets destroying empty homes. Some of the civilians had been killed, either by artillery fire or, to Blake's disgust, by Schutztruppen who had dragged them from their huts and executed them on the spot. Blake hadn't believed the worst of what Kaptein Morengo had told him, but now it appeared it was true. It was also true that he'd had enough of war and had been reluctant to join this struggle, but it would have been harder for him to ride away now that he had seen for himself what the Nama were up against.

The time it had taken the Germans to sweep the plateau had allowed the fleeing civilians to move further out of reach.

Blake took aim at a running soldier, felt the kick of the rifle in his shoulder, and saw the man fall. He looked for a new target and saw movement on the firing line; the mountain guns were too far away for his rifle, but he could see that the artillery pieces were being adjusted. 'They're aiming at us.'

Morengo nodded. 'As we knew they would. Prepare to move, men!'

Blake slid backwards on his belly, over the loose rocks that were warming with the sun's ascent. Just before he lost sight of the guns he saw the first puff of smoke from a barrel and heard the screech of an incoming shell. The projectile detonated just below the edge of the cliff and sent up a fountain of red-hot shrapnel. Dislodged rocks rained down around Blake and he put his free hand over the back of his head as he was peppered with dirt.

On either side of him rebels were making their way to their horses. The German gunners adjusted their fire and two shells from the next salvo detonated on Blake's side of the ridgeline. A man he had just seen running disappeared, obliterated by the explosion of steel and fire. A horse rolled on the ground.

'Come,' Morengo said to him.

'Where's Liesl?' Blake asked. The last time he had seen her, in the pre-dawn darkness as Morengo had issued his final orders, she had been assigned the duty of caring for the Nama's horses in preparation for them falling back from the ridgeline.

Morengo took his horse's reins from a small boy. He hoisted himself up into the saddle. 'I don't know, but she passes for a grown woman these days.'

Blake took control of his horse and addressed the boy. 'Where is Liesl?'

The boy nodded his head towards the plateau they had been overlooking. 'She told me to take the horses because she was going down to be with the old people in the camp.'

'Bloody hell,' Blake said. He leapt up onto his horse, spurred it and rode off, in the opposite direction to Morengo and the others.

'Where are you going?' Jakob called.

'To find your niece.'

Blake didn't wait to hear Jakob's reply, concentrating instead on the narrow path that led down a winding route to the plateau. He had to be careful, as he knew that if the Germans saw him coming they would work out the route up to where the rebels had been lying, and their Boer outriders might be able to negotiate the trail and come after them. Morengo's success now depended on his being able to make a clean break from the Germans.

Blake went about halfway down to the plateau then stopped and dismounted behind a large boulder. He tethered the horse's reins to a gnarled tree that grew from a crevice. He took his rifle and crept lower.

From here he could see the smoking ruins of the huts and the chaos of the Germans as they tried to regroup and pursue Morengo and his men.

Blake heard rifle shots and took out his binoculars from the leather pouch hanging from a strap across his body. He saw two Schutztruppen, standing and firing, and when he followed their line of fire he saw a lithe figure running. She was in pants and a broad-brimmed hat, but Blake recognised Liesl immediately. She was carrying a child, a boy of nine or ten by the look of it, on her back. Blake saw the red stain his wounded foot was making on Liesl's buckskin coat.

Blake chambered a round and rested his Lee Enfield in the cleft of two rocks, taking aim at the soldier on the right. He breathed and squeezed and the man fell. His comrade dropped to one knee, half hidden by a mat house. Blake worked the bolt and fired again through the flimsy wall, but couldn't tell if he had hit him or not.

Of more concern was a man on horseback, who had clearly also seen Liesl's flight and looked to have decided to ride her down. The man had his rifle over his shoulder, but as he galloped towards her he drew his long bayonet from its scabbard with the hand not holding the reins and held it up, pointing forward like a cavalry sword.

Blake aimed for him, fired, but missed. Hitting a moving target, especially one on horseback, was never easy.

The rider swivelled his head, looking for where the shot had come from, but unable to see the danger, he carried on. He was rapidly closing the distance between him and Liesl. Blake led the man, aiming ahead of the horse, knowing that he needed to allow for the speed of the animal and the distance it would cover before the bullet reached its target.

The rider was almost on Liesl and the boy and it looked like he was aiming to skewer her through the child's back. Blake saw the grim fury in the man's face as he fired.

The horse's breath must have been on the boy's back when the man toppled from the saddle. The horse carried on past the fleeing girl and the child, the dead man hanging from one stirrup, his head and body bouncing over the mercilessly rocky ground. Blake saw Liesl's mouth open wide in horror.

Blake stood and hopped from rock to rock, coming lower so that he might meet Liesl, who was less than a hundred metres away from him now. There were another two men on horses following the dead rider, but Blake knew he would get to her first, as long as Liesl kept up her pace.

One of the men on horseback fired a wild shot which missed, but Liesl instinctively glanced over her shoulder to see where the danger was coming from, and fell.

Blake swore.

The fall cost Liesl her lead. The little boy screamed in pain as he was catapulted off her. Blake looked at the distance between them and it could have been a hundred miles for all the good it would do him. He brought his rifle up and aimed at the man closest behind Liesl. The rider was coming straight at him from this angle, so there was no need for him to aim off, but just as he was about to pull the trigger Liesl scrambled to her feet and blocked Blake's view of man and horse.

He held his fire, but kept his aim steady, ready to pull the trigger as soon as he got a clear shot at this man, or the one riding up immediately behind him.

Blake wanted to scream at Liesl to get out of the way, but he was sure she wouldn't hear him over the drum of the horse's hooves. She turned to face the riders and shepherded the boy behind her, to shield him from the oncoming fury.

Courage, Blake thought.

He could see that the man in the saddle, probably an officer, had a pistol out, and Blake gritted his teeth, dreading the worst. So help him, if this man shot an unarmed girl dead in cold blood Blake would die trying to kill him.

Liesl reached up with one hand and Blake thought it might be the death of her, but she pulled off her hat and her long hair cascaded down. The German officer pulled up, dust obscuring Liesl and the boy for a second. When it settled Blake saw that the man had dismounted and was pointing his pistol at the fugitives. He seemed, from what Blake could see, to be laughing at something, perhaps Liesl's clever ploy to show she was a woman.

The German's hat had fallen off, Blake saw, and he had blond curly hair and a uniform that was different from the normal Schutztruppe brown. The tunic under his open oilskin coat had green facings and Blake knew that the man was Landespolizei, a volunteer police officer. He tousled the boy's hair, and though the lad recoiled from the touch, the officer appeared to pose them no immediate harm.

Nevertheless Blake took aim at the officer, but he was thwarted again when Liesl once more unknowingly stepped in the way of his shot. By this time the other rider had arrived, and two more were cantering up. Blake hoped they might let Liesl go, but another officer arrived, Schutztruppe this time, and gave orders to one of the troopers, who dismounted, fetched some rope from his saddlebag and tied Liesl and the boy's hands.

There was nothing more Blake could do – he was outnumbered. He retraced his path through the boulders back to where his horse was tied. He climbed into the saddle, grabbed the reins tight and set off to catch up with Morengo and the others.

Blake consoled himself with the fact that Liesl had not been shot on sight – clearly not all Germans were as evil as Morengo made them out to be. However, he was not sure she was out of trouble. She was young and pretty and Blake feared what a bunch of lonely soldiers far from wives and sweethearts and the orderliness of their European home might do once they took a good look at her. Even if she were not raped en route she would be taken to one of the camps that people spoke of, where she would be worked to death.

He was not prepared to forget about Liesl, but he had to trust Morengo and the strategy they had worked out together. Their plan was to draw the Germans deeper into the mountains, exhaust them, and eventually 'disappear'. When the northern column turned home for Keetmanshoop the rebels would fall upon it from the rear. Blake hoped Liesl could stay safe until he and Morengo came after the column. He would make it his business to rescue her when they did.

He spurred his horse on over a rise and in the distance caught a glimpse of the last of Morengo's men disappearing into a rocky gully that he might not have been able to find if he'd been a minute later.

The Black Napoleon was about to lead his colonial masters on a dance of death.

CHAPTER 38

Karas Mountains, Namibia, the present day

Anja lowered her iPad. 'My battery is nearly dead.'

Nick contemplated the barren plateau below them. He tried to imagine shells bursting, machine guns firing and wily rebel horsemen disappearing along hidden trails. Namibia today was empty and peaceful; it was almost impossible to imagine the country at war, but of course it had been during the latter years of the twentieth century, in an equally bloody struggle for independence.

For now there was silence.

'Do you know much about this Dr Peter Kohl?' Nick asked, after a while.

'Yes. He has been part of my research for some time. He and his first wife, Claire Martin, bred horses, as well as owning three cattle farms, though it seems most of their horses went to the war effort. After the conflict was over he went back to breeding horses. One theory is that the desert horses are descended from his stock, that he let them loose when South African troops fighting on the British side invaded German South West Africa in 1915, in the early days of the First World War.'

'Just before Dr Kohl ended up in the British prisoner of war camp.'

'Yes,' Anja said.

'And we know from the start of his manuscript that Claire died just before Blake.'

'Yes. The same month, September.'

'So not long after the battle you were just reading about, at Narudas,' Nick said.

'Yes.'

'Kohl says she drowned at sea – the coast is a long way from here,' Nick said.

Anja nodded. 'Yes. I found an old item from a newspaper from 1907 that confirms this, where Dr Peter Kohl had announced his wife was still missing, presumed dead, after falling overboard from a passenger vessel that left Lüderitz in September 1906, two days before Blake was killed. I wonder if she was trying to get away from the colony, maybe with some of her gold? Kohl says she was waiting with a boat for Blake. I wonder what they had planned.'

'Me too,' Anja agreed. 'It's one more mystery I hope his papers clear up. Anyway, where to next? We can go to Aus, if you like, where I stay. I need to charge up my iPad at least. Also, I have skimmed ahead in the manuscript, looking for places I'm interested in. There are several mentions of Aus and Lüderitz. We'll be heading in the right direction, and Lüderitz was the home of one of the most infamous places in Namibian history, the concentration camp at Shark Island, sometimes referred to as Death Island.'

'Doesn't sound good.'

'No,' Anja said. 'It's not known how many Nama and Herero internees died there, but some estimates put the figure at three thousand. It's not a big island, only about forty hectares and joined to the mainland by a causeway built during the war, but it was a terrible place, exposed to the rain and winds off the Atlantic. People died of typhoid and scurvy or they were worked to death.'

'I'm in your hands from now on, as to where we should go.'

They got in their cars and Nick followed Anja out to the M26 gravel road and the B1, which took them via the town of Keetmanshoop. Nick imagined the German Schutztruppe column more than a hundred years earlier, men, cannons and machine guns, trudging down this same route, then just a dusty track, on their way to the

Karasberge. Anja called Nick on his phone as they approached the town and told him she needed to stop for fuel.

The town was low-rise, utilitarian, a place for farmers to shop for essentials and locals to get business done. It was much smaller than Upington and less prosperous.

A warm wind coated the town in dust as they filled up at a service station. Nick bought Cokes for both of them in the shop and tried his best to politely deter one young man who was begging and another who was insisting he clean Nick's car. Anja ignored them when they came to her.

'The Nama are marginalised,' she said as she leaned against his car, drinking her cola while his car was filled. 'The government is dominated by Ovambo, a tribe which was not much involved with the colonial war against the Germans. The Ovambo played a major role in the fight for Namibia's independence, which put them in power, and while they pay lip service to the role the Nama played in the uprising – their most famous commander, Hendrik Witbooi, is on the Namibian hundred-dollar note – the Nama people feel as though they are at the end of the queue for government funding and infrastructure.'

Nick looked up and down the main thoroughfare. Here and there were people living off the street, one man sitting against the building with a wine bottle between his legs. His overall impression of the town was one of a place at the far reaches of care.

There was a bustle about the place, though. It was clearly the largest settlement for hundreds of kilometres and people were coming and going from a supermarket. The traffic, while not heavy by any stretch of the imagination, was quite chaotic.

'Do you know the Schützenhaus? I'm not sure if I pronounced that correctly,' Nick asked.

'Of course,' she said. 'It's the best place to stay and eat in Keetmanshoop, and no doubt it was the same when Peter Kohl and Claire Martin lived here. We could go have a quick beer and a burger there.'

Nick checked his watch. 'It's only just gone twelve.'

She laughed, the first time he'd seen her do so, and it was like a different person had jumped into her body. 'This is Africa, Nick. The normal rules don't apply. Come.'

'What the hell, OK.' He paid the pump attendant and followed Anja through town and down a side street, jinking wildly to the left at one point to avoid being sideswiped by a mall taxi.

Anja drove to a boom gate, spoke to a security guard and drove into a fenced compound. The Schützenhaus was an historic-looking stone building, with newer accommodation units tacked onto the back. Another block had sprouted up out of the dirt car park and Nick saw a swimming pool enclosed behind a fence topped with barbed wire as he got out of his car.

Anja led him to a side entrance and through sliding glass doors into the older part of the building. They entered the bar and it was like stepping back in time.

On the wall was a picture of Kaiser Wilhelm II, emperor of Germany at the time South West Africa was his colony. While Anja went to the bar and spoke to the white bartender in German, Nick wandered slowly around the walls, taking in the colonialera memorabilia.

'This place was the first German club in the colony,' Anja said. 'The name actually means shooting club, or marksmen's club.'

'So I gather from these pendants.' The flags were encased in clear vinyl, which was just as well as the protective coating was stained brown from past decades of exhaled smoke, but they dated from the colonial era and showed motifs of rifles and targets.

Anja took two Tafel lagers from the barman and handed one to Nick. 'I've ordered us burgers.'

They clinked bottles and Nick lowered his voice. 'This place is like a time capsule.'

She smiled. 'A little old-fashioned, but people here are proud of their German heritage. Despite everything that happened during the Herero and Nama wars, and then later in the seventies and eighties in the liberation struggle, people in Namibia get on with each other these days. It's a harmonious country where different cultures are respected.'

As he drank Nick studied photographs of settlers from the early 1900s. 'It's funny to think that Dr Kohl and Claire Martin might have been in this very room.'

'Well,' Anja said, 'this was not the original building. The original Schützenhaus was made of timber. This stone structure was built later, though it's still very old.'

All the same, he thought, they had been here, maybe even on this spot, and while Keetmanshoop now had supermarkets, fuel stations and a few other twenty-first-century trappings, he guessed it had still had the same dusty edge-of-the-world feel in 1906 as it did now. Their food arrived and they ate in silence, both of them hungry.

Nick stared up into the Kaiser's unsmiling eyes. The Germans had only officially ruled South West Africa for thirty years, until South Africa took it off them in 1915, but they had left their mark indelibly on this desert land.

He finished the last of his food. 'How did studying horses lead you to the story of Cyril Blake and Claire Martin?'

'Claire and Peter's horse stud was one of several established by order of the imperial German government in the early years of the colony. The settlers knew they would need a good supply of horses to explore and open up the interior of Namibia and the demand increased dramatically when the Herero and Nama wars started. I was searching the archives in Germany for mentions of both of them and Claire's name started coming up in documents from around the turn of the century. That's where I found her dispatches from South Africa, during the Anglo-Boer War. To be honest, I didn't think those papers would help me with my research, but I became fascinated by the story of a young Irishwoman spying for the German government, and her letters mentioned Blake again and again.'

Nick thought back to his first meeting with Susan. 'When Susan Vidler came to visit me in Australia she told me that Cyril Blake had fought with the Nama against the Germans, but that was before anyone, presumably, even knew about Dr Kohl's manuscript, which to the best of my knowledge wasn't published. Who made the connection?'

'It was Susan who first mentioned Blake to me, in the context of him living in Upington and trading with the Nama. Blake used an alias, Edward Prestwich.'

Nick nodded. 'Yes.'

'Prestwich is actually in a couple of books on the history of Namibia and about the Nama and Herero wars. They both mention an Australian, Prestwich, who rode and fought with Jakob Morengo, and was assassinated on German orders.'

'So who worked out that Prestwich was, in fact, Blake?'

'Susan, I think, or perhaps this Scott Dillon she worked for who is fascinated by the Boer War. There is a book about an irregular unit that your Blake was part of ...'

'*Steinaecker's Horsemen*. I've got it.'

'Exactly. If you look in the back of the book there is a list of all the men who served in the unit and what happened to them. Edward Prestwich died of malaria at Komatipoort in 1902, the day the war ended, and the same day Blake and Claire Martin slipped across the border from South Africa into Portuguese East Africa. Susan or Scott Dillon must have noticed a mention of Prestwich in the book about Steinaecker's Horse and put two and two together.'

'And they came up with the right answer.' Nick finished his beer.

'Yes. Dr Kohl's manuscript confirms the theory. What we don't yet know is if there will be more clues to where the gold might have been hidden, assuming no one found it before Claire Martin died at sea. Now, I need to have a look at Scott Dillon online – I charged my iPad in the Land Rover.'

Nick looked on as she typed Dillon's name into her web browser. The same links and images that he had seen came up.

Anja nodded. 'Yes, it's him.'

'Then we need to confront him. Are you up for that?' Nick asked.

'I am. If he is the man who arranged for me to be attacked, I want to face him.' Anja went back to translating the manuscript on her iPad. Nick's mind churned with thoughts of Susan and the gnawing worry that she might have befriended him merely to gain his trust and spy on him. But what, he wondered, had happened when she went back to Cape Town?

He felt restless, impatient to hear the rest of Dr Kohl's story. If Scott Dillon was indeed after Claire Martin's stash of Kruger's gold, then they would have to work fast.

From Kohl's manuscript and Anja's research they knew Claire had died young, around the same time as Blake, and that she'd had some of her hoard stolen by Jakob Morengo's men just a few months before. There was also a reference to a missing cache of her gold somewhere near Lüderitz, where she had drowned at sea.

Anja looked up from the device. 'I've just worked out how the Cape police knew Blake's real identity, I mean, that he wasn't Edward Prestwich.'

'How?' Nick asked.

'Your great-great-uncle was an amateur photographer.'

CHAPTER 39

The Karasberge, German South West Africa, 1906

'What are you looking at?' the Schutztruppe guard asked Liesl in German.

Liesl rolled over in the sand, onto her belly, but she felt the man's fingers on her forearm, biting into her flesh. She was fluent in German and despite his order she was not going to let him see what she had been looking at.

'Let me see.'

She tried to resist, but her hands were tied together with rope and her ankles were manacled and chained to the wheel of a wagon. She had no blanket, no cover against the elements, and Liesl thought she was the coldest she had ever been – until then.

The soldier grabbed a handful of her hair, wrenched her head back, and forced her to roll over. He set down his rifle and his hands roamed over her breasts, under her jacket and between her thighs. She tried to scream but he put a palm over her mouth and drew his bayonet, holding the blade against her neck.

'If you scream I will kill you.'

She blinked away tears and he found the photograph.

'A white man?'

She sneered at his outrage and the guard slapped her face and spat on her.

*

For three days Blake rode at Jakob Morengo's side as the Black Napoleon drew von Deimling's forces deeper into the eastern Karasberge, teasing them with occasional glimpses of his men on ridge tops, infuriating them with the odd volley of fire and a casualty here and there.

Blake chafed at the rebel leader's insistence that they stick to the plan, and that did not involve Blake riding off on a solo mission to rescue Liesl from the Germans.

'Will we go for her today?' Blake asked Morengo on the dawn of the fourth day as they paused at a place where water had pooled in a shaded chasm, to allow their horses to drink and the men to refill their water bottles.

'Now we leave the Germans and we circle around them and position ourselves on the road to Keetmanshoop,' Jakob said as he broke off half a stick of biltong and handed it to Blake.

Blake took the salty dried gemsbok and chewed on it. 'What makes you think they're ready to turn back?'

'They have wounded, and their supplies are limited. The German commander will want to return and report a victory, that he has routed us and our remnants have fled their military might. He knows he won't catch me or my people in these mountains.'

'You seem sure.'

Morengo shrugged. 'There is no such thing as surety in warfare, you should know that.'

Blake nodded.

'And,' Morengo continued, 'you should know I could not allow you to risk capture by heading off on your own after Liesl. I know the Germans. They would not risk sending their doctor and their wounded back to Keetmanshoop alone, or with a light escort, but nor can the Schutztruppen live out here indefinitely. This is a good plan that you and I hatched together, Blake; you must stay the course. Liesl is of my blood and I care for her as well.'

Blake knew Morengo was right, and the fact that he had not ridden off in hot pursuit of Liesl either did not mean that Jakob cared less for his niece than Blake thought. Morengo had not earned his German nickname by being an impetuous romantic.

They rode hard all that day, down out of the rocky hills onto the flat desert, skirting the range and looping north and westwards. By late afternoon they could see an orange dust cloud hanging long and low in the distance, backlit by the setting sun.

Jakob called a halt and the Nama settled in between low dunes covered with scrubby, hardy grass. The night passed slowly, the temperature below freezing as men and horses huddled close to each other for warmth. The fighters could not afford to make a fire as the flames would have been easily seen by German pickets. Blake saw the warm glow of campfires on the horizon and envied his enemies.

He lay on his back, his horse blanket pulled up over his nose, and looked up at the night sky ablaze with stars. There was so much beauty in this place, and the same infinite supply of bloodshed and sadness. All the same, his heart had been captured by this wide open land despite, or perhaps because of its attendant danger.

Liesl was out there, hopefully still alive and inviolate, and if she had the courage to fight for her people and their freedom then it was not for him to run away. He cared for her, but he found his thoughts returning to the red-haired woman who had been seen in Upington between his forays in and out of the desert.

What if it was Claire?

He had guessed she might return to German South West Africa, where she had spent time before heading to South Africa. She would have a hard time getting a wagon load of gold into some European port, he imagined, but she was well connected in Germany's African colony and would have had connections on the docks thanks to her first husband, who had run a shipping company. He was sure she could have smuggled old Paul's treasure into Lüderitz Bay by greasing the right palms.

It was ironic, he thought, that at some point when the fighting died down Jakob would pay him for the horses, guns and ammunition, with gold Blake may have helped steal.

There was a squeak of feet on sand behind his head and Blake rolled over, shrugging off the blanket, his finger already on the trigger of the Lee Enfield. He'd learned in his war against the Boers that a rifle could seize up from frost on the open veld and sleeping with your weapon meant it was warm and ready.

'It's me,' Jakob whispered.

'Are we moving?' Blake asked.

'No,' said the rebel leader. 'I wanted to talk.'

Blake set his rifle down. 'What about?'

'Liesl.'

'I hope she's still alive,' Blake said.

'So do I. You care for her.' It wasn't a question and Blake didn't answer, so Jakob carried on. 'As do I. We will find her, at the rear of the column, and if we can, we will rescue her. But if she is chained to a wagon, we will not take the time to break her bonds while the Germans regroup. Do you understand?'

'Yes,' Blake said.

'Do you understand that I cannot jeopardise the lives of the majority for the sake of one person?'

Blake looked into those eyes, as cold as the night air. 'I do.'

'Then you will not take part in the morning's attack on the column.'

'What?' Blake was taken aback.

'You are a good shot, Blake, you proved that in the mountains. However, I cannot let the Germans see that a white man is riding with me. Von Deimling will take casualties, maybe lose some wagons and supplies to us, but if he sees you he will be duty-bound to report a foreigner fighting with the Nama. The Germans will come for you, and for me, instead of returning to lick their wounds in Keetmanshoop and claiming a false victory.'

Blake bridled. He knew Jakob wanted him out of sight not just because of the colour of his skin, but because he was worried he might do something foolish in order to rescue Liesl. 'Do you want me to leave?'

'No. I want you to find a high spot, in the dunes, and cover us when we raid the wagons.'

Blake let out a long breath. 'All right.'

The Nama broke camp an hour before dawn and circled around the Germans, who would take some time to get on the move. The rebels took up ambush positions two kilometres further on, in the direction of Keetmanshoop, hidden in the dunes.

Jakob waited until the column had moved past them. Blake lay next to him, just below the crest of a dune. 'The sand is soft here,' Jakob said.

Blake looked through his binoculars. He could see a German wagon driver at the end of the column savagely whipping his oxen. The supply wagons, still laden with enough food and ammunition for the long drive back, and burdened with artillery shells that had found no use, were making hard work of the soft surface. As usual, Jakob had enlisted the help of the land he lived in, and knew so well, in his fight against the enemy.

'The escorts are moving out,' Blake said. The German commander, von Deimling, probably realising progress would be slow on this section, had been smart enough to issue orders for small parties of Schutztruppen to range out to the flanks in search of any rebels who might be lying in wait.

'Yes,' Jakob said. 'I sent two men ahead, and off to the right of the column. They should make themselves known some time soon.'

Blake was impressed. Jakob was a step ahead of the enemy, as always. He had let the entire column get past them, knowing that the Germans would not send their flankers out until they were already on the move, and now he had given them some bait.

Sure enough, they soon heard shots fired to the right of the column, and the Schutztruppen on horseback galloped off in pursuit of the two Nama who had just opened fire. The Germans who had been scouring the left flank cut through the column and joined their comrades on the right in pursuit of the pair of rebels who had set up the diversion.

'Hendrik and Johan are two of my best men, on our fastest horses. The Germans will not catch them,' Jakob said, smiling. He started to get up. 'It is time. If Liesl is alive, I will find her and do my best to rescue her.'

Blake gave a reluctant nod. 'I'll move abreast of the wagons.' He got up, slung his rifle and mounted his horse. Moving between the dunes, Blake allowed Bluey to gallop, then pulled him up within easy shot of the rearmost wagons. He dismounted, scaled the loose slope and set himself up with a sniper's view of the floundering column below.

Jakob and his band mounted up, galloped over the crest of the dune and descended on the struggling wagons like vultures swooping down on a dying beast. Through his binoculars Blake could see that the wagon masters hadn't spotted the dust cloud rising up like a gathering storm, and had no idea of the hell approaching them from behind.

The need for the Germans on the left flank to join their comrades on the right in pursuit of Hendrik and Johan had cut the column in two, and five supply wagons at the rear, those that had to wait for the Schutztruppen to pass in front of them, were now lagging even further behind. These were Jakob's target.

Blake sighted down the barrel of his Lee Enfield, and with the practised ease and weary resignation of a blacksmith pounding a horseshoe or a clerk scratching in a ledger he worked the rifle's bolt and took up the slack on the trigger.

The driver of the last wagon was the first to turn his head, perhaps on hearing the muffled yet insistent beat of hooves digging sand. It was the last gesture of the man's life. Blake's bullet took him from his seat and the oxen, momentarily spared the lash, slowed to a stop.

By the time the soldier sitting next to the fallen man realised what was happening, and tried to scrabble for his rifle, Jakob Morengo was galloping abreast of him, pistol drawn, and he shot the German through the head.

One after the other the gaggle of wagons was overtaken and the soldiers on board dispatched.

From his grandstand position Blake saw even more evidence of the Black Napoleon's tactical genius. While these tail-end supply wagons had been struggling through soft sand, made even harder to negotiate by the fact that the rest of the column had already churned it, Blake could now see that the ground ahead quickly changed to a hard-packed rocky surface. Because of this, the horses and wagons that had already passed through the sandy patch had picked up speed and were throwing up a dust cloud that obscured their view of those behind them. Hendrik and Johan's fire had spurred the rest of the train onwards at a gallop. As a result, the last five wagons were now half a kilometre behind.

Some of Morengo's men had dismounted and were ransacking the wagons, cutting ropes and pulling off tarpaulins, unloading boxes and prising them open.

A wagon driver, wounded and mistaken for dead, got to his feet and found his rifle lying nearby. Shielded by a team of oxen he brushed the sand from his weapon and chambered a round. He was beginning to take aim at a Nama when Blake killed him with a shot through the chest.

Blake watched for other targets. One of Morengo's men struck a flint and lit some desert grass. He touched the burning embers to some papers and held them, in turn, to a tarpaulin, and soon the first of the five looted wagons was burning.

The third-last wagon had a canvas cover. A rebel climbed up into the back of it and a knife blade appeared from inside, slashing open the cover. Two other men outside started ripping away the fabric, exposing what was inside.

People.

Blake set down his rifle and took up his binoculars. As the canopy came off he could see four or five men lying inside, blood-stained bandages showing they were wounded Schutztruppen, lying on stretchers. A soldier with a red cross armband stood and held up his hands.

The Nama fighter who had climbed into the wagon shot him.

Blake felt the bile rise in his chest. War was war, and no matter how right or wrong the cause, conflict brought forth both devils and angels. He closed his eyes for a second, but when he opened them he regretted having done so. The Nama on the back of the wagon swung his rifle around, pointed it down and shot a wounded German. Methodically, the man chambered another round, took aim again and killed another man on a stretcher. He carried on until he was out of helpless targets, then clambered over some boxes to get to the front of the wagon, where both he and Blake had just glimpsed movement.

Half-a-dozen mounted Schutztruppen, perhaps realising the col-umn had been severed and worrying about the wagons at the rear, had wheeled around and were emerging from the dust cloud and bearing down on the rebels, most of whom were on foot and therefore easy prey.

A Nama man was shot dead before he could pick up his rifle from where it rested against a wagon.

Jakob Morengo, identifiable from his broad-brimmed black hat and suit, climbed onto his horse. Blake could see he was holding something, like a stick, in his hand. He rode up to one of his men who had just set fire to a wagon. The man passed Jakob a burning scrap of canvas. Blake didn't know what the kaptein was up to and didn't care for now, as he had targets.

Blake fired once at a rider, missed him, worked the Lee Enfield's bolt and sent the man falling from his saddle with his second shot. He searched for another rider, but the five remaining Schutztruppen were among the rebels and it was difficult for Blake to get a clear shot at them.

He looked to the wagon, where the rebel had shot the medic. The same man was now firing at a German, but the trooper, firing from horseback, executed his revenge on the Nama, who fell among his victims. The rider carried on, searching for more rebels, but a figure stood up at the front of the formerly covered wagon; it was the person Blake and the executioner had both caught a glimpse of. Though she was wearing pants and a man's top, Blake could tell immediately it was Liesl.

Blake stood, slung his rifle, jumped on his horse and thundered down the slope of the dune he'd been lying on. He rode hard towards the wagons.

*

Liesl had crawled to the far end of the wagon. 'Don't shoot me, I'm Nama,' she cried in Afrikaans.

However, when she peeked around a box of medical supplies she saw that the man who had shot the medic and the prisoners, Frans, was no longer there. She looked over the side and saw Frans' body lying in the sand but, she noticed, he had dropped his rifle on the wagon's floor. Liesl crawled as close to the weapon as the chain tethering her would allow and, stretching her body over the boxes of supplies, she was just able to grab it by the sling. She pulled the rifle to her, turned it in her hands and placed the tip of the barrel against one of the links of the chain that had hobbled her ankles. She bent over, holding her shoulder against the butt, and pulled the trigger. The recoil knocked her backwards, but the chain broke. With her next shot she severed the chain that linked her to the wagon.

Liesl crawled to the dead medic and took a knife from a sheath on the man's belt. Gripping the handle between her knees she sawed through the rope binding her wrists. As she worked she couldn't help but see the lifeless eyes of the non-combatant, and the dead soldiers. As much as she hated the Schutztruppen she had been shocked by what Frans had done. His family had been captured by the Germans so she could only guess that he had slaughtered the wounded in revenge. *What have we become?* She felt sick.

Gunfire raged around her and men cried in pain and anger. Finally, Liesl's hands were freed and she clambered to the front of the wagon. As horrific as the dead bodies were, she realised there were plenty of supplies here they could use. She rolled the dead driver from his seat and snatched up the reins of the bellowing ox team in one hand and the whip in the other. She cracked it in the air and the beasts, probably eager to get away from the tumult, turned to her command and set off.

A man in a big black hat galloped past and tossed a stick of dynamite into the bed of the wagon in front of her. He wheeled back and, brandishing a pistol, galloped across her front. 'Uncle Jakob!'

He lowered his pistol and waved his hand vigorously at her. 'Get down!'

Another German came riding out of the disappearing dust cloud in front of them; it seemed the rest of the column had all but forgotten the stranded wagons. It was the blond-haired doctor in the Landespolizei uniform, the one who had captured her and she had later seen treating the wounded men. He, too, was brandishing a pistol and he fired at Jakob.

The oxen had almost completed their turn. The doctor came up to the rear of the wagon, reined in his horse, jumped down from his saddle then climbed up onto the back of the slow-moving cart. He looked down at the men he had treated, all of whom were dead. '*Mein Gott.*'

Liesl dropped the whip and picked up Frans' rifle.

The German pointed his pistol at her. 'You ... you killed these men in cold blood.'

The wagon swayed as the oxen completed their turn and picked up pace. The doctor looked down at the dead men again, his face ashen. Liesl brought the rifle up as far as her hip and pulled the trigger. Nothing happened.

The doctor stared at her again and pointed his pistol at her once more.

'No!' Liesl cried. 'I didn't. Don't shoot me.'

'You are Morengo's niece. I heard you calling before.'

Liesl saw another horseman from the corner of her eye, but forced herself not to look at the man, who was galloping towards the wagon, out of sight of the doctor. As the horseman gained on them she saw it was Blake.

The doctor glared at her; his blue eyes, which should have been beautiful, looked frozen. 'You murderess. You are coming with me.'

Blake rode up alongside the wagon and before the doctor could register and turn to check the noise behind him, Blake had leapt from his still-moving horse onto the wagon. He careened into the German, knocking him down and onto the corpses. The doctor shrieked. He started to get up and Blake punched him in the jaw, sending him falling backwards. Blake looked over his shoulder. There were more Schutztruppen heading their way and the rebels were fleeing.

'This wagon's too slow.' Blake whistled to his horse.

The German doctor lay among his dead patients, seemingly unconscious.

'Don't shoot him,' Liesl said, 'he's a doctor.'

'I don't do that sort of thing.' Blake's horse trotted up beside them. He held out his hand to her but she hesitated. 'Come on. Let's get the hell out of here. I'll take you away from all this, back to Upington.'

Liesl had begun to reach out her hand when the wagon in front them, full of artillery ammunition, exploded.

CHAPTER 40

After their lunch at the Schützenhaus Nick and Anja drove to the Klein-Aus Vista Lodge's Desert Horse Inn and Nick booked himself into a chalet as well.

Dusk brought a chill to the air and as tempting as it was for Nick to stay under his hot shower, he hurried, wanting to catch up with Anja, who had been carrying on with the translation in her room during the afternoon. He got out, dried himself, and dressed in jeans, shirt, hiking boots and a rugby jersey. He put his fleece on over the top. He was glad he'd brought it with him, even though when he'd hastily packed in Australia he had asked himself why he was bothering bringing cold weather gear.

He remembered. Susan had told him to.

Thinking of her brought up a surge of grief as he went out into the cold. He swallowed hard. Instead of going straight to Anja's chalet he detoured via the lodge bar and bought a bottle of red wine. He walked under a cold clear sky, already showing a tantalising sprinkling of stars.

The manuscript was proving to be a treasure map that might yet lead them – and Scott Dillon – to whatever was left of Kruger's gold. Peter Kohl's story had already hinted at several locations where Claire had buried her stolen booty, on her three farms and somewhere in or near the port of Lüderitz.

They knew now, sadly, that Blake and Claire Martin had died within days of each other. Was that a coincidence? Did it mean some of the gold was still missing, unspent by Claire, or would Peter Kohl end his tale by telling them that he had squandered his late wife's fortune on wine and women? Nick was impatient to learn the truth, and was ready to work through the night to find out, but it was Anja who was doing the translation. While he had agreed to her request to let her work in private for a few hours, they both needed to eat.

His phone rang, a call from a private number.

'It's Joanne Dillon,' said the woman's voice on the other end of the call when he answered.

'Hello. Good to hear from you.'

'I've found out where Scott is,' said Joanne without preamble. 'I spoke to a friend of his, one I'm still, shall we say, close to.'

'OK. Where is he?' Nick asked.

'Lüderitz. He should be there for a few days, I'm told. He's staying in the Lüderitz Nest Hotel. Where are you now?'

'Aus,' Nick said.

'You're not far from Lüderitz, only about a hundred and twenty kilometres. What's your plan?' she asked.

'To be honest, I'm winging it.'

There was a pause. 'If you meet him, Nick, make sure it's in public, with lots of people around, not on your own out in the desert.'

'You think he's that much of a threat?'

'He's after whatever you've got, and he's getting closer to you by the sound of it. Maybe he knows more than you do?'

'That's possible,' Nick conceded. 'Tell me, does Scott speak German?'

'No; at least he didn't when we were married. He does have some buddies in Namibia. He's got a past that he doesn't talk about too much. He served in Koevoet – it means "crowbar" in Afrikaans – an elite police anti-terrorist unit during Namibia's independence war. There were quite a few German Namibians in the unit.'

'So he was a policeman?'

'Koevoet was more a paramilitary unit. They were ruthless guys, Nick, and not even Scott, who was a blowhard, would talk about all the things he must have seen and done. They were killers, and membership of this unit is not something a wealthy property developer would boast of publicly – if he did many people would not want to deal with him.'

Nick had wondered if a real-estate mogul would really get involved with the murky world of muggers and hit men, but now that he knew a little more about Scott Dillon it didn't seem so far-fetched.

'Are you going to meet him?' Joanne persisted.

'Yes.'

'Then let me come with you,' Joanne said. 'I can be in Namibia tomorrow.'

'I don't know ...'

'If he's on the trail of a hoard of gold, I want to make sure I get what's owing to me,' she said. 'Also, he's not going to try and kill you or have you beaten up if he sees me by your side. There would be no way he could cover up his involvement if anything happened to me.'

'That's very brave of you, Joanne, but ...'

'To hell with brave. I just want my money, and if that bastard thinks he can get rich quick by finding buried treasure and then just take off to Buenos Aires or somewhere, he's got another think coming.'

'I don't suppose I can stop you,' Nick said.

'You can't. I'll be in Lüderitz tomorrow. There's a restaurant called Essenzeit; I'll see you there for dinner tomorrow night and we can talk through our options.'

Joanne ended the call. Nick continued on to Anja's chalet, knocked on her door and she opened it. She had a towel turban on her head and he could smell bolognese in a saucepan on the two-burner hob in the kitchenette.

'We're going to Lüderitz tomorrow,' he said. 'Scott Dillon's wife just phoned me. Scott's there.'

Anja nodded to her iPad on her bed. 'I'm not surprised. That's where the people in Dr Kohl's story are headed, too.'

'Really?'

'Yes. I wonder how much further ahead Dillon is in the manuscript?'

'Joanne says he has some old army buddies here of German descent. They were in a unit called Crowbar or something together.'

'Koevoet.' Anja gave a low whistle. 'Those guys were super-efficient.'

'I heard that, as well.'

'He would know plenty of guys who wouldn't be afraid to rob and mug people, or even kill, for money.'

Nick told Anja about Joanne's planned trip to Namibia.

'I guess if this is some kind of showdown, then having another witness won't hurt,' Anja said. 'You can drain the spaghetti, please.'

He readied the pasta and he and Anja served up.

Anja gestured with her fork towards the iPad. 'I will tell you what I have learned.'

CHAPTER 41

German South West Africa, 1906

Blake came to as the last warmth of the day was being swallowed by the cold desert night. Bluey nuzzled him.

He reached up and touched the animal's muzzle. Blake looked around, and the simple action of turning his head sent jolts of pain through his skull. He was alone, just him and Bluey.

Blake stood, also painful, and dusted himself down. He carefully touched his forehead and felt a sticky wound and a round bump. One side of his face, he realised, was covered in dried blood, as was the collar and top of his shirt and jacket.

Liesl was gone. He closed his eyes and tried to remember what had happened. After the explosion had knocked him off the wagon he had come to for a few seconds, he guessed, because he had a memory of the German doctor grabbing Liesl, throwing her across his horse and galloping away. After that Blake had passed out again.

Blake found his hat and his Lee Enfield and got up on Bluey. In the distance was the wagon on which Liesl had been held, with its silent cargo of dead soldiers. The oxen, startled to a stampede by the explosion, had come to rest five hundred yards away, where they were nibbling on some tufts of dry desert grass.

He nudged Bluey gently in the ribs and headed to the wagon. The oxen bellowed, but seemed to lack the energy to flee, so Blake dismounted and climbed up on the wagon. He checked the dead men, by now covered in flies, and found one whose uniform was reasonably unbloodied. He undertook the grisly business of stripping the man as quickly as he could, then put on the dead German's clothes. He bundled his own and tied them to his horse's saddle.

Blake rode off, hoping someone, either the Germans or the rebels, would come for the oxen, and headed towards Keetmanshoop.

He rode through the night and caught up with the column just before dawn, when he could see their watch-fires burning on the horizon. Blake found a place to tether the horse, unbuckled his bedroll and lay down. Within minutes he was asleep.

After two hours he woke with the sun. It wasn't enough sleep, but he was charged with the thought of what might be awaiting Liesl. He needed to get close enough to the column to see how and where she was being transported.

Through the morning he tracked them, knowing that with each step they were getting closer to the German stronghold at Keetmanshoop. Would they keep her there, he wondered, or take her to the Shark Island camp on the coast?

Occasionally there was a sign of settlement, a modest farmhouse or a telltale plume of smoke from a far-off chimney. Blake kept an eye out for resourceful outriders who might double back to check if the column was being tailed, but even with the knowledge of Morengo's successful ambush fresh in their minds the Germans behaved like most soldiers getting closer to base; they dropped their guard. Blake knew this part of South West Africa reasonably well as he had roamed close to Keetmanshoop, and towards the Rietfontein border post further north with his horse and cattle trading.

Blake was able to keep the force in sight by its dust cloud, which also obscured him from anyone who might look over their shoulder. That was, at least, until the lone horseman left the column.

Blake wheeled Bluey to the right and galloped away off the pounded trail into some low dunes covered with scrubby grass. Taking out his binoculars, he dismounted between two sandhills and crawled on his belly to the crest of the one closest to the column.

The rider wore the uniform of the Landespolizei, and Blake had seen only one man in the column dressed like this, the same one who had taken Liesl. He was alone, now, and Blake followed his progress through the glasses along what he now saw was a rough track that led to a stand of trees. In between the foliage, green from a spring or well, he caught glimpses of whitewash. When the man had disappeared Blake climbed up on Bluey and took his own circuitous route to the farmhouse through the desert.

He had it in mind that he might take the man prisoner. As a part-time officer he might break more quickly and easily than a professional soldier, Blake thought. He would find out what had happened to Liesl. If they had killed her, the same way they had dispatched civilians in cold blood in Morengo's *kraal*, he might exact some measure of revenge on the man. His stomach had turned at the sight of the slaughtered German soldiers in the wagon, but now his own blood lust was simmering.

Blake dismounted away from the farmhouse and crept forward.

*

Claire saw the rider a long way off. She took the Mauser down from the wall and chambered a round.

It wasn't long before she recognised Peter's horse and his distinctive solid build. Even though she knew it was him she didn't feel she could completely relax. She kept the rifle in her hands as she walked out onto the *stoep* to meet him.

Normally he would have leapt from the horse and come running, but instead he slid wearily off the animal. He took two heavy steps then hung his head.

Claire walked towards him, looking around as she did so. A trio of gemsbok, oryx as they were also known, took flight in the distance. It could be a predator lurking, she thought. When she reached him she took his horse's reins from his hands. He stared at her, and there was no trace of his trademark grin. His eyes looked beyond her, into the distance. Claire tethered the horse to a post. She put a hand on his arm.

'Let's get you inside.'

He blinked, not seeming to hear her. When he looked at her he screwed his eyes, as if he was having trouble focusing. 'Claire. It was …'

She gave a small nod and hooked her arm through his. 'War.'

'No, a butchery.'

She led him to the house and in through the kitchen. She had just lit a fire in the stove and he stood there, watching the flames.

'Innocents,' he said.

She rubbed his broad back with her palm. 'I'll get some coffee on.'

She prepared the pot, then went into the lounge room and took a bottle of schnapps from the carved wooden bar. Back in the kitchen Peter was still staring at the little fire through the open door of the cooker. She poured a glass and handed it to him.

His eyes were red.

'She – someone – shot our wounded, murdered them in cold blood.'

That didn't sound like Morengo's style, she thought, but said nothing. Good commanders led by example, but it still didn't stop individual men from giving in to the devil within. But a woman? 'She?'

'Morengo's niece, a … young … thing. I found her on a wagon the rebels had taken from us. She had a rifle and there were five dead soldiers lying at her feet, all men who I had treated, who probably would have lived. The blood, Claire …'

She nodded. 'It won't help their cause, an act like that. Von Deimling will make sure the whole of Germany hears about it and the natives will be doubly damned.'

Peter shook his head. 'You don't understand, Claire. We … we are just as bad. Von Deimling ordered the mountain guns to open fire on Morengo's *kraal*, knowing there were only women and children and old people there. I watched men drag women from the huts and shoot them in cold blood.'

She put her arms around him and ran her fingers through his curly hair. Then she drew his face to her breast, where his tears soaked her dress. At least, she thought, he could cry. He was a doctor, a good man, despite his weaknesses. She shouldn't have married him, but part of her did still love him, in an inconvenient way. He sniffed.

When he lifted his head she gave him the drink and he downed the schnapps in one gulp. They sat and she poured him coffee and more of the liquor.

In time he composed himself and looked at her. 'There was a white man, riding with the Nama.'

A chill ran through Claire and she tried not to let it show. 'Really? That's odd. An Englishman?'

Peter shook his head. 'Von Deimling says he is Australian. The girl, Morengo's niece, was carrying a photograph of him. We have been warned about this man in the past. His name is Prestwich.'

Claire dropped her coffee cup and it shattered on the flagstone floor.

Peter jumped to his feet and reached for a cloth. 'Are you all right, Claire?'

'I'm fine. Silly me. I can't afford to be breaking perfectly good cups. It must have slipped from my fingers. You ... you never told me about this man before.'

Peter shrugged. 'Actually I should have told you about him. He's from Upington. The colonel says he's a cattle and horse thief who has traded with the rebels. He's furious that a white man is riding and fighting with the Nama. Maybe he has our cattle?'

Claire looked away from him, but he came to her. It was his turn to hold her. 'Are you all right? You look pale.'

'I'm fine, Peter, just tired is all.'

He took her in his arms, gently, and stopped her from fussing over the spilled coffee.

She wondered how long Peter had known the name of the man she had left behind in Portuguese East Africa. Claire had dared to think, dream perhaps, that the mysterious Australian in Upington might possibly be Blake, perhaps come to find her after all. And it was him. He was using the alias she had secured for him all those years ago.

'I don't know how much money we have, Claire,' Peter said, and she had to concentrate to hear his words, 'but I do know we have enough for a new coffee cup, for a hundred fine china sets, most likely. What's wrong? Has something happened while I've been away? I haven't even asked how you are, or what's been going on.'

'Nothing, nothing at all.'

The kitchen door burst open and a man in a bloodstained German military uniform stared at them, his eyes wide when he saw Claire. He pointed a rifle at Peter, who held up his hands.

Claire drew a breath.

It was him, after all these years.

*

Blake stared at her. Claire had cut her hair and her eyes were red, as though she'd been crying or was about to. She was dressed in men's riding clothes that accentuated rather than hid her figure.

The man in the Landespolizei uniform, who Liesl had said was a doctor, drew her closer to him and moved so he was protecting her. He said something in German.

She didn't scream out Blake's name or run to him or from him. Instead, she held his eye and gave a tiny shake of the head, as if telling him not to reveal that they knew each other. Blake's mind reeled. He owed this woman nothing, and yet his stomach was flipping and his heart pounding at the sight of her.

'You speak English?' Blake said to the doctor. His mind raced. Was this man her husband?

The man nodded.

'What's your name?' Blake asked.

'I am Dr Peter Kohl. You are the man who rode with the Nama rebels. I saw you, on the wagon, with my patients. You hit me.'

'Please don't hurt him,' Claire said to Blake, adding, 'whoever you are.'

His eyes still on Claire, Blake said, 'I won't hurt him or you if he does as he's told. You understand, Doctor?'

'Yes.'

'I want the girl, the one who was on the wagon when you arrived, just before the explosion,' Blake said. 'I want you to find out what they've got planned for her.'

Dr Kohl's hands turned into fists by his side. 'She murdered four wounded men.'

Blake shook his head. 'She did not. I was watching the attack. The man who did that was named Frans – one of your soldiers killed him. Justice was done, Doctor.'

'Nonsense, there were four wounded men lying helpless in that wagon. What that man did was unforgivable.'

'Like shelling and machine-gunning innocent women and children in their huts?' Blake countered.

'If I get caught,' Peter said, changing the subject, 'if the authorities suspect I am asking about her and she is then later freed, it will go badly for me.'

'If she goes to one of your camps,' Blake said, 'she'll be lucky to live.'

Peter braced himself, as though he was on a parade ground. 'I am sure she will be treated honourably.'

Blake tossed his head towards Claire, keeping the rifle trained on the doctor. 'If you want to see your wife again, you'll do as I say. Where are your people taking her?'

Peter seemed to vacillate so Blake raised the rifle and took aim between the German's eyes.

'The prisoners from Narudas will be kept at Keetmanshoop for now, but there are only the prison cells there. I don't know where she will be sent, or when.'

'Then you'd better find out,' Blake said. 'You have my word, nothing will happen to your wife – as long as you hold to your end of the deal.'

'I could return with a company of Schutztruppen. You would not stand a chance,' the doctor said.

'Correct, and neither would your wife here. It's up to you.'

'Peter, please listen to him,' Claire said in a beseeching tone, 'we have no choice.'

Blake bit his tongue. People always had choices. Claire could have stayed with him in Portuguese East Africa, or got word to him somehow when he was convalescing. Now, however, she was trying to get her husband to leave, so maybe she had something to say to him after all this time.

The doctor glared at her. 'You would have me betray my country for a young girl?'

Claire nodded. 'Yes. They've got no business seeing a child off to some camp. You said it yourself, Peter, there've been too many innocents slaughtered already.'

Blake suppressed a smile. *That* sounded like the Claire Martin he had known.

The doctor sighed.

'Get out of here,' Blake said. 'I'll be here, with your wife, until you get back. Just remember that.'

Peter squared up to him again. 'If you harm her in any way, or touch her, I will kill you.'

Blake nodded. 'Let's make this easy on all of us, sport. Just find out where they're taking the girl, and when. That's all I want to know. Then you can have your wife back.'

Peter went to Claire, and Blake didn't try to stop him. He kissed her and she gave him a hug.

'Off you go, now,' she said, 'I'll be fine.'

The doctor left, his face red with frustrated rage, and Blake watched through the window as he mounted his horse and galloped off.

Blake lowered his rifle. He was still recovering from the shock of seeing Claire and finding her here, of all places, four years after he had last seen her. He said the first thing that came into his mind: 'Why did you leave me?'

Claire put her hands on her hips. 'Why the hell didn't you follow me?'

What right did she have to be angry at him? 'Because I had no idea where you went. When I was fit enough I went to the docks and asked around and I worked a passage to Cape Town, but couldn't find any trace of where you'd gone to.'

Claire's shoulders sagged. 'The *note*, Blake?'

'What bloody note?'

'I left a letter with Dr Machado. He seemed a decent enough man. Did he not even give it to you?'

Blake shook his head and wanted to curse and yell over the twist fate had taken. 'He *was* a decent man, Claire. There was a fire at the hospital and Dr Machado was killed trying to rescue a patient. It was before I was fully conscious.'

Claire put a hand over her mouth. 'Oh no! The poor man. I left a message for you, Blake, telling you that Walters was on to me. I had to leave. He survived the lioness attack and –'

He nodded. 'I know. He's still alive. He's a colonel in charge of the Cape Mounted Police now, in South Africa.'

She took a step towards him. 'I said you should write to me care of the Lüderitz port offices, Blake.'

He had hardened his heart. They had only made love the once, he had told himself so many times over the years, and he had convinced himself that she had used him, merely to help her get to the gold and shift it. And all the while she had been hoping to hear from him.

'I waited,' Claire continued, 'for a year, and hoped you might come, but I thought you mustn't want to be with a thief after all. I wrote to Dr Machado and, of course, never heard back from him, so I assumed you'd read the note and torn it up in front of him. I met the German fellow, Peter. He's a good man, Blake, but ...'

The word hung between them. Did she not love the doctor who had just vowed to kill him if he harmed her? The news was still sinking in. 'You're married.'

'I am.' She sniffed and wiped the corner of her eye. 'Would you, Blake ... would you have come for me if you'd received the note I left with Machado?'

In a heartbeat, he thought. He would have dragged his still-wounded body onto the first ship bound for Lüderitz. However, it was all moot, because she was a respectable married woman now. Also, Claire had been a spy and a thief; as much as the sight of her stirred old passions the thought crossed his mind that the story about the note might have been just that, a fiction. 'Do you have children?'

'No. You didn't answer my question, Blake.'

He wanted to grab her and crush her to him and make love to her. He had felt hurt, then angry, then betrayed, and he had let the scar tissue harden his heart, but now he felt it trying to burst free from his chest. 'I would have come looking for my share of the gold.'

Her face hardened. 'Aye, well, I should have expected that. For your information, there's not much of it left that's readily accessible.

Some of it was recently stolen by the Nama and there's a sizeable stash hidden near Lüderitz. If ...'

'What?' He scowled at her. 'If I help you find it you'll give me a share?'

She came to him and for a moment he regretted his words, thinking she was going to throw her arms around him. Instead her hand shot out as fast as a black mamba striking its prey and she slapped his face. 'I saved your life, damn it.'

'That just made us even.'

She glared at him. 'I'll get you your gold, or at least what I can afford to give you.'

'Will your husband betray me?'

She shook her head. 'No, I don't think so. He's a good man and he cares for me, but he knows I don't love him enough, Blake. He sleeps around with floozies and I haven't gone out of my way to change his ways or give him children. He wasn't the man I wanted, Blake, he was the one I settled for.'

Blake mulled over her words and at the same time his eyes roved over her. She was as beautiful as ever.

'What are you going to do now, Blake? Rob me?'

'I've come for the girl, Liesl.'

'You and her ...?'

'It's the cause she loves, not me,' he said, and it was the truth.

They held each other's gaze, old passions, lusts and the missed opportunities of four years boiling inside them.

He took a deep breath to steady himself and his feelings. 'You're happy here, otherwise?'

'I wanted to start again, start a better world,' she said.

'And?'

'And instead I've ended up in another war,' she continued, 'where the rich have dispossessed the poor. As always, when the have-nots dare to rise up against the haves, they're slaughtered, just like in Ireland.'

Blake raised an eyebrow. 'You own three huge farms, don't you? Haven't you taken the best land from the Nama?'

'I *bought* it, and before this blooming war started I was building schools for the Nama, and Peter, for all his faults, was providing healthcare in the village clinics I'd started and learning about traditional healing from the bushmen. We were making progress.'

'Not fast enough for Jakob Morengo and the other Nama, it seems, who wanted their own land back, not just some charity from a farmer's wife. If your brave new world involves taking someone else's land, how does that make you any better than the British?'

She sighed. 'I don't know. I thought that all this land in South West Africa was so empty, compared to Ireland and Europe, that we could start again, have a place that was pure, with greater equality. I was told there was no one living out here, but there was, the Nama and the bushmen, and they're all worse off now.'

He could see the despair in her eyes. It seemed that neither Claire nor he could get away from war and killing. He couldn't tell her how easy it had been to slide back into a soldier's life.

Perhaps she missed it, as well.

She held a hand to her forehead. 'Oh, Blake, I'm so glad you found me.'

He took her in his arms and they fed off each other with their kisses. While Claire undid his belt buckle he hurriedly undid the buttons of her blouse, exposing those glorious pale breasts he had never quite forgotten. He suckled on her as she freed him and grabbed him. She was brazen, and he loved it. 'The bedroom ...'

'I can't wait, Blake.' Claire backed up against the heavy old timber kitchen table and slid up onto the smooth-worn surface.

'Your husband?'

Claire smiled. 'He'll be a few hours.'

Blake pulled off her riding boots, taking his time, revelling in the wanton look in her eyes, then slid down her breeches and her knickers. She was ready for him and he entered her, in one long fluid movement.

There was no need for more talk, not now, he thought. They had only lain with each other once, that night in the bush, but it had been unlike any other time he'd been with a woman. She clung to him, the pain of her fingers digging into his flesh only arousing him further. He leaned over her, kissing her deeply as he joined with her, as they erased the longing and the loss of the missed years with their bodies.

When they were done, out of breath, they went to her bed, un-dressed fully and got in. She lay on her side, facing him, and he traced her contour with his fingers, lingering on the swell of her hip above the thatch of red hair.

'It's like we were never apart,' he said.

She smiled. 'I was thinking the same thing.'

'Tell me, did you ever plan on going through with the deal, sell-ing guns to the Boers in exchange for the gold?'

She looked away, as if remembering. 'Maybe. If Nathaniel had lived and brought me the gold, I would have sold him the guns, probably, but he was having second thoughts himself.'

'Did the Afrikaners not come looking for their gold?'

Claire shook her head. 'Very few people other than Nathaniel knew the location of the gold. Hermanus' rogue commando got wind that Nathaniel and his American boys were escorting some gold and Hermanus ambushed them and killed them all except for Nathaniel and Christiaan, the loyal Afrikaner man who was at the trading post raid. Walters must have got a lead on Nathaniel from a Boer prisoner or some other source.'

'What do we do now, Claire?'

'I don't know,' she sighed. 'I came here looking for a paradise in the desert, an escape, but it was just a dream. Instead I've ended up in a war that's even worse than the one you fought in South Africa.'

'Come back to the Cape Colony with me, after I've found Liesl. I've been saving money, to brief a lawyer, to make a case against Walters.'

She smiled at him. 'Sure and you're the one dreaming, now, Blake. *If* you ever catch up with this girl and free her you'll have half the German army chasing you across the desert. Tell me ...'

'Yes?' he said.

'You and this girl ...'

'We were close once,' he said, and he felt her stiffen against him, 'but it's as I said, it's the cause she's devoted to, not me. She's too young, Claire, and she doesn't deserve to be worked to death or condemned to a slower end as a soldiers' whore.'

Claire seemed to accept his explanation and gave a little nod of understanding, then kissed him. She rolled over on top of him, flattening her breasts against his chest. He loved the feel of her, every inch of her pressed into him, yet she was no burden. He felt he could sleep like this, with her body giving him warmth against the chill desert night.

But she had other ideas. He opened his mouth to speak, but she put a finger to his lips as she drew herself up and straddled him. She leaned over him, her nipples brushing his chest, and he could feel her hand around him again, guiding him into her. She was even warmer there and they melded into one like two metals being poured into a crucible. Claire sat up, arching her back, and he covered her breasts with his hands as they moved against each other.

He looked at her, at her eyes half closed, her slightly crooked smile, and he felt he could stay like this, joined to her, for eternity. The pleasure rolled up like a wave's swell, created from deep within an ocean. The peak rose and he knew that if he could he would have frozen this moment, poised forever on the crest, weightless in the swell.

Claire crashed against him and cried out loud.

CHAPTER 42

Rietfontein, Cape Colony, near the border of German South West
Africa, 1906

The camel dropped to its front knees and Colonel Llewellyn
Walters gratefully and painfully dismounted. A coloured levy
took the cantankerous beast's reins and a white constable saluted.

Walters narrowed his eyes against the glare. Even by African
standards this was a godforsaken middle-of-nowhere place. The police post and lockup were made of brick and tin but the dozen or
so other dwellings were mean little places of mud and whatever
rubbish some trader had bothered bringing this far into the rocky
desert and abandoned. He'd been assaulted by the sun throughout
the journey and now the ground was trying to burn him from the
soles of his boots upwards.

The lioness had taken a good deal of muscle and tendon from
his right leg in 1902, and he suffered when he had to sit for extended periods. He had survived because he'd kept a cool head and
feigned death. The lioness that had attacked him was the biggest
in the pride and she had spent some time fighting off her sisters.
This had given Walters time to draw a knife that Hermanus' Boers
had missed, hidden inside his belt. When the lioness returned for
him she had clamped her jaws over his shoulder and dragged him,
between her forelegs, deep into the bush. When Walters was sure
they were away from the rest of the pride he had reached up under

her and stabbed her in the heart. Bleeding profusely he had managed to climb a tree, where he spent an agonising night out of reach of the other lions. When they lost interest, at daybreak, he had seen one of the dead Boers' ponies trotting down the nearby track and had called to it. The horse had come to him and he was able, with great difficulty, to get into the saddle and ride as far as the main railway line, where a patrol from Steinaecker's Horse had come upon him and taken him to Komatipoort. From there he was put on a British hospital ship, which had been moored in Delagoa Bay in neutral Portuguese East Africa. Seriously wounded British soldiers were taken there for surgery. Though far from recovered, when he had regained consciousness after being operated on he had thanked whatever force had landed him in the same port Claire Martin would no doubt be shipping her stolen gold from. Unfortunately, he narrowly missed her. Before he could board another ship for Cape Town his wounds became infected. He believed it was his sheer will to find the woman and the gold that had brought him through the fever.

His convalescence was long, but the story of his brush with the lion spread and Walters decided it would be to his advantage to stay in Africa. A fellow officer organised his posting to the Cape Mounted Police and he found his ability to sniff out and take over as many rackets as he broke up earned him money and higher rank. He spent his spare time investigating the whereabouts of the gold and his early queries ascertained that Sergeant Cyril Blake had died of malaria in Komatipoort at the war's end.

Claire Martin had disappeared, or reinvented herself somewhere. Walters had befriended the German consul in the Cape Colony and the man had made enquiries on his behalf – in repayment for a goodly number of cigars, women and bottles of the Cape's finest wines. It seemed the Germans had no record of Claire arriving in the Fatherland, and the consul's queries across the border in South West Africa had drawn blanks.

But now, four years on, he had two new leads.

Walters touched his giraffe's tail fly whisk to the peak of his pith helmet.

'Welcome to Rietfontein, sir.'

Hell, more like it, Walters thought to himself.

'You'll be wanting to freshen up, sir?' the constable continued.

'The understatement of the new century, constable,' Walters said, 'but where are the Germans?'

'Waiting, sir, at the border post. They sent word this morning that the German colonel, von Deimling, had only just arrived. We hear there's been quite a bit of fighting to the south, sir, at a place called Narudas. Von Deimling let the rest of his column carry on to Keetman-shoop, but he's ridden here to meet you. Perhaps you'd like to freshen up, let them cool their heels, sir? I could show you around, like.'

The constable seemed impressed, and so he should. Walters knew he wielded considerable power in the Cape, yet he was under no illusions that a German colonel would go too far out of his way to meet with the Cape Mounted Police if there wasn't something of importance to von Deimling as well. 'No. It's them I'm here to see.'

The constable looked ever so slightly crestfallen. 'Very well, sir. We can take a horse from here.'

Thank God, Walters thought. As tempting as the idea of a bath was, he was here on a mission, one that he had deemed worth the arduous journey from his comfortable digs in the Cape.

'It's just, that, well, sir ...'

'Out with it, Constable ...?'

'Laidlaw, sir, Malcolm Laidlaw. It's just that it's not every day we get the commandant of the Cape Mounted Police paying us a visit and if you'd like to see the station ...'

'I would not. Ready the horses, Laidlove.'

'Laid*law*, sir.'

'Hop to it, man.'

Walters fought a brief and losing battle with the flies and took a sip of warm water from his canteen while Constable Laidlaw fetched the horses.

The horse was marginally less uncomfortable than the lurching gait of the camel that had taken him over the longest and worst stretch of his journey to reach this, the remotest police outpost in the northwestern corner of the colony.

A mile down the track they found four Germans on horseback. A *Leutnant*, a lieutenant who introduced himself as Kurtz, saluted

Walters and welcomed him to German South West Africa. He was accompanied by an NCO and two Schutztruppen who gave curt nods and cool stares to Laidlaw.

Kurtz led him another mile into the desert where a small camp had been set up. An older man stepped out from under the awning of one of three canvas tents. He had a moustache modelled on the Kaiser's and iron-grey stubble on his head, which he covered with his cap as they approached. The riders all dismounted and the German officer stood.

'May I present Colonel Walters of the Cape Mounted Police, sir,' Lieutenant Kurtz said with a click of his heels.

'Colonel,' Walters said. The two men shook hands and von Deimling gave a sharp nod of his head.

'Welcome to German South West Africa, please take a seat.' Von Deimling gestured to a canvas and timber safari chair. 'A drink? Beer, wine, schnapps?'

'Water, please, if you have it,' Walters said.

Von Deimling spoke German to Lieutenant Kurtz, who then saluted and left, making for the next tent. Walters noticed Kurtz walked with a pronounced limp and von Deimling followed his gaze.

'My aide was wounded in action.'

'I must commend you on your English, Colonel,' Walters said. 'I picked up some Afrikaans during war, but I don't speak your language.'

'I trust your journey was not too arduous,' von Deimling said.

Walters eased himself, somewhat gratefully, into the low-slung chair and crossed his legs. A soldier handed him a glass of cool water, a balm for his lips, which were cracked from days of exposure to the sun and dry, hot wind. Lieutenant Kurtz had also returned, carrying a folder. He stood behind the colonel and if his wounded leg troubled him his posture or face did not betray it. 'My journey was fine, thank you.'

'Good. I will, as you would say, get to the point – I am eager to return to Keetmanshoop. As I said in my telegram to my superiors, which you received through diplomatic channels, there is a British subject serving with the Nama rebels.'

'Technically,' Walters set his glass down on a folding side table, 'the man is Australian and they seem to have taken matters of government somewhat into their own hands since becoming a federation, but, yes, the man in question is still a subject of the crown.'

'This man, Edward Prestwich,' von Deimling snapped a finger and Kurtz handed him the folder, 'took part in the battle at Narudas earlier this week. He subsequently was involved in an ambush of my forces who were returning to Keetmanshoop after a successful engagement with the rebel commander Jakob Morengo in the Karasberge. We inflicted serious casualties on the rebels.'

Yet they were still able to ambush you on the way home. Walters kept his thought to himself and simply smiled and nodded.

'Several wagons at the rear of our column were cut off. Three were destroyed but of more concern was the murder of four wounded German soldiers by the rebels. Prestwich was last seen by one of our officers standing on the back of the wagon where the murders took place.'

'You believe he was responsible?' Walters said.

Colonel von Deimling gave a small shrug. 'Of that I have no proof – I would hope that a white man would not stoop so low, but your colonial troops in your last war had a reputation for shooting prisoners of war, did they not?'

Walters pursed his lips. 'What else do you know about this man?'

'From our *sources*,' Von Deimling reclined in his chair and brought his fingers together, 'we know that this Prestwich is an Australian who served with the British Army in the war against the Boers in an irregular horse unit. He has been known to us for some time as a thief, trading in cattle stolen by the Hottentots, the Nama as they call themselves, and supplying horses and perhaps arms and ammunition to the rebels. It would be of assistance to German South West Africa if your police could perhaps exercise greater diligence in controlling the illegal trade in livestock back and forth across the border.'

Walters did not need some Hun telling him how to run his police force. Ordinarily he would have sent an underling to a meeting about some miscreant colonial scoundrel, but this case was of particular interest to him. A particularly diligent lieutenant on his staff, on receiving the cable from the foreign office, had shown great initiative by searching for the service record of Edward Lionel Prestwich. Two things leapt out from the briefing the lieutenant had prepared for him.

Firstly, Edward Prestwich had been a member of Steinaecker's Horse and he had died of malaria in 1902 at Komatipoort; secondly, when Walters had consulted his notes from that period he confirmed that Sergeant Cyril Blake had been reported as dead on that same day.

On top of all that, just two days ago Walters had received a routine report from a patrol officer when he passed through Upington which mentioned a red-headed European woman visiting the town in search of missing cattle some time earlier. Her name was Claire Kohl, wife of a German doctor-cum-farmer across the border.

There had been no sign of the alleged Prestwich in Upington, and no one seemed to know where he was or when he would be back, so Walters had come to Rietfontein to discuss the man with his German counterparts across the border. He also wanted information on the red-headed woman.

'What would you like me to do about this, Colonel?' Walters asked, punctuating his feigned disinterest with a swish of the giraffe's tail.

Von Deimling gave a tight smile. 'I am tempted to say your job, Colonel, but I do not wish to sound flippant or rude.'

Walters ignored the criticism. 'Naturally, the Cape Mounted Police take all allegations of illegal activity seriously and I am sure our government would take a dim view of a British subject, colonial or otherwise, acting as a gun runner or armed rebel.'

Von Deimling stroked his moustache. 'For my part, I have put a price of three thousand Marks on the head of this man, Prestwich. He seems to be overly sympathetic towards the natives. There are even reports of him cohabiting with a coloured girl in Upington from time to time. If this man was to brag of his exploits, perhaps spreading falsehoods of Morengo's successes around Upington, then he might sow the seeds of rebellion among your own native people. I'm sure the Cape Colony and your masters in England would not like to have to deal with the type of uprising and banditry that we are faced with.'

'Quite,' Walters said. 'I see you have a file.'

Von Deimling nodded. 'In the interests of international cooperation I would be pleased to share what we have with you, and in return perhaps you could give me some sort of assurance that I could pass on to my superiors.'

It was Walters' turn to negotiate. 'Perhaps you might be able to assist me with something?'

'Of course.' Von Deimling spread his hands wide. 'If it is in my power. I am but a humble soldier.'

'While you are concerned about an Australian entering your territory illegally, I have recently had reports of a woman, possibly of Irish or American descent, red hair, a farmer's wife I believe, crossing from your side of the border into the Cape Colony at Upington.'

Von Deimling brought his hands together again, on his chest. 'There would be very few women of that background in South West Africa. There are precious few women in colony still, in fact, and most of them come by ship from Germany.'

'So I've heard.'

'May I ask your interest in this woman?'

'It dates back to my time during the war against the Boers. I was involved in investigations then, much as I am now.'

Von Deimling broke into a wide smile, which was as pleasant and lifelike as dried skin stretched either side of a corpse's jaw. 'Come, come, Colonel, it's known to us that you were an officer in British military intelligence during the war. As that conflict is over and our two nations are not at war I'm sure we can be frank with each other, as one old soldier to another.'

Walters didn't return the smile. 'There was a woman I was investigating, a half-German half-Irish Fenian, the daughter of one of our own "rebels", named Claire Martin, who sympathised with the Boers. She had spent time in America and had also been infected with that country's moral lassitude. Miss Martin was, we believed, spying for your government and acting as an intermediary between a German arms manufacturer, her cousin, Fritz Krupp, and the Boers.'

Von Deimling looked impassive. 'The Imperial German Government had no involvement in your war with the simple farmers of South Africa, although it's no secret a number of our citizens felt so aggrieved by the treatment of the Boers that they fought alongside them – without official approval, of course.'

'Of course, and even if you knew of the lady's involvement in intelligence matters then I'm sure you wouldn't confide that you did.'

Von Deimling put a finger to his lips. 'There is a woman, a farmer's wife with red hair. I've seen her in the Schützenhaus, the marksmen's club in Keetmanshoop. I believe I did hear someone say that the woman was a foreigner.'

Walters raised his eyebrows. 'A humble farmer's wife?'

'Well, perhaps not so humble. If this red-headed woman is the Claire Martin you are looking for then her surname would now be Kohl as she is the wife of the town's doctor – one of my reservist officers. They have three farms, each quite large. They have sheep and cattle and breed horses for the *Kaiserreich*.'

'Three farms? Is that unusual?'

He spread his hands wide as if to encompass the nothingness around them. 'South West Africa is a land of great opportunity for hard-working Germans, and those who are drawn to our way of life and views. Many settlers from the old country, and quite a few from South Africa, have found prosperity here. Between you and me, though, I've heard it said that the doctor left a mound of debts and more than one broken heart back in Germany before he came here.'

'And in Africa he made enough money to buy three farms?'

Von Deimling shrugged. 'Perhaps the woman, this red-head you are so interested in, came from means? If I may be blunt, what is your interest in this woman, Colonel – your war has been over four years now?'

'She stole a good deal of money from the British Army – she was part of a gang that held up a payroll wagon that was under my supervision.' Walters relaxed into the story. Though it was a lie he had told it enough times to almost believe it himself. 'They got away with a hundred thousand pounds. The thieves were tracked down and ambushed by a detachment of my soldiers and whilst they killed the men involved the woman, Claire Martin, got away with the wagon. Apart from the fact that she stole a good deal of money from the crown, my career suffered as a result of the initial theft and my inability to get the funds back and bring her to justice.'

Von Deimling nodded. 'I can see why this is a matter of interest to you. But from what I know of Dr Kohl, it seems like she has spent your missing money.'

'That should not stop her from being investigated, I'm sure you would agree.'

'Perhaps,' von Deimling said, 'but the lady is now a subject of the Kaiser, living on German territory.'

Walters stroked his moustache. 'Just as Edward Prestwich is an Australian living, ostensibly, in the Cape Colony.'

'Touché, Colonel Walters.'

'Any more information you can provide about Frau Kohl, even a confirmation of her first name and maiden name, would be of great help to the Cape Mounted Police, Colonel, and very much appreciated.'

Von Deimling snapped his fingers. 'Kurtz?' The aide stepped forward and von Deimling asked him a question in German.

'Claire, Herr Oberst,' Kurtz replied.

Walters could barely contain himself.

Von Deimling at last passed him the file. 'That is the doctor's wife's Christian name, Claire.'

Walters fought to still his breathing. He opened the dossier and a face he recognised immediately stared back at him.

'One of my men found this picture in the possession of a coloured girl we captured at Narudas,' von Deimling said. 'She is a *friend* of the man, it seems, a whore most likely. Our doctor from Keetmanshoop, coincidentally the husband of the woman you are seeking, confirmed he saw this man during the battle, climbing onto one of our wagons just as another carrying ammunition exploded. The coloured woman was a prisoner, but she had managed to free herself. Prestwich was attempting to rescue her, but was blown from the wagon. Herr Doktor Kohl said he saw the white man crawling in the sand, injured but alive, as Kohl retreated with the coloured woman under his charge.'

Walters stared at the picture, willing his hands to stay still so as not to pique the German's interest. Walters' hunch was correct – Cyril Blake had switched identities with the late Edward Prestwich at Komatipoort – for the man staring back at him from the photograph was most certainly Claire Martin's partner in crime.

In the interests of fairness Walters told von Deimling that Prestwich was an alias and that the man the Germans were looking for was really Cyril Blake. Von Deimling beckoned to Kurtz and relayed the news to his aide – Walters caught the use of Blake's name.

'Some wine, now, Colonel?' von Deimling said.

Walters was lost in thought. The painful journey here had been worth it. Women were Blake's weakness and he had been trying to rescue his coloured lover. Was he also trying to find Claire Martin in South West Africa?

A lesser man might have been worried that Blake was alive, that he might try to expose Walters' deeds during the war. Perhaps the man was plotting his revenge – who knew? – but the fact was, Walters could use Blake to get to Claire Martin. If von Deimling kept an eye on the woman then Blake might fall into the Germans' hands, but Blake was canny and careful. If Walters could get a tail on Blake, someone he trusted, then Blake would lead him to the woman, and to the gold. Walters was sure now that Claire Kohl was, in fact, Claire Martin – the story of the penniless doctor and the red-haired foreigner being able to afford to buy a large chunk of German South West Africa told him that she had indeed made her way to that colony with a sizeable portion of Kruger's gold. The question was, how much of it was left, and how could he get his hands on it?

Von Deimling cleared his throat. 'Colonel?'

Walters looked up, realising his opposite number had asked him something, though he could not recall what.

'I asked if you are ready for some wine now?'

'Oh, yes, of course.'

'You look like you have just seen a ghost, as the English say.'

No, he thought, not a ghost, but a soon-to-be dead man and a woman he would make talk.

CHAPTER 43

South of Keetmanshoop, German South West Africa, 1906

They slept in each other's arms, but Blake woke before dawn, a soldier's habit, and washed himself and dressed. He made tea and woke Claire, who greeted him with a grin and a kiss.

'We need to be ready if your husband shows up,' he said, handing her the cup.

She gave a wave with her free hand. 'I don't care if he finds out. I still like him but it's been over between Peter and me for a long time, Blake. We live together out of convenience these days.'

'All the same, it's a complication we'd do best to avoid at the moment.'

Claire nodded and sipped.

They ate breakfast and Blake went outside to brush, feed and water his horse. He saw a dust plume on the horizon and fetched his rifle. It was one man, mounted. The doctor.

Peter rode up to his house, his face still marked with a scowl. 'Where is my wife?'

'Claire's inside.'

'Claire? She is a married woman and it is impertinent of you to use her Christian name. Please address her as Frau Kohl.'

Claire came up behind him. 'It's all right, Peter.'

The doctor looked to her and then to Blake, as if puzzled the Australian was not holding a gun to her head. His eyes narrowed as suspicion dawned.

'You ... know one another?'

Claire nodded. 'The truth of it is that we met in South Africa, Peter, during the war. Blake helped me when the British, one officer in particular, were after me.'

Peter frowned. 'Well, it seems another British officer is after you. I was talking to a young officer friend of mine, Kurtz. He told me to warn you that the Cape Mounted Police are looking for you. Von Deimling has made a deal with a British police colonel that he would provide information about an Australian riding with the Nama in return for information about, you, Claire.'

'Me?'

'Unless there is another red-headed Claire with an Irish-American accent in the colony. The British officer said you robbed a British military payroll shipment and that you killed British soldiers in cold blood. Is that where our money comes from, Claire?'

Claire's eyes met Blake's. It was a good enough cover story.

'This British colonel,' Claire said, 'did Kurtz by any chance give you his name, Peter?'

'Walters. Louis, or something like that.'

'Llewellyn,' said Blake and Claire in unison.

Peter looked at both of them. 'You know him.'

Blake nodded.

Peter addressed him: 'And von Deimling has put three thousand Marks on your head, the same bounty being offered for the capture or killing of Morengo. You are a very wanted man, Mr Blake.'

'The Germans know me as Blake?'

Peter nodded. 'Yes, this Colonel Walters has told von Deimling that Prestwich is an alias, your *nom de guerre*, as it were.'

'Shit,' Blake said.

'Why should I not inform on you, Mr Blake, and collect three thousand Marks? As you and my wife are ... acquainted ... it seems unlikely you will harm her.'

'That was my idea to drop the charade, Peter,' Claire said. 'I was going to be honest with you, whatever news you brought back. Do you know what's happening with the girl?'

'Yes,' Peter frowned. 'She is being taken to Lüderitz along with the other prisoners, to the Shark Island concentration camp.'

Claire went to her husband and took his hands in hers. 'Peter, this man, Walters, he's a criminal. He wants what I have, my fortune. I didn't rob a British payroll wagon, but nor did I inherit my money. Walters was a British intelligence officer, but what he really wanted was to get his hands on a share of Paul Kruger's gold, the wealth of the Boer republic.'

'You took Kruger's gold?' Peter looked incredulous.

Claire nodded. 'Some of it.'

Peter closed his eyes for a few seconds, then opened them. 'So you are a thief.'

'Well, in a manner of speaking, yes, though I prefer to think of it as spoils of war. Peter, Walters set Blake up, and he murdered a man who was my contact with the Boers, an American. He was ... a good friend, and Walters tortured and shot him to try and find out the location of the gold.'

'And this man, this American, just gave you the location of the gold?'

'Yes.'

'Why?' Peter asked.

Claire blushed.

Peter looked away from her.

'Come now, Peter, don't play the high and mighty aggrieved husband with me, learning about your wife's sordid past. We both know what you've been up to, and in all honesty it actually feels quite good to tell the truth about this. You might try it yourself some time.'

Peter looked back at her, slightly shamefaced, then to Blake. 'And this one, Claire?'

Blake stepped up to him. 'I'm searching for the woman who was taken by your people. She's who I'm after, not your wife, Doctor.'

Blake and Peter both turned to Claire, who frowned. Blake was pleased she didn't carry on with her new-found openness and tell Peter all of what had happened. He sensed the doctor had probably guessed, but did not want to hear it spelled out for him.

'There is nothing we can do for her,' Peter said. 'She and five other prisoners will be taken under escort to the Shark Island camp.'

'Who are the other prisoners?' Blake asked.

Peter looked sheepish. 'Three old women and two children, a boy and a girl.'

Blake shook his head. It was like South Africa all over again; rounding up the women and the children to deprive the foe of their families and support. It sickened him. 'I'm going to get her, Claire.'

'You won't change your mind, and slip back across the border?' she said.

'And leave you again, knowing Walters is after you? No.'

'Then I'll come with you,' Claire said.

Peter's face turned red. 'You will not, woman!'

Claire bristled. 'Don't you be calling me "woman", I'm not some slave. I'll do what I want. I've seen enough innocents locked up and starved to death or sent to an early grave through dysentery or fever. I'll not stand by and see it done again.'

Peter sat down on a wooden chair and put his head in his hands. 'What is happening? Are you leaving me for this rebel, Claire?'

'*This*,' said Claire, 'is war, Peter. This is what it's about, not dressing up in your police uniform and holding court at the bar in the shooting club telling tall stories and laughing at the natives; you've seen it for yourself. To tell you the truth, I'm pig sick of it out here in the desert. The Nama are robbing me blind, the German military doesn't care about helping the sick or educating the native children, and you could be killed next time you ride out with the Schutztruppe. This isn't the place I thought it would be.'

Peter looked up, angry. 'So, you will leave me, your lawfully wedded husband, for another man?'

Claire sighed. 'I'll miss you, Peter, but I think we both know we're better as friends than we ever were as husband and wife, and it's not like you can cast the first stone, is it? I've known about Andrea, and Helga, for some time.'

He lowered his gaze to the floor. 'What do you want from me? To betray my country and my uniform?'

'I want you to behave like a decent human being, Peter. There's a young girl who's off to face God knows what horrors and the Brits are after me. I'm going to the coast whether you come or not. I've business to attend to in any case.'

351

Peter stood up. 'I need to think about this, Claire. You are right, I have not been a perfect husband, far from it, but this has come as something of a shock to me.'

She nodded, but said no more, not wanting to rub in her betrayal of him, no matter what he had done in the past.

He took a deep breath. 'I need a bath. Excuse me.'

When he had left the room, Blake said: 'You've got business to attend to?'

'Unless he's told someone else, which I doubt, Walters is the only person in the world other than you and Peter who knows I made off with some of Kruger's gold. Now he knows I'm in South West Africa. You were right before, Blake, he'll hunt me down.'

'So what, you're running off to Europe?'

'Somewhere.'

'And what about me?'

'If you're smart you'll leave here now and catch a boat back to Australia. I'll give you the price of a ticket and enough to buy yourself a little house back in Sydney town in repayment for your help. Maybe we can meet there. What do you say to that?'

'I'm not smart, and you tried to leave me once before. I'll not let you go again, Claire.'

*

The three of them, Blake, Claire and Peter, rode along the desert road from Keetmanshoop towards Aus. Blake was still in his German Schutztruppe uniform; their cover story was that he was an escort for the doctor and his wife.

The sound of metal clanging on metal and a woman's scream told Claire they were nearing the railway line that was being built across the southern part of the colony from Lüderitz on the coast to Keetmanshoop in the interior.

They crested a dune and Claire saw the cause of the noise.

A group of women had been carrying a length of steel track and one had clearly fallen. Somehow the others had dropped the track and it had landed across the woman's leg. She was screaming in pain while the others tried in vain to free their fellow worker.

Behind them men dressed in rags were ignoring the unfolding tragedy, hammering spikes into place.

A uniformed guard carrying a *sjambok*, a leather whip, went to the fallen woman and beat her, as if it were her fault that she had been pinned to the ground.

Peter spurred his horse and galloped ahead of them. Claire and Blake followed. 'Hang back,' she said to him over her shoulder. Blake nodded and kept his distance.

Claire reached Peter as he was dismounting and unstrapping his medical bag from his saddle.

The overseer stepped away from the screaming woman and met Peter on foot. 'What do you want?' he asked in German.

'I'm a doctor. What are you doing beating that woman?'

'It's none of your business.'

Claire stepped in and addressed the overseer 'This man is also a *Hauptmann* in the Landespolizei, and you will accord him the respect he deserves.'

The overseer, a slovenly man whose uniform was missing a button thanks to his bulging stomach, glared at her, but slowly brought himself to attention and gave Peter a lazy salute. 'The prisoner fell deliberately, *sir*, in an attempt to sabotage construction of the line. We are on a tight schedule.'

Peter ignored him. He dropped to his knees and opened his bag.

Claire looked at the poor wretches who stood around the woman. They were painfully thin and dressed in rags, and from their features she guessed them to be a mixed group of Herero and Nama women. She looked to the nearest woman and addressed her in German. 'What happened here?'

The woman cringed away from her and cast a terrified glance at the overseer, whose snarl kept her silent.

'Don't look at him. I am asking you a question,' Claire said.

The woman backed away.

'Lift this bloody piece of steel,' Peter said to them.

'You're wasting your time, Doctor,' the overseer said. 'I've seen injuries like this. She'll lose the leg and die soon enough.'

Claire pushed her way between the women and bent to try and lift the piece of track. It was far too heavy for her to even budge it. Reluctantly, and keeping a wary eye on their guard, the women came to her, in ones and twos. Eventually twenty of them were kneeling, getting a grip on the piece of track.

The injured woman screamed even louder as the steel was lifted from her. Peter had tied his belt as a makeshift tourniquet around her thigh and he put his hands under her armpits and dragged her from under the track. Panting, he fell backwards on the sand. He got up and went back to his medical bag.

As Peter was taking out his supplies the overseer went to the woman, drew his pistol, aimed between her staring, pleading eyes, and shot her.

The other women winced and one cried out.

'You bastard!'

Claire went for the guard, who held up his arm, but did not point the pistol at her. Claire slapped at him.

Peter was fuming, but he took hold of Claire and dragged her away.

'Sir, take control of your woman,' the overseer said.

'Where is your commanding officer?' Peter said, not trying to disguise his disgust.

The man looked lazily over his shoulder. 'Coming, now.'

Peter and Claire saw a young lieutenant striding towards them.

'What's all this ...?' The man stopped, clicked his heels together and saluted when he saw Peter. 'Sir.'

'Your man ... just shot this woman in cold blood.'

The officer looked from Peter to the overseer, who shrugged. 'She would have died anyway.'

'*I* would have been the judge of that,' Peter said. 'And in any case, what right does this underling have to become judge, jury and executioner? What have these women done wrong?'

The lieutenant's face was red with acne, but his eyes were those of an old man, not a teenager. 'They are sympathisers of the Herero and Nama rebels. Our job is to get this railway line built, on time, at any cost. We are a long way from the nearest town, and we cannot waste resources, sir, on transporting prisoners to a clinic when they would surely die on the way.'

'How many have you lost, so far?' Peter asked, his fists clenched in barely contained fury.

The young officer scratched his head under his peaked cap. 'Hard to say, sir, maybe five or six hundred. There are plenty more where these came from, in Lüderitz on the *Todesinsel*, so there is no risk that we will not make our target. Trust me, sir, these women are happier out here in the desert than back in the camp at Shark Island – they say some Herero kill themselves when they learn they are to be sent there.'

Peter's jaw dropped. He looked to Claire who just gave a small shake of her head, as if to tell him to drop it. She had reined in her anger, for now at least.

'Have you seen a shipment of prisoners head through here in the last day or so, *Leutnant*?' Claire asked.

The man nodded, as if relieved to be asked a civil, easily answered question. 'Yes, madam, yesterday, from Keetmanshoop. The escort said they were taken during the fighting against the Nama rebel Morengo.'

'I will make a formal report of what I have seen here today,' Peter said to the young officer.

He nodded and saluted, but the overseer just gave a half-grin.

Claire looked at the cowering women and her stomach churned. She remembered the squalor of the South African concentration camp she had passed through. At the time she had thought it terrifying and brutal, but here, in her own homeland, it seemed these innocent victims of war faced not only the prospect of life in a camp, but also being worked to death on the railway line. She found it hard to imagine how life on Shark Island could be worse than this. Two women were ordered to drag the dead woman away, where she was dumped a few metres from the railway line. The overseer barked at the women to get back to work.

Claire and Peter mounted up and as the three of them moved out of earshot Blake brought his horse next to hers.

'What was that all about?'

She explained, still using the word the officer had used to describe the camp.

'What does *Todesinsel* mean?' Blake asked.

'Island of death.'

CHAPTER 44

Aus, Namibia, the present

Nick and Anja had stayed up late the evening before in her chalet at the Desert Horse Inn, where she had continued to read and translate for him.

They met again, as planned, at seven in the morning in the main building for breakfast.

'I'm sorry to have kept you up last night,' Nick said as he came to her table. By habit she had arrived five minutes early.

He had a sad face, she decided. He could become animated at times, such as when she came to a particularly interesting part of Dr Kohl's story, but he was troubled, mostly. All the same, she found she enjoyed his company. 'No problem.'

He took a seat and they both ordered coffee from a waiter.

'Can I ask you a question, please, Nick?'

'Sure,' he said.

'You and Susan Vidler …?' she said, leaving the question open.

'It was terrible, what happened to her.'

He was not giving much away. 'Yes, I agree. As much as she could be annoyingly persistent, I would not wish what happened to her on anyone. Nick …?'

'Yes?' He looked at her.

'Were you and Susan … close?'

He looked away and she had her answer. 'I'd only known her a very short time, but yes, we were close.'

356

Now she felt embarrassed and she was sure it showed on her face. Anja knew what had interested her in the story – some possible supporting evidence for her theory of the origins of the desert horses – but she wondered what had motivated Nick to come all this way. 'What are you looking for?'

He frowned. 'I don't know. I mean, this is important to me because Blake was a relative, but I can't really convince myself that there is a fortune in gold buried somewhere here in Namibia, no matter what Scott Dillon thinks.'

'So you're not in this for the money?'

He gave a small smile. 'I didn't even realise there was money involved when I decided to come. Plus, I gave up thinking that I would die a rich man a long time ago. I liked writing for newspapers, but I guess I didn't have drive, you know?'

She regarded him. 'I don't think you lack drive – you are here pursuing a story more than a hundred years old, and possibly on the trail of a man who will rob and kill to get what he wants. No, I think if you have lacked anything it was maybe a purpose.'

He seemed to think about that. She hoped she hadn't offended him; Anja was nothing if not direct, which was a polite way of saying she was bossy and intolerant of other people's flaws. An ex-boyfriend had called her arrogant, which had hurt her.

'I'm sorry,' she said, meaning it. 'I have put my foot in it, again.'

Nick poured coffee into both their cups. He was quiet for a few seconds, and the longer the silence drew out the harder her heart beat. He smiled. 'You may be right.'

'Phew.'

They laughed.

'Seriously,' he said, 'my work was everything to me when I was young, working in journalism, and I thought I was the king of the heap, even though I was a very ordinary reporter. I was never going to be a big name on a major daily newspaper or on TV. I didn't like getting in people's faces.'

'There is nothing wrong with that, some reporters can be very rude.'

'Rudeness, determination, call it what you want, I didn't have it. I think if I had my time over again I'd write a novel, maybe.'

'And why do you have to have your time again? Why not start now?'

He shrugged. 'Bills to pay, my age.'

'Now you are sounding defeatist. You will have a story to tell when we get to the end of this – we both will.'

'Maybe.' He smiled. 'When I first contacted you, you didn't want to know me.'

Anja felt embarrassed. 'I was foolish, jealous, overprotective of my work, and maybe of myself.'

'What about you? Is there someone waiting somewhere for you?'

She felt herself blushing. 'No, just my research. And the desert horses.'

'As awful as it is, what happened to Susan and Lili and you, I feel … I don't know … alive? Is that terrible?'

'No. I'm excited as well, and I want to know how the horses fit into all this,' she said.

'Really?' he said slowly.

Anja could see that Nick was not surprised by her comment. His question had been, she thought, more one of admiration, or respect. 'Yes.'

'That shows incredible dedication, Anja.'

'Thank you. Some gold would be nice, as well.'

He laughed.

'We have to do this, Nick,' Anja said, serious again. 'This Dillon man needs to be shown he cannot treat people the way he did, and if he killed Susan, or had her killed, then he must be brought to justice.'

'I agree. We go to the cops as soon as we confirm our suspicions, yes?'

She nodded. 'Yes. We are not investigators, or vigilantes. As much as I hate what those men did to me I will not take the law into my own hands.'

'I wonder how Blake and Claire Martin would have handled someone like Dillon,' Nick said.

'With Mauser rifles, I imagine.'

They set off straight after breakfast and when they hit a straight, smooth road she did nothing to discourage him from sitting on the maximum speed limit. He slowed as they passed the desert horse waterhole at Garub and even after years of research Anja still pressed a hand to the window, lovingly, as they passed a mare with a young foal. He drove on.

The road followed the course of the railway line.

'It's terrible to think of the people who died building this,' Nick said, 'and that poor woman who was shot after the piece of track fell on her.'

Anja contemplated the cost in silence. She had read about the concentration camps and the work parties. 'It's said that of the two thousand Herero and Nama who worked on the line about thirteen hundred of them died during construction.'

Nick shook his head.

The countryside became even more foreboding, if that was possible. The stubbly grass the horses fed on gave way to a wide valley amid sand dunes. As they come closer to Lüderitz a billowing curtain of sand was being blown across the road.

'No point trying to speed through the sand,' Anja said. 'If you go faster, trying to outrun a sandstorm, you just make the abrasiveness of the grains worse.'

Nick nodded and kept his speed steady. After an hour and twenty minutes, most of it spent in silence, they saw old buildings coming up on the left.

'That's Kolmanskop,' Anja said. 'It was a diamond mining town, from the boom after the First World War. It was said that champagne was more plentiful and cheaper than water there during the town's heyday. Now it's a ghost town that's been reclaimed by the desert.'

Nick looked over at the grand mansions and mining buildings where wind and sand had broken down doors and windows and half filled the interiors. It was a bizarre sight. 'If the desert can swallow a town, someone like Dillon might never find a stash of buried gold, even if he knew where to look. This place is so desolate, it's a wonder anyone ever bothered to settle here.'

'The British claimed the best port on the Atlantic coast, at Walvis Bay, and kept it to themselves as a separate enclave for decades,' Anja explained. 'The Germans had to make do with

Lüderitz, even though it had no fresh water. They used condensers to desalinate sea water.'

Their first views of Lüderitz revealed it for what it still was, a small town clinging to the edge of the desert, with its back to the Atlantic and Europe beyond. Even from their first glance they could tell that in many ways not much had changed since the early 1900s.

'It looks like a German village that's been prefabricated and dropped into Africa,' Nick said.

'That's exactly what it was.'

Anja directed him through the compact coastal town. Normally a trip to Lüderitz was either a pleasant diversion from life in the desert, or a necessary chore, depending on how she was feeling. In either case she rarely thought about the seaside village's sinister past.

On Hafen Street she pointed to a shopping complex on the right and the restaurant where Joanne Dillon had suggested they meet, Essenzeit. 'That's the old waterfront area.' On the left, across the road, was an historic building perched high on a bluff, now a cafe but once the headquarters of the Woermann shipping line, she explained to Nick.

'Let's go to Dillon's hotel,' Nick said.

Anja shook her head and took a deep breath. 'Maybe let me handle this, Nick?' Anja said. 'I did meet Dillon in Windhoek and maybe he doesn't know that you and I are working together. If he's the one who ended up with all my stolen data then he would have seen that I didn't have a copy of Peter Kohl's manuscript at that time. He might be more willing to meet me.' She nervously took out her phone and a beer coaster and started composing an SMS.

'What are you writing?' Nick asked.

Anja showed him the coaster. 'Scott gave me his number in Windhoek and he knew that I was going to be in this part of the country. I'll send him an innocent message asking if he wants to catch up. I'll tell him I'm going to Shark Island; we can finish reading the manuscript while we wait for him.'

CHAPTER 45

The desert east of Lüderitz, German South West Africa, 1906

Blake, Claire and Peter had to wrap their faces and keep their eyes screwed to slits to keep out the worst of the sand as their horses trekked wearily through the desert.

Blake drew alongside Peter. 'And you and Claire paid money to buy a piece of this bloody place?'

Peter laughed. He was that sort of bloke, Blake had learned, someone who could manage to keep his spirits high and a smile on his face most of the time. Having said that, Blake knew the battles at and around Narudas had affected the doctor.

Blake had come to like the affable German in the days since the incident at the railway line. Peter had been shaken by the killing of the woman and they had talked about it, around the fire, as well as about some of the things Blake had seen in his time in Africa.

'In Australia you have the desert as well, yes?' Peter said.

'Yes, mate, but you won't catch me going there, especially after this. I've seen enough sand to last me a lifetime.'

'Yet still you stay, Blake. Will you ever leave Africa?'

'Might have to, the way I'm going now. I'd like to find a beach again. The water's probably the only thing I miss about Australia.'

Peter gestured ahead. 'Where we are going there is nothing but beach! However, the water is so cold that you will freeze to death, and if you don't, the lions that roam the coastline feeding on dead whales and seals and shipwrecked sailors will kill you.'

Claire looked over and managed a smile for both of them. She was beautiful, but that simple smile hurt Blake. He had a terrible sense of foreboding. There was something about this journey to rescue Liesl, the helplessness of it, that made it feel, more than any other mission he'd been on during the war, like a one-way trip.

They hadn't formulated a plan and Blake had seen there was no need to restrain or intimidate Peter. Blake sensed Peter was on this journey to learn for himself what was happening with the Nama and Herero prisoners, not because he was being coerced. The fact was that he could have easily slipped away in the night and ridden back to Aus and raised the alarm, but somehow Blake knew that he wouldn't.

Early the next morning Blake saw a cliff face of fog hanging on the horizon, beyond the dunes.

'That is the Atlantic,' Peter said. 'We are nearly there.'

He almost sounded sad, Blake thought, as if he were sorry they were approaching their destination.

They had found signs of the Nama prisoners and their escorts: still-warm embers from campfires, wagon ruts in the sand and, worst of all, as they neared the coast, the body of a young woman who had been mauled by hyenas in the night.

Blake and Peter had scooped out a hollow in the sand and buried the girl.

They stood next to the grave in silence for a minute and Claire said a Hail Mary softly. Blake saw the tears rolling down her cheeks. Peter nodded to him and Blake went to her and put an arm around her. She buried her face in his chest.

Peter went to his horse and, without looking back at them, mounted and rode off slowly. They caught up with him soon enough, but Blake sensed they had crossed yet another invisible line. They said nothing as they approached the town, which was close enough now to detect the fresh tang of sea salt and the stench of human waste, and walked their tired horses up the final rise.

'My God, it's grown,' Claire said, as they paused atop the dune and took in the sight below.

'The war,' Peter said.

Blake could see Peter was right. It seemed every second person they saw on the street below them was in the uniform of the Schutztruppe. A platoon of soldiers was marching in step down the road while others lounged outside a line of stores. There was the sound of orders barked, a donkey braying and the shriek of a woman from somewhere.

Claire pointed out the docks and warehouses and he followed the sweep of her hand to a promontory from which columns of smoke scribbled grubby lines on the clear blue palate of the sky. 'Shark Island.'

They rode slowly into town. The *Feldwebel* in command of the marching troops saluted Peter as they passed and Peter returned the sergeant's courtesy.

Lüderitz was the main disembarkation and embarkation port for troops and supplies destined for the war in the south of the colony, and for troops returning home. Blake felt nervous with so many Schutztruppen around, but his anxiety eased a little when he noticed a few of the marching soldiers appraising Claire with sideways glances. All attention would be on the pretty red-headed woman rather than him in his dusty and stained uniform. Blake could see as they moved past lounging soldiers that they seemed to be a mix of newcomers in fresh, clean uniforms, and old hands, perhaps on leave or on their way home to Germany, whose clothes were as dusty, stained and patched as his.

Peter stopped his horse next to a corporal in an unbuttoned sand-coloured corduroy tunic. The man gave a sloppy salute. Peter spoke to him in German, apparently giving him something of a dressing-down, as the man did up his buttons and stood straighter, then answered some questions.

When they rode off again Blake gave his horse a nudge and drew alongside Peter and Claire.

'Peter asked that man if he'd seen a fresh crop of prisoners,' Claire said quietly. 'He said he had, this morning, so we were close to them. He says they've gone to Shark Island.'

Blake cursed. If they had been able to catch the wagons carrying the prisoners in the desert they might have been able to sneak up to them at night and free Liesl and whomever else was with her, but now that they were in Lüderitz, and inside the camp by now, he wondered if there was anything they could do for her.

Peter looked to him. 'We are going to the island.'

Blake was a little surprised. He had forced Peter to be involved in this search for Liesl and now the German would have been justified in turning back. 'Why?'

'I am a doctor. I'd heard rumours, but after seeing what happened at the railway line I want to see for myself what is happening in this camp. I need to look for a Dr Bofinger.'

Blake looked to Claire.

She nodded. 'I want to see Shark Island as well.'

'It's risky,' Blake said.

'I didn't come all this way for nothing,' Claire said firmly.

They heard a high-pitched scream come from a narrow alleyway and Peter spurred his horse on. When Blake caught up with him he saw Peter still in the saddle, kicking a soldier. The man had his pants around his ankles and Blake could see, lying slumped on the ground, a skinny boy no more than ten or eleven years old. The boy had his hands over his face.

The soldier tripped and fell. Peter dismounted and grabbed the man by his collar, lifted him and punched him in the face. The soldier reeled again and fell, and Blake wondered if he was drunk. Peter kicked him again, viciously. The soldier crawled away, desperately trying to escape and pull up his trousers at the same time. As Peter knelt to check on the boy the soldier made good his escape, up the alleyway.

Blake got down out of his saddle. 'Bloody hell.'

Peter looked up at him, his face red with fury, his eyes welling with tears. The boy, also pulling up his pants, got up and darted away, in the opposite direction to his attacker. Peter stood.

'My God. This is my country, Blake. What is happening to it?'

Blake clasped him on the arm. Peter gently freed himself, sniffing. He reached into his medical satchel and pulled out a bandage.

'What's that for?' Blake asked.

'We don't want anyone talking to you. Hold still.' Peter took the bandage and wrapped it snuggly around Blake's neck, though not tight enough to restrict his breathing. He wiped his knuckles, which were cut and bloodied from the blow he had landed on the soldier, on the white of the bandage, colouring it a little in front of Blake's Adam's apple for effect. 'If anyone talks to you in German just point to your mouth and show them you can't speak.'

'All right.' The doctor was committed to this folly now, Blake thought, and felt a rush of gratitude. 'Thank you.'

'Don't thank me,' Peter said, 'I am not doing this for you.'

*

They remounted and left the alley and its stink of urine and vomit and spilled beer. Claire had been shocked by the attack on the street urchin. Lüderitz had boomed, thanks to the war, but the influx of soldiers had brought trouble.

Peter led them down the main road through town. The streetscape was more of the same: soldiers, poor Africans either making a living as labourers or in some form of service, whores and the occasional civilian. Peter stopped again by a pair of officers of the same rank as he, walking side by side.

'Good morning,' Peter called.

'And to you, Mr Policeman,' the nearest said, then nudged his comrade. 'Seems we have done something wrong, Heinz, the law has stopped us.'

Peter laughed. 'Not at all, although I have some serious business. We've just ridden in from the desert and my escort here took a bullet fragment to the neck.'

'Nasty business,' said the officer who had spoken. He saw Claire and touched a hand to his Südwester. 'Ma'am.'

Claire smiled at the men. 'Please, can you help us, our brave soldier here protected us from a rebel ambush.'

'Yes,' Peter continued. 'I am looking for a Dr Bofinger, who I am told practises here.'

It was the turn of the second officer, the one called Heinz, to laugh. 'Yes, but you mustn't value your good man too much – none of Bofinger's patients leave his surgery alive.'

'He can't be that bad,' Peter said.

The first officer shrugged. 'Well, he is one of only two doctors in the garrison and they're both based at the island.'

'Can you give us directions, please?'

'Of course,' Heinz said, 'and you can do me a favour.'

'With pleasure,' Peter said. 'What is it?'

Heinz reached into his uniform pocket and pulled out a piece of paper. 'I've come from the railway line. Bofinger is always after statistics and information. These are figures for prisoner deaths through illness and injury. Bofinger's got it in his head that the hard work in the open air is a cure or preventative for scurvy.'

'Really,' Peter said, 'sounds interesting.'

The two officers looked at each other and laughed. 'Scurvy's the least of their problems out in the desert! The hyenas will get them whatever happens. Hey, we should shoot a hyena and get Bofinger to perform one of his scientific autopsies on it and see if it caught scurvy off a native!'

Peter took the list, forcing a smile, and the three of them took grateful leave from the officers.

'Autopsies?' Claire asked when they were out of earshot.

Peter shrugged.

Claire felt a sense of foreboding as their horses' hooves echoed off the walls of the warehouses along the waterfront and a foul smell wafted towards them on the breeze.

They crested a rise on which there was a port building and a sentry post. Below them, jutting into the bay, was a picture of misery.

The island, now more of a peninsula thanks to a work gang below that was busy with picks, shovels and wheelbarrows filling and widening a causeway that linked the rocky outcrop to the mainland, was teeming with people. From what Claire could see the inhabitants, who might number as many as a thousand, had no fixed structures or housing, but had cobbled together rudimentary shelters made of mats, old blankets and other pieces of rubbish. The workers were barely clad, their skeletal bodies exposed to the sun and the wind whose keen cold presence now cut through her riding clothes.

There was not a tree or bush on the island and no sign of a convenience. Claire supposed people made their ablutions in the icy water of the Atlantic, but she could smell the mess of the teeming mass of prisoners acutely now. A guard yelled at a worker on the causeway and, as on the railway line, reinforced his order with the lash of a *sjambok* whip. Claire flinched.

Peter took her gently by the arm. '*Schatzi*, I can go ahead, find this Dr Bofinger, and find out where Liesl is. I can't see what hope Blake has of rescuing her. Look at this place – there's only one way in across this causeway and there are guards everywhere.'

'I'm going onto the island, Peter. I want to have a look at this new causeway. It wasn't here when my ex-husband ran the shipping line.' By force of habit and perceived necessity Claire had always kept some things secret from Peter. She didn't tell him why, but she needed to see for herself the extent of the causeway, because she was searching for something very valuable.

A sentry with a Mauser rifle slung over his shoulder came out of a hut to meet them and saluted Peter.

'I am looking for Herr Doktor Bofinger,' Peter said.

'Your name, sir?'

'Dr Peter Kohl. I have important papers for Dr Bofinger.'

The soldier glanced at the others and touched his Südwester's brim in greeting to Claire.

'This is my wife and the man is an escort. I need to take him to Dr Bofinger's clinic for treatment.'

The sentry widened his eyes. 'Clinic?'

'Yes, Corporal. Hurry, I haven't got all day,' Peter added imperiously.

The corporal saluted and summoned a soldier. 'Take the doctor and his party to Dr Bofinger's *clinic.*'

The soldier showed them where they could hitch their horses and asked them to follow him. Then he seemed to have second thoughts and went back to the corporal and whispered something to him.

'Sir,' the corporal said to Peter. 'The lady … it might not be wise if she …'

'Claire?' Peter tried.

Claire had wandered away from the sentry post to the edge of the causeway. She was peering over the rocky edge, into the water, looking back and forth from the original mainland to where the new spit of land met the rocky island. She looked up at the sound of her name.

'The lady will stay with her husband, Corporal,' Claire said in fluent German.

The corporal ignored her, his eyes fixed on Peter. 'Sir, I am not sure if you are aware of the extent of Dr Bofinger's research.'

'I've worked as a nurse assistant to my husband,' Claire interjected. 'I've seen amputations, gunshot wounds and the clap in all its many horrible forms, Corporal.'

The soldier who was to escort them sniggered, but the corporal steadfastly refused to look at or listen to Claire. 'Sir, there is disease in that building. And worse.'

'My wife has said her piece and your concerns are duly noted, Corporal,' Peter said. He turned to the escort. 'Come. My man needs treatment.'

The corporal shrugged then gave a nod to his underling to proceed.

As they passed under a raised boom Claire heard the corporal ask Blake in German what had happened to him.

Blake obviously didn't know the man was addressing him because he continued walking. Claire stepped in.

'This is our escort, Corporal,' she said. Blake stopped at the sound of her voice and turned. 'He fended off a Nama rebel at close range, and was shot in the neck. He is also partially deaf from his proximity to an explosion.'

Blake seemed to get the gist of what was going on and he pointed to the bloodstained bandage at his neck. The corporal just shrugged again.

The soldier led them past the work gang. Claire caught the jaundiced eye of a man dressed only in a loincloth. The man quickly went back to digging as an overseer approached. A woman cried out and Claire turned and saw the painfully thin prisoner being whipped, seemingly for dropping her pick.

They reached a building made of timber and corrugated iron, the only permanent structure on the island. 'This is Dr Bofinger's *clinic*,' the soldier said.

Claire felt a shiver. The disdain with which the soldiers referred to Dr Bofinger's practice filled her with unease. Claire saw that at the far end of the long building two women, one Nama and one Herero by the look of them, were stirring a big pot of boiling water or food. At least there might be something warm for the poor wretches, Claire thought.

They walked inside and Claire held her hand up to her mouth. There was the smell of faeces and vomit coming from the emaciated patients who lined both walls of the long, narrow room, and barely any space between each simple wood and rope bed.

A white man in uniform, a surgical mask over his face, looked up from where he stood, bending over a patient. The uniformed man had a syringe in his hand, which he plunged into the prisoner's arm. He turned, handed the syringe to a cadaverous-looking German orderly and came over to them.

The man removed his mask, clicked his heels together and nodded to Claire. 'Can I help you?'

'Dr Bofinger?' Peter said. 'I'm Dr Peter Kohl and this is my wife.'

'Herr Doktor, Frau Kohl.' He extended his hand. 'Hugo Bofinger, charmed.'

Claire took his hand and nodded. His palm was damp and his handshake limp.

'And our escort,' Peter nodded to Blake, 'wounded in action, but recovering. It will be a while before he sings opera again.'

Dr Bofinger smiled at the joke, 'To what do I owe the pleasure of this visit?'

Peter reached into his uniform pocket. 'First, I bring you this list, from two of your officers who have returned from the railway. They said you needed this information.'

Bofinger adjusted his rimless spectacles, unfolded the paper and studied it. 'Yes, yes, very good.'

'The officers told me you are conducting research into scurvy?'

'Yes, that is my current project. Forgive me, but what is your interest, Herr Doktor Kohl?' His eyes flitted to Claire, who made herself smile back at him.

'Me? Oh, I'm just a humble physician from the outer extremes of the colony. My military duty with the Landespolizei brought me here in search of one of your prisoners, but I am actually fascinated by the field of medical research. I have heard of your work and was wondering if you might be able to tell me a little of what goes on here in the camp?'

Bofinger gave a curt nod, but his attention kept returning to Claire. 'I would be happy to show you around, Doctor, but I fear that Frau Kohl ...'

'I will be fine,' Claire said, beaming pleasantly. 'And I, too, have an interest in science in all its many forms. I would be very interested to learn more of your work here. A life in the wilds of Africa on a farm has inured me to rigours that might cause other women to faint.'

Bofinger gave a tight-lipped smile. 'Then come with me, please.'

He led them further along the row of beds. Men and women lay there, dying. Claire breathed through her mouth, such was the stench.

'These natives are all suffering from scurvy; it is rife on the island,' Bofinger said.

Peter stopped and looked at a patient. 'Classic symptoms. Hair falling out, gums bleeding. The teeth will go soon. What are they feeding these people? Some lime juice or citrus fruit would help them soon enough.'

Bofinger shook his head. 'I don't subscribe to the old-fashioned idea that scurvy is related to diet, and as you yourself know, Dr Kohl, fresh fruit is a luxury here, even for those of us who deserve it. No, I am convinced scurvy is a bacterial disease, spread by germs. You're aware of the new science, I presume.'

'Of course,' Peter said.

'I believe that hard work and exercise assists in the prevention and treatment of the disease,' Bofinger continued. 'I've been experimenting with a range of treatments here in the camp as well. I just administered opium to this patient.'

If nothing else, Claire thought, the man would hopefully die in peace.

They continued through the room, with Bofinger reeling off a list of the illnesses the prisoners on the island suffered.

'Surely survival, and productivity, would be increased if these people were fed a little more?' Peter said. 'Everyone I have seen is malnourished.'

Bofinger clapped him on the arm. 'Come, come, Doctor, we know there are many Herero, and increasing numbers of Nama, to supply labour for the colony. No, this operation is very economical. Workers are farmed out to the railway and other capital projects around Lüderitz and the work gets done. That's what's important.'

Not human life, clearly, Claire thought. It almost seemed as if the mission of this island was not to supply labour for the colony, but to meet the twin aims of successfully completing the building projects on time and getting rid of unwanted people. The camps in South Africa had been inhumane and people had died of disease, but that been due more to neglect than because of an underlying intent to wipe out the Afrikaner people. It seemed the people in this camp had little chance of survival. Claire was sickened, not just by the sights and smells of this place, but by the underlying evil. This was worse than anything she could have imagined.

Peter and Dr Bofinger walked on ahead, towards the end of the building. Claire shot a glance at Blake and he mouthed the word 'Liesl'.

'Herr Doktor Bofinger?'

He looked over his shoulder. 'Yes, Frau Kohl?'

'What happens to newly arrived prisoners? Surely they are in good health and in demand for work parties.'

'Yes,' he coughed into his hand, 'and other duties as is seen fit by the camp commandant.'

Claire shuddered inwardly.

'It is my job to give them a medical examination.'

Bofinger leaned in close to Peter as they neared the far end of the ward. Peter stopped and waited for Claire to catch up. He spoke quietly. 'Bofinger says you might want to stay inside and wait for us.'

'I'm not staying in this house of death a moment longer than is absolutely necessary,' she whispered in English, so that Blake could understand them. 'And anyway, what can be worse than the filth and suffering in here?'

'I don't know,' Peter said, 'but he says, "you have been warned". It's something to do with another research project.'

'Doctor,' Claire said aloud in German, striding towards Bofinger and feigning a nonchalance she certainly did not feel, 'I appreciate your concern but I have a strong constitution. Please lead on.'

Bofinger nodded and opened the door for her. With a sweep of his arm he ushered her outside towards the women stirring the big, black cast-iron cooking pot, which stood waist high to the reed-thin inmates. The women looked at her with blank eyes.

'This is a project being supervised by my colleague, Dr Eugen Fischer,' Bofinger said to Peter and Claire, including them both now. Blake stayed to one side, his expression blank with incomprehension. Claire noticed, though, that his eyes kept moving, taking in everything around him. 'He is studying racial characteristics, ground-breaking work which will scientifically prove, once and for all, the superiority of the white European peoples over Africans.'

Quite what that had to do with food preparation, Claire had no idea. Behind the women tending the pot, she saw, were half-a-dozen more, standing with their backs to the visitors but clearly working on some sort of processing or preparation at a long table. She noticed that one of the woman was holding a fragment of glass wrapped in a rag, perhaps some kind of simple knife or scraper.

Behind those workers was a detail of four German soldiers who were stacking round objects the size of footballs, wrapped in leather by the look of it, into a wooden packing crate the length and width of a coffin.

Intrigued, Claire moved towards the pot, to see what was going on here.

'Perhaps not too close, Frau Kohl,' Bofinger said.

'Nonsense.' She spoke to the women in German. 'What are you cooking there?'

One of the women looked away, while the other's lower lip started trembling.

'I can't say it smells like fine cuisine; rather meaty.' At least, she thought, these poor people might get some protein in their diet.

She waved away the steam from the boiling vat so she could get a better look, and when she leaned over and peered inside she saw bobbing in the boiling water, three human heads.

CHAPTER 46

Shark Island, Namibia, the present day

'Heads?' Nick said. 'You're fucking kidding me.'

Anja looked up from her iPad. 'I'm afraid not, Nick. Have you not read anything about the history of Shark Island?'

'Not enough, clearly.' He looked out over the barren rocky outcrop. He could barely imagine how a thousand people could fit on the promontory, let alone the atrocities that had gone on there. 'However, I shouldn't be shocked. There were British scientists taking the skulls and skeletons of Australian Aboriginal people for research back in the day. The whole supposedly civilised world has a lot to answer for.'

Shark Island was now a national park and they had paid a modest entry fee to a parks officer at a little wooden cabin on the causeway that linked the island to the mainland. Nick and Anja sat on a bench in a paved observation area on a high point, where the island proper began.

The only physical evidence that something brutal had happened there was a white tombstone-like memorial to one of the Nama rebel leaders, Captain Cornelius Fredericks, and the men and women of his Bethanie Nama clan who had died on the island. There was a carved picture of Fredericks holding a smoking rifle. Nearby was a smaller bronze plaque depicting the bespectacled trader, Franz Adolf Lüderitz, who founded the settlement for Germany.

Ironically, this place where thousands had sought shelter amid the boulders, under flotsam and old blankets, and had died of illness, overwork and exposure, was now a camping ground. Nestled among the rocks was a South African couple with a Land Cruiser and an off-road caravan. Despite the early hour – it had just gone eleven – the man sitting in a fold-out chair had just opened a can of Castle Lager and was reading a novel.

They got up and walked along a track that led to other camping sites and the end of the island.

'Dr Eugen Fischer was exporting the skulls of dead Herero prisoners to universities in Germany. Like Bofinger said, there were studies going on at the time to try and prove the superiority of the white races. This sort of thing predated Hitler and the Nazis by thirty years, but there's a book that theorises that what happened at Shark Island and other forced labour camps at Swakopmund and Windhoek were a trial run for the Holocaust.'

'My God,' Nick said.

'The women in the camp were given the job of boiling the heads of dead prisoners and the softened skin was scraped off by other inmates using shards of glass. Some of the skulls have been returned to Namibia, but not all of them.'

They walked briskly to counter the effect of the cold wind. Nick wondered what it would be like just trying to sleep on this island without shelter, with wind and rain howling in from the Atlantic, let alone to keep up one's strength after long days of hard manual labour and scant food.

'How many people died here?' Nick asked.

Anja shrugged. 'We don't know exactly. So many people came and went, and died on the railway and other work projects. It's thought that maybe half of the seven thousand people who passed through the island died. It's hard for me, as someone of German background who was born here in Namibia, to come to terms with, but even harder for the Nama and Herero people.'

'This country,' Nick said, pausing and looking around, searching for words, 'from what I've seen it just seems so peaceful, so quiet.'

Anja nodded. 'It is. Our saving grace is that today Namibia is, by African standards and even by world standards, a peaceful, tolerant country. Everyone's culture and history is respected, mine included.'

Other than the South African campers there was no one else on the island, and they both turned at the sound of a vehicle pulling up in the car park behind them.

Nick recognised the man who got out of the BMW. 'Scott Dillon.'

'Yes,' Anja said. 'That's the man I met in Windhoek.'

He looked around, saw them, and walked over. Dillon smiled as he approached them. 'Anja.'

'Hello again, Scott,' she said.

'This is a pleasant surprise.' Scott put out his hand and she took it. He looked to Nick. 'Hello there.'

'Hello, Scott,' Nick said.

'Do we know each other?'

He was smooth, Nick thought. 'Maybe if I talk a bit more you'll recognise my accent.'

Dillon's eyes widened. 'Nick ... remind me?'

'Eatwell.'

The smile left Dillon's face. He looked to Anja. 'I didn't know you two knew each other.'

'You do now,' Nick said. 'Do you want to tell us what's going on?'

'I've come here to meet Anja, that's all. But if you two are busy, I'll be on my way.'

Nick held up a hand. 'Not so fast. What are you doing here, exactly?'

'None of your business,' he said.

'I'd like to know, Scott,' Anja said. 'Did you know I was assaulted and robbed just after I saw you in Windhoek?'

'My God, I'm sorry to hear that,' Dillon said. 'I wish I'd walked you home.'

Nick admired Anja's cool and Dillon's acting ability. He sensed that he should keep quiet and let her play the role of the good cop in questioning Dillon. He was too angry – he kept thinking of Susan.

'So what brings you to Lüderitz, Scott?' she asked.

'It's that development I was telling you about.'

'The golf estate? I thought that was in Windhoek.'

'It is,' Scott said, ignoring Nick for now. 'It's important to me, but to tell you the truth I'm having trouble getting approval from the environmental and planning authorities. A ... well, a potential business partner has come up with a plan that might help smooth the way.' He looked at Nick. 'It's a little trick I learned in Australia – when you have a big property development application, the local councils over there sometimes expect an investment in some sort of community facility, such as a library or parkland. I know Lüderitz pretty well – I come here for the crayfish season in May sometimes – and it always struck me as a shame that there wasn't more information here about what happened on Shark Island, with the camp.'

'You're right,' Anja said. 'Apart from a couple of plaques there isn't a lot here for tourists or even local visitors.'

'Exactly,' Scott said. 'I'm going to propose to the government that I build an interpretive centre here. Nothing too big or over the top, but a nice, tasteful building that explains the history of the island and its significance during the Herero and Nama wars. It'll function like a combined memorial and a museum and there will be a gallery space for local artists and craftspeople to showcase their stuff for tourists.'

Nick studied Scott. The man was impeccably groomed, well dressed in a polo shirt, chinos and loafers, and as handsome as his online profile picture. The BMW had Namibian plates so Nick assumed it was rented. The word was that Scott Dillon was nearly broke, but Nick assumed the man needed to project an image of confidence and wealth if the government and his investors were going to take his development plans seriously. The interpretive centre sounded like window-dressing to Nick, a slick bit of PR that ticked all the boxes – culturally sensitive, politically correct, uplifting for the local community and probably tailor-made for some politician's family company or cronies to make a profit out of the construction work.

'Lüderitz is a long way from Windhoek, where your golf estate's supposed to be,' Nick said.

'Yes, but as a *journalist*, Nick, you'll know the issue of compensation for the Herero and the Nama is in the news once again in Namibia. Even with a substantial contribution I can't afford to build the centre here by myself – my co-investor thinks we'll be almost guaranteed of funding from the German government. They might be stopping short of paying compensation to individuals, but they've shown they're willing to acknowledge what happened during the wars and to try to make amends.'

'Where exactly would you build it?' Nick asked.

Scott looked around. 'That's one of the reasons I'm in Lüderitz, to do a preliminary survey. As you see, it's a rocky island. Ideally, to save money, it would need to be on the flattest ground we can find.'

'The causeway,' Nick said, pointing to where they had driven onto the island, 'built during the development of Shark Island as a concentration camp.'

Dillon looked as if he hadn't thought of that. 'Maybe. Not a bad idea, actually.'

'Scott?' Nick said.

Dillon showed him his even, perfect white teeth. 'Yes, Nick?'

'Why did you kill Susan Vidler?'

*

Even though he was two hundred metres away, Hannes Nel could hear every word the two men and the woman were saying. It was a beautiful sunny day and the cool breeze off the Atlantic was not enough to distort the audio coming through his headphones from the long-range directional microphone.

The allegation of murder was what he was waiting for. He shifted the crosshairs on the telescopic site atop his Sako hunting rifle so that they were over the chest of the Australian, Nicholas Eatwell.

Hannes knew Scott Dillon well. Even though Dillon was an *Engelsman*, a *soutpiel* with one foot in South Africa, the other in England, and his prick dangling in the Atlantic, Dillon had been accepted into Koevoet as a member of that elite police unit and had proved himself a good operator and a more than capable killer during the Border War in South West Africa in the late eighties. Hannes and Scott had fought side by side and killed more than their fair share of communist guerrillas, but those same terrorists were running the country now known as Namibia. Dillon might present like a Cape Town *moffie* in his pink polo shirt, but Hannes knew Scott was a ladies' man, most certainly not a homosexual.

Hannes was the overall commander of the operation and it was he, along with Wessel, another old comrade of his and Scott's, who had robbed and intimidated the German woman, Berghoff, in her Windhoek B&B. Charl, another former comrade, had posed as Eatwell's neighbour in Skukuza and Hannes had used WhatsApp to send orders to Karl, now living and working as a greenkeeper in Sydney. Poor Karl – his wife had forced him to take her and the children from South Africa to Australia and Karl had found the country very expensive. He needed cash, and burgling Eatwell's aunt's house and roughing up the German girl had been easy, well-paid work for the old soldier. Wilfried, in Munich, had botched the robbery on Berghoff's mother – there would be no more work for him.

They had thought that Eatwell and Berghoff would fold, that the failed journalist would not have the balls to go after Scott and the scientist woman would have spent so much time in Germany that she would have lost her Namibian toughness and become soft and fearful of confrontation.

Not so.

But that was why Hannes was there, with his sniper's rifle and his directional microphone. He took a breath, aimed, took up the pressure on the trigger and fired.

*

Anja realised someone was shooting at them before Nick did.

'Get down!' she said.

Nick was looking around, trying to work out what had made the noise and why the fragment of rock next to him had been exploded away from the boulder. Scott Dillon was running from them.

'What is it?'

Anja grabbed Nick's collar and pulled him down, behind the rocks.

'Someone's shooting at us.'

Anja crawled and Nick followed her. The island was so desolate that whoever was targeting them must be somewhere on the mainland. Anja peered around an outcrop and was rewarded with a shower of stone fragments.

'He's up there, in the direction of the Felsenkirche,' she said, pointing. The old church sat atop a hill that dominated the small port town. It made sense, Anja thought, that a sniper would look for high ground with a view.

They heard a high-revving car engine.

'Dillon,' Nick said. 'He's bugging out. You think he ordered this?'

'Of course he did!' Anja said. 'It happened as soon as you mentioned Susan's name. Maybe Scott gave some signal, or maybe the whole thing was a set-up.'

Nick's phone beeped. They seemed safe enough at the moment, though his heart was racing. He took out the phone and checked the screen. It was a message from Joanne Dillon, saying she had arrived in Lüderitz and asking him what was happening.

He tapped, quickly: *Your ex-husband set us up and we are being shot at on Shark Island.*

Shot at? she replied.

Yes.

ON MY WAY!

CHAPTER 47

Shark Island, Namibia, the present day

Joanne Dillon raced up to the Shark Island car park in a Toyota Fortuner a few minutes later. She must have been close by, Nick reflected, but then again nowhere was far from anywhere else in Lüderitz.

Joanne manoeuvred the car as close as she could to them, even driving the front wheels up onto a smooth boulder to give them extra cover as Nick opened the back door and bundled Anja in ahead of him.

Two bullets fired in quick succession sent stone chips ricocheting into the bodywork of the SUV as Joanne reversed.

'Go!' Nick shouted.

Joanne stayed low behind the wheel as she accelerated away along the causeway, past the port authority buildings and fish market and then, tyres screeching, left into Hafen Street.

'Where are we going?' Anja asked from the back.

'Out of town, I think that's the safest, don't you?' Joanne asked.

'Yes,' said Nick.

'Tell me what's going on,' Joanne said as she watched the road ahead and indicated to overtake a four-wheel drive with a roof tent. 'Why did Scott spring a trap on you?'

'He must know what we know,' Nick said, thinking out loud, 'as we have to assume he is working off the same information that we are, a manuscript written in 1915, but set mostly during the Nama and Herero wars.'

Joanne nodded. 'And you think Scott wanted it because he thought there was a reference to Kruger's gold in it?'

'There is definitely mention of the gold,' Nick said. He thought about what they had read so far. Anja, meanwhile, had taken her iPad out of her daypack and he could see she was reading ahead.

'Is there a precise location given for the gold?' Joanne asked.

Anja looked up. 'There's more information here. I'm nearing the end of the document.'

They left town and Joanne accelerated to a hundred and twenty on the smooth blacktop.

'Listen to this,' Anja said.

Lüderitz, German South West Africa, 1906

Blake and Claire left Lüderitz and rode into the desert where they made camp for the night. Claire said she couldn't bear to stay in a town full of drunken soldiers within sight of the misery and horror of Shark Island for another minute. Blake agreed.

Blake had escorted Claire off the island after she'd nearly fainted, but Peter had stayed behind to talk to Bofinger. He had told Claire that he would catch up to them.

'Find Liesl,' Blake had whispered to Peter as he left.

'I will, I promise,' Peter had replied.

The emptiness of Africa had at times confounded him and driven him close to madness, but now he relished its clean sands, its open, unpolluted skies and cool, crisp air. He remembered the cooking smell coming from the big pot and his stomach turned. He saw the lifeless eyes staring up at him and wondered what would be the worse fate for Liesl: being worked until she died in a brothel or on the railway, or dying of disease on the island, her head cut off and sent to Germany to be studied. He shuddered.

They had climbed a dune that afforded them a view of the railway line and the sand road to Aus and Keetmanshoop so they would have plenty of advance warning of Peter's arrival, or of a search party if for some reason he had been compromised or betrayed them.

Blake unstrapped the blanket and saddlebags from his mount and lay them on the sand, which was still warm from the day but would soon enough become chilly.

Claire had said little on the ride, staring straight ahead. What she had seen on the island had clearly left her shaken to the core. She came to him and he enfolded her in his arms.

'You should rest,' he said.

She looked up into his eyes. 'I'm not some feeble creature, Blake. We have to do something.'

'Peter's going to –'

'I know, I heard you two whispering. Peter's going to find out about your precious Liesl and –'

'Claire –'

Claire held up a hand. 'It's all right, Blake. What I mean is, I need to do something to help more than one pretty girl. I want horses, as many as you can find across the border in South Africa.'

'I'm broke, Claire. I got separated from Jakob Morengo before he could pay me what he owed me, with your gold.'

'I've got enough stashed at the farm for a hundred horses. That's the last of it.'

Blake was fairly sure he loved this woman, but she had lied to him on more than one occasion. 'You can't have spent that much, buying farms in South West Africa.'

'And building clinics for the natives and sinking boreholes for their villages. But, yes, you're right,' she said. 'I had to dump close to half of the gold in Lüderitz Bay back in 1902.'

'What happened?'

'I'd paid a few stevedores to help me move the stuff off the ship from Delagoa Bay. They were transporting the boxes in a lighter, from ship to shore, and then into a wagon I'd bought. It was quite an exercise, let me tell you. Anyway, one of these scoundrels took a peek in one of the boxes, which he rightly reckoned were too heavy for artillery shells. He found the gold and threatened me so I shot him. That caused quite a commotion. The captain of the ship was a good man, loyal, a friend of my first husband. He was worried about the fact I'd just shot a man, and concerned the Landespolizei would come and start poking their noses around. The captain believed me when I said I was moving pirated ammunition. He wanted to scarper up the coast to Walvis Bay, British territory, and lie low, but I told him I needed to get ashore and tend to my wagon. He wasn't happy, but I told him he could dump the stevedore's body and the remaining crates in Lüderitz Bay. He was right to be worried as a port authority boat did come out to check on us, but by then the gold was at the bottom of the bay, between the mainland and Shark Island.'

Blake remembered how Claire had told Peter that she wanted to see the causeway, which had struck him as odd, and how when Peter had been talking to the sentry at the boom gate leading to Shark Island Claire had been snooping about the edge of the new land bridge, looking into the water. 'Where the causeway is being built now?'

'Yes. I always figured that the gold was safe enough where it was under the sea and that one day, when I needed it, I could make up some excuse as to why I'd have men in pearl divers' underwater suits poking around on the bottom of the bay. The war and this island of death seem to have put an end to that plan – my loot's buried under a few thousand tons of rock and dirt now.'

The temperature plummeted with the disappearance of the sun and through the cold night air and across the empty desert Blake heard the jingle of a horse's bridle. He climbed the crest of the dune. 'It's Peter.'

Blake showed himself and Peter rode up the dune to them.

'I found out what happened to Liesl,' Peter said without preamble as he dismounted.

'You did?'

'I told Bofinger I knew her, that she was a maid on our farm at one time. I told him that she and I had been close. Bofinger said he could have her certified fit to be sent to a military brothel, but I told him I didn't want that. He said he would say that she had venereal disease and recommend that she be sent to work on the railway. He said ... he said death would come quicker that way and be kinder than dying of exposure or scurvy on the island or ...'

'I understand,' Blake said. 'How soon will she be moved?'

'Bofinger says there is another shipment of prisoners due to be sent up the railway line in a week's time. She will be among a group of fifty Nama men and women, the fittest alive on the island. She'll survive until then as long as she can evade the guards.'

'Thank you, Peter,' Blake said.

'Did he do all this for free?' Claire asked.

Peter shook his head. 'No, it took the last of my money. Blake, I saw her.'

Blake nodded. 'I can't let her die.'

'Neither can I,' Peter said.

Blake saw it in Peter's eye. Liesl had an effect on men, usually from the moment she caught their eye. It was why Rassie had been right to keep her out of the bar in Upington, and why Blake had fallen for her. She was still so young, and she deserved none of the fates that lay in wait for her.

'Will you two old buffalo bulls stop giving each other the eye, for goodness sake,' Claire said, 'and let's think of a plan to save her.'

CHAPTER 48

The desert east of Lüderitz, Namibia, the present day

Joanne looked over her shoulder at Anja, seated in the back of her car as they sped along the blacktop through the desert. 'Do you usually stay in Lüderitz?'

'No,' Anja said, 'I'm based at Klein-Aus Vista when I'm working on the horse project.'

'Cool, I'll take you there just now.'

'We have a car in Lüderitz,' Nick said.

Joanne shook her head and checked her rear-view mirror. 'We can go back for that later. I think it might be too risky right now. Scott and his thugs will be staking out your car, waiting for you. We need to get someplace where we can assess what's happened and call the Namibian police in on this.'

'That's the most sensible thing I've heard today.' Anja exhaled. 'I can't believe someone shot at us in Lüderitz, at a national park.'

'This is Africa, after all,' Joanne said. She glanced back at Nick. 'Bet you didn't get too many "sniper shoots at tourists" stories on *The Australian*, hey.'

Nick thought about that for a moment. 'Um, no. Not at all.'

They went over a hill and on the downward slope Nick heard and felt Joanne's car start to chug as if the power was going off and on.

'Something's wrong,' Joanne said. 'Maybe one of the bullets hit my fuel tank or something.'

Nick leaned over a little to try to see the gauge. 'How's your fuel?'

'I've got plenty,' Joanne said, 'it just seems to be coming and going to the engine.'

'Maybe a fuel line was damaged?' Nick didn't really know much about cars. The engine's note was rising and falling. He got out his phone.

'What are you doing?' Joanne asked.

'Googling intermittent fuel flow.'

'Seriously?' Joanne said.

'Yes.'

'Well, keep an eye out behind us as well, in case that bloody ex-husband of mine has sent his old Koevoet *boeties* after us to finish you two off.'

Nick wasn't, however, on Google. He was checking Facebook. He did a search, found the account he was looking for, hit the 'Friends' button and scrolled down. Nick sent an email to Anja, whose phone pinged beside him.

'Keep reading and translating, please, Anja,' Joanne said. 'I can't get enough of this story.'

'OK,' she said.

Near Aus, German South West Africa, 1906

A week after they had visited Shark Island, Blake, Claire and Peter were hiding amid the boulders of a rocky *koppie* overlooking the railway line, east of Aus. The pre-dawn morning air was bitingly cold. A score of Jakob Morengo's men waited at the foot of the hill, on the side away from the line.

Claire looked down at them and in the pink morning light she saw the breath of horses and men hanging momentarily frozen in the air.

What they were about to do was madness. It was treason, punishable by death for her and Peter, even though her husband had made it clear he was there only to administer first aid and would not be carrying a rifle or shooting any German soldiers. Blake, too would swing from a rope or face a firing squad as an enemy agent, out of uniform.

Thanks to the stillness of the air and the vast emptiness of the desert they heard the train coming a long way off.

Blake looked at her and she at him. On impulse she kissed him, full on the lips, not caring that Peter would see nor that her cheek would be smudged from the black charcoal makeup Blake had rubbed into his face. 'Go carefully, my love.'

Blake gave her a grin, teeth white against his sooty skin. 'I will. Don't run off and leave me again.'

She nodded.

As Blake hopped from rock to rock, making his way down, Claire saw that Peter had indeed been watching them. He gave her a sad smile as if to confirm that what had remained of their marriage was over.

Claire had sent Blake to her farm and told him to bring the twenty horses from the stud. These animals which, apart from her small supply of gold and her land, represented much of her fortune, were with the men and other horses below. Claire was burning her bridges here in South West Africa, of that she was sure.

Below she could see Blake moving across the sandy valley floor, staying low in case an eagle-eyed driver or footman on the train picked out his shadow or silhouette. She saw him reach the railway line and lie down.

*

Blake could feel the vibration of the approaching train through his body and hear the tracks singing as he lay next to the rails.

Placed already in a hole was a bundle of dynamite with the fuses twisted into one. Blake had learned a bit about explosives during the Boer War from former goldminers, of whom there were quite a few in the ranks of Steinaecker's Horse. He had prepared the fuse to give himself two minutes to retreat from the place of the blast; he had spied a depression between two small dunes which he hoped would give him enough cover. The trick, now, was to light the fuse at the right time – too early and the driver might have time to stop the train and for the guards on board to rouse themselves and deploy into good all-round defence, and too late and the explosion might go off after the engine and carriages had passed over the dynamite. An even more horrifying thought was that the blast might kill the innocent prisoners on board.

Blake had timed the approach of a train the day before and done his calculations accordingly. Down the line he saw steam staining the horizon and the black blob of an engine. He took out his pocket watch and exactly ten seconds later he struck a match and held it to the wick.

Satisfied that the fuse was sputtering nicely he got up and ran at a crouch to the dip in the ground. He threw himself down and peeked over the brow of the dune. The train was chugging along and there were no signs that the driver or anyone else on board had seen him. Seated on top of the second and the last of the six carriages were guards, rifles sticking up from the cocoon of blankets they had wrapped around themselves.

Blake lowered his head. There was nothing more to be gained by watching.

The blast shattered the peace of the morning air and was followed a moment later by the piercing screech of brakes. Blake popped his head up and held his breath as he saw sparks flying from the wheels of the locomotive. For a moment it seemed as though the train would stop before the break in the line, but then the engine left the line and skewed off into the sand. The locomotive rolled onto its side, taking the second carriage with it until the whole train ploughed to a halt.

For a second there was silence, but then Blake felt a vibration of a different kind. He looked over his shoulder and saw the Nama rebels galloping across the desert, rifles drawn. Blake brought his Lee Enfield to bear and looked for targets. The sentry closest to the front of the train had been thrown from his perch, but the second had somehow managed to hang on and was taking aim at the horsemen. Blake aimed and fired and the sentry toppled backwards off the roof of the carriage.

Stunned soldiers were climbing down from the carriages but some of the Nama horsemen had already dismounted and were pushing forward, firing from the hip. Another rebel had crossed the lines and circled the train. He found a carriage full of Schutztruppen all looking the other way and he tossed a lit stick of dynamite inside. The blast blew out several windows.

Blake got up and ran forward. An officer crawled out of the toppled first carriage and pointed a pistol at him, but Blake fired first and the man fell back inside. Blake then saw a man in a grimy undershirt and trousers lying next to the loco, his face bloodied – the driver, he thought. Blake ran to the next carriage, a cattle car. He heard voices inside and fists pummelling on the wooden door.

'Stand back inside!' he called. He chambered a round and fired at the padlock securing the car. The lock pinged and fell off and Blake hauled the heavy door open. Men and women began jumping down. 'Horses, over there!'

Blake looked to the rebels and, as planned, four riders were each leading five more tethered horses. To his surprise, Blake saw that one of the riders was Peter Kohl, his face also blackened now. Peter charged towards him.

'The driver's wounded,' Blake said to Peter as soon as he was near.

Peter nodded and once he had handed over his spare horses to the Nama prisoners he dismounted and ran to the locomotive driver.

The battle was almost done. The Nama had overrun the train and Germans were being rousted out of carriages. The second prison car had been opened and its inhabitants provided with horses, some of them two to a mount.

Blake found Gert, the leader of the Nama war band. 'Take the injured to the far side of the train, away from the other prisoners – I don't want able-bodied men identifying the doctor later.'

'Yes, Blake.'

'Have you seen Liesl Morengo?' Blake asked.

'No.'

Blake looked around. Smoke was billowing from two of the carriages. 'What's happening there?'

'I ordered my men to burn the train,' Gert said. 'The railway line will allow the Germans to move more men and weapons to where they're fighting us.'

It was a smart move, Blake thought, but if Liesl had been on this train she was still in one of those carriages. Blake climbed into the first of the cattle cars, the one whose lock he had shot off. Inside it smelled of urine and sweat. It took his eyes a moment to adjust to the gloom but when they did he saw a form lying curled in a corner. Heart pounding, he went to the person and laid down. He put a hand on a cold arm and rolled the woman over. It wasn't Liesl.

He climbed out of the carriage and to his horror saw that the second car that had held the prisoners had smoke billowing from the doorway. He went to the opening, but just as he tried vaulting up into the burning wagon Peter Kohl appeared in the doorway.

'Here, take her!' Peter handed a limp form to him.

It was Liesl. Peter jumped out as flames consumed the wooden car. 'Lie her down, Blake.' He coughed.

Moving away from the burning car, Blake placed Liesl on her back. Peter knelt and took her wrists and lifted her arms up and down, over her head and back. He lowered his mouth to hers and blew into it.

'What are you doing?' Blake asked, horrified.

Peter blew into Liesl's mouth then looked up. 'I have done this with newborn babies who don't breathe. Sometimes it works.'

'Sometimes?'

'Push down on her chest, Blake, try to get some blood moving from her heart.'

Before he had a chance, Liesl coughed then groaned in pain.

Blake started. For all his assurances Peter looked as surprised as Blake felt as Liesl came back to life in front of them.

'She must have been knocked unconscious and then she was breathing in smoke. She was not breathing, Blake.' Peter carried on with his examination of Liesl, telling her to stay as still as she could. 'She has a broken arm as well. I will bandage it now and put her on my horse. You go, sort out the Nama and the prisoners.'

Blake told Gert to strip the German soldiers of their weapons, ammunition and food and to send them walking back down the line.

'We should just kill them,' Gert said.

Blake shook his head. 'There's been enough of that.'

Once the prisoners had been stripped and sent on their way Blake helped load the captured rifles onto a spare packhorse. Claire, seeing that the enemy troops were almost out of sight, rode down from the *koppies*. She dismounted and came to Blake.

'Well done,' she said. 'And Liesl?'

Blake, arms full of rifles, indicated with a nod. Peter had Liesl in his arms and was taking her to a horse. The girl was looking over Peter's shoulder, towards them. Blake handed the confiscated weapons to a grateful Nama rebel. Claire got up on her toes, put an arm around Blake's neck and kissed him.

'We need to get out of Africa, Blake,' Claire said into his ear as she broke the kiss.

He looked into her eyes. 'Whatever you want.'

She took a deep breath. 'There's just one thing.'

He gave her a crooked grin. 'Does it involve gold?'

'Yes and no. Like I said, I want to do something to help these people. It will involve money and horses.'

He raised his eyebrows. 'Are you growing a conscience, Claire Martin?'

She gave him a playful punch on the arm. 'Sure and you're the one who said he'd had enough of war, and now you're blowing up trains and rescuing fair maidens. Our work isn't done here, Blake, not while I've still got some of Kruger's gold left.'

Colonel von Deimling's headquarters, Keetmanshoop, German South West Africa, one week later

Colonel Berthold von Deimling was poring over a map of the Karasberge, looking for a way to get back into the mountains and rout Jakob Morengo's forces once and for all. A knock on his door made him look up. 'Enter.'

Leutnant Kurtz, his young aide, opened the door, limped in and saluted. 'One of the Boer scouts, du Preez, is here to see you, sir.'

'I'm busy, Kurtz. Find out what he wants and make a time this afternoon.'

'He says it is about the Australian fighting with the Nama.'

'Ah, show him in, quickly now, Kurtz.'

The aide saluted and left and du Preez entered, taking off his hat.

'Sit, sit,' von Deimling said.

'I have word of the Australian, Prestwich,' du Preez said.

'I have learned his real name is Blake, but carry on,' von Deimling said.

'Our source in Upington –'

'Yes, the barman. What is his name?'

'Erasmus, Colonel. He says Prestwich – Blake – has been gathering horses, a good many of them, perhaps fifty. Erasmus told me that the British Cape Mounted Police have been paying him for information and supplying him with their own intelligence on Blake's movements. Blake has been gathering them in Upington and is planning on delivering them to one of Morengo's men on our side of the border.'

Von Deimling tapped his lip. 'We can catch him.'

Du Preez shook his head. 'With respect, Colonel, Blake will sniff out an ambush by the Schutztruppen a mile away. *I* can catch him, because I know how he works. I've passed word to Blake via Erasmus that I have a herd of cattle to sell, on this side of the border. Blake has said he is interested and can meet me on the twenty-fourth of the month. Erasmus believes that this is when the Australian will be bringing horses to Morengo's man.'

'You know what is expected of you when you meet Blake, du Preez?' von Deimling said. 'High command has no wish for a trial, even one that will end in a hanging, nor of meddling from the British government or their colonies.'

Du Preez stood and nodded. 'This man is an enemy of your Kaiser, operating in civilian clothes, as a spy. He fought against my people and his kind took joy in executing prisoners taken on the field of battle. In addition he is a traitor to his race. Trust me, Colonel, you will not have to worry about Blake after I see him.'

Von Deimling gave a curt nod. 'Very good. Send in *Leutnant* Kurtz on your way out.'

Du Preez put on his battered hat and left. Von Deimling felt a rush of excitement. Blake was almost within their grasp and according to du Preez, the British colonel, Walters, had helped deliver the time and the place of the Australian's next border crossing via the double-dealing informant Erasmus. That meant it was time for von Deimling to honour his side of his deal with Walters. The young officer entered.

'Kurtz, you know Frau Kohl, the doctor's wife?'

'Yes, sir.'

'I want you to talk to the Landespolizei commander and have charges drawn up against her, for sedition. She was most strident in her criticism of conditions on the railway line and the camp at Lüderitz. I suspect her of aiding the rebels and she is wanted for questioning on the British side of the border for an historic crime in South Africa. She is to be taken into protective custody, until further notice.'

Kurtz looked surprised. 'Ah, sir, she is a lady of some repute in the colony. Do we perhaps have some evidence that I can cite or take to the –'

'Kurtz? You dare to defy me? I might have the Landespolizei arrest you instead. You of all people with your wounded leg should feel no sympathy for those who support our enemy. Now get to it.'

'Yes, sir.' Kurtz saluted and left.

Von Deimling shook his head at Kurtz's impudence. He would need to get word to Walters that he was taking the woman into custody, but not via *Leutnant* Kurtz. The foolish young officer was correct in that the woman would have some standing in the community, but Claire Kohl was not pure German and, as such, lacked the strength and moral courage of his people. She was a liability to the colony with her soft liberal views, even if they might be shared by certain weak-willed people back in Germany. It would do no harm to his command or South West Africa if she was delivered into the hands of the British to face justice for her crimes in South Africa.

*

Leutnant Thilo Kurtz leaned on his walking stick as he limped out of the headquarters building onto the dusty Keetmanshoop Street. A Nama woman carrying a skinny baby hurried out of his way and crossed the street to avoid him.

Kurtz had come to German South West Africa full of the patriotic zeal to protect his country's interests against a murderous heathen enemy. What he had seen had both surprised and disenchanted him. The Nama were mostly Christians, poor people who had nothing any more, no land or possessions, and who had initially fought on Germany's side. Von Deimling had said Kurtz should hate them, but he didn't. He had watched in horror on that day in Narudas how some of his soldiers had slaughtered innocent civilians, and how the mountain guns had zeroed in on the Nama's homes. This, he had thought, was no way for a professional soldier to wage war.

Dr Peter Kohl was a kindly, jovial man, and he had saved Thilo's life and his leg with his quick first aid and, later, surgery. Thilo had met Peter's wife, Claire, once, and she had struck him as being as opinionated and headstrong as she was beautiful. She reminded him of a girl he had left behind in Munich.

Von Deimling had told him to advise the Landespolizei of his intention to have Frau Kohl arrested. Well, Thilo thought, Peter Kohl was a policeman, and as Claire's husband he should be notified of the crimes she was about to be accused of. It was late in the day, the sun turning the desert dust red gold. Dr Kohl would be propping up the bar in the Schützenhaus, which happened to be on the way to the Landespolizei station. Thilo walked up the stairs of the shooting house.

CHAPTER 49

The desert east of Lüderitz, Namibia, the present day

Joanne's car engine cut out and she drifted off onto the left-hand side of the road.

Nick glanced at Anja.

'Nick, won't you get out and have a look under the bonnet, please?' Joanne said. 'I'll try and start the car when you tell me.'

'I'm a city boy, a journalist, I'm no mechanic,' Nick said. 'Anja's spent a lot more time in the bush than me, maybe she should take a look as well.'

Joanne frowned. 'Well, I suppose so, but she's an academic, isn't she?'

'*She*,' Anja said, opening the back door, 'has fixed her uncle's old Land Rover plenty of times. If it's a leaking fuel line we might be able to fix it.'

'OK, no offence meant,' Joanne said.

'None taken,' Anja said.

Nick got out and lifted the bonnet when Joanne popped it. Anja joined him. Nick had a quick look around the engine bay.

'I can't see anything obvious, Joanne. Maybe give it another try?' he called.

'OK.'

Nick heard a faint click from inside the car, but there were no noises from the engine bay.

'There's a car coming, from the Lüderitz side,' Anja said.

Nick peered around the open bonnet lid and looked where Anja was pointing. As the car came closer he recognised it. 'It's Scott's car.'

Joanne got out. 'Shit.'

Nick heard another engine and turned the other way. From the direction of Aus, to the east, he could see a white pick-up with a green box-like rooftop tent. It looked like one of the many hired safari cars he had seen since entering Namibia. The truck was travelling fast, while Scott was slowing.

Nick stepped out into the road as the tourist vehicle closed on them. He put his hand up.

'What are you doing, Nick?' Joanne called. 'Come back.'

He ignored her. 'Anja, come here.'

She went to his side and he lowered his voice to a whisper as he continued waving. 'Read the email I sent to your phone a few minutes ago. We need to stop this car.'

The driver of the hire vehicle, perhaps worrying that Nick meant him some harm, tried to swerve around him, but Anja moved further out onto the road, preventing the driver from passing them. The vehicle stopped.

Nick went to the driver's window and rapped on it. Anja moved quickly in front of the truck to stop the driver from leaving.

A blond man wound down the window.

'Take this woman to Lüderitz, to the police, please. This is an emergency and people's lives are at risk.'

'Nick!' Joanne called.

Again he ignored her.

'Blimey mate, are you serious?' the man asked in an English accent.

'Deadly, mate. Take Anja here, please.'

The man looked to his female companion, who shrugged helplessly. Nick saw that, thankfully, the vehicle was a double cab, with room in the back for Anja. Before Anja could protest Nick guided her in. 'Get the cops.'

'OK,' she said to Nick, then to the driver, 'go!'

Joanne got out of the car, carrying her handbag. She reached into it and pulled out a pistol. Nick looked her in the eye.

Joanne pointed to the BMW sedan which had pulled up a hundred metres from them. 'That's Scott's car.'

'I know,' Nick said. 'You think he's going to try and shoot you, or me? He could have killed us on Shark Island.'

'That's not his style these days,' Joanne said, 'he gets other people to do his dirty work. That's why he had a sniper open fire on you. He screamed away to make it look like he had nothing to do with it. Just listen to what he says now.'

Joanne hung the long strap of her handbag on her right shoulder, but kept the gun out of sight in the bag, still gripping it.

Scott got out of the BMW, but stood behind the open door.

'Nick,' Scott called, 'come over here.'

'Are you crazy?' Joanne said back to her ex-husband. 'You tried to have him and the German woman killed on Shark Island.'

Scott shook his head. 'You're one of a kind, Joanne. Nick, I had nothing to do with that attack on you.'

'What are you doing out here?' Nick asked. 'How did you know where to find us? You left before Joanne arrived.'

Scott looked to Joanne, then to Nick. 'She SMSed me, told me where you were heading.'

'Really?' Nick raised his eyebrows in feigned surprise and looked to Joanne.

'He's lying, he followed us,' Joanne said. 'You can't trust a word he says.'

'I am not lying,' Scott said.

Nick sensed movement in his peripheral vision and turned his head quickly. He was worried a sniper might appear from nowhere. It was, instead, a group of three desert horses – it looked like a big stallion, a smaller mare, and a very small foal. Nick remembered that Anja had seen a newborn. He hoped she would return soon with the police. Joanne and Scott were locked in a tense stand-off and Nick was acutely aware of the gun in Joanne's hand.

'Anja's gone to get the police, Scott.'

'Good,' Scott said. 'Hopefully they can catch whoever was shooting at us.'

Joanne laughed. 'You can't talk yourself out of this one.'

'I really do not know what you're talking about, Joanne.'

Nick interrupted. 'You've got the manuscript, Scott, you know where the rest of Kruger's gold is, where Claire Martin dumped it.'

'What the hell are you talking about? What manuscript? I do not bloody well know where any gold is, but maybe you can enlighten me, since you believe I know already.'

'Paul Kruger's gold is ...' Nick had his eye on Joanne, and as soon as he saw her hand start to come out of her handbag and glimpsed the black metal of the pistol he leapt on her, grabbing her right arm and pushing her to the ground. 'Help me, Scott, she's got a gun!'

Nick had knocked Joanne over and was trying to twist her arm behind her back and force her to drop the pistol, but it was harder than he thought and she was far stronger than he'd imagined. She twisted in his arms and sank her teeth into his shoulder, biting down hard.

Nick screamed and relaxed his hold on her enough for Joanne to move her hand between them. Then Nick heard the boom of a gunshot and felt like he'd been punched in the gut.

CHAPTER 50

The desert south of Klipdam Farm, German South West Africa, 1906

Blake crossed the border under the cover of darkness. Beside him rode Dawie, the young Nama man who worked for Rassie. Blake needed him to help keep the fifty horses they trailed under control, and then to take the cattle they expected to collect from the Boer, du Preez, back to Upington.

Blake would not be returning to the Cape Colony.

Blake had taken the gold that Jakob Morengo owed him – Claire's gold – and some of her remaining stash from her farm, and used half of it to buy the fifty new horses. The remainder would pay for the cattle du Preez would sell him. When the deal with the Boers was done Blake and Dawie would part company and Dawie would take the cattle to Upington and deliver them to Morengo at the Spangenberg farm. The money Dawie would make for on-selling them in the Cape Colony would go to help the Nama refugees in the camps on the British side of the border.

After leaving Dawie, Blake would take the horses a short distance further to Gert, Morengo's man who commanded a new band of rebels the Black Napoleon had formed in the Klipdam area. Morengo had decided it was time to escalate the war against the Germans.

Blake and Dawie led their mob of horses along a gully, the way ahead clearly visible thanks to a night sky ablaze with stars. Thoughts of Claire kept the chill from cutting through his oilskin.

The longer Claire and Blake stayed in Africa the greater the risk of the Germans or Llewellyn Walters catching up with them, but Claire was adamant that she wanted to leave some sort of legacy behind. They had discussed it and Blake had agreed to help her implement her plan to supply a last herd of horses to Morengo. He knew this was important to her, perhaps to atone for the theft of the gold in the first place. As tired as they both were of war they knew that Jakob Morengo and his people would have to continue the fight after they were gone.

Blake and Dawie rode on through the long, cool night. Their strategy was to rest up during the day to avoid German patrols.

Blake decided he would miss Africa's enchanting night skies, not to mention the sunrises, but after the horses were delivered and Dawie was on his way with the cattle he was looking forward to a new life. To the east Blake saw the red sun peeking above the dunes and the silhouettes of two men on horseback.

Blake looked to Dawie, who nodded, indicating he had seen them too. Dawie took his Lee–Metford rifle, an older but well cared for predecessor of Blake's Lee Enfield, from its holster by the saddle and chambered a round. Dawie cradled the rifle across his lap. Blake opened his oilskin coat to make sure his Broomhandle Mauser was within easy reach.

The two riders closed on Dawie and Blake, and as they got closer the sun climbed, and Blake recognised them.

'Du Preez, de Waal,' Blake said, nodding to the two Afrikaners.

Blake reined in his mount, stopping twenty metres short of the Boers. Both men were traders, like him, and he knew from barroom talk that the pair had been on commando, fighting against the British and colonial forces during the war in South Africa. That in itself was not unusual for men of their age, but they had moved to German South West Africa rather than live in their birth country under British rule. They were frequent visitors to Upington and de Waal was the man who had tried to molest Liesl in Rassie's bar. While he and Blake had traded blows that night, they hadn't fought since.

'I'm curious,' Blake said. 'Who would have told you that I was moving horses?'

Du Preez shrugged. 'It's hard to keep the movement of fifty animals a secret in a small town like Upington. I tried to buy some myself to sell this side of the border and old Stephanou told me you'd bought up all his stock.'

Blake nodded. The story checked out.

'Where are the cattle?' Dawie asked the men.

De Waal indicated with a flick of his head. 'Over that far dune, grazing.'

'All right,' Blake said. 'Let's have a look.'

They walked their horses to the base of a dune.

'We must dismount here,' du Preez said. 'It's quicker if we climb the dune rather than ride all the way around to the valley.'

'Take your rifle with you,' Blake said quietly to Dawie, who nodded.

Blake got off his horse and lagged behind as du Preez set off with Dawie beside him. De Waal was between him and the others. Blake noticed the two Boers had both left their rifles on their horses.

'I like your rifle, boy,' du Preez said to Dawie. 'Lee–Metford? An old one but a good one.'

'Yes,' Dawie said, pride evident on his young face.

'Can I have a look at it?'

'It's loaded,' Dawie said.

'I know how to handle one of these almost better than I do a woman.' Du Preez laughed.

'Dawie,' Blake called. He would never hand another man his weapon, unless it was unloaded and cleared.

Dawie looked over his shoulder but he was already passing his treasured weapon to du Preez.

Du Preez took the rifle, swung around and fired from the hip, shooting Dawie in the chest.

The young Nama was blown backwards and rolled down the hill. Blake reached for the Mauser at his belt as de Waal spun around to face him. De Waal lifted a Colt revolver but Blake fired first, two shots from his automatic, and knocked him down.

As de Waal fell Blake could see that du Preez had brought Dawie's Lee–Metford up to his shoulder and was taking careful aim, waiting for his moment. Blake pulled the trigger again, but du Preez was fifty yards up the dune. It was long range for a pistol, but not a rifle.

Blake fell onto his back, and while he felt no pain immediately he put his fingers on his belly and they came away red.

Du Preez half jogged, half slid down the loose sand of the dune and came to Blake. He looked down at him. 'If you think I'm going to put you out of your misery, you're wrong, Blake.'

Blake stared up at him, meeting the other man's eyes. Du Preez knew his real name; this was not just a crooked deal. He had been betrayed.

'You don't deserve a quick end for what you've done. You can bleed, burn or freeze to death, depending on whether the bullet, the sun or the cold night take you first.'

Du Preez spat on him, then turned and walked away. Blake said a prayer for Claire and closed his eyes.

CHAPTER 51

The desert east of Lüderitz, Namibia, the present day

Nick looked up past Joanne and saw Scott running towards them. He hoped that Scott would be able to tackle her and get the gun off her before she could shoot him as well.

There was a whizzing sound, like Nick had heard on Shark Island, and then a puff of red spray erupted from Scott's chest and he pitched forward into the sand.

Joanne stood and looked at the two men at her feet.

'It didn't have to be like this,' Joanne said.

'It was you,' Nick said. He had his hand on his belly and when he looked down he could see blood oozing from between his fingers.

'You stopped me going for my gun,' Joanne said. 'How did you know?'

'You ... you said something to me earlier, about my time on *The Australian*. I never told you the name of the newspaper I worked for. Susan, though, had researched me. I wasn't sure – maybe you googled me and found some of my old bylines ...' He coughed and the pain came, at last, unwelcome, 'so I checked Facebook in the car.'

'Bloody Facebook,' she said.

Nick managed a small nod. He felt himself getting weaker as his shirt became increasingly wet. 'I looked at your profile, at your friends, and found your sister. Trudy Walters.'

Joanne sighed. 'Yes. There are millions of Walterses in the world, Nick.'

'Yes, but your great-grandfather, or whatever he was, Llewellyn Walters, was the man who set up my relative and Claire Martin to be killed. It was you, not Scott, who was obsessed with finding Kruger's gold, and I'm guessing that fixation was handed down to you through the generations.'

Joanne looked away from him, just for an instant, and waved to someone in the distance before giving them a thumbs-up.

'The same sniper who fired at us on Shark Island?' Nick said.

'Yes. One of my ex-husband's old Koevoet buddies, but he works for me these days. Money's stronger than any ideology. He could have killed you there, Nick, and the woman. You were meant to be scared off, just like everyone else who came into contact with the manuscript.'

'What ...' his vision was starting to grey, 'what about Susan? She must have worked for you, as well as Scott. Was she in on your plan all along?'

Joanne frowned. 'I can't let you live, Nick, but I'm not so cruel as to let you die without knowing about Susan. I sent Susan to Australia with a cover story about writing an article, to search the archives and find a descendent of Cyril Blake, to see if she could turn up some new evidence about what happened to Kruger's gold. When she found out about your manuscript I told her to get a copy immediately, to steal one if you wouldn't hand it over straight away. She told me to wait, that she had convinced you to share it with her, but I didn't want to wait for some German kid to translate it, or for you or anyone else to get to the gold before me. Susan objected, telling me she was a PI, not criminal, and wouldn't be a part of any thieving.'

'She ... she went to you.'

'Yes,' Joanne said, 'she came to Cape Town and threatened to call in the police and expose me. As well as objecting to my methods I think she genuinely fell for you, Nick. Shame. However, I think she needed time to break the news to you that she'd been less than honest with you. After she stormed out of my office, I followed her in my car, called her and convinced her to pull over. She stopped and we talked, but she didn't see reason. Stupid.'

Nick felt the bile rise in his throat and he didn't know if it was his wound or his revulsion for this manicured woman who stood over him, talking as if she was recounting a bothersome business meeting. 'You shot her.'

Joanne stared at him, but said nothing.

He could see it in those cold eyes. 'You made it look like a carjacking and you sent me that SMS, pretending to be Susan breaking up with me.'

Joanne smiled.

'Fuck you,' Nick croaked.

'No, Nick, fuck you. You lose, and now I know where the gold is.'

'The ... the museum and visitors' centre on Shark Island. That was your idea, not Scott's, so you could look for the gold while the foundations were dug.'

'My very ex-husband was as appalling a lover as he was a businessman. Even though we divorced it was in my interest for his ludicrous Windhoek golf estate to proceed; I still have shares in his company. The development approval was looking shaky but as soon as I learned about the gold buried at Shark Island I planted the idea of the cultural centre in his head. It all came together nicely – the Namibian Government loved the idea, and now that Scott's dead I can take over the company and proceed with both the estate and digging up the causeway.'

'You've got what you want, Joanne.' He coughed and winced.

'Yes, I have. I'd offer to let you live, but this is too messy. You had plenty of chances to run away like the failure you are. Ironically, Susan gave you a set of balls you never had. Now, if I hurry I'll catch Anja before she gets to the police. In my car I shouldn't have any trouble hitting two hundred per hour on the road to Lüderitz. I'll easily catch that tourist wagon, but it's time for us to say goodbye. Sorry, Nick.'

Joanne lifted the pistol and took aim at Nick. He stared at her, not wanting to give her the satisfaction of closing his eyes. Before he died he said a prayer for Anja, and for Susan.

CHAPTER 52

The desert east of Lüderitz, Namibia, the present day

'Stop the car!' Anja had seen the Hilux pick-up on the side of the road, with no one in sight.

The bonnet was not up, indicating engine trouble, and a quick inspection when Anja got out showed that none of the tyres were punctured. Ray and Anne, the English tourists who were driving her, had suffered a blowout before picking her up. The hired vehicle's jack and wheel spanner were sitting on the backseat next to her, where they had been tossed, awaiting proper stowage.

On the far side of the Hilux Anja had seen a single set of footprints leading away into the desert.

Anja had been in two minds. There could be a perfectly innocent explanation for the vehicle being there, but she couldn't think of one. She looked out into the desert and a glint of light, a reflection on glass, caught her eye.

'Go to the police in Lüderitz!' she said to Ray as she reached into his vehicle and grabbed the wheel spanner. 'Get them to send someone back here, immediately. Tell them it's murder. Send an ambulance as well, just in case.'

'What about my spanner?'

'I'll give it back to you when you bring the damn police!'

Ray drove off, probably grateful to be rid of her, Anja thought. She walked into the desert and saw now why the *bakkie* was parked where it was. Ahead of her was a dune that ran perpendicular to the road. It was high and would have an unobstructed view over the point where Joanne had stopped, less than half a kilometre away.

An easy shot for a trained sniper.

Anja remembered her time hunting with her father. She stooped low as she moved, which she did as quickly and as quietly as she could. The sand muffled her footprints.

She saw the man's boots first, just below the crest of the dune. He had nestled his body into the sand and was peering intently through the rifle's telescopic sights. She caught sight of his right hand and recognised the liver spots and scar she had seen on the man who had assaulted her.

Anja saw the slight jerk of the man's shoulder and heard the muffled report of the bullet leaving the barrel. As her father had told her, there was no such thing as a truly silenced rifle.

Anja started to run. She prayed she would not be too late.

The man was still peering through his scope. As Anja got closer she could see over the ridge of the dune. Joanne was standing, a hand outstretched. Both Scott and Nick were lying on the ground. Anja felt a wave of nausea wash over her. Did this mean she was seconds too late? Rage overtook her and she ran at the prone man.

He must have heard the squeak of her shoes on the sand because he started to roll, but not before Anja swung the spanner and brought it down hard on the side of his head.

The sniper fell back, either out cold or dead from the blow. Anja didn't have time to check his pulse. She lay down behind the rifle and sighted through the scope. As the figures below came into focus she could see that Nick was moving a little, lifting one hand as if gesturing while speaking, though his other hand was over his belly.

Joanne raised her pistol and took aim at Nick.

Time suddenly seemed to slow down. Without thinking anything at all, Anja stilled her breathing, worked the bolt on the rifle to chamber a round, took aim, and fired.

Joanne fell to the ground. Anja studied her through the scope. Her heart was racing and her brain was not quite able to process the fact that she had just shot someone, and possibly killed her. She watched Joanne for a few seconds, but the woman did not move. Nick crawled across to Joanne, obviously in pain, and took the pistol from her hands.

Anja set down the rifle and went to the man she had hit. She checked his pulse and found he was still alive, but unconscious. Casting about for something she could use to secure him with, she saw that he was wearing a bracelet made of braided parachute cord. She pulled it over his hand and quickly unravelled it before using it to tie his wrists behind his back. Then she checked his pockets and found the keys to the Hilux. Anja picked up the rifle, ran down the dune to the *bakkie*, got in and sped down the road to Nick.

She would need something to treat him with, she realised. Jumping out, she searched the back of the Hilux and found a first aid kit which she ran with to Nick.

'You ...' he said as she dropped to her knees next to him, almost out of breath.

'Yes.' She took out a wound dressing and unwrapped it. 'Place the pad against the bullet hole and hold it there, as hard as you can.'

'The sniper?'

'He's out cold, tied up.'

Anja couldn't help but notice the look of admiration on Nick's face. 'Where ... where did you learn to shoot like that, to do first aid, to beat up and tie up a gunman?'

She smiled. 'Africa.'

*

As Anja had hoped, they met a police car and ambulance with lights flashing on their way back to Lüderitz.

Paramedics carried Nick out of the Hilux, where Anja had helped him lie across the back seat, and loaded him into the back of the ambulance. After giving the police a brief rundown of the crime scene that awaited them further along the road to Aus, Anja got in the back of the vehicle with Nick.

While a paramedic checked him and ran an IV line into his arm Nick managed to hang on to consciousness. 'Anja ...'

'Yes, Nick?' She took his hand and squeezed it, as hard as she dared. Anja looked into Nick's eyes and had the sudden realisation that she did not want to let go of him.

'Read the ending for me, please,' he said, 'but don't let go of my hand.'

EPILOGUE

Aus prisoner of war camp, the former colony of German South West Africa, now a British protectorate, 1915

On this cold night in the desert I have come to the end of our tale.

Colonel von Deimling heard from the Boer, du Preez, that he had left Blake wounded, to die in pain like a dog in the desert. The colonel was a man driven by efficiency and wanted proof that Blake, the man also known as Edward Prestwich, was dead. He ordered a patrol under his aide, *Leutnant* Kurtz, to go into the desert to where the ambush had taken place and ascertain that Blake had indeed perished.

As the Landespolizei doctor, I was ordered to accompany the patrol and ensure that Blake did not return alive. Von Deimling was furious that Claire had escaped and Kurtz and I were told that unless we confirmed Blake was dead he would have both our heads.

I confess I was surprised to find Blake still alive. How he survived nearly twenty-four hours in the desert, under the burning sun and through the freezing night, blood oozing from the hellishly painful wound in his belly, I have no idea.

Perhaps it was his innate strength. Perhaps it was love.

The members of our little patrol that set out from von Deimling's forward headquarters at Klipdam Farm that day were hard men, many of whom had lost comrades to the Nama. I am sure they felt little if any sympathy towards Blake, who had run guns an

410

horses to the rebels and killed his fair share of German boys. However, it is thankfully a rare breed of soldier who has the stomach to shoot an unarmed wounded man in the head.

Although I was 'only' the doctor, and a mere police reservist, I outranked Kurtz, so I was able to announce to the patrol that I would check on Blake and do what needed to be done. The other Schutztruppen talked among themselves and lit pipes and cigarettes and looked away from the deed that was about to be done, but they were close enough to hear my conversation with Blake.

He was delirious from pain and fever but the first word he said to me was 'Claire'.

For the benefit of my military comrades, listening in, I told him Claire was dead, that she had drowned.

I told him I had come to kill him. I confess, dear reader, that for a moment I thought of doing just that. I loved Claire, just as Blake did, and my career, possibly my life, were in jeopardy from my superiors if they found out I had assisted the Nama and facilitated my wife's escape to the coast. Kurtz, too, would have suffered if it had come to light that he had helped us.

However, I had developed a grudging respect for Blake and I was, in truth, envious of the love he and Claire shared. At the same time, I was falling in love with someone else and I could not go to her in the knowledge that I had executed a man she had once cared for deeply. There had been enough killing in my beloved corner of Africa.

My anger at everything that had happened was real, but my aim was not true. I fired a bullet into the sand next to Blake's head. I surreptitiously reached into my medical bag and took out a dressing, which I put into Blake's hand and had him press against the bullet hole. Young Kurtz came over and he clearly saw that Blake was still alive, yet he simply told his men to 'mount up', and he and I both told Colonel von Deimling what our commander wanted to hear.

That night I stole out of camp, with the ambulance cart drawn by two horses and two spare mounts tethered behind us. I would not have been surprised to find Blake dead for real, but he had managed to hang on through the rest of the day. Though Blake had lost a good deal of blood the bullet had, miraculously, missed his vital organs and exited out his side. I cleaned his wound as best I could and laid upon it a poultice made from the *kraalbos* plant. The bushman healers I had met used this to good effect in the treatment of skin conditions and wounds that were putrefying.

The horses that Blake and his dead comrade had brought with them were grazing on desert grass nearby, as was Blake's faithful mount, Bluey. I could not take the animals with me and it seemed cruel to leave them tethered to each other. I unsaddled Bluey and untied the rest of the animals. One-by-one, they galloped off. Bluey seemed at first unwilling to leave Blake and trotted along behind the wagon for the first hour or so. The other horses had formed a loose herd and moved parallel to us. Eventually Bluey left us to join the others and they drifted away. I am sure that at least some of them survived and bred as, occasionally, over the years since, I have seen wild horses and foals at a distance in the desert.

I partially dressed Blake in German uniform and the two of us journeyed once again across South West Africa, westwards, towards Lüderitz. I scrounged food and water for us and the horses at Aus and told my story, several times over, that I was taking the wounded son of a prominent German politician to Lüderitz for treatment and a ticket home to the Fatherland.

The decay had begun to set into Blake's wound and he cried and yelled through two nights, most often calling the name of the woman he loved. It wasn't Liesl, it was Claire.

In time the bushmen's herb worked its magic; Blake's fever broke and the stitches I had placed in his wound looked clean. When Blake was lucid I told him that I had lied about Claire's death, and spread the word through Keetmanshoop that she had drowned at sea. Blake cried and, I think, would have hugged me if he'd had the strength.

On our journey I quizzed him, as I had Claire, about his recollection of events in South Africa and in our colony, about Walter and his love for my wife. He told me everything, just as Claire had explained her relationship with the American, Belvedere, and his motivation for stealing the gold. Claire had also told me where the gold was buried, on Shark Island, though at that time it was clea that I could not very well start digging up the causeway leading to the concentration camp. I told Claire that if I ever did find the gold I would keep it for her. Well, some of it.

The next day the billowing curtains of sand and dust gave way to the sparkling icy blue of the Atlantic.

I found Claire in hiding in one of the warehouses her first husband had once owned, down by the docks in Hafen Street. She used the last of her gold from the farm, other than what she had given Blake to purchase the horses, to buy the yacht and had spent time with a couple of old salts who ran the warehouse, relearning how to sail it. The two sailors, friends of her first husband, who were hiding her on the promise of gold, had reported her disappearance to the port authorities and a search had been mounted.

Claire ran to Blake and enfolded him in her arms when we arrived. 'You made it,' she said, after she had finished kissing him.

'Thanks to Peter,' Blake said.

I gave my wife a sad smile and a hug and she kissed me goodbye.

I asked Blake if he had an address in Australia, so that I might write to him and Claire one day, when the war was over. He gave me his mother's details and while I never did write I will send her a copy of these scribblings, just in case she never heard from her son again.

The yacht was a fine ketch whose owner had been killed in the fighting against the Nama and Claire said she could sail it single-handedly, although once Blake made a full recovery the job would be easier.

I bade farewell to Claire and Blake that night and tossed the mooring line onto the deck. The yacht slipped away on a mercifully calm sea and I never saw nor heard from either of them again.

After the war against the Nama and the Herero ended and the death camp on Shark Island closed, my new wife, Liesl, and I discussed what to do about the gold buried beneath the causeway.

'Nothing,' Liesl told me. 'The ghosts of too many of my people haunt that place, Peter, and they cannot be disturbed in the name of something as trivial as greed. Gold is a metal, cold and unfeeling, and pursuit of it brings only tears and death.'

She is a good woman, as brave and as principled as her uncle Jakob was. Her people's rebellion was crushed, but she lived and bore me three fine children, two boys and a girl. They are all safely out of this war, being cared for by her family. At the time we discussed the gold Liesl was pregnant with our first son and I remember she put my hand on her swollen belly. 'This is what is most important, Peter.'

'Life?' I asked her.

'Love.'

HISTORICAL NOTE AND ACKNOWLEDGEMENTS

Much of this story is true and some of the characters are real, or based on real people.

While some of the events in *Ghosts of the Past* took place in real life, I have been a bit creative with historical dates in order to accommodate all of the elements I wanted to squeeze into my story. The battle of Narudas and the plot to kill the real person represented as Cyril Blake actually occurred in 1905 (not 1906, as mentioned in the book). Likewise, the Schützenhaus in Keetmanshoop did not open until 1907, the same year much of the railway line from Lüderitz was built, and the Shark Island concentration camp only began taking in Nama prisoners in 1906. For these reasons I decided to split the difference between the three years over which all these events took place and set Part Two of *Ghosts of the Past* in 1906.

Here are some of the facts behind this work of fiction:

On September 24, 1905, a real life Australian, 24-year-old Edward Lionel Presgrave, from Hurstville, Sydney, lay dying in the remote desert, south of Klipdam in German South West Africa (modern Namibia), near the border of The Cape Colony (South Africa). Presgrave had been shot in the gut and left to die by one of two Afrikaners, named du Preez or de Waal, who were spying for the Germans. The Germans had put a price on the head of Presgrave, who had been trading guns and horses with the Nama and fighting on their side.

Du Preez reported to the Germans that he had successfully ambushed Presgrave. A patrol under the command of a Lieutenant Beyer, including a military doctor named Erchardt, was dispatched from Klipdam to check on the Australian. Against the odds, they found Presgrave still alive, bleeding from a stomach wound 20 hours after he had been shot. On the orders of Lieutenant Beyer, Presgrave was executed by a Baster (a coloured soldier) named Dirk Campbell.

Back home in Australia Presgrave's parents tried to have the matter investigated and for those responsible to be held accountable. Perhaps fearful of provoking an international incident over the actions of an upstart colonial, the governments of Australia, Britain, Germany were all, to varying degrees, complicit in sweeping the matter under the carpet.

I have assumed for the purpose of this novel that Berthold von Deimling knew of the plot to kill Presgrave, given that he was the commander of the troops Morengo and Presgrave fought against, even if the order did not come solely or directly from him. I should note here, for the record, that von Deimling became a committed pacifist and a director of the German Peace Society later in life, perhaps due to his experience in German South West Africa and/or later as a General in the First World War.

I based the character of Sergeant Cyril Blake on Edward Lionel Presgrave. Like Blake, Presgrave fought on the British side in the Anglo-Boer War in an irregular unit, though he served with Brabant's Horse, not Steinaecker's Horse. For reasons we will never know Presgrave decided to stay on in South Africa after the war and found 'work' in the Cape Colony, making his living as a horse and cattle trader, based in Upington.

Blake's unit, Steinaecker's Horse, was real. As portrayed in this novel, they were a colourful band of hunters, poachers, miners and traders who roamed the malaria and lion-infested bushveld on the border of the Transvaal and Portuguese East Africa (now Mozambique). It's said that 10 members of the unit were killed by either lions or crocodiles.

In case you think the ability of Captain Walters to survive a lion attack in this story is fanciful, I should acknowledge here that h actions are based on the true story of how Harry Wolhuter, an early ranger in the Kruger Park area and veteran of Steinaecker's Horse, fought off and killed a lioness.

I don't know what Edward Presgrave thought of the war in South Africa, but several accounts I read during my research for this book indicated that many of the Australians who fought against the Boers were uncomfortable with British commander Lord Kitchener's scorched earth strategy, which included burning farms and interning Boer women and children. Soldiers who had joined the fight full of patriotic fervour, wanting to defend the British Empire, eventually found they probably had more in common with the Afrikaner farmers they were fighting than the British high command running the war.

No one really knows what happened to the gold reserves of the two Boer republics, the Transvaal (South African Republic) and the Orange Free State. However, the legend of 'Kruger's Gold' and its purported whereabouts lives on in South Africa today. Every few years there is a newspaper report of someone claiming to have found part of the haul in a new location.

Claire Martin and Nathaniel Belvedere are fictitious, although it is a fact that many foreigners, including Germans, Dutch, Irish and Americans served on the Boer side during what is now known as the Second Anglo-Boer War of 1899-1902.

A Confederate engineering officer, Gab Rains, did invent and deploy the 'sub-terra torpedo', the precursor of the modern landmine, during the American Civil War, though I have no evidence these heinous weapons were used in the Anglo-Boer War.

Germany supplied many of the weapons used by the Boers, most notably Mauser rifles. Blake's Mauser C96 Broomhandle semi-automatic pistol was prized by soldiers and officers on both sides of the conflict, including Winston Churchill who reported on the conflict as a British war correspondent.

Jakob Morengo was real and was known as the 'Black Napoleon' by his foes, who developed a grudging respect for him. As mentioned in this book he was well educated, multilingual, and a man ahead of his time who granted women the right to speak at his council meetings before any other kaptein. Edward Presgrave took part in several engagements, including the battle at Narudas, with Morengo during 1905. I have tried to reflect the sequence of events at Narudas as accurately as possible. Morengo did indeed draw von Deimling and his troops into the Karasberge, by moving his people out of their mat houses before the German attack. He then harried the main German column on its return march to Keetmanshoop. Von Deimling's two-pronged attack from Warmbad and Keetmanshoop failed in its objective of wiping out Morengo and his supporters; instead the Germans returned to their bases tired and bloodied.

Ironically it was the British, across the border in South Africa, who put an end to Morengo's effective insurrection against the Germans. At Germany's behest the British authorities in the Cape arrested Morengo and imprisoned him for a time at Tokai (now known as Polsmor) Prison. Morengo was later released on the condition that he never again cross into German South West Africa. Morengo, however, ignored the terms of his parole and returned to his homeland to continue his fight. On one of his forays back into South Africa he was detected by the British and cornered by a joint British-German force in the southern Kalahari Desert and was killed.

How do I know all this?

I'd like to say I undertook months of painstaking research, trawling archives in South Africa, Germany, Australia and Britain and interviewing descendants of the real people involved in this story, but someone else did all that.

I am enormously indebted to Dr Peter Curson, Emeritus Professor at the Department of Health Systems and Population a Sydney's Macquarie University, who researched the life, times and untimely death of Edward Presgrave and wrote a non-fiction book of his findings, *Border Conflicts in a German African Colony Jakob Morengo and the Untold Story of Edward Presgrave*.

I first came across Edward Presgrave's story in brief reference from two books I read on the history of Namibia while researching one of my earlier novels set in that country, An Empty Coast. He mentioned in *The Kaiser's Holocaust, Germany's Forgotten Genocide and the Colonial Roots of Nazism*, by Casper W. Erichsen an

David Olusoga; and *A History of Namibia* by Marion Wallace and John Kinahan. I remember thinking when I read these books that Presgrave's story would make a great premise for a novel.

Like me, Peter Curson read those books some time ago and decided to do his own research on Edward Presgrave and write his book about him, which I read. When I started to get serious about researching *Ghosts of the Past* I contacted Peter and he suggested I write a novel based on Presgrave (which was what I hoped he would say). The rest is history, pun intended. Peter read a draft of the manuscript and provided feedback, for which I am extremely grateful.

I have tried my best in this novel to accurately reflect life and death in the concentration camps of the Anglo-Boer War in South Africa, and during the Herero and Nama wars in German South West Africa. These two conflicts, and in particular what happened to the non-combatants interned in these camps, remain contentious subjects in South Africa and Namibia to this day. I have tried to play a 'straight bat' when writing about these emotive subjects, but if I've cause offence to anyone by my interpretation of history I'd like to take this opportunity to apologise.

As well as Peter Curson's book, and those already mentioned, I also benefitted from *Steinaecker's Horsemen* by the late William (Bill) Woolmore, and *Scorched Earth* by Fransjohan Pretorius, a comprehensive analysis of Kitchener's strategy in the Anglo-Boer War and the British concentration camps.

A number of other people helped with the research and proofreading of *Ghosts of the Past*.

On his last foray into the desert Edward Presgrave was accompanied by his friend, a Dane by the name of Frode Sahlertz. Frode was taken into custody into by the Afrikaner spies and spent time in German prison. Via Peter Curson I was able to correspond with Frode's granddaughter, Lucretia Sahlertz, living in South Africa. I am grateful to her for sharing with me her own knowledge and documents from the time.

My aunt, Sue Park, like the fictitious Nick Eatwell's aunty Sheila, is passionate about researching our family history and I am grateful to her for explaining the rather complex manner in which Susan Vidler would have been able to track down Nick in Australia.

Thanks, too, to friend, fellow author and horse lover Karly Lane for checking and correcting my references to horses and to horse trainer Gerald Egan for his advice about moving mobs of horses across country.

The wild horses of Namibia still exist, although as mentioned in this story their numbers have decreased in recent years due to drought and predation by hyenas. I have tried to accurately portray their plight, although I must stress that the theory that the horses are descended from mounts released during the war between the Nama and Germany is fictitious. The most commonly accepted theory on the horses' origin is the one I have also referenced in the novel, that the first horses escaped during the bombing of the South African military camp by a German aircraft in 1915. I am grateful to Christine Swiegers from the Namibia Wild Horses Foundation, based at the lovely Klein-Aus Vista lodge, for answering my questions about the horses.

My good friend in Sydney, psychotherapist Charlotte Stapf analysed my characters, corrected their behaviours and my German, and gave me some descriptions of Munich – thank you, again

In South Africa my go-to person for all matters African and Afrikaans, Annelien Oberholzer, once more read and corrected the manuscript. Baie Dankie, my friend.

Firearms expert Fritz Rabe again deserves my thanks, this time for delving into history to make sure my aim was true in relation to firearms and ammunition. Friend and former Army comrade Dave Morley also read the manuscript and I'm grateful to him for his corrections and suggestions, including the reference to sub-terr torpedoes.

I'd also like to thank historian Bruce Gaunson, author of Fighting the Kaiserreich, Australia's epic within the Great War, for passing on his knowledge of early German military espionage and his suggestions for Claire Martin's family background.

In Namibia I am particularly grateful to my good friend and the general manager of HitRadio Namibia, Wilfried Hähner, and to my new friend Charl Viljoen, a keen student of German South West Africa's history, for reading the manuscript, correcting errors and providing feedback.

As I have tried to explain in *Ghosts of the Past*, while the conflict between Germany and the Herero and Nama peoples is still a matter of debate to this day, Namibia remains a beacon of peace, harmony and stability in a continent often riven by conflict. I urge you to visit this stunningly beautiful and friendly part of the world.

As in most of my books good people have paid good money to great causes to have their names assigned to characters. I'd like to thank the following people and the charities they supported: Claire Martin (via Brett Martin, Friends of Robins Camp, Hwange National Park); Nick Eatwell (via Pete Chilvers, ZANE – Zimbabwe, a National Emergency); Llew Walters (African Icons, in support of widows and orphans of South African Police Service personnel); Scott Dillon (Dine for Rhino/Wild Support/Saving the Survivors); Peter Appleton and Ian Heraud (Juvenile Diabetes Research Foundation); Susan Vidler (via Melanie Oldland, Heal Africa Hospital in the Democratic Republic of Congo); the late Pippa Chapman (via Lauren Chapman-Holle, Breaking the Brand – a charity focusing on reducing demand for rhino horn in Vietnam); and Sheila MacKenzie (via Greg Hargrave, Heal Africa Hospital).

In Australia my deepest thanks, as always, go to my unpaid editing team who have been with me for all 23 of my novels and biographies – wife, Nicola; mother, Kathy, and mother-in-law, Sheila. I couldn't do it without you.

My transnational work family, Pan Macmillan in Australia and South Africa, allows me to continue living my dream in the countries I love. Thank you to Cate Paterson, Danielle Walker, Brianne Collins, Terry Morris, Andrea Nattrass, Gillian Spain, Veronica Napier, Eileen Bezemer and everyone else who helps get a book from my laptop into your hands. I'd also like to thank the late Patricia Paterson, whose support I valued from the very first book, and my fellow Pan Macmillan author Peter Watt for his friendship and promotion of my novels.

And if you've made it this far, thank you. You're the one who counts most.

Tony Park
www.tonypark.net

If you've enjoyed this book and would like to connect with Tony Park or receive more information about future novels, please visit www.tonypark.net where you can sign up for Tony's newsletter.

Tony is also on Faceboook, Twitter and Instagram as tonyparkauthor

MORE BESTSELLING FICTION FROM TONY PARK

Scent of Fear

Afghanistan veteran Sean Bourke's world explodes when an IED detonates in South Africa's Sabi Sand Game Reserve.

On a routine anti-poaching patrol, Sean and his tracker dog Benny watch in horror as over-eager rookie Tumi Mabasa is almost killed, and her dog gravely injured, in the explosion.

Along with Tumi and best mate Craig Hoddy, Sean is determined to hunt down the elusive bomb maker who has introduced this destructive weapon to the war on poaching.

But Sean is his own worst enemy. Haunted by nightmares of the war and racked with guilt from driving away his ex-wife, Christine, he soon discovers she and Craig in the midst of an intense affair.

And there's another enemy at play …

As bombs target Sean's unit, can he get himself back on track and win the fight for Africa's wildlife – and Christine – before it's too late?

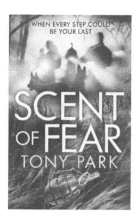

Captive

A very eager – and rather naive – Australian lawyer Kerry Maxwell flies into South Africa to volunteer at a wildlife orphanage run by notorious vet, Graham Baird.

Graham is as jaded and reckless as Kerry is law-abiding and optimistic. When Kerry arrives at the animal sanctuary it's to the news that Graham is imprisoned in Mozambique following a deadly shootout with elephant poachers.

Kerry's earnest sense of justice takes her to Massingir to help Graham with his case, and into a world of danger. Kidnapped, chased, attacked and betrayed, Kerry learns the bitter truth about the complexities and deadly nature of the war on poaching.

'One of our best and most consistent thriller writers' CANBERRA TIMES

'(Park) successfully conjures up vivid scenery and stunning animal encounters.' AU REVIEW

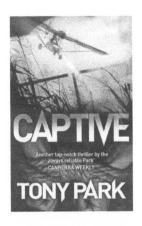

The Cull

Former mercenary Sonja Kurtz is hired by business tycoon Julianne Clyde-Smith to head an elite squad. Their aim: to take down Africa's top poaching kingpins and stop at nothing to save its endangered wildlife.

But as the body count rises, it becomes harder for Sonja to stay under the radar as she is targeted by an underworld syndicate known as The Scorpions.

When her love interest, Hudson Brand, is employed to look into the death of an alleged poacher at the hands of Sonja's team, she is forced to ask herself if Julianne's crusade has gone too far.

From South Africa's Kruger National Park to the Serengeti of Tanzania, Sonja realises she is fighting a war against enemies known and unknown ...

'Gripping from beginning to end, with some evocative descriptions of the countryside thrown in, it makes for an entertaining and thought-provoking read.' CANBERRA WEEKLY

'The story starts off at a pace and never slows down – purehard core action. His passion for his characters matched with his experience and familiarity with southern Africa is probably unequalled, or a very close second to Wilbur Smith ... you can feel the author's enthusiasm on every page.' ARMY NEWS

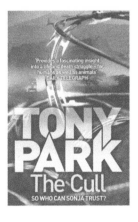

Lightning Source UK Ltd.
Milton Keynes UK
UKHW011816281219
355994UK00001B/66/P

9 781925 78